Buzzard's Bluff

A BEN SAVAGE, SALOON RANGER WESTERN

BUZZARD'S BLUFF

WILLIAM W. JOHNSTONE
AND J. A. JOHNSTONE

WHEELER PUBLISHING
A part of Gale, a Cengage Company

Following the death of William W. Johnstone, the Johnstone family is
working with a carefully selected writer to organize and complete Mr.
Johnstone's outlines and many unfinished manuscripts to create
additional novels in all of his series like The Last Gunfighter, Mountain
Man, and Eagles, among others. This novel was inspired by Mr.
Johnstone's superb storytelling.
Wheeler Publishing Large Print Western.
The text of this Large Print edition is unabridged.
Other aspects of the book may vary from the original edition.
Set in 16 pt. Plantin.

**LIBRARY OF CONGRESS CIP DATA ON FILE.
CATALOGUING IN PUBLICATION FOR THIS BOOK
IS AVAILABLE FROM THE LIBRARY OF CONGRESS.**

ISBN-13: 978-1-4328-8754-4 (softcover alk. paper)

Published in 2021 by arrangement with Pinnacle Books, an imprint of
Kensington Publishing Corp.

Printed in Mexico
Print Number: 01   Print Year: 2021

BUZZARD'S BLUFF

CHAPTER 1

Wilfred Tuttle stood in the open door of his store and watched the two riders he could see in the distance, approaching his store. As his eyes were no longer as sharp as they used to be when he was a younger man, he squinted in an effort to identify the two men. Tuttle had operated his little store, perched on the bank of the Brazos River, for more than twenty years, and he had seen his share of good and bad men. At this particular time, he hoped the two approaching now were a better sort than the two who had left his store that morning. At least, he was sure they weren't the same two, for those men were following the river trail down the Brazos. The riders he was looking at now were traveling from the west to intercept the river trail.

After a few moments more, his scraggly whiskers parted to make room for a grin when he recognized the familiar form of

Texas Ranger Ben Savage. The fellow with him, riding one of those horses called a Palouse, was still unfamiliar to him. He walked on out to the porch to wait for them. "Howdy, Ben," Tuttle sang out when he pulled up at the hitching rail and dismounted. He had grown to like the broad-shouldered, easygoing Ranger in the last twelve years since Ben had made his first visit to his store. "Who you got with you?" Tuttle asked.

"Howdy, Wilfred," Ben responded. "This is Ranger Billy Turner. He's come down from Fort Worth." They tied their horses and stepped up on the porch.

"Howdy, Billy," Tuttle said. "Welcome to my store." Turning back to Ben, he asked, "You wouldn't happen to be lookin' fer two mangy-lookin' saddle tramps ridin' the down-river trail, would ya?"

"As a matter of fact," Ben answered. "When did they leave here?"

"This mornin'," Tuttle said. "About eight-thirty I'd say, and I was glad to see 'em go. Who are they?"

"They're stagecoach bandits," Ben answered. He paused before going on. "Billy, here, came down from Fort Worth to give us a hand in catchin' up with 'em."

"Pleased to meetcha, Mr. Tuttle," Billy

said and extended his hand.

"Same here," Tuttle answered and shook his hand. "Who are those two? Anybody I've ever heard of?"

"I doubt it," Ben replied, "Samuel 'Big Foot Sam' Kelly, and his partner, Jack Queen."

"Nah, I ain't heard of 'em. You say they robbed a stagecoach? Where was that?" He knew there was no stagecoach line out this way.

"North of Dallas," Ben said. "They killed one of the passengers and wounded the fellow riding shotgun. We got word they were headin' this way. Billy and I tried to see if we could head 'em off, but if we're still half a day behind 'em, we're gonna have to ride hard to make up that ground."

"We've been ridin' pretty hard since sunup," Billy said, "so we're gonna have to rest the horses here. I don't know 'bout that dun of yours," he said to Ben, "but my horse is tired." He grinned at Tuttle then. "Ben told me we could buy something to eat when we got here. Said you had a Mexican woman who would cook us up some breakfast."

Tuttle laughed and nodded to Ben. "Rosa," he said. "He's right about that, as long as it *is* breakfast, somethin' she can

9

cook up right away. 'Course it's past dinnertime right now, but this ain't no restaurant, so it's a good thing you're thinkin' about some breakfast."

"Breakfast is what I was countin' on," Billy assured him, " 'cause I ain't had none today." He rubbed his belly and complained, "Ben wouldn't wait for breakfast this mornin'."

His comment seemed to amuse Tuttle. He chuckled and said, "Well, take care of your horses and I'll tell Rosa to fry up some sowbelly and eggs. There's always a pot of coffee on the stove, but I'll tell her to make up some fresh for a couple of Rangers. Will that do?"

"That'll do," Billy answered.

"Wouldn't hurt if she was to have some biscuits left over from dinner, too," Ben suggested.

Tuttle laughed again. "I expect she's got some left over. If she don't, she'll most likely bake some fresh ones when she finds out you're here."

"Tell her not to go to that much trouble," Ben insisted. "I just thought if she still had some cold ones, we'd try to catch her before she throws them to the hogs." He turned to face Billy then. "Come on, Billy, we'll go water the horses."

10

He led the way behind the store to a little grassy clearing that ran down to the water's edge. "Rosa?" Billy asked. "Is that Tuttle's wife?"

"No," Ben answered. "Tuttle's wife, Mildred, died about four years ago, after she took a fever one evenin' and passed on the next. Rosa Cruz is a young Mexican woman that's been cookin' for him since then. She takes care of him, but not like a wife, more like a daughter."

"He said she'd probably bake fresh biscuits when she found out you were here. Just tell me it ain't none of my business, if you want to, but is there something goin' on between you and her?"

His question brought a laugh out of Ben. "No, ain't nothin' like that goin' on. Rosa's mother and father were murdered by a gang of outlaws led by Frank Bodine down near El Paso. Bodine rode off with the girl, who wasn't but about nine years old at the time. I was ridin' with almost a whole company of Rangers sent out from Austin to run him and his gang to ground. We caught up with 'em about five miles south of here. I was able to slip in and snatch Rosa away from 'em before the shootin' started. After it was over, we were stuck with a nine-year-old little girl. I knew Tuttle and his wife, so I

11

brought Rosa here and they took her in. It turned out to be a good fit. They didn't have any children of their own and raised her like she was their natural daughter."

"Well, I reckon she is glad to see you when you show up," Billy said. "Let's hurry back to the store and maybe she'll roll out some more biscuits."

His remark turned out to be an understatement, for Rosa was waiting for them in the store, and as soon as they walked in, she ran to give Ben a hug. "Papa says you're hungry," she said. "I'll fix you some breakfast. Fresh coffee is already boiling. I'll make biscuits, if you're here long enough."

"We'll be here long enough to rest our horses," Ben told her.

"Good," Rosa said. "I got time."

"Say howdy to Billy Turner."

"Pleased to meet you," Rosa said politely, then spun on her heel and returned to the kitchen, where she had already begun rolling the biscuit dough. A few minutes later, they went in the oven and she started working on the bacon and eggs.

Back in the store, Ben was asking Tuttle about Kelly and Queen. "They were two rough customers," Tuttle said. "I told Rosa to stay outta sight. That big one, the other feller called him Sam, he kept askin' me

12

where my missus was. I kept tellin' him I didn't have one. The other one wanted whiskey, and I told him I didn't sell no whiskey. Then they wanted some breakfast, and I told them I didn't sell no food. That didn't suit 'em too good, so Sam asked me how I'd like it if they tore this place to the ground. I told 'em I didn't think I'd like that a-tall. I think he was considerin' doin' it, but the little one told him they'd best get goin' 'cause there might be some Rangers after 'em, and they needed to get to Houston. So they walked out with a few things, some tobacco, some rollin' papers, matches, some coffee. When I told 'em how much they owed me, the big one said to just put it on his bill. I told him he didn't have no bill with me. So he said, 'Good, I don't owe you nothin' then.' And they got on their horses and rode off down the river. I figure I got off pretty cheap."

"You might have, at that," Ben remarked. "How much do they owe you? Maybe when we catch up with 'em, I can collect your bill for you."

Tuttle walked over to the counter and picked up a sheet of paper. "Comes to six dollars and fifty cents," he said and handed the paper to him. Ben folded it and stuck it in his pocket.

■ ■ ■ ■

After a big breakfast and the horses were rested, Ben and Billy paid for the meal, even though Tuttle insisted it was not necessary. "It's hard to show much profit if you're gonna give your food away," Ben declared.

"Or if a couple of outlaws take it without payin'," Billy added.

"You take care of yourselves," Tuttle warned. "Those two characters you're goin' after ain't the kind to listen to reason."

Ben assured him and Rosa that they would be careful, then rode back on the river trail, heading south. He was of a strong opinion they would catch up with Kelly and Queen in the little town of Navasota, which was a wide-open little pocket of lawlessness with everything to attract those seeking saloons, whorehouses, and gambling houses. It was only a twenty-mile ride from Tuttle's. Ben didn't tell Billy about it when they left Austin, or he would have asked why they didn't head straight for Navasota. And Ben didn't want to explain that he wanted to check on Tuttle and Rosa because they were in Big Foot Sam Kelly's path to Houston. *Besides,* he thought, *might as well go to Navasota with a good breakfast under your belt.*

Located at the north end of town, the stable was the first business they came to, so they pulled up there to talk to the owner, Lem Wooten. They figured if the two outlaws they trailed planned to stop in Navasota for a night or two, they would most likely stable their horses. "Afternoon, Lem," Ben said when Wooten walked out to meet them.

"Ben Savage," Wooten responded. "What brings you over this way?" His tone was not unfriendly, but it was short of outright warmth. Wooten's first thought was spoken then. "Which one of my customers are you lookin' for?"

"Always appreciate your help, Lem," Ben answered. "We're lookin' for a couple of fellows that rode into town earlier today. Thought they mighta left their horses with you." He turned and nodded toward Billy. "This, here, is Billy Turner. He's come down from Fort Worth to help us run 'em down. Billy said the reports they got up there was that one of 'em rides a flea-bitten gray, the other'n a paint. That sound like anybody you've seen today?"

Lem looked instantly relieved when he realized he wasn't going to lose any customers. He became cooperative then. "Ain't nobody like that come in here today," he replied, "but I saw two fellers ride by here on horses like that. They was headin' on into town, leadin' packhorses."

"Much obliged, Lem," Ben said. He turned to leave because that told him the two outlaws weren't planning to stay in Navasota long.

He paused when Wooten asked, "What did they do?"

"Held up a stagecoach, killed a passenger, and wounded the guard," Ben answered.

"Anybody famous?"

"Nope. 'Preciate it, Lem."

They wasted no more time. In the saddle again, they walked their horses down the middle of a surprisingly busy street. As Ben led them past one saloon and then another without stopping to question anyone, Billy finally had to ask if it might be a good idea to check them out. "We'll check the Texas Rose first," Ben answered him. "That's at the other end of town, and it's the likeliest place they'd stop. It seems to be the favorite for drifters and outlaws. The question is, how long did they stop there? And sometimes the folks at the Texas Rose suddenly suffer from loss of memory when a lawman asks a question." He was hoping Kelly and Queen were in no hurry and had maybe stayed long enough to shorten the distance between them. It would depend on how much they drank and whether or not they availed themselves of the opportunity to spend some time with the soiled doves that worked the saloon. He got his answer before they reached the saloon because they saw the two horses they had described to Lem Wooten tied out in front of the saloon.

"Looks like we're in luck," Billy said when he saw their horses. "It ain't that late in the afternoon. Maybe they've had time to get a little drunk, though. Make it easier to get the jump on 'em."

"It'd make it a whole lot easier if we knew what they looked like," Ben commented. "You say you ain't ever seen 'em, and I sure as hell ain't, so we're gonna have to go in and find 'em first. Let's cover up these badges, so we don't start a riot as soon as we walk in. We wouldn't know which ones to chase after, if more'n two ran out the back. If we knew what they looked like, one of us could go in the front, and the other one in the back."

"I reckon to be sure," Billy suggested, "we could just wait 'em out and catch 'em when they come out and get on their horses."

"There ain't no tellin' how long they'll be in that saloon," Ben said. "Why don't we just walk on in kinda easy-like and look the

17

room over? I've talked to the bartender here more than a few times, and he's always been pretty straight with me. Maybe he'll point 'em out for us. If that don't work, we can just take their horses down to the stable and wait for them to come get 'em." Billy couldn't suggest anything better, and like Ben, he preferred not to wait for Queen and Kelly to come out, so they went in the saloon.

"Ben Savage," the bartender stated when they walked up to the bar.

"Cal," Ben returned. "You got a right smart crowd here for this time of day. He turned and looked over the crowded room. Back to the bartender, he said, "This is Billy Turner. He's down from Fort Worth to find a couple of killers. Billy, meet Cal Devine."

"Who you lookin' for?" Cal asked.

"Big Foot Sam Kelly and Jack Queen," Ben answered. "Just point 'em out, and we'll try to arrest 'em with as little fuss as we can, so we don't interrupt your business too much."

"I don't know anybody by those names," Cal said at once. "Hell, Ben, you know I don't ask every stranger his name. The only thing I ask is what they want to drink. So I'll ask you and Billy, whaddaya want to drink?"

Ben smiled at him. "I reckon I could handle one shot of corn whiskey, even though I'm workin'. How 'bout you, Billy?"

"I'll have the same," Billy answered. Like Ben, he hoped if they bought a drink, Cal might feel more cooperative.

Ben watched Cal pour a couple of whiskeys, then suggested, "You don't know anybody by those names, but maybe you can point out the two strangers that belong to that flea-bitten gray and the paint horse at the rail."

"Damn it, Ben, I don't look to see who's ridin' what when somebody walks in the door," Cal complained, obviously feeling a certain amount of loyalty to his customers, even if they were killers.

"I was hopin' we could do this quietly," Ben said, "instead of closin' down the bar while we question everybody in here."

Cal paused to release a sigh of frustration. "All right, I still don't know any names, but the skinny feller settin' at that table with Eunice is one of 'em. His partner, a big feller, is upstairs with Nell."

"What room?" Ben asked and was told her room was the second door on the right. He looked at Billy then and asked, "Up or down?"

Billy answered him with a sly smile. "I'll

let you take the big one upstairs, since you're more likely his size. I'll take the skinny one."

"I shoulda said we'd flip a coin," Ben replied. "But at least, you can pay for the whiskey."

"My pleasure," Billy said with another grin. They tossed the whiskey shots down and Billy paid Cal while Ben headed for the stairs and the rooms on the second floor.

CHAPTER 2

After paying for their drinks, Billy walked casually back past a couple of card games in progress to a table next to the one where Eunice and the skinny outlaw were sitting. He took a seat and waited for what he expected to happen upstairs. Ben, meanwhile, went to the second door from the top of the stairs and quietly tried the doorknob. It was locked, so he politely tapped on the door. There was a long pause with no response, so he tapped on the door again, this time a little bit harder. Again, there was a pause until finally, the woman called out. "Who is it?"

"Fellow downstairs sent up a bottle of whiskey, Nell," Ben answered.

He could hear some conversation between Nell and her customer, then finally, he heard the key turning in the lock. A moment later, the door opened just enough to allow a bottle of whiskey to pass through and a curious woman's face to peer out. It was obvious she didn't recognize the voice. "Who the hell are you?" she asked when she didn't see a bottle, only moments before Ben pushed the door wide, moving her backward in the process.

"Best sit yourself down on that chair in the corner, Miss," Ben ordered. "Your lover, here, is under arrest." Her eyes opened wide when she saw the Colt six-gun in his hand and she backed quickly out of the way.

"What tha . . ." was as much as Big Foot Sam got out before he started to reach for his gun hanging on the back of a chair close to the bed.

"That would be your last and biggest mistake," Ben warned him and cocked the hammer back on the Colt. "You're under arrest for the murder of a passenger on the stage you and your partner robbed." He pulled his coat aside far enough to let him see the star he wore on his vest. Kelly hesitated, half off the bed, still weighing his chances. "It's up to you," Ben urged. "You'll be a helluva lot more trouble to take to jail than it would be to bury you, so it don't make any difference to me."

Convinced that the Ranger meant what he said, Kelly sat back down on the bed. "You ain't lookin' for me," he claimed.

"That was Jack that shot that feller."

"That right?" Ben asked, knowing now that the man he was arresting was, in fact, Big Foot Sam Kelly. "How 'bout the fellow ridin' shotgun on that stage? Did Queen shoot him, too, or was that you?"

Kelly didn't answer right away, still weighing his odds. "I ain't shot nobody. You got the wrong person," he said after another long moment.

"Samuel 'Big Foot Sam' Kelly is who I'm pretty sure I've got. So pull your trousers back up and grab your hat. Let's go." He started toward the chair to get Kelly's gun and holster, but at that moment, Nell decided she might not get paid for services rendered. So she suddenly jumped out of her chair and bolted toward the dresser and Kelly's wallet. Ben automatically reacted to meet any threat from her. It was no more than a quick turn in her direction, but it was enough to cause Kelly to lunge toward his gun. Ben turned back in time to fire a shot that struck the gun belt hanging on the chair and knocked the chair over backward before Kelly could reach it. "That was a warning shot," Ben said. "I don't give but one. The next one will save you a trip to jail."

"All right! All right!" Kelly exclaimed and

sank back on the bed again. "I was just tryin' to keep her from stealin' my money."

"He owes me for lettin' him wallow all over me!" Nell blurted.

"I suppose he does," Ben said. "How much do you charge for a trip up here?"

"Fifteen dollars," Nell answered.

"You lyin' bitch!" Kelly spat. "Five dollars is what I agreed to, and that's more'n she's worth."

"Take five dollars," Ben said, "and put the rest back on the dresser."

"You believe his word over mine?" Nell cried.

"I reckon I do," Ben told her. "I expect that money will be goin' back to the stage company."

She did as he said, took five dollars, and put the rest back on the dresser. "It'd take more'n that to do it again," she pouted. "Big Foot Sam, hah! Maybe his foot's big, I don't know. I wouldn't let him take his boots off, but I've seen the rest of him."

"Sit down over there and shut up," Ben said, afraid if she didn't, he might have to shoot Kelly to keep him from going after her. "Come on, Kelly, let's get movin'."

Downstairs in the saloon, all conversation stopped suddenly when the shot was heard overhead. Everybody waited to hear if there would be more, all except Jack Queen. At once concerned about his partner up there with the prostitute, he got up from his chair, intending to find out. "Just hold it right there, and I won't have to shoot you," Billy Turner said, standing behind him now. "I wanna see both your hands in the air," Billy told him, and when Queen did so, Billy slipped the .44 up out of his holster. "I'm a Texas Ranger, and I'm placin' you under arrest for shootin' two people in a stage-coach holdup."

Queen was about to claim that Billy had the wrong man but saved his breath when he saw Kelly coming down the stairs with Ben behind him with a drawn six-gun. Sam had made no more attempts to jump the lawman, hoping that Ben was alone, leaving a possibility that Jack would shoot him down when he tried to escort him out the door. His hopes sank when he saw there were two Rangers, and the other one had already arrested Jack. "Heard a shot," Billy said. "Any trouble?"

"No," Ben replied, "just a warnin'. Let's get some bracelets on these boys." While Ben held his gun on the prisoners, Billy clamped their hands together behind their backs and they marched them out the front door. "Sorry to interrupt your afternoon entertainment, folks," Ben said to the spectators as they escorted the two out.

Outside the saloon, they helped their prisoners up into their saddles. Once they were settled on their horses, Ben and Billy had to decide how they were going to handle them. They had to transport them to Austin, which was a hundred miles due west. They now had two prisoners and two extra packhorses to contend with. Their own horses had already gone forty miles that day. They didn't know how long the prisoners' horses had rested. On top of all that, it was getting close to suppertime, not a good time to start on a hundred-mile trip. They decided to water their horses, then start out for Austin, but planned to stop and make camp after only ten miles or so. Ben had traveled the old trail between Navasota and Austin many times before and he had a spot in mind to camp. They agreed it was best to get the prisoners out of Navasota. So they rigged up a line for all the packhorses and departed Navasota in the late afternoon. Their plan was to start out early the next morning and make Austin in two days' time.

Evening was fast approaching when they reached the bank of the creek Ben had in mind. So after handcuffing their prisoners' hands around a couple of small trees, the Rangers unloaded the horses and left them to water. Only after the horses were taken care of did they think about starting a fire and cooking something for their prisoners and themselves to eat.

"Hey, Ranger," Sam called out, "you gonna cook us somethin' to eat, too?" The two oaks he and Jack Queen were embracing were close enough for the prisoners to talk to each other. They were the only two trees in that spot small enough to lock their arms around comfortably. Otherwise, Ben would have parked them on opposite sides of the campfire, so they couldn't talk quietly to each other. That often led to plans to escape.

Billy didn't bother to answer Sam's question, so after a minute or two, Ben answered. "Yeah, we'll feed you, but don't expect a fancy supper. It'll be the same thing we're eatin', so any complaints will just be wasted breath."

"We're goin' to a helluva lot of trouble carryin' these two back to jail," Billy commented, his words too low to be heard by the prisoners on the other side of the fire. "Too bad we jumped 'em before they had a chance to fight. Be a lot easier to shoot the devils."

"Yeah, I reckon it woulda," Ben replied, "but our orders are to bring 'em in for trial, if possible. So I reckon that's what we'd best do."

Billy still saw no sense in it. "The boys in my company in Fort Worth pretty much think we're just bringin' fellers like these two in for a rope necktie that's waitin' for 'em. So what's the sense in goin' to the trouble to transport 'em all that long way?" When he saw the skeptical look he got from Ben, he was quick to explain. "Hell, I ain't talkin' about horse thieves and bank robbers that ain't shot nobody. We carry them back to trial. But when you're haulin' a couple of murderers like these two, that's liable to kill you if you was to get careless, it makes sense to save the hangman the trouble."

Ben took a long pause before he responded. "Well," he finally said, "I reckon that is one way of lookin' at it. I expect it depends on the company you're in. F-company has always been one to see a prisoner get his day in court and let the executioner do his job."

Billy was clearly disappointed, and not looking forward to a hard two-day ride, hauling the two prisoners. He was sorry to hear Ben's reluctance to eliminate the possibility of trouble, as well. He reached over and picked up a couple of small limbs and stuck them on the fire. He bit his lip and shook his head and sighed as he watched them catch fire, "It's gonna be a long ride from here to Austin."

"Reckon so," Ben replied, "always is." His opinion of Billy Turner had dropped considerably in the last few minutes. There were often times when a Ranger was given no choice in the question of life or death. There were lots of times when you transported a corpse back from an arrest attempt. But to outright execute a bound prisoner to save yourself some trouble couldn't be classified as anything short of murder, which made you no better than the outlaw you were sent to arrest.

As both Rangers expected, Big Foot Sam and Jack were already discussing the prospects of a possible escape. "It ain't gonna be easy," Sam said, speaking just above a whisper as their captors went about the business of cooking some sowbelly and boiling coffee.

"It's a long way from here to Austin," Jack replied. "I heard 'em say they was gonna make it in two days. They're liable to slip up sometime, we just got to watch for it. If they get us locked up in Austin, it's gonna be the hangman's rope for us and that ain't no lie." He paused when Billy walked close by on his way to fill the coffeepot with water. "You see what I see?" Jack continued after Billy passed by. "Look at them packs they took off our horses. They tied our gun belts to 'em. Now, that's mighty careless."

"I expect they emptied the guns," Sam said. "Don't you reckon?"

"Not while I was lookin'," Jack replied, "and I've been watchin' 'em pretty close. They ain't likely gonna leave 'em like that, but maybe we'll get a chance if they unlock us to eat."

The two outlaws were not the only ones to take note of the gun belts hanging conveniently on top of the packs stacked over away from the fire. When Billy came back with the coffeepot filled with water, Ben nodded toward the packs. "I expect we'd best carry those gun belts on our horses."

"Yeah, I was thinkin' the same thing," Billy replied. "We'd better do that. Ain't no need to worry about it right now, though. I emptied the cartridges outta the guns, just in case. I'll take care of 'em after we eat. Right now, this sowbelly looks like it's ready, and they're wantin' somethin' to eat. I'll go unlock 'em. Get ready to cover 'em." He got up from one knee and went at once to unlock the prisoners. His actions surprised Ben, since Billy just seemed to take command of the situation without consulting him.

Ben hesitated for a minute, but there wasn't time to put the belts and holsters out of sight, so he drew his weapon preparing to guard the prisoners while they ate. Billy's actions were unbelievably careless, but Ben figured there was no real danger, since the guns were empty. Even if they made a play for them, it would all be over once they found out there were no bullets in them. "Bring 'em around this way, Billy," he said when the prisoners started toward the fire on the side closer to the packs. When Billy didn't respond, it suddenly struck Ben what he was up to. "You pecker-head!" he uttered, then yelled at the outlaws. "Stop right there!" But it was too late. Jack Queen bolted toward the packs and the .44 sitting conveniently waiting to be drawn. He was downed by a shot in the back before he reached the weapon.

In a panic then, thinking the Rangers planned to kill them both, Sam saw no alternative other than an attempt to save himself. Ignoring Ben's commands to stop where he was, Sam lunged toward the packs and snatched the .44 out of the holster. "It's

31

empty," Ben told him. "Drop it."

Billy stood, waiting, his pistol cocked and ready, watching for Sam's next move. Convinced that he had no choice, Sam aimed the weapon at Billy and pulled the trigger, only to hear the lifeless click of the hammer on an empty cylinder. His eyes wide with fright, he pulled the trigger again and again. Ben looked at Billy to see a cynical smile of contempt an instant before Billy cut Sam down with a shot in the chest. Feeling Ben's look of total disbelief, Billy turned to him with a smug smile on his face. "What?" he asked.

"You sick mongrel," Ben responded. "You set those men up to murder 'em."

"Murder?" Billy blurted. "The hell it was! It was self-defense. They were goin' after that gun."

"You set it up for them," Ben insisted. "I shoulda known you were up to something as low-down as that — shoulda known that gun settin' up there was nothin' but bait, so you could shoot 'em."

"What the hell is your complaint?" Billy responded. "They didn't know the gun wasn't loaded. They woulda sure as hell shot us if it hadda been. So what's the difference? They was on their way to a hangin', anyway, so we did 'em a favor and did us one, too. Now, we don't have to worry about all the trouble of haulin' their sorry asses all the way to Austin." It was obvious to him that Ben wasn't buying his attitude, so he began to worry that he had made a mistake in judgment. From all he had ever heard about the big lawman working out of F-Company, he assumed that Ben Savage was stone-cold hard on outlaws — and far from a by-the-book Ranger. "You ain't gone goody-goody on me, have you?"

Ben didn't answer him for a long moment. It was the first time in his twelve years as a Texas Ranger that he was tempted to shoot a fellow Ranger. When he felt he was calm enough, he answered Billy. "I reckon you and I don't see this job in the same way. You don't seem to have any problem with what you just did. And I have a helluva problem with it. It ain't your job to execute a prisoner. It's just your job to catch him. If you're so damn anxious to shoot a man, then give him a loaded gun, too. Maybe you oughta apply for a job as a hangman."

"So now what?" Billy asked. "You gonna go runnin' to Captain Mitchell complainin' about me shootin' two worthless saddle tramps? Maybe you oughta been a deacon instead of a Ranger."

"No, I'll let you take your two prisoners

33

in by yourself. Make up any story you want about how brave you were, standing up to two killers. Then get your ass back up to Fort Worth and don't ever cross my trail again. I won't be ridin' back with you. If you're thinkin' about shuttin' me up the same way you did those two, you need to remember that my gun is loaded." He left Billy standing there while he went to saddle his horse and load his packhorse, having decided that he wouldn't risk riding back with him, since Billy knew what he thought of his actions against two defenseless men. He didn't trust Billy enough now to close his eyes with him in his camp. He believed there was a real possibility that he might be another fatality in Billy's heroic gun battle when he would report to the Ranger captain, Randolph Mitchell. Maybe he should report Billy's actions to the captain, but somehow, Ben was reluctant to report any transgressions committed by a fellow Ranger. He didn't know what to do about it, if anything, so for that reason, he just decided to let Billy take the credit for doing the job he was sent down here to do, knowing he'd never work with him again.

Back by the campfire, Billy poured himself a cup of coffee and called out to him, "Ain't you gonna eat some of this sowbelly?"

"Nope," Ben answered, still picturing the way Billy had waited before taking his second shot, obviously wanting him to shoot one of them. "You can have it all. I just lost my appetite."

"Where you goin'?"

"Somewhere else," Ben answered and continued loading up his packhorse.

"You leavin' me to clean up this mess?" He pointed toward the two bodies.

"It's your mess," Ben answered. "You take care of it any way you see fit."

"It's your responsibility to guide me back to Austin," Billy protested.

"You don't need a guide. Just stay on this wagon road. It goes to Austin." When he was finished loading up, he climbed on his horse and rode off into the growing darkness, leaving Billy still sitting by the fire. After he was out of sight, he turned and circled back toward Navasota. "Sorry, Cousin," he told the big dun gelding. "I know I've worked you pretty hard today, but I'm hopin' Lem Wooten ain't locked up the stable yet. I'll give you a good rest and a portion of oats when we get there."

Back in town, he went straight to the stable and was glad to find Lem Wooten still there. "Good thing you came when you did," Lem greeted him. "I was fixin' to go to supper. Where's your partner?"

"He went on to Austin," Ben said. "I decided to stay here tonight. I was hopin' I'd catch you before you locked up. I wanna leave my horses here tonight. Like to sleep with 'em if it's all right."

"Sure," Lem said. "Bring 'em on in. You wanna feed 'em?"

"Yep. I'd like to feed myself, too, but I don't reckon I've got time before you lock up."

"Why don't you go to supper with me?" Lem invited him. "I eat up the street at Mabel's Table. Can't get any better chuck in Navasota than Mabel's. Matter of fact, you can't get anything that's fit to eat anywhere else in town. After that, I'll let you back in the stable for the night. Whaddaya say?"

"That suits me just fine," Ben answered and led his horses into the stable. After the horses were watered and fed, he and Lem walked up the street to a small building between the post office and the dry-goods store.

"Evenin', Lem," Mabel Rivenbark greeted them when they walked in. "I was startin' to wonder if you was takin' supper somewhere else. I was fixin' to throw the rest of the cornbread out."

36

"If I'da knowed you baked cornbread tonight, I'da been here a lot sooner," Lem said, and looked at Ben. "Best cornbread in the state of Texas, and every time she bakes it, I ask her to marry me."

Mabel threw her head back and laughed. "You do carry on," she declared. "Who's this you got with you?"

"This, here, is Ben Savage, Texas Ranger," Lem announced. "He came all the way from Austin to arrest me for sellin' horse meat to you." She just shook her head, pretending to be out of patience with him. "I told him you cooked the best horse in town." She looked at Ben, still shaking her head.

"Ma'am," Ben said and removed his hat.

"Well, I'm happy to meet you, Ben Savage," Mabel said, "in spite of the company you keep. We're outta horse meat tonight, but we're servin' some beef stew that I hope you'll enjoy."

"That sounds a little bit more to my taste," Ben said.

"Doris!" Mabel called out. "Bring a couple of cups of coffee for Lem and his friend." Thinking to check then, she asked Ben, "You do want coffee, don't you?"

"Yes, ma'am," Ben answered.

The cooking proved to be as good as Lem had claimed. The stew wasn't skimpy on beef, and the cornbread was as good as he had ever tasted. For a brief while, Ben was able to forget the trouble he had just experienced with Billy Turner. He had never had much exposure to Lem Wooten before, so he was surprised by his sense of humor and his teasing of Mabel Rivenbark. Before the supper was half-finished, however, Lem asked about the two outlaws Ben had enquired about when he first hit town. "Did you find them fellers?" he asked even though he already knew about the arrests made in the Texas Rose. "So your partner went on with your prisoners, huh?"

"He took responsibility for the two men we arrested and he's on his way to Austin with 'em," Ben answered. "I gotta tend to something else tomorrow, so I decided to stay here tonight."

"Well, I reckon they weren't too hard to handle," Lem said.

"No, they weren't too hard to handle. He won't have any trouble takin' them to Austin." The topic was something Ben didn't want to discuss, and Lem finally sensed it, so the conversation got back to Mabel's cooking. When they had finished, they walked back to the stable where Lem threw down some fresh hay for Ben's bed before retiring to his little cabin behind the stable.

Ben spread his bedroll on the fresh hay Lem had provided, removed his boots, and made himself comfortable. He lay there for a while, listening to Cousin snuffle, unable to rid his mind of the incident earlier with Billy Turner. In his twelve years as a Ranger, he had certainly known there were Rangers who would kill for convenience, but this was the first time he had ever ridden with one. He was still working on it in his mind, whether or not to make a complaint to Captain Mitchell about it, or just let it ride, since Billy wasn't in his company. He still hadn't decided by the time he fell asleep.

CHAPTER 3

"Didn't expect to see you back this way so soon," Wilfred Tuttle said when Ben pulled up at the hitching rail in front of his store. "Did those two you and your partner were lookin' for give you the slip?" He glanced back toward the path leading down to his store. "Where is your partner? He ain't with you?"

"No," Ben answered. "Billy ain't with me. We found Kelly and Queen and arrested 'em. Billy's takin' 'em back to Austin, so I decided to come back this way, so I could have another one of Rosa's fine breakfasts and pay you for what those two took." His answer brought a grin to Tuttle's face. Ben didn't volunteer the fact that Billy had shot the prisoners down like a couple of dogs with rabies. "I'll rest my horses, then start back the way I came yesterday."

"I expect Rosa will be tickled to see you," Tuttle said. "I'll tell her while you take care of your horses."

Ben purposefully took the occasion to enjoy a leisurely breakfast visit with Wilfred and Rosa before starting back to Austin. He needed to get his mind off Billy Turner.

It was past suppertime when he rode into Pritcher's stable in Austin and left his horses in Fred Pritcher's care. He had kept Cousin there for several years, since the stable was convenient to the rooming house he lived in. It had been two full days since he left Tuttle's store and he figured Billy would have arrived early enough to report in before Captain Mitchell left for the day. Hoping that would be the case, he intended to wait and report the next morning, a meeting he was not looking forward to. Mitchell was going to want a hell of a lot of explaining to account for him and Billy arriving separately. Ben wasn't sure he could give him a satisfactory explanation. He would have to wait and hear what Billy's version of the arrest was.

By the time he finished talking to Fred Pritcher, it was too late to get anything to eat at the boardinghouse, so he settled for some jerky from his packs, figuring that would hold him until breakfast.

■ ■ ■ ■

After breakfast at the boardinghouse, during which, he exchanged idle but polite conversation with the other few early risers, he walked down to the F-Company Ranger headquarters. It consisted of one small office for Randolph Mitchell in the back of an annex to the courthouse. When he walked in, he found Mitchell coaxing a coffeepot to boil on the tiny iron stove in his office. The captain turned when he heard the door open. When he saw who it was, he just stared for a long moment while he formed his question. "Ben, what in the hell happened in Navasota?"

"What did Billy Turner say happened?" Ben responded.

"That ain't the answer to my question," Mitchell said. "Ben, you've been in this business for twelve years — the last four under my command in F-Company. I've never known a Ranger who was any better at the job than you. And I sure as hell never heard any report of you backin' away from a dangerous situation."

"I'll ask you again," Ben said. "What did Billy say happened? He brought the bodies of Big Foot Sam Kelly and Jack Queen back

42

yesterday, didn't he? He didn't need any help from me to do that."

"He didn't bring their bodies. He just brought their weapons and their horses. Said they didn't have any money on 'em." He paused then and studied Ben's face for a moment. "How did they die?" Mitchell asked.

"I expect that was in Billy's report, wasn't it?"

Mitchell hesitated. He could see that Ben wasn't going to give his version of the confrontation with the two outlaws, so he finally answered. "Billy said him and you arrested the two outlaws in the Texas Rose Saloon. You started back to Austin and made camp about ten miles from Navasota. He admitted that you both were a little care-less about packing their weapons out of reach but decided to let the prisoners go ahead and eat. He said he released them and both of you had your weapons drawn to guard 'em." Mitchell paused, watching Ben's face carefully before he continued. "He said Queen saw the weapons on top of their pack and made a try for one, so he had to shoot him down. Kelly made a move for the weapon and got his hands on it while you just stood there like you were frozen. So he had to shoot Kelly before he shot you.

He said you were still actin' strange after he killed both of the outlaws and didn't hang around to help bury 'em — just got on your horse and rode off."

Ben didn't protest during Mitchell's accounting of Billy's report. He hadn't planned to make much fuss about what happened to Kelly and Queen, as long as Billy just made a simple statement that the prisoners resisted and gave them no choice. But now that he heard the picture Billy had painted for Mitchell, depicting him as having been frozen with fear and forcing him to save his life, Ben couldn't hold his tongue. "Sounds like Billy was havin' trouble rememberin' all the details of that confrontation, and I reckon I am to blame for that. I shoulda come back with him, so you could get a full report. I reckon Billy forgot the part about when he emptied the bullets out of those two handguns, then set 'em up so they'd be tempted to make a play for 'em. That was a little something he forgot to tell me until it was too late. Did he mention that Queen was shot in the back? 'Course, if he'd brought the bodies back, you coulda seen that for yourself. He was right about me standin' there, facin' Kelly after he got hold of that gun. I didn't shoot him, and I kept tellin' him the gun he had wasn't loaded, but Billy shot him." He paused then and studied Mitchell's face for his reaction. "So now you've got two versions of what happened on that little creek bank the other night. I reckon it's up to you to decide which one to believe. The reason I didn't come back with him was because I just refused to ride with the lowlife."

Mitchell was visibly relieved, having already found the charge of cowardice leveled against a man he knew to be the direct opposite of a coward hard to believe. "He wanted to make the ride back from Navasota easy, right?" was his first response. Ben nodded. "Well, rest assured I'll take the report from a man I know as well as I know you over one I just met. So don't worry about this thing. You might as well take a little rest, since I don't have anything pressing right now." He got up and extended his hand. "Sorry you got paired with Billy Turner. Oh, I almost forgot, there's a letter that came here for you day before yesterday."

"A letter? Who from?" Ben asked. "Does it say?"

"Yeah, there's a name on it." He reached into his drawer and looked at the return address before tossing it on the desk in front of Ben. "Here it is. Attorney at Law Robert T. Spencer. You know him?"

"Nope, never heard of him. Wonder what he wants?"

"You got any relatives that mighta been sick, maybe passed away or something?"

"Hell, Cap, you know I ain't got no family a-tall," Ben said, "least none I know about." He opened the letter and read it, then explained to Mitchell, who was every bit as curious as he was. "Says he needs to meet with me in the settlement of a will. He's right here in Austin." He looked up at Mitchell and shook his head. "There wouldn't be anybody leavin' me anything. I think this came to the wrong person. I don't know how he wound up with my name."

"Go by and see if he's really wantin' to talk to you," Mitchell advised. "If it ain't you he's lookin' for, at least you can let him know that."

Attorney Robert Spencer opened the door to his office, which was located in a little white frame house near the edge of town. He looked the tall, broad-shouldered man up and down before asking, "Can I help you?"

"You Mr. Spencer?" Ben asked.

"I am."

"You sent me this letter. Said you wanted to talk to me 'bout something." He handed

46

the letter to Spencer.

"Of course," Spencer said when he glanced at the envelope and saw Ben's name. "Ben Savage. Come on in."

Ben didn't go in right away. "What's this about?"

Spencer smiled. "You've been named as an heir in a will. Come on inside and we'll go over it."

"I'll be honest with you, Mr. Spencer, I'm pretty sure you've got the wrong person. I don't know of any relatives I've got anywhere."

"You are Benjamin, no middle name, Savage, right?"

"Yes, sir, I am," Ben answered. Then Spencer asked if he could prove it, and Ben was stuck for a moment. "No, I reckon not. I ain't got any papers or anything that says I'm Ben Savage. I expect you could ask Captain Mitchell if I'm Ben Savage. He's the captain of the Ranger company I work for."

"Have you got a Ranger badge?" Spencer asked, unable to think of anything else.

Ben pulled his coat open to reveal the badge on his vest. "It ain't got my name on it," he said.

"Where is the Ranger headquarters?" Spencer asked and when Ben told him it was behind the courthouse, Spencer said, "Fine, when we get through here, we can walk over there and let someone identify you. Is that all right with you?" Ben shrugged and said that it was. "Do you know a man named James Howard Vickers?"

"I can't say as I do," Ben declared, then caught himself. "Wait a minute, are you talkin' about Jim Vickers?" Spencer nodded. "Of course, I know Jim Vickers," Ben said. "Jim's an old friend of mine. He was a Ranger. We rode many a trail together till he got a little too long in the tooth to keep at it." He had to chuckle when he thought about it. "James Howard Vickers," he announced grandly. "I never knew him by any name but Jim — ain't seen him in years, and now you're tellin' me Jim's dead?"

"That's right, he's passed on, and without any family or other heirs, you were the only one he named in his will."

"Jim's gone," Ben stated. "That's sad news, I reckon, but knowin' Jim, I expect he's more'n ready for whatever was waitin' for him. So you say this letter was what this was all about? Jim left me something in his will?" He paused to wonder what it could be. "I used to admire a saddle he used to have pretty much, maybe he remembered that. What did he leave me?"

"A saloon," Spencer said.

Ben hesitated, not sure he had heard correctly. A long moment passed while he waited for Spencer to explain. "I thought you said a saloon," he said.

"I did," Spencer replied. "You are the new owner of the Lost Coyote Saloon in Buzzard's Bluff, Texas. I've got the deed right here to prove you are the owner. Do you know where Buzzard's Bluff is?"

"Well, sure, I know where Buzzard's Bluff is, but I ain't been there since they grew up a town there. It's right where Buzzard's Bluff strikes the Navasota River. The last time I was there, there wasn't nothin' but a tradin' post and a fellow with a blacksmith shop." He paused while he pictured it. "But that was four, maybe five years ago."

"Evidently, it's a lot bigger than that now," Spencer said, as he pulled a legal folder from a desk drawer. It contained some papers for Ben to sign. "According to what I've seen, the saloon is operating at a profit."

Just beginning to realize what was about to transpire, Ben balked. "I don't know anything about runnin' a saloon. I'm ridin' with a Ranger company. That's what I know how to do. Can I sell it, if I want to?"

"You can do whatever you want with it,"

Spencer answered. "It's yours. But if you want my advice, you might want to take a ride to Buzzard's Bluff to see what you've got. I know that Mr. Vickers had been ill for quite some time, and the saloon is still doing well. So there's evidently someone managing it."

"I don't know." Ben was still very much against owning a saloon. "Maybe whoever that is that's managing it would wanna buy it."

"You do yourself a favor, go there, and look it over. Then decide. We'll just sign these papers and you'll be all set."

"You want me to sign before we go over and let Captain Mitchell tell you I'm Ben Savage?"

"Yes," Spencer said. "Hell, I believe you're Ben Savage."

It was going to take a while before he could realize that he had just walked into a lawyer's office and a saloon literally fell on him. When he left Spencer's office, he felt the need to visit just such an establishment as the one he had inherited. He thought about Jim Vickers, an older, experienced Ranger who had taken raw recruit Ben Savage under his wing. He had no idea that Jim had built a saloon after he retired from the

Rangers. Now, he felt remiss for not keeping in touch. He had always thought a lot of Jim, but he was astonished to find that Jim thought so much of him that he would leave him an operating business. As soon as that thought entered his mind, another one struck him. *How in the world could I manage a business?* He stopped in the first saloon he came to.

"What'll it be?" the bartender asked when Ben stepped up to the bar, while looking the barroom over. It was a small saloon and empty except for one customer sitting slumped over at a table.

His attention returning to the bartender then, Ben ordered a shot of corn whiskey. Nodding toward the man slumped in the chair, he said to the bartender, "Looks like you ain't too busy this time of day."

"We never are," the bartender said. "Ol' Charlie, there, is the only customer I've had before you this mornin'. He's got a couple of pals that usually show up, but I ain't seen 'em today. It's got to where it don't take but three or four shots before Charlie passes out. He's had three this mornin' and his head's almost down all the way. When his chin rests on his chest, I usually wake him up and tell him it's time to go home."

"Don't seem like you can make much

money with business as slow as this," Ben speculated aloud.

"I reckon not, if it was like this all day long," the bartender replied, "but it'll soon start in about an hour or so. You gonna have another'n?"

"I believe I will," Ben answered. "Just one more. I ain't much for drinkin' in the mornin', but this mornin' I'm in the mood for a couple of shots of whiskey."

"Is that right? What happened? Did your wife tell you she's leavin' or something?"

Ben chuckled and replied, "Nope, I ain't got that kinda trouble. I just found out I own a saloon, and I don't know the first damn thing about runnin' one."

"No foolin'?" the bartender asked. "Here in town?"

"Nope. Buzzard's Bluff," Ben answered.

"Buzzard's Bluff? Where the hell is that?"

"About ninety miles northwest of here on the Navasota River, and I just made up my mind that I'm gonna head out that way this mornin'." That said, he paid for his whiskey and left his second shot untouched. The bartender shook his head, amazed when Ben walked out the door, so he picked up the drink and downed it himself.

With his mind made up to ride to Buzzard's Bluff right away, Ben went back by

Randolph Mitchell's office and told him he was going to take some time off to have a look at a piece of property he had been left in an old friend's will. He didn't tell him the property had a saloon on it that was his, as well. Mitchell was agreeable, "Take all the time you need," he said. "I've been working you pretty hard for the last few weeks, so just come on back when you're ready."

"I 'preciate it, Capt'n," Ben said. When he left Mitchell's office, he got his horses and possibles ready to leave before noon. He planned to arrive in Buzzard's Bluff at noon, two days later.

He had expected to ride forty-five miles a day, but both Cousin and his packhorse seemed to be willing to go farther. So he traveled about fifty-two miles, as close as he could figure, the first day. It shaved a little off the distance for the second day, so he crossed the river and arrived at the town of Buzzard's Bluff a little before noon. Entering the south end of the town, built where Wolf Creek emptied into the Navasota, he pulled Cousin to a halt and took a look up the main street. It was hard to believe his eyes when he thought of the last time he had been there. In the length of the street, there were three two-story buildings. The first one was a hotel. He rode past to the next one which was obviously a saloon. However, when he stopped in front of it, he read THE GOLDEN RAIL on the sign. *Competition,* he thought. He didn't linger for more than a few moments there, anxious to see his new property. He nudged Cousin and the big dun gelding walked him slowly up the main street while Ben looked at the stores and shops as he passed. When he came to the last two-story building in the center of the businesses, he stopped to read the sign, LOST COYOTE SALOON. Two large windows framed the batwing front door, and a porch ran the width of the front façade that was in need of some carpentry repairs at one end. While he watched, a couple of men that looked like ranch hands passed on either side of him and tied their horses up at the rail. *Well, there's some business,* he thought, and urged Cousin to continue on up to the north end where he could see a stable.

"How do?" Henry Barnes greeted Ben when he pulled up to the stable. From habit, he made an obvious appraisal of the man, the horses, and his gear. "You wantin' to leave them horses here?"

"That's what I had in mind, if you don't

charge too much," Ben answered.

"That depends on whether you're thinkin' about leavin' 'em here for a month or just for the night," Henry said.

"Let's start out with overnight."

"Fifty cents a horse," Henry quoted. "That's water and a stall. Portion of grain is twenty-five cents extra."

"That adds up to a dollar and a half," Ben said. "That's kinda steep, ain't it?"

"I can give you a lot better rate if you were boardin' 'em here longer." He waited for Ben to consider it, then said, "I won't charge you for the oats. All right?"

"All right," Ben said and started pulling the saddle off Cousin. They turned his horses out in the corral and Henry helped him stow his packs and saddle in a corner of a stall. "How much if I wanna sleep in the stall with him?"

"A quarter, I reckon, but you have to be here when I lock up at seven o'clock," Henry said.

"Fair enough. Where can I get something to eat?"

"The hotel's the best place to get you a good dinner or supper," Henry said. "If you'll settle for a slice of ham in a biscuit, you can get that at the saloon." He waited for Ben to think that over, then asked,

"What's your name, mister? — so's I'll know whose horses I'm boardin'."

"Ben Savage. What's yours?"

"Henry Barnes. Hope you find what you're lookin' for in Buzzard's Bluff."

"Obliged," Ben said and walked out to take a walking tour of the town before he made his inspection of the Lost Coyote Saloon.

CHAPTER 4

He walked back the length of the main street, just to get a feel for the town, past the hotel, the sheriff's office, the post office, and Howard's General Merchandise. Then he turned around and headed back to the Lost Coyote Saloon. When he stepped inside the door, he paused there a few seconds to look the room over. He recognized the two cowhands who had ridden by him when he had stopped to look at the saloon before. They were seated at a table playing cards with two other men. At the far end of the bar, the bartender, a huge man, was talking to a woman who had a cup of coffee on the bar before her. Always an imposing figure, Ben attracted a looking-over by the bartender and the woman as well. After a moment, Ben walked over to the bar. "Howdy," the bartender moved down the bar to serve him. "Whatcha gonna have?"

57

"Howdy," Ben returned and touched his hat brim politely as he nodded to the woman. "Tell you the truth, I'd like to have a cup of that coffee the lady's drinkin', if you sell coffee."

"Sure thing," Tiny Davis said. "We'll sell you some coffee."

"I'll get it for you," the woman said to Tiny, then to Ben she said, "If you need something to eat with it, we sell that, too." She waited for his decision. "You're in luck today. Annie's husband killed a deer this morning and she cooked up some stew with that fresh venison."

"That sounds pretty good," Ben replied. "I'll give that a try."

"You won't be sorry," the woman said. "Sit down at a table and I'll bring it to you." She went to the kitchen while Ben settled into a chair at a table close to the bar.

Tiny walked over to talk to him while he waited for his coffee. "You just ride into town? I know I ain't ever seen you in here before."

"That's a fact," Ben answered. "The last time I passed through here, there wasn't anything but a store and a blacksmith."

"Man, that was a long time ago," Tiny responded. "What brings you back this way? You thinkin' about lookin' for some land around here?"

"I reckon you could say that," Ben answered. "I thought I'd like to get a feel for the town — see what you folks are doin' with the town."

"You couldn't find a town with a better future than Buzzard's Bluff," Tiny claimed. "We're seein' more families movin' here every year." He paused then to introduce himself. "I'm Tiny Davis." Ben wasn't surprised by the name. He offered his hand just as the woman came with the coffee and stew. Tiny stepped aside to give her room. "And this is Rachel Baskin," he said. "She's the manager."

"Ben Savage," he said, "pleased to meet you, ma'am." She extended her hand and they shook. "So you're the boss," Ben commented.

"Well, no, not really," Rachel said. "I guess you could say I manage the saloon. The owner was the boss, but he just passed away recently, so I'm the boss temporarily until we get a new owner, I guess. We heard that the saloon has a new owner, but we don't know what he'll do with it. I don't even know if I'll still have a job, once he gets here. My hope is that he'll be just as clueless about running a business as Jim was. I don't think Jim would have made it six months on his own. But that doesn't mean we didn't love the man."

"Have you been workin' here a long time?" Ben asked.

"Since the day Jim Vickers officially opened the door for business," she said. "He didn't have any family to help him, and I needed to make a living for myself."

"I woulda thought, if the owner didn't have any family, the saloon mighta just gone to you when he died."

"That's what I thought," Tiny commented. "Jim was in such poor health for the last year or more, so Rachel was runnin' the business. We figured that when he died, the saloon would just keep operatin' with Rachel runnin' it."

"It didn't happen that way, though," Rachel said. "Come to find out, Jim had a will and left the saloon to somebody. The lawyer said it would probably be sold, because he said the new owner wasn't likely to keep it."

"And he didn't tell you who the person was that inherited it?" Ben asked. They both shook their heads. "Well, I can understand why you're wonderin' what's gonna happen." He would have told them what was going to happen, but he wasn't sure, himself, at this point. The only thing he was sure of he did comment on, however. "You know, you weren't lyin', this stew is good. Reckon I could have another cup of that coffee?"

Rachel smiled and was about to respond when she was interrupted by an outburst from the card game. They looked toward the table to see one of the players on his feet. A stubby little man with red hair and beard, he was pointing at one of the cowhands and exclaiming loudly. "I'd best see what that's about before Tuck gets himself shot," Rachel said.

"You'd best let me go see about it," Tiny said. "We've had trouble with that pair from the Double-D before."

"No," Rachel insisted. "You go over there and you're liable to get yourself shot. They're not gonna get rough with a woman. Go on back to the bar in case you need the shotgun. Sorry, Mr. Savage," she apologized to Ben as she walked away.

"They ride for the Double-D Ranch," Tiny felt a need to explain. "We don't usually see any of their crew in here but once in a while. But it seems like every time we do, they cause trouble. Their usual hangout is the Golden Rail, down the street."

Curious to see how the woman was going to quiet the disturbance before it became violent, Ben turned his chair partially

61

around so he could watch. "What is the trouble back here, Tuck?" Rachel asked when she approached the table.

All eyes turned toward her. "These side-winders are low-down cheaters!" the gnarly little man declared. "And they ain't even good at it. That one," he pointed at one of the cowhands, "is tryin' to deal off the bottom of the deck, and I've caught him at it twice. Me and Ham were havin' a friendly little game of two-handed poker and these two wanted to play. So we let 'em play. I reckon they was figurin' on skinnin' two old codgers."

Rachel spoke directly to the man Tuck had accused. "Why don't you and your friend move over to another table and we'll give you a couple of drinks on the house."

One of the cowhands, a large surly-looking bully, waited until Rachel finished before speaking. "I didn't hear anybody ask you to put your two cents in, bitch. This ain't none of your business, but if this redheaded little turd don't set down and shut his mouth, I'm gonna shoot the snake down."

"All right," Rachel responded. "I think you and your friend have had enough to drink. I think it's best if you leave now before anybody gets hurt."

"I ain't goin' nowhere till I hear this little

maggot tell me he's a lyin' piece of dirt," the bully informed her. He crossed his arms and sat solidly in the chair. "If you wanna throw me outta here, sweetie-pants, you're gonna have to pick me up and tote me 'cause I ain't movin' outta this chair."

They were clearly at a standstill with the bully parked in the chair like a pouting child, daring anyone to try to move him. His partner, obviously enjoying the woman's helpless situation, added to Rachel's problems when he openly solicited her for a roll on a mattress upstairs. It was at this point that Ben figured he'd had enough of the bullying. Very quietly, he got up from his chair and walked up behind the bully's chair. The other cowhand became alert and, with his hand resting on the handle of his handgun, he waited for Ben to make a move. But Ben didn't say anything. Instead, he reached down and grasped the two back legs of the chair the bully was sitting in. Then in one swift, powerful motion, he jerked the chair out from under him, dumping him on the floor. Before the bully's backside hit the floor, Ben threw the empty chair to land in his partner's arms, causing him to stagger backward while trying to get out of his chair and pull his pistol at the same time. By the time he was free of the chair, he found himself staring at Ben's six-gun, already out and aimed at him. "Go ahead, if you feel lucky," Ben invited.

The cowhand hesitated for a moment before reconsidering. "Yeah, you'd like that, wouldn't you? Put that gun back in the holster and we'll see who shoots who."

"Do I look that damn stupid? I oughta go ahead and shoot you just to rid the world of another moron. Get on your feet and get on outta here." He glanced at Tiny, standing wide-eyed and gaping. "Are they paid up? They owe anything?"

"No, they paid for the whiskey," Tiny answered.

"All right, we're goin'," the surly-looking bully said and got up from the floor. He glared at Ben while he dusted his pants off. "Another time things might be a whole lot different," he said.

"I expect you'd be the same loudmouth lookin' for trouble and showin' no respect for ladies," Ben said. He kept his gun on them until he marched them out the door and stood in the door until they untied their horses and stepped up into the saddle.

"I'll be seein' ya," the bully said.

"Not if I can help it," Ben said and went back inside where Tuck and Ham were grilling Rachel and Tiny about the stranger. Ben

64

was heading back to the table to finish his coffee and the one biscuit he was just getting ready to eat before he decided to get involved with Rachel's predicament. Glancing at the gnome-like little man watching him, he saw Tuck's eyes suddenly open wide. It was all the warning Ben needed.

"Look out!" Tuck yelled, but by then Ben had already spun around and fired. The cowhand bully dropped to his knees, his drawn pistol clattered to the floor, then he sank facedown, a bullet in his chest. Waiting only a few seconds to make sure he was dead, Ben ran back to the saloon door only to see the dead man's partner race away up the street, leading the bully's horse.

Frozen in a moment of amazement over what had just occurred, Rachel finally broke the silence that followed the gunshot. "I guess we'd best go get the sheriff, but he'll probably be here in a few minutes, anyway, if he heard the shot."

"I'll go get him," Ham volunteered and went out the door, being careful to step around the body lying in the way. He was gone for less than a minute before he came back in the door, Sheriff Mack Bragg right behind him.

The sheriff walked in and nodded to the stunned woman standing near the bar. "Rachel," Bragg acknowledged, "you wanna tell me what happened here?" He never took his eyes off the formidable stranger standing in the center of the room.

"It was strictly self-defense, Mack," Rachel said at once. "If Mr. Savage had not been alert, he would have been killed. Everyone here will tell you that." She looked around at them, and they all nodded. She went on to tell the sheriff all the details that led up to the shooting. He seemed satisfied that it had all happened just as she said, so he turned to Ben.

"Well, I'm sorry you had to get your first look at our town in such a bad light, Mr. . . ." He paused to recall the name.

"Ben Savage," Ben quickly announced. "I'm sorry, as well. But I already had a good impression of your town before I met up with this fellow and his partner. I feel responsible for lettin' him come back in here. He was on his horse and fixin' to wheel away from the hitchin' rail when I came back in here. I misjudged him. I shoulda watched him till he rode outta sight."

"You just passin' through Buzzard's Bluff?" Bragg asked, immediately impressed after hearing the details of the shooting from Rachel.

"I was," Ben answered, "but I might decide to stick around for a while. Seems like a nice town, and judgin' by everyone's reaction to that fellow, maybe things like this don't happen as a rule."

"We like to think so," Bragg said. "What line of work are you in, Mr. Savage?"

Ben reached in his vest pocket and pulled out his star. "For the past twelve years, I've been a Texas Ranger."

His announcement caused a minor explosion of exclamations. "By Ned, I knew it!" Tuck blurted. "When he turned and popped that sidewinder, I knew it wasn't the first time he'd handled a six-gun!"

The others had the same reaction. Tiny grinned at Rachel and shook his head as if to say they should have suspected. The sheriff was as surprised as anyone. "Are you here on some Ranger business that has something to do with Buzzard's Bluff? Maybe I can help you out."

"No, thanks just the same, but I'm not here on Ranger business."

Bragg nodded. "You know something that's kind of a coincidence? The fellow that used to own this saloon was a Ranger for years before he got into this line of work."

"Same thing for the new owner," Ben said. His statement was met with confused stares from them all. Having just made the decision moments before, he thought he'd better make it a little clearer. He glanced at Rachel. "Your new owner was a Texas Ranger, too, starting a couple of days ago."

Still confused, Rachel tried to understand what he was saying. Then it suddenly struck her. Totally stunned then, both eyes and mouth opened wide as she tried to speak. "You don't mean . . ." she started. He nodded. "Oh, my God!" she managed. "You're the new owner?"

"I'm afraid so," Ben answered. "I've got the papers to prove it."

Amid the hooting and hollering, Rachel was trying to remember all that she had just told him and wondered if she would still have a place there. There were comments she had made about Jim Vickers and his lack of business sense that might come back to strike her. She looked at Annie, who was standing there grinning, and speculated on the chance she might work in the kitchen with her. "I guess you'll want to go over some things in the office and catch up on things," she suggested, lamely.

"I expect that would be a good idea. Maybe we'll do that tonight sometime and get it over with," Ben told her.

"Certainly, Mr. Savage."

"First thing we'll take care of is my name's Ben and I don't intend to call you Miss Baskin. Is that all right with you?"

"Of course," she blushed. That was as far as they got for the moment, because there was the matter of a dead man lying in the front door. In the middle of it, Tuck Tucker and Ham Martin were eager to meet the new owner of the Lost Coyote. Bragg asked for a little help in relocating the cowhand's body to the porch to await Merle Baker's handcart, so Ben helped him carry the body outside.

Once that was done, the sheriff went to fetch Merle, who acted as the town's undertaker. But before he walked away, he felt inspired to offer an opinion. "I ain't about to tell you how to run your business, but for what it's worth, Rachel Baskin is a fine woman, and she's done a good job takin' care of this saloon."

"I 'preciate what you're sayin', Sheriff. That was my first impression of Rachel, as a matter of fact. I was just as surprised as everyone else here a couple days ago when I found out I owned this saloon. I rode a few years with Jim Vickers. He was the one who broke me in as a Ranger. And just like Jim, I ain't got a grain of experience runnin' a saloon, so it looks like Rachel's got another greenhorn to break in."

"I'm glad to hear you ain't bringin' in new people to replace the ones workin' here now," Bragg said. "And I hope you do well here in Buzzard's Bluff."

" 'Preciate it, Sheriff," Ben said and went back inside. When he walked in the door, the conversation at the end of the bar between Rachel, Annie, and Tiny stopped immediately. All three stared at him, waiting to see what instructions he might have for them. He was not insensitive to their concern, so he thought it best to set them at ease as soon as possible. Starting with Annie and Tiny, he asked them how long they had worked there in the saloon. Both had been on the payroll for more than two years. "I reckon if Jim thought you were doin' a good job, then I do, too, so everything's the same for you two." He looked at Rachel then. "But not for you, Rachel. Let's you and I go in the office and take a look at those books you mentioned before."

She was not quick enough to hide the instant look of concern as she turned at once and led the way to the office, which was immediately behind the barroom. When she passed by Annie, the cheerful little woman touched her arm and said, "Don't worry, honey, I've got a good feeling about this man."

When she and Ben walked in the office door, she started to sit down at the desk, but thought better of it, and sat down at a straight-back chair against the wall instead. He paused in front of the desk and said, "Why don't you go ahead and sit down at your regular place. I'll pull this chair over by the desk." When she did as he directed, he said, "Now, I'm wonderin' if you can show me how much it costs to run this place — how much we take in and how much we pay out."

"I can," she replied and pulled a set of ledgers from one of the desk drawers. She showed him the balance sheet and pointed out her's, Tiny's, and Annie's salaries, and showed him that the saloon was showing a profit every month. This was even after the owner's share was taken out. He was impressed. When he had asked to see the books, he had actually expected to hear there were no books. "Well, that's about it," she said. "We're gonna need a new shipment of whiskey in the next week or two, so some of that money will be needed to pay for that. That usually runs me about six hundred dollars. The kitchen pantry is well stocked, Annie keeps it that way, and there's a little over nine hundred dollars in the safe.

You wanna count it?"

He didn't tell her that he had not the slightest idea what he was looking for, but he studied the ledgers intently, noticing expenditures generated by Jim Vickers's personal expenses. He was looking to make sure expenses like costs for stabling his horses were included. When he had satisfied himself that the saloon would more than support his needs, he closed the ledgers and handed them back to Rachel. "I reckon that'll do for now. I don't need to count the money in the safe. In case you ain't figured it out yet, but I expect you already have, I don't know any more about runnin' a place like this than Jim did when he started. So I want you to do the same job you've been doin', but I don't think your salary is right for your job. I think the fairest thing to do is to make you a partner in the business. Whaddaya say? Fifty-fifty, we'll split the profits down the middle. Does that sound fair to you?"

She was struck speechless for a few moments. Jim Vickers had paid her a generous salary, but nowhere near the income she would enjoy as an equal partner. She could not imagine why he would give up half of the profits of a going business when there was no reason to do so. When she had still not replied after several more seconds, he suggested, "You're good at things like this, so you could draw up a partnership agreement, if you like, and we'll sign it. Take it to the bank and let them notarize it. Whaddaya say?"

Finally recovering her emotions, she answered him. "I don't know what to say. I mean, of course I accept. I just didn't expect you to be so generous." Then she quickly sought to assure him. "I will do my best to make sure you don't ever regret this. I'll surely take care of your business for you."

"Our business," he corrected her. "I'd be very surprised if I've misjudged you."

"I have to ask," she insisted. "Why would you do this? I would work just as hard if you kept me on at my regular salary."

"I figured you would, and that's one of the reasons I wanted you as a partner. Look, I'm pretty much in the same boat Jim was. I ain't as old as Jim was when he quit the Ranger service, but I don't have any family, and I don't need much money to live on. So why not pay the person who's really operatin' the saloon?"

When they returned to the saloon, they found Tiny and Annie waiting by the bar, anxious to try to read the expression on Rachel's face. They relaxed their concern at once when they saw her beaming happily. Waiting with them were two women of uncertain age, but obvious occupation. Only then did it occur to the new owner that he had seen no trace of the soiled doves that are typically found in saloons. Whereas he was surprised to see them now, he told himself that, of course, the Lost Coyote had saloon gals, like every other saloon in the wild west. Sensing his surprise, Rachel said, "You were probably wondering where the girls were. I was wondering, myself." She motioned for them to come over. "Meet the new owner of Lost Coyote Saloon, Ben Savage. Ben, this is Ruby and Clarice." Addressing them directly, she asked, "Where were you two hiding while all the fuss was going on down here?"

Clarice, the larger of the two and obviously a little older, answered Rachel. "We were both stayin' in our rooms as long as those two fellers from the Double-D were down here. Didn't neither one of us wanna see those two animals again. Then Ruby came into my room when we heard the shot down here and we stayed there till we were sure everything was all right."

Back to Ben then, Rachel said, "Clarice and Ruby sell a lot of whiskey for us. They keep a lot of customers coming back here, instead of going down the street to the Golden Rail."

Both women looked at the imposing man who was their new boss, wondering if they were to be at his call whenever he needed company, and if it would be without compensation. "Pleased to meetcha, Ben," Clarice managed.

"Me, too," Ruby seconded.

"Ladies," Ben returned the greetings. "Just to set things straight, I'm the new half-owner. Rachel's now an equal partner." Back to her, he said, "I reckon I might as well move in. Did Jim have a room here?"

"Yes," she answered. "He had a room here behind the kitchen. He also kept a room at the hotel he'd sleep in. It was a little too noisy here in the saloon sometimes, so he would go to the hotel some nights. I think he liked to eat breakfast in the dining room there, too. Come on and I'll show you his room. I guess it's about time I showed you around the whole place, isn't it?"

She led him through the kitchen, where Annie had finally gotten back to her cleanup. From the kitchen, Rachel led him through a door back to a long hallway that led to several rooms. The first two were storerooms for the kitchen. The last two were bedrooms. "Jim's room is the last one before the outside door."

"What's the other one?" Ben asked.

"That's my room," she answered, waiting for a typical male remark, but there was none.

"That'll be handy," he said, causing her to change her mind back to her original thought. "I can bring the stuff off my packhorse right in the back door, there." She hoped he didn't notice her little flush of embarrassment. He walked past her room and tried the doorknob on his, but found it locked.

"Here, let me," she said and stepped up to the door to unlock it. "When we go back to the office, I'll get your key to the room and the key to the outside door. We usually keep that outside door locked." When the door was unlocked, she pushed it wide and stepped back to let him enter. "Probably need to open a window and let it air out a little," she suggested.

He walked in and went straight to the window to open it. "It'll be all right in a little while. It'll beat where I was plannin' to sleep tonight, in the stable with my horses." He looked around for a moment at the bare furnishings, primarily a bed and a dresser. "This'll do," he said. "What's up-stairs?"

"Bedrooms," she answered. "Four of 'em, Clarice and Ruby have rooms up there, and Tiny lives in the last one."

"Might as well have a look," he decided, so they went upstairs and he took a quick look at the rooms, just so he would know the whole building. "What happened to the side of the porch out front?" he asked when they were back downstairs.

"Freighter let his mules get away from him when a couple of drunk cowboys started shooting up the town. The sheriff put 'em in jail, but not till after one of the mules killed itself when it tried to jump up on the porch."

"Anybody in town do carpentry work?" Ben asked.

"Ham Greeley," Rachel said. "That was him playing cards with Tuck and the two cowhands."

"Maybe we oughta talk to him about fixin' that porch. We don't want strangers comin' through town and goin' to the Golden Rail for a drink 'cause they think the Lost Coyote looks run-down."

She laughed. "I guess you're right. We'll talk to Ham."

"Why do you call him Ham?" Ben wondered, thinking it to be a nickname and probably had a story behind it.

" 'Cause that's his name. He says his mama named him Hammer, hopin' it would encourage him to wanna be a carpenter when he grew up, like his daddy." She paused to let him think about that for a few seconds. "Well, you've seen the whole place, except the outhouses."

He nodded and said, "I reckon I'll wait on seein' that till my insides tell me to go see it." He started to walk toward the stairs but paused to ask one more question. "How'd Jim come to name this place the Lost Coyote?"

She smiled as she recalled. "When he started building the place, one morning a coyote came up from the creek. Just one coyote, and Jim said it was the mangiest coyote he'd ever seen. And it would just stand off about fifty yards and watch. It came back the second day and one of the men helping him build the saloon said it looked like it was lost. Jim hadn't been able to decide on what to call the saloon, so he said that coyote was a sign and he called this the Lost Coyote." She laughed when she remembered. "I asked him if he was sure he wasn't supposed to call this place the Mangy Coyote, but he said Lost was the sign. He said that coyote came back

78

every morning for the next four days and then they never saw it again."

CHAPTER 5

He left the saloon and walked up to the
stable at the end of the street. He found
Henry Barnes cleaning out some stalls in
the back of the stable. "You decide you ain't
gonna stay in town tonight?" he asked when
Ben walked in. Everybody in town knew
about the shooting at the saloon, so Henry
thought Ben might be thinking about getting out of town, in case some of the cowhand's friends came looking for him.

"No," Ben answered. "I decided I'd stay a
while. I'll bunk in the Lost Coyote. Right
now, I'll need my packhorse to carry my
possibles down to the saloon. Then I'll bring
him back and I'll want the monthly rate for
boardin' both of 'em. I'll expect the same
rate you gave Jim Vickers. Fair enough?"

"Fair enough," Henry answered, then
shook his head as if astonished. "It's true
then. Tuck Tucker said you came into town
and bought the saloon after you shot that

man down."

"Well, that ain't exactly right. I already owned the saloon before I rode into town. I shot the man after that." He loaded the sorrel up rather loosely for the short trip back to the saloon, leaving Henry standing in the door of the stable shaking his head.

After he unloaded his belongings into his room in the saloon, he returned his packhorse to Henry's care. Before he left for the night, he spent some time with Cousin while Henry stood talking to him. When he decided it was time to go to the hotel dining room for supper, since Annie didn't cook supper at the saloon, he gave Cousin's face a good scratching and asked, "Is Henry treatin' you all right? You just let me know if he ain't." He looked at Henry then and said, "He'll tell me if you ain't."

Henry chuckled. "Well, I'll keep that in mind," he said. *But I ain't likely to do anything that might rile you up,* he thought, recalling Tiny's description of the stranger in action.

He walked in the outside entrance to the River House Hotel dining room and was met at the door by Lacy James, who was serving as hostess. She gave him a good looking over before asking, "Welcome to the River House, stranger. Are you by any chance the new owner of the Lost Coyote?"

An attractive woman, he had to admit, but with a bit of smugness in her tone. "That's a fact," he answered her. "I'm hopin' you permit saloon owners to eat in your dinin' room."

"You're in luck," she joked. "Today's Tuesday and we let all manner of riffraff in on Tuesdays." She gave a hearty chuckle in appreciation for her wit. "Come on in, Mr. Ben Savage." When he looked surprised, she said, "Word gets around fast in this little town, especially when newcomers make as big an entrance as you did."

"I can see that," he replied.

"Let me officially welcome you to our dining room," Lacy said grandly, "and invite you to leave your firearm with the others on the table." She fairly beamed at him while he unbuckled his gun belt. "Will your family be coming to Buzzard's Bluff soon?" she asked.

"You're lookin' at the whole family," he informed her.

"Well, we'll treat you like family here. Jim Vickers used to eat supper here every day and sometimes breakfast, too. Nice man," she commented. "We'll miss seeing him come in." She waited for him to put his gun belt on the table, then asked, "You wanna sit at the big table?"

"How 'bout one of those little tables against the wall?" he answered.

"Anywhere you want, you're too big to argue with," she said cheerfully. "Cindy will take care of you," she said when a young girl came out of the kitchen. "Enjoy your supper." She spun around and hurried off to greet a couple of men, then escorted them to the large community table in the center of the room. Then she disappeared into the kitchen.

"Was that him?" Myrtle Johnson asked when Lacy came in.

"Yep," Lacy replied. "That's him, all right. Freeman said he heard he was a Ranger, just like Jim Vickers, but he looks a lot younger than Jim was when he came here."

Cindy came into the kitchen then and headed for the coffeepot. "He wants the special, Myrtle," she said as she poured a cup of coffee. "Seems like a nice enough man, kinda quiet."

Lacy laughed. "I don't know if that cowpoke from the Double-D would agree with you or not," she said. "He made quite an impression on him. First day in his new business and he shoots one of his customers. I'm gonna have to get the whole story from Rachel Baskin."

"I guess I'd better be careful not to make him mad," Cindy joked. "Fill him up a big plate, Myrtle. I bet a man his size needs a lotta food." She picked up the cup of coffee and headed back out the kitchen door. "There's Freeman now," she said as she went out.

Freeman Brown, the owner of the hotel, came in the entrance from the hotel hallway. Spotting the big man sitting alone at a small table, he walked over, arriving there at the same time Cindy got there with Ben's coffee. "Ben Savage?" Freeman asked.

"That's right," Ben answered.

"Just wanted to welcome you to Buzzard's Bluff. I'm Freeman Brown. I own the hotel." He extended his hand and after they shook, he asked, "Mind if I join you for supper?"

"Not at all," Ben responded, "have a seat."

Freeman pulled a chair back and sat down. "Cindy, bring me a cup of that coffee, will you?" She asked if he was going to have supper and he said he thought he would, so she went to get his coffee. Back to Ben, he said, "Jim Vickers used to keep a room here in the hotel. Are you plannin' on a room here, too?"

"Tell you the truth, Mr. Brown, I haven't even thought about it. I've got a room in

84

the saloon. I don't know why Jim wanted one in the hotel. Maybe whatever drove Jim to need a place out of the saloon will drive me there, too. I'll have to wait and see."

Freeman chuckled. "I reckon he just needed a little peace and quiet sometimes. Well, I just wanted to let you know I gave Jim a special rate. If you decide you need a room, too, I'll give you the same rate."

"I 'preciate that, Mr. Brown," Ben said. "I'll keep that in mind."

"Please, call me Freeman. That's what my friends call me, and I hope we'll be friends, too."

"All right, Freeman. I don't see why we wouldn't be."

They were interrupted then by the arrival of Cindy with two heaping plates of beef stew and a plate with four biscuits on it. "I declare," she said to Freeman. "I went to get your coffee, and clear forgot it. I'll be right back."

"She's a fine young lady," Freeman said after she left, "a little bit scatterbrained sometimes, but what girl isn't at that age?" There was a short period of silence while both men launched the initial attack on the plates of stew in front of them. After a few moments, Freeman resumed the conversation. "I heard about your rather rough

85

welcome to town at the saloon today. And I think it would be remiss of me if I didn't offer a word of caution. I don't know if anybody told you, but the man you shot was one of the Double-D hands. And you're gonna find out that the town has had its share of trouble from that bunch. A fellow by the name of Daniel Dalton owns the Double-D, and he's never been one to keep a tight rein on his men. So it would be wise for you to keep a cautious eye about you just in case. You know what I mean?"

"I think I do," Ben answered. 'Preciate the warnin'."

Changing the subject slightly, Freeman, like Sheriff Bragg had, saw fit to tell him how competent Rachel Baskin had been in her role as manager of the Lost Coyote Saloon. "You're mighty lucky to have had Rachel taking care of that place. She was running the saloon even before Jim Vickers died."

"That's what the sheriff told me," Ben replied. Unable to resist japing Freeman, he added, "I had a meeting with her earlier today and fired her from that job." He saw the immediate results of his remark in Freeman's face. Before Freeman could respond, he said, "I made her an equal partner in the Lost Coyote." The hotel owner's face, flushed moments before, relaxed to form a wide grin. Ben was beginning to think that his new business partner might be the most popular person in town.

Freeman made it a point to tell him a lot more about the town and the people who had chosen to cast their lot on a settlement that grew from a trading post and a blacksmith to the bustling little town that it had become. "I'm sure all of us will give you our cooperation to help your business continue to be successful. Most of us hope you will run it the same way Jim did, and Rachel does now."

"I reckon we'll see," Ben said.

Before they finished their supper, they were joined by another merchant, Cecil Howard, owner of Howard's General Merchandise. Seeing Freeman sitting at the table with the newly arrived owner of the Lost Coyote, he walked over to meet Ben. "Rachel said I might find you here," Cecil said. "I wanted to say hello and welcome to Buzzard's Bluff before you met some of our lower-class citizens, but I see I'm too late."

Freeman snorted a chuckle in appreciation for Cecil's attempt at humor. He turned to Ben and said, "You'da had to meet him sooner or later, Ben. This is Cecil Howard. He's the mayor, and we're all still

87

trying to figure out how he ever got elected. Maybe it was out of respect for his patient wife, Sarah, who's had to put up with him at home for a good many years."

"General store, right?" Ben asked as he shook hands with Cecil.

"That's right," Cecil answered.

"Ben just told me he's made Rachel an equal partner in the Lost Coyote," Freeman said. The statement brought a big smile to Cecil's face.

"I swear, that's good news," Cecil responded. "Maybe that means you'll let it run the way it always has, ever since Jim Vickers built it. We've got the Golden Rail Saloon with all its gambling and whores, knifings and gunfights. We don't need another one."

Ben understood now the compliments for Rachel Baskin from Bragg and Freeman. Evidently, Lost Coyote was the saloon of choice for the citizens of the town, while Golden Rail was the saloon that attracted drifters and troublemakers. "From what you're tellin' me, the Golden Rail is wide open and the place that attracts the kind of people that make trouble. Well, I found out the hard way that Lost Coyote attracts troublemakers, too. And we do have two prostitutes that I've met."

"Well, sure, Lost Coyote gets a few of the wrong kind of customers," Cecil replied, "can't avoid that — but not like Golden Rail. And Ruby and Clarice are just there for some of the men's comfort. They're there, if you need 'em, and good company when you're drinking, but they ain't like the brazen prostitutes at the Golden Rail."

They talked a while longer until finally Cecil said he had better go home before Sarah threw his supper out for the coyotes to feed on. Freeman got up when Ben did and insisted on paying for Ben's supper. "It's my pleasure," he said, "now that I found out you ain't thinking about turning the Lost Coyote into another sin den."

Lacy James met them on their way out. "Well, how was your supper, Ben Savage?" He allowed that it was as good as advertised, and she would definitely see him in there again. He said goodnight to them all and took his leave, desiring to take a little walk around town before returning to the Lost Coyote. Outside, he paused to strap on his gun belt and exhaled a couple of deep breaths to expel the heavy air inside his lungs and replace it with clear evening air. As he walked the already deserted main street, he found it strange to believe he had actually decided to keep the saloon and try to run it. *I might change my mind in the morning,* he thought, knowing there was no harm done. As far as Captain Mitchell knew, he was still a Ranger just taking a short leave of absence. Thoughts of Captain Mitchell led to thoughts of Billy Turner, which prompted him to reassure himself that it was time to quit the Rangers. Thanks to Jim Vickers, he could walk away from Texas law enforcement, a job he had never cared for, but one of the few he was qualified to do. Instead of waiting until he was too old to cut it and forced to retire, he could walk right into ownership of a going business. *Thanks to the management skills of Rachel Baskin,* he quickly reminded himself, having already been informed of this three times.

When he came to the blacksmith's shop, he decided he would take Cousin in after breakfast in the morning. It was time to have the big dun fitted with some new shoes. He wasn't really looking forward to the everyday business of running a saloon, so he decided he was every bit as glad as Freeman and the others to have Rachel Baskin to oversee the daily operation of it. When he got back to the Lost Coyote, he went inside to find a moderate collection of customers. He imagined he could feel every eye in the place on the new owner. Seeing Rachel standing at the far end of the bar, he made his way back to join her. "Don't you go for supper?" he asked.

"Sometimes," she answered. "Most of the time, I like to be here to judge the evening crowd and see if everything's running smoothly." She smiled at him when he looked as if about to question. "Everything seems to be going fine this evening." She could see that he was at a loss, thinking he should be doing something to help her, but without the slightest notion as to what that might be. "Don't worry, there's nothing you need to be doing. And don't think I'm going hungry. I went into the kitchen a little while before you came in and made myself some coffee and ate a cold biscuit with it."

"Do we ever close?" He had to ask.

She laughed. "Yes, we usually close at one o'clock in the morning. Sometimes there may be one or two customers that would stay all night, if we'd let them. And sometimes we'll let a poker game go on past that time, if it's big enough to sell a lot of whiskey. But most of the time we close the doors at one. Our regular customers are used to that, and most of them don't stay that late, anyway." She watched his reaction to everything she told him and figured he

91

would be no more help than Jim had been. She preferred it that way. "Don't worry," she said, "I'll take care of everything. Right now, how about a drink to celebrate our first day in business as partners?"

"I think that's a good idea," he agreed at once, thinking of a long road ahead before he would ever feel comfortable in his new role.

"Tiny," she said, "let's have a couple of glasses and hand me a bottle of the good stuff. Get a glass for yourself and join us in a toast to the new partnership." She took a quick glance at Ben for his okay.

"Right," Ben said. "Join us, Tiny."

"Don't mind if I do," Tiny replied, and filled three shot glasses with the expensive whiskey. They drank to the health of the Lost Coyote.

From that moment on, there was a sense of loyalty of purpose. Tiny picked up the three glasses and dropped them in the bucket of rinse water he kept under the bar. Then he took a long look at the two of them and decided this was going to be a good thing, as long as Ben was smart enough to stay out of Rachel's way. And Tiny thought he was.

As Rachel had predicted, the crowd began to thin out well before the midnight hour, and when the clock behind the bar struck one o'clock, there were only two customers to be escorted to the front door. Ben retired for the night in the room where his benefactor Jim Vickers had slept, wondering what time he would wake up in the morning, since he was in the habit of going to bed hours before one o'clock.

CHAPTER 6

He surprised himself the next morning, waking up close to his usual time of five-thirty, even though he had gone to bed later than normal. He guessed it was because he had spent more time on a horse, in a hurry to get someplace else for so many years. He climbed into his clothes, pulled his boots on, and picked up his gun belt, then he hesitated. As a reputable businessman now, would it be proper for him to wear a Colt six-gun? Undecided, he put the weapon back on the chair and opened the door. Even though he had a hankering to try breakfast at the hotel, since his supper had been so good, he thought it might be better if he had breakfast in the saloon. He didn't want to start off his first morning by insulting Annie Grey, his cook. So he stepped out into the back hall, but he stopped before closing his door. The long hall was still dark at this time of day, one window the only light. He just didn't feel right. It had been too many years, so he went back inside his room, picked up his gun belt, and slapped it around his hips. Feeling dressed now, he went back into the hallway and started toward the kitchen.

It seemed awfully quiet, and it occurred to him that he didn't hear a sound inside the saloon save that of his boots on the hardwood floor as he strode toward the kitchen door. At five-thirty, there should be sounds of Annie in the kitchen, but he heard no such sounds. Thinking he must have forgotten to wind his watch, he pulled it out, held it up to the window, and gave it another look. It was still running. He walked into the kitchen to find no one there, and the room almost as dark as the hallway. The big iron stove still felt warm from the night before, so he figured he might as well get it going again while there were still some live ashes left. Looking around the stove, he spotted a basket of kindling, next to a stack of firewood close to the outside door.

In a short time, he had a fire going and the stove began to heat up. Satisfied with that, he picked up the big gray coffeepot on the edge of the stove and walked out the back door to the pump. He was in the process of filling the pot with water when he became aware of someone standing behind him in the doorway. When he turned to see who it was, he found himself confronted by an obviously surprised Annie Grey. "Good mornin'," he greeted her. "I was startin' to worry about you."

"Why?" she asked, still astonished to find him stumbling around her kitchen at this early hour.

" 'Cause it's gettin' pretty late and you weren't here, so I figured I'd best get a fire goin' in your stove."

"Why?" she asked again, waiting for an answer that made sense to her. When he failed to answer right away, she asked, "Have you been wanderin' around the saloon all night?" He said that he had just gotten up. She realized then what his problem was. "I ain't late," she said. "I reckon you'll have to get used to a new schedule." Then she thought to say, "Unless you change it — you bein' the owner and all. But ain't nobody gets up early in the saloon 'cause they stay up so late before closin'. Rachel don't usually open up till eight-thirty or nine. There ain't no need to because there ain't no customers that early, except one or two drunks and they'll sleep on the porch till the doors open."

"I reckon I just never thought about it like

that," Ben confessed. "I thought you'd already be out here rustlin' up breakfast, and I was sleepin' late."

She smiled at him and admitted that she was a little earlier than usual this morning, primarily because she wanted to be sure not to be late on the first morning the new owner was there. "I usually have something cooked up around seven-thirty. That's the time when Rachel usually has her breakfast. But hand me that coffeepot and I'll fix you up with something in a jiffy. You'll have to wait a little while for the biscuits to bake, but I'll fry you up some eggs and bacon. All right?"

"I don't wanna trouble you," he said. "I can wait for your usual breakfast time."

"No trouble a-tall," she said, "just have to wait for my pan to get hot. Shouldn't take too long, since you've already got my stove going."

He had to wonder if their breakfast hour played any part in Jim Vickers's keeping a room in the hotel and eating breakfast in the hotel dining room. He felt sure the hotel dining room opened by six o'clock every morning. "If you're sure it won't upset your routine, I'd be obliged." A thought occurred to him then. "Don't often find a saloon that offers fresh eggs. Where do you get 'em?"

"Same place we get the bacon," Annie answered, "my husband, Johnny. I brought four dozen fresh eggs with me this morning."

By the time the coffee was ready, the stove was plenty hot enough to cook his eggs and bacon. Ben sat at the table and talked to Annie while she prepared her kitchen for the day after she set his breakfast before him. He figured it a good time to get to know her, so he wasn't in a hurry, although he planned to go to the stable to take Cousin to the blacksmith for shoes. As the clock on the wall inched up closer to six-thirty, she seemed to be concerned, for she took frequent glances at it. He soon realized what caused her apparent nervousness when he heard the back door open and a man walked in shortly before seven. Seeing Ben seated at the kitchen table, the man hesitated before coming on in. When he stood there for a long moment, Annie said, "Oh, come on in, Johnny, and say hello to the new owner." Back to Ben, she said, "This is my husband. He usually eats his breakfast here. I hope that ain't a problem. Johnny, this is Mr. Ben Savage." Looking at Ben again, she said, "Rachel knows Johnny eats here in the morning. Half the time, she shows up for breakfast before he finishes, but if it's a problem . . ."

"It ain't a problem for me, unless he expects me to cook it for him," Ben interrupted. "Come on in, Johnny, and sit down. Your wife and Rachel are tryin' to break me in as a co-owner of the Lost Coyote. Right now, everything depends on whether or not those biscuits are fit to eat. And I think she was just fixin' to take 'em outta the oven when you came in. So you can help me judge 'em."

Johnny laughed good-naturedly. "Well, I can already tell you I guarantee 'em to be the best you'll find in the whole state of Texas." He could tell from the first that he was going to like Ben Savage, having expected someone completely different. When Annie had told him about the reactions of the man when threatened by one of the Double-D riders, he had pictured a deadly steely-eyed gunman. He had wondered if the Lost Coyote was going to be competing with the Golden Rail for all the troublemakers that chanced to drift through town. After talking to Ben for a little while, he was convinced that the new owner was focused more on not losing the present business attitude.

By the time they were eating hot biscuits, Rachel appeared. "Looks like I'm late for the party," she said upon finding Ben and Johnny still at the table. "Morning, Johnny. I see you've met the new owner." He returned her greeting. "Morning, Ben," she said then. "You were looking so sleepy by the time we closed last night, I thought we wouldn't see you until noon."

"He had a fire in the stove and was making a pot of coffee when I got here this morning," Annie informed her.

"I'm gonna have to reset the clock inside my head," Ben said, "so I ain't in Annie's way every mornin'." Annie was quick to state that he was welcome to fire up her stove and start the coffee every morning, if he wanted to. "Right now, I reckon I'll walk up to the stable and take my horse to the blacksmith. I understand he's good at shoein' horses."

"That he is," Johnny remarked. "Jim Bowden, he'll treat you right."

"Mornin'," Bowden offered cautiously when Ben walked up to his shop, leading Cousin. Like Johnny Grey and everyone else in Buzzard's Bluff, Bowden had heard about the confrontation in the Lost Coyote and had formed the same picture as Johnny had. The size and intimidating bearing of the man seemed to enhance that image.

"Mornin'," Ben returned. "I think Cousin, here, is about ready for some new shoes. Accordin' to what Johnny Grey says, you'll do a good job at a fair price. Is that about right?"

Bowden laughed. "I reckon it is, if Johnny says so. Jim Bowden's my name, and I'd be glad to take a look at him."

"Ben Savage," he said and shook Bowden's hand. " 'Preciate it."

Bowden took Cousin's reins and led him back behind his forge and proceeded to take a look at the dun gelding's hooves. "You're right," he told Ben, "he's about ready for some new shoes, but his hooves look to be in good shape. Looks like you take good care of him."

"He always takes good care of me," Ben said, "so I reckon I owe him that."

Bowden began the work of removing Cousin's shoes and fitting him with the proper shoe to fit his hoof. As far as Ben could tell, Bowden was a careful farrier, taking about fifteen to twenty minutes on each hoof. While he worked, he asked Ben how he thought he'd like the little town of Buzzard's Bluff. Ben said he didn't know, but he liked what he had seen so far. "Well, from what I've heard," Bowden said, "you're plannin' to operate that saloon pretty much the same way Jim Vickers did. Is that right?"

"Don't see any reason to change anything," Ben answered. "Looks to me like Rachel has been takin' care of business."

He fully expected to hear Bowden compliment Rachel, just as everyone else had so far, but he didn't. Instead, he fell silent for a moment, staring beyond Ben, then muttering, "Uh-oh."

Ben turned to see what had captured his attention and saw a pair of riders walking their horses toward the Lost Coyote. He continued watching them until they pulled up at the hitching rail in front of the saloon. "You know those fellows?" Ben asked.

"I know who they are," Bowden said. "They ride for the Double-D ranch. At least, I know who one of 'em is. That one on the right is Ed Hatcher. He shot a man down in the Golden Rail about six months ago in a fight over a card game. I don't know the name of the fellow with him." He paused to give Ben an intense look. "He's the fellow that was with the one you shot yesterday."

That tweaked Ben's interest right away. "This Ed Hatcher, how come he's not in jail?"

"Mack Bragg would have arrested Hatcher," Bowden said. "But the fellow he shot went for his gun, too, and Hatcher outdrew him. Everybody in the Golden Rail said it was a fair fight, that Hatcher was just too fast for the other fellow. But Mickey Dupree, the bartender at the Golden Rail told me that Hatcher baited that fellow till he had to face him, or crawl outta the saloon like a yellow dog. Maybe it's a good thing you ain't at the saloon."

It didn't take much thinking to figure out the reason the two Double-D riders came to pay a visit to the Lost Coyote this early in the morning. "You mind takin' my horse back to the stable when you finish shoein' him? And I'll come back and settle up in a little while."

"You goin' over there?" Bowden blurted, fairly astonished.

"I expect I'd better," Ben said. "I don't want 'em causing Rachel any trouble." When Bowden started shaking his head in disbelief, Ben said, "I'll come back to pay you. If I don't, you'll have my horse. Fair enough?"

"Mister, you're crazy!" Bowden exclaimed. "That Hatcher fellow is a professional killer."

"Whaddaya sayin' I oughta do," Ben asked, slightly perturbed, "hide out here and let 'em raise hell with my people in the saloon? I'll be back to pay you." He started toward the saloon, striding as fast as he could without breaking into a trot.

When he reached the door of the saloon, he stopped to take a look before walking inside. As he had anticipated, the man called Hatcher was hassling Rachel and Tiny. He could hear Rachel repeating several times that Mr. Savage was not in the saloon. When he heard Hatcher say he was going to search the entire saloon if she didn't produce him, Ben figured it was time to put a stop to it. Seeing a young boy walking past the saloon, he stepped away from the door and called to the boy, "What's your name, son?" When the boy told him, Ben asked, "You wanna make a nickel, Sammy?" The boy said he did, so Ben reached in his pocket and pulled out some change and gave the boy a nickel. "Run down the street and tell the sheriff he's needed at the Lost Coyote. Can you do that?"

"Yes, sir," Sammy said and took off running.

Stepping back up on the porch, Ben pushed on through the batwing doors, his Colt six-gun in hand. "Something I can help you fellows with?" he asked. Surprised, they both spun around. Hatcher started to reach for his .44 but stopped short when he saw the weapon already in Ben's hand.

"Well, ain't you the brave one?" Hatcher taunted. "Why didn't you just shoot us in the back and be done with it?"

"I considered it," Ben answered. "Now, suppose you tell me what you're lookin' for me for. Have you got a complaint about this saloon, or about somebody who works here? We're always ready to help you with any complaints, but I don't allow anybody to harass the employees or the owners."

Both men were speechless for a moment, unprepared to hear this type response. Then Hatcher's partner blurted, "You shot Bob Wills down in here yesterday!"

"Was that his name?" Ben asked the man with Hatcher. "I didn't catch yours, you left in such a hurry. That's a fact, though. I shot Bob because he tried to shoot me in the back after I told you to leave. We've got a rule here in the Lost Coyote — no back shootin'. That's why I won't shoot you in the back, if you turn around and walk on outta here now. But we ain't got no rule against shootin' you in the front, if you make a move toward those guns."

"Who the hell are you, mister?" Hatcher finally demanded. It occurred to him that he might be calling out somebody with a reputation. "I'm wonderin' if Bob Wills had a fair chance when you shot him."

"I reckon that depends on how you look at it," Ben said. "When Bob came back in and was fixin' to shoot me in the back, it mighta been unfair for me to turn around and shoot him first. To tell you the truth, I thought he and this other fellow with you today were already on their way outta town and nobody hurt. But he came sneakin' back in here like the yellow dog he was. I expect you never got the true story of how he got himself killed. So, now that you know, you'll most likely ride on outta town peaceful-like and no harm done. I'll even buy you a drink to show you there's no hard feelin's, and you can go back to the Double-D and tell 'em you took care of everything."

Hatcher was not sure if he was talking to a lunatic or being japed by a fast talker. Whichever, he decided, there was no doubt in his mind, the man was trying to talk his way out of a gunfight between the two of them. Marty was not sure how fast this fellow was, but he said that he had turned around and shot Bob Wills before Bob got off a shot. That was something to consider, but he still could not discard the idea that the big man was trying to avoid facing him man to man. And that could be nothing less

106

than outright cowardice. He decided to do what he had ridden in with Marty Jackson to do. "I'm tired of hearin' you runnin' off at the mouth. It's time for you to own up to what you did. I'm callin' you out to stand up for killin' Bob Wills. So holster that six-gun, and we'll settle this thing man to man."

Ben slowly shook his head to exhibit his impatience before he replied. "Now, Hatcher, I believe that's your name, ain't it?" Hatcher did not answer but continued to glare at the big man holding the Colt on him. Ben continued. "Not only have you come after me for defending myself against Bob Wills, but now you're insultin' me by insinuatin' that I'd be dumb enough to holster my pistol when I've already got it ready to blow a hole in you." He glanced briefly in Tiny's direction and said, "Tiny, take that shotgun from under the counter and hold it on Mr. Hatcher's friend, there, in case he's got a case of stupidity, too." Tiny quickly drew the shotgun out, having already anticipated a need for it.

Almost to the point of exploding, due to the situation he had fallen into, Ed Hatcher could only snarl insults in reply. "You yellow devil," he charged. "You ain't got the guts to face me man to man. Walk out in the street and we'll see who comes out on top. You're too yellow, ain't you?"

"Is that what this is all about?" Ben asked. "If I say I'm afraid to face you in a gunfight, that'll satisfy you, and you and your friend, here, will ride on outta town? Why, hell, I'll do that to keep from killin' you. I'm afraid to face you. How's that? Your friend heard me say it, so you two can get back on your horses and never come back to the Lost Coyote. And that oughta make everybody happy."

Eaten up with frustration and the knowledge that he was being made a fool of, Hatcher fumed for a full minute before he could speak. "Dead man!" he finally managed. "You're a dead man. Sure as the sun comes up in the mornin', I swear I'll kill your sorry ass."

"Well, now you've done it," Ben said. "Before, you just challenged me to a duel and that's all right. But now you've threatened to murder me, so I'm afraid I'm gonna have to arrest you and your partner for threatenin' my life in front of these witnesses." He reached into his vest pocket and pulled out his badge. "Under my authority as a Texas Ranger, I place both of you under arrest for threatening my life."

"Wait a minute!" Marty Jackson blurted. "You didn't say nothin' about bein' a

108

Ranger. And, anyway, I didn't say I was gonna kill you!"

"Don't matter," Ben responded. "You brought him back here for that purpose. You're under arrest for aidin' and abettin' ol' Hatcher, here."

Marty looked at Hatcher, frantically looking for help. "Maybe we oughta just go on back to the ranch, Ed, if he'll let us go like he said at first."

"He ain't no Ranger," Hatcher said. "He's just tryin' to get outta facin' me. He knows I can beat him." Back to Ben, he said, "You're gonna slip up sometime, and when you do, it'll be me that puts a bullet in your brain."

"What's the trouble here?" Mack Bragg called out, surprising the two ranch hands standing before Ben. His .44 drawn, he walked up behind Hatcher and Jackson and pulled the pistols from each one's holster. "You havin' some trouble here, Rachel?" Ben, still holding his six-gun on Hatcher, let her answer the question.

"Those two came here with the idea of killing Ben," she said. "That one," she pointed to Hatcher, "challenged Ben to a gunfight and Ben told him he wasn't interested. So then he threatened to kill him, anyway, and Ben put him under arrest —

both of them."

Bragg looked at Ben, who smiled and confirmed what she said with a nod. "You arrested them?" he asked. When Ben nodded again, Bragg said, "I thought you retired from the Rangers."

"I have," Ben said, "but it ain't official till I notify Captain Mitchell. I thought it would be better than shootin' 'em. Maybe a night or two in jail would be good for 'em — let 'em know we don't like gunfightin' in Buzzard's Bluff." Bragg didn't look like he was especially tickled with the idea. "I'll help you herd 'em over to the jail," Ben offered.

"You'll sure as hell hear from Mr. Dalton if you throw us in jail, Sheriff," Hatcher warned. "He's gonna be mad as hell."

"That's what I was thinkin', too," Ben remarked. "Might give us a good chance to talk to him about some of the trouble I hear his hands are causin' here in town."

"That'll be the day," Bragg replied and shrugged. "But I reckon you and Rachel have just cause to complain about these two making threats and disturbin' the peace. So let's walk 'em down to the jailhouse. Maybe after a day or two they can get some sense into their heads."

"What if I don't wanna go to your damn jailhouse?" Hatcher protested. "You gonna shoot me?"

"That's as good an answer as any," Bragg said. "Sure would make it a lot less trouble for me. Is that the way you want it?" He looked at Jackson. "How 'bout you? Is that the way you want it, too?" He cocked the hammer back on the Colt .44 he was holding.

"No, sir!" Jackson exclaimed immediately. "That ain't the way I want it! I'll go to jail!"

"Shut up, Marty!" Hatcher barked. "He ain't gonna shoot you. He's just tryin' to scare you."

"Are you ready to walk down to the jail now?" Ben asked Hatcher.

"I ain't walkin' nowhere," Hatcher said. "You want me in that jail, you're gonna have to carry me."

Ben couldn't help thinking about the last cowhand from the Double-D who took that stance. He ended up shooting him and that's what started all this trouble. "If you and Tiny keep 'em covered for a minute, I'll be right back," he said to the sheriff. He went out the front door and returned shortly with a coil of rope. "I figured every good cowhand had a coil of rope on his saddle." He made a loop in one end of the rope, then walked up to face Hatcher, who gave him a smirk for his efforts. "Hold your arms

111

straight out to the sides, like you've got wings. Like this," he demonstrated, holding his arms straight out to the side. With a defiant sneer, Hatcher clamped his arms down tight against his sides. Ben instantly dropped the loop over Hatcher's shoulders and drew it up tight, trapping Hatcher's arms against his sides. He then wrapped the rope around and around the surprised man until he had his upper body bound securely. Hatcher stood there helpless and furious when he realized how easily Ben had tricked him into cooperating. "All right, let's get along, little doggie," Ben said and led him toward the door with the other end of the rope.

The sheriff prodded Jackson in the back with his Colt and said, "Get movin'." And they followed Ben and Hatcher to the door before Hatcher realized he could still refuse to cooperate, so he dropped to the floor.

Ben took a strong grip on the rope and managed to drag Hatcher through the door to the porch. He let him sit there for a few moments, long enough to untie one of the horses from the hitching rail. He led the horse up to the edge of the porch so he could tie the end of his rope to the saddle horn. He smiled at Hatcher and said, "You're a pretty big fellow, but my money's on the horse. Come on, boy," he said to the horse and led him out into the street, dragging Hatcher off the porch. He thought he heard his prisoner let out a "yow" just before he heard him hit the boardwalk in front of the porch. If he had to guess, he would have bet the "yow" might have been a splinter Hatcher picked up on his slide across the porch.

The defiant cowhand maintained his determination until about halfway down the street to the jail. But after bumping and scraping across the roughest ruts Ben could find to lead him over, he started yelling. "All right! All right! I'll walk to the damn jail. Stop the damn horse."

With an air of casual patience, Ben helped Hatcher to his feet. Then he untied the rope from the saddle horn and led him the rest of the way to the jail. Bragg and Jackson followed along behind them. Bragg, his gun in hand, watched while Ben removed the rope trapping Hatcher's arms to his sides. Then he put him in the cell with Jackson. That done, he joined Ben in the office to talk about their punishment. It was blatantly apparent that the sheriff wasn't too happy about Ben's actions, which had resulted in an arrest. On the other hand, he could hardly find fault with Ben's handling of Hatcher because it prevented a shooting.

However, knowing Ed Hatcher and his passion for violence, he could not imagine this arrest to be the end of the trouble over Ben's shooting of Bob Wills.

"I reckon I can hold 'em in jail for a couple of days, then turn 'em loose and tell 'em to get outta town," Bragg speculated. "That's what I usually do with anybody makin' too big a fuss in one of the saloons, as long as it doesn't lead to a shootin'. And that's all this has boiled down to so far." He paused to think about that for a few seconds. "I don't have any idea what Daniel Dalton's liable to say about this. I'll tell you the truth, Ben, it ain't beneath Dalton to send a few more men in here to settle up with you for killin' one of his hands. And he ain't gonna be too happy with me for puttin' two of 'em in jail."

"Reckon we'll just have to wait and see," Ben responded. "You want me to lead their horses up to the stable for you? I gotta pick mine up from the blacksmith, so I'm headin' that way."

114

CHAPTER 7

Ben led Marty Jackson's horse back to the Lost Coyote to pick up Ed Hatcher's horse, still tied at the rail. Tiny and the women were all standing on the porch and watched as he untied the horse. "You gonna want somethin' to drink when you come back?" Tiny asked, thinking he might need one.

"Just a cup of coffee," Ben answered. "I won't be long."

Jim Bowden was standing in the middle of the street talking to several other spectators who had happened to see Hatcher's rough trip to the jail. "Damned if you ain't somethin'," Bowden declared. "I didn't hear no shots, so I was glad nobody got killed."

"Did you finish shoein' my horse?" Ben responded.

"No, I didn't," Jim replied. "I was too anxious to see if I was gonna be the new owner of that dun you ride, but it won't take long to finish him up."

"I gotta take these horses to the stable, then I'll be back to get Cousin," Ben said.

"Didn't look like ol' Hatcher wanted to go to jail," Bowden commented, obviously desiring more details on what happened inside the saloon.

But Ben was not inclined to paint a picture for him. "Reckon not," he said and kept on walking toward the stable. "I'll be back in a little bit."

"Boy, there's gonna be hell to pay when ol' Daniel Dalton finds out about this," Henry Barnes announced with a chuckle. "He ain't used to havin' his boys locked up in the jailhouse, and right after you shot another one." He pulled the saddle off one of the horses. "I swear, Ben, you've stirred up more trouble in two days than we'd had all year."

"Why do you say that?" Ben asked. "None of this trouble is my doin'. I never went after any of Dalton's men. They came after me and for no reason that I gave 'em."

"I reckon you're right about that," Henry admitted. "I reckon it's because the Double-D hands expect to have their way in Buzzard's Bluff. Rachel and Jim never had much trouble with 'em because Dalton's men usually did their business with

116

Wilson Bishop at the Golden Rail. Most of us folks here in town want it to stay that way. That's why we're tickled to hear you ain't thinkin' about changin' the way the Lost Coyote does business."

"I ain't sure my partner would let me make any changes," Ben said with a chuckle. "I'll tell her that you and the rest of the town think she's doin' a good job. Now, I'd best get back down to Bowden's place and pick up my horse."

As was the usual case, the news spread throughout the little town pretty quickly. Seated at a table in the Golden Rail with a rugged-looking woman called Charlene was one of the few people in town who was unaware of it. Having been dragged out of Charlene's bed just barely half an hour before, Elwood Moore had finally awakened to find his pockets empty of all money — paper and coin. He could not remember anything after climbing on the bed after a night of drinking, and Charlene was trying to tell him that he had simply passed out. "You just went out like a lamp, honey," she said. "I tried to wake you up. I wanted to make sure you got your money's worth, but you were out cold. But you had a real good time last night. You just remember that, honey."

"What time is it?" he kept asking, unable to believe it was late the next morning. "I'm gonna be in a world of trouble. I was supposed to be back at the ranch before breakfast. Spade's gonna kick my ass from here to Sunday," he said, referring to Spade Gunter, the foreman.

"Just tell him you ate some bad food and took sick, sugar," Charlene said.

"Damn," Elwood remarked in response, even then envisioning the intimidating foreman when something triggered his temper.

Overhearing Elwood's lament, bartender, Mickey Dupree, said, "You ain't the only Double-D hand that ain't gonna make it back to the ranch this mornin'."

"What are you talkin' about, Mickey?"

"I'm talkin' about Ed Hatcher and Marty Jackson coolin' their behinds in Sheriff Bragg's jailhouse," Mickey answered.

"You're japin' me now," Elwood said.

"Hell, I am," Mickey came back. "While you was upstairs between the sheets this mornin', Ed and Marty rode into town, lookin' for that feller at the Lost Coyote that shot Bob Wills. Word is, they found him, all right, only he got the jump on 'em and hauled 'em off to jail. Mack Bragg locked 'em up. That ain't the fun part about it. Feller was in here earlier, said he saw it. Said Ed was all tied up and refused to walk down to the jail, so that feller drug him down the street with one of their horses."

Elwood didn't say anything for a long moment while his simple mind tried to grasp the idea that anybody could do that to Ed Hatcher.

Charlene broke into his thoughts then. "There you go, honey. You can take that news back to the Double-D, so they'll know what happened to Ed and Marty. You tell 'em you stayed around to help 'em, if they needed it."

Her suggestion lit a spark in his alcohol-numbed brain. "Right," he said, then turned to Mickey again. "Was there anybody else from the Double-D in town last night?"

"Nope," Mickey answered. "If they was, they didn't come in the Golden Rail."

"That just might save me an ass-kickin'," Elwood said. "I gotta get goin'." He jumped to his feet and would have fallen across the table had Charlene not been quick enough to steady him.

"You'll be all right, sugar," Charlene said. "Mickey, pour him a cup of that coffee. He's still got some cobwebs in his head." Back to Elwood, she said, "You get back on that horse, and the fresh air will straighten you out by the time you get back to the Double-D." She stayed with him until he downed a cup of coffee, then she walked him to the door. "You come back to see me, darlin', when you save up some more money." She remained there in the doorway, watching him as he struggled to climb up on his horse. Her only real sympathy was for the poor horse that had stood there at the hitching rail, saddled, all night long.

When he had gone, she turned around and went back inside to meet a grinning bartender. "That is one messed-up cowboy," Mickey said. "He don't remember nothin' past ten o'clock last night. I ain't ever seen anybody that whiskey hits harder than ol' Elwood."

Charlene laughed with him. "Every time he'd start to wake up, I'd pour him a little more outta the bottle of whiskey he bought. And I'd tell him he'd just had another ride, and he'd best try to get a little sleep. He thinks he had about four rides last night." That brought another spell of laughing.

"You better have one helluva good reason why you're just now draggin' your behind up here to the barn this mornin'," Spade Gunter barked as he walked out to meet

Elwood. "Where the hell have you been?" He walked around the weary horse, taking note of the condition of the animal.

"I got good reason, Spade," Elwood implored. "I was tryin' to help Ed and Marty. They ran into trouble with that feller that shot Bob."

"What kind of trouble?" Spade asked. He was well aware of the two men's ride into town to settle up with Ben Savage. Mr. Dalton had okayed it, himself. "Did they get that damn gunslinger?"

"No, they didn't," Elwood answered. "That feller turned the table on 'em and Mack Bragg locked 'em up in the jailhouse." He shook his head sadly. "And I couldn't find no way to help 'em, but I figured I could at least stay there till I found out they were all right in the jail." He went on to tell Spade all the details about their capture as Mickey had related them to him. "I feel bad I couldn't figure out a way to try to help 'em, but there was too many people helpin' to take them into the jail. Then I got back here as quick as I could, so you'd know what happened." When he finished his piece, he watched Spade to see how he was going to react.

"Well, I reckon there wasn't much you coulda done about it," Spade said, his mind

121

already working on how best to give Dalton the news. The boss wasn't going to like it very much. No longer concerned by Elwood's failure to show up for work this morning, he said, "Put your saddle on a fresh horse and get out to Crawfish Crick. Deacon's got a crew out there gettin' ready to move that bunch of cows over closer to the river with the main herd."

"Right, Spade," Elwood responded smartly. "I'll get right on it." He turned the weary horse toward the horse herd, grazing south of the ranch headquarters, rode into the middle of it, and dismounted. He pulled his saddle and bridle off the horse, then shook out a loop in the rope he carried. With his head still feeling as if it had been packed with sawdust, he suffered several attempts before he succeeded in cutting out a fresh horse.

Having been in the process of preparing to saddle a horse, himself, Spade decided he'd best go tell Mr. Dalton about the turn of events that happened in town. He could check on the men later. Dalton would want to know that some of his men were being held, so Spade walked up to the back door of the ranch house and rapped on it. He waited only a few seconds before the door opened. "I need to talk to Mr. Dalton," he said to Maria Gomez. "Has he finished his breakfast?" Spade had met with Dalton before breakfast that morning when Ed Hatcher wanted to go into town right away to settle with the new owner of the Lost Coyote for the killing of Bob Wills.

"Sí, Señor Gunter," Maria answered. "He eat long time ago. He in study now. I go tell him you want to speak." She held the door open for him, and he stepped inside to wait in the kitchen. In a few minutes, she returned to tell Spade to go into the study.

"What is it, Spade?" Dalton asked. He was sitting at his desk, an open ledger before him. "Have you heard back from Hatcher, already?"

"No, sir," Spade answered. "Elwood just got back from town. He said Ed and Marty are both in jail. He said that fellow, Ben Savage, got the jump on Hatcher, and Sheriff Bragg threw Ed and Marty in jail for attempted murder."

"What?" Dalton exclaimed. "Attempted murder?"

"That's what Elwood said," Spade answered, "or maybe it was for threatenin' to kill Savage. Elwood said Savage dragged Ed down the middle of the street to the jailhouse."

"How in hell did they come up with that?"

123

Dalton wanted to know. "Hatcher was supposed to call Savage out, man to man. Bragg can't put him in jail for that! He wasn't supposed to bushwhack him."

"I ain't sure he tried to," Spade said. "I think Elwood's got the story mixed up. Maybe I oughta go into town and see if I can get the straight of it."

"No," Dalton said, "I'll go into town and talk to the sheriff. I can't have him holding my men in jail on some cockamamie charge. I wanna know more about this new owner of the Lost Coyote, anyway. That damn woman that runs that saloon is up to something. We finally get rid of Jim Vickers and suddenly this stranger shows up." He paused and sat there fuming for a few moments. His interest in the competition between the Golden Rail and the Lost Coyote ran deeper than the harassment of his cowhands when they were in town. Daniel Dalton was the money behind the building of that saloon, so he was protective of his investment. He had thought the competition between his saloon and the Lost Coyote was finally coming to an end when Jim Vickers's health started to deteriorate. With a woman left to run the saloon, he figured it a matter of days before their doors would close. But the bitch held on, somehow, and then this mysterious stranger showed up. He glared at Spade and demanded, "Why wasn't Ben Savage put in jail when he killed Bob Wills? And they throw my men in jail for challenging Savage to a duel?"

"You want me to ride into town with you?" Spade asked. "Wouldn't hurt to have somebody along to watch your back."

"Maybe you're right," Dalton said. "Saddle the black Morgan, and I'll be out as soon as I change into some riding clothes." He walked Spade to the study door and yelled, "Maria!" When the gentle Mexican woman appeared in the hallway, Dalton said, "Lay out my riding clothes, I'm going into town."

"Sí, señor, you want I tell the señora?"

"No, you go ahead and lay out my clothes. I'll tell Estelle." He walked down the hall, past his bedroom, to his wife's room, and went in. His wife sat in a large stuffed chair by the window, still dressed in her nightgown. "Aren't you going to get dressed at all today?" he asked.

"I didn't think there was any hurry," she answered. "So I thought I'd work on this shawl I've been knitting while the morning light is still coming in the window."

"Morning light?" he replied, impatiently. "It's damn-near noon." He was thinking that her ass was going to take root in that chair before long, but he didn't express it. "I'm going into town. Don't know how long I'll be. Just tell Maria if you need something. She'll take care of you." He paused a moment, then added, "Wouldn't hurt you if you got outside for a little while and get some fresh air."

"I'm fine here," she replied. "I'll tell Maria to make me some tea. She's good about taking care of me." *She sure as hell takes care of you,* she thought. It aggravated her that Daniel thought she didn't know. He always blamed her for not being able to provide him with any sons. But he didn't move out of their bedroom, and into one of his own, until she began to dry up inside. "Will you be back tonight?" Sometimes he stayed overnight in the hotel when he went into town.

"Yeah, I'll be back, probably for supper. I've just got some business to take care of, and I don't know how long it'll take." He went out and closed the door behind him, then went into his room and changed into the outfit Maria had laid out on the bed for him. She was in the kitchen when he walked out the back door. "I'll be back for supper," he told her, as well.

She watched him from the back window

126

as he strode briskly across the yard toward the barn where Spade was saddling the big Morgan gelding he preferred to ride. Thinking then of the frail woman who spent so much of her life sitting in her bedroom, moving about the rest of the house only when her husband was away. He never had a kind word for her. Maria decided to make her a pot of the tea she seemed to enjoy. *Maybe I can make her some of those little tea cakes she likes,* Maria thought. She wished she could do more to brighten up the poor woman's life.

It was an hour's ride from the Double-D headquarters to the town of Buzzard's Bluff without pushing the horses too hard, so they arrived at the jail soon after the noon hour to find a padlock on the front door. "I reckon the sheriff's gone to dinner," Spade commented.

"I expect so," Dalton said. "It's time to eat something, anyway, so let's go to the hotel to see if he's there. I doubt if he eats at either one of the saloons."

"I'm pretty sure he don't eat at the Golden Rail," Spade said. He didn't express it, but he was feeling fortunate to get an opportunity to eat at the hotel dining room.

Their speculation turned out to be accurate, for they saw the sheriff sitting at a table by himself when they walked in. When Dalton started to pass the weapons table, Spade pointed it out. "Have to get rid of your shootin' irons, or they won't feed you, boss." He unbuckled his gun belt and left it on the table.

"I'm not wearing a gun belt," Dalton said. "That doesn't apply to me." He straightened his coat to make sure the pocket pistol he carried was not obvious.

Lacy James came forth to meet them. "Well, guests from the Double-D," she greeted them with a wide smile for Dalton. "We don't see you in town as much as we used to. Quite a coincidence, though, 'cause we're feeding a couple of your men down at the jail." She couldn't resist.

Dalton returned her smile with a smirk of his own. "We'll ask the sheriff if we can join him," he told Lacy.

Having seen them come in, Bragg watched them carefully from the moment they left the weapons table and started in his direction. *Damn it,* he thought, *why couldn't they wait till after I'd finished?* He had warned Ben Savage that there was going to be hell to pay when Dalton found out about his two men in jail, but he didn't expect to see him show up this soon. Too bad Savage wasn't here to meet with them, so he could do the explaining. Since Bragg remained silent, even though he had heard Dalton's remark to Lacy, Dalton addressed him directly.

"Mind if we sit down with you, Sheriff?" Dalton asked, but didn't wait for Bragg's answer before pulling a chair out and seating himself directly across from him. Spade couldn't help grinning as he pulled a chair and sat down, too.

"Why, no, Mr. Dalton," Bragg answered him, "make yourself at home."

"Thank you," Dalton said. "I was telling Spade, here, that as a servant of the people of Buzzard's Bluff, the sheriff is always willing to talk about any issues that involve the citizens." He was interrupted then when Cindy Moore came up to ask what they wanted to drink. "We'll have coffee and what's that the sheriff's eating?" When she said it was roast pork, he promptly ordered the same for him and Spade. "Don't get a chance to eat pork very often," he commented before getting down to business. "I understand you have two of my most valuable men in your jailhouse."

"I got two of your men in a cell, all right," Bragg said. "I didn't know if they were two of your most valuable men or not. That didn't make no difference in the matter of why they was arrested."

"I see," Dalton responded calmly. "And why, exactly, were they arrested? Did they shoot anyone? Destroy any property? Attack any women?"

"They were arrested for makin' death threats," Bragg answered.

"Don't men drinking in a saloon often make threats they don't intend to follow through with?" Dalton insisted. "Just the liquor talking, nobody pays any attention to it."

"Your men weren't drinkin' when they made the threats," Bragg replied. "Ed Hatcher came to town with one purpose, to kill Ben Savage. He called Savage out, but Savage wouldn't do it, so Hatcher told him, as sober as you can get, that he was goin' to kill him, anyway."

Dalton saw right away that Bragg wasn't going to budge on his stance. He paused for a moment when Cindy brought their plates, then tried another approach. "I agree with you, Sheriff, the boys mighta shot their mouths off a little too much. So I'm suggesting you let me deal with them. How about if I take them off your hands and discipline them back at the ranch? Save you some trouble and save the town some money for feeding them. Whaddaya say, Sheriff?"

Spade could readily see that Dalton's reasonable approach was not working with Mack Bragg, so he concentrated on the plate before him, eating the pork roast as fast as he could get it down. He was only halfway through the beans and cornbread that came with the roast when Bragg answered Dalton's request.

"I can understand you wantin' to get your men outta jail," Bragg calmly answered. "But I think it'd be a good idea to let those two set and think about it for a while. I was plannin' to keep 'em locked up only till day after tomorrow, then let 'em go with a warnin'. I don't want no killin' in this town."

"Looks to me like it's all right to kill Double-D men and not even get arrested," Dalton charged. "Else, Ben Savage would be locked up right now."

"Like I done told you," Bragg insisted, "that was a case of pure self-defense. Your man, Bob Wills, didn't give no warnin' or nothin'. He just tried to shoot Savage in the back. There weren't no question about it, and plenty of witnesses saw it."

Straining to control his frustration with the sheriff's bullheaded determination, Dalton said nothing more on the release of his men. After a few long moments, he asked if he could talk to the two prisoners.

Bragg agreed to that. "Sure," he said. "you're welcome to visit your men, as long as it's a short visit. I'm about done here. You eat your dinner and come on down to the jail when you're finished." He got up from the table and walked over to a sideboard where Myrtle was filling two army mess kits with his prisoners' dinner.

When Lacy walked out of the kitchen, carrying a cloth-covered plate of cornbread for his prisoners, she commented, "I hope your dinner wasn't spoiled by your eating companions." He answered with no more than a wry smile and a shake of his head.

CHAPTER 8

"You got some visitors comin' to see ya," Sheriff Bragg told his prisoners when he passed the food through the bars of their cell. "I'll make you some coffee to go with that grub."

"Who's the visitors?" Hatcher asked.

"Your boss, and he's got one of the other men with him," Bragg answered as he went out the cell room door.

Hatcher looked at Marty and grinned. "I didn't think he would let us rot here in this damn jail. We might be gettin' outta here before we thought." He yelled toward the open cell-room door then, "When's he comin'?"

"When he finishes eatin', I reckon," Bragg yelled back.

While he waited for Dalton and Spade to show up, Bragg opened the door between his office and the cells all the way back against the wall and put a chair in front of it to make sure it stayed open. In about a quarter of an hour, they showed up, and when they walked in, Bragg got up to meet them. "I'll have to have you both lay your guns on my desk," he told them. When Dalton looked as if he was insulted, Bragg said, "It's the same for anybody who visits a prisoner, no sense in takin' a chance."

Spade pulled his .44 and laid it on the desk, but Dalton said, "You can see I'm not wearing a gun." He turned to go into the cell room but stopped when the sheriff dropped his hand on his pistol.

"Your coat looks like it's hangin' a little heavy on one side, there. You musta forgot about that pocket pistol you're carryin'."

Dalton flushed slightly but recovered quickly. "You're right, I forgot I had it in my pocket. I'm not sure it's even loaded." He pulled it out of his pocket and laid it carefully on Bragg's desk. "All right?"

"All right," Bragg echoed and stood aside to let the two men from the Double-D inside the cell room. He had figured the wide-open door would be enough for him to hear most of what conversation was passed between them, but he changed his mind, picked up the shotgun he had propped against the desk, and walked in behind them. Inside the cell room, he went to a chair sitting against the far wall and sat down. "Don't mind me," he said. "Just go on like I ain't even here."

It plainly irritated Dalton, but he tried to ignore the intrusion, and turned his attention to the anxiously awaiting pair in the cell. "Hatcher, what in hell happened?"

Extremely conscious of the sheriff sitting against the side wall, listening to every word, Hatcher said, "It was all a mistake, boss. I swear. I challenged that son of the devil that shot Bob to a shoot-out between just me and him. The coward wouldn't do it. Then he told the sheriff I said I was gonna shoot him whether he faced me or not. It's just the same old story they always pull against the cowhands from the Double-D."

Dalton turned to address Sheriff Bragg. "What's this I hear about dragging one of my men down the street behind a horse?"

Bragg shrugged. "Well, he's too big to tote, and he refused to go, so we had to get him here the best way we could."

"Ask him who was the one that done it, boss!" Hatcher blurted. "It wasn't him. It was that SOB, Ben Savage. He let Savage drag me behind a horse."

"That's a fact," Bragg volunteered before Dalton could ask him if that was true. "Your man, there, was refusin' to walk. I was glad to get a little help from Ben Savage."

Dalton could see that he was getting nowhere with an aggressive attitude, so he tried one more approach. "Sheriff, I know these men got a little bit rowdy in here yesterday, but I'm sure Hatcher wasn't serious when he threatened the owner of the Lost Coyote." He paused and looked at Hatcher. "That's right, ain't it, Hatcher?"

"That's right, boss, I was just japin' him," Hatcher replied. "And Marty didn't do nothin'. He was just standin' around."

Back to the sheriff then, Dalton said. "That's what I thought. So, as owner of the biggest saloon in town, as well as owner of the biggest cattle ranch doing business here in Buzzard's Bluff, I'll ask you to do me the favor of releasing these two in my custody. I'll see that they are properly disciplined."

The sheriff was caught in a position he didn't feel comfortable in. What Dalton said was true. As much trouble as his men caused, his ranch and saloon were still responsible for a lot of business for the merchants of Buzzard's Bluff. On the other hand, he knew without doubt that Ed Hatcher had come to town with one objective, to kill Ben Savage. "I'll tell you what, Mr. Dalton, let's you and me go talk to the owner of the Lost Coyote. He's the one who's pressin' charges against your two boys. If he's satisfied that they've been locked up long enough, I've got no reason to hold 'em."

Dalton hesitated. He hadn't expected that and it didn't seem like there was much use to meet with Savage. After thinking about the prospect of meeting this mysterious new owner of his competition for a few minutes, he changed his mind and decided it might be to his advantage to meet his adversary. "I think that's a good idea," he said, to Bragg's surprise.

"You want me to stay here and make sure your prisoners don't escape?" Spade Gunter couldn't resist japing.

"I expect you'd best go with us," Bragg told him and they walked outside while Bragg locked the cell-room door and the front door to the office.

"If I tell you who's come to see you, you ain't gonna believe it," Tiny Davis said when he stuck his head inside the door of the office behind the bar.

"Who?" Ben asked.

"Mr. Daniel Dalton," Tiny said. "He's out here with Sheriff Bragg and one of the Double-D hands, Spade Gunter, I think.

They said they came to see you. Rachel's talkin' to 'em now."

"Well, you're right," Ben responded. "I find that damn hard to believe." He got up from the desk, where he had been trying to familiarize himself with the books Rachel gave him to study, and followed Tiny back to the bar.

When the two saloon owners confronted each other for the first time, both men studied the other carefully. "Ben," Sheriff Bragg opened the meeting, "this is Daniel Dalton. He came to see me about the two men I've got in jail. And since you're the one pressin' the charges against 'em, he's wantin' to see if you might see fit to withdraw 'em, so he can take his boys back to the ranch. He says he'll punish 'em there."

The two adversaries continued to stare at each other for a long moment before Ben broke the heavy silence hanging between them. "Well, Mr. Dalton, I've heard a lot about you in the short time I've been in Buzzard's Bluff. I'm glad to finally meet you in person."

"I have to say I haven't heard much about you at all," Dalton responded. "Matter of fact, I heard you sorta popped up out of the prairie, like a cactus, surprising Miss Baskin, here, and everybody else in town. Where did you come from, anyway?"

"Like you said, I just popped up outta the prairie," Ben answered. "I never figured I'd meet the owner of my competition right away. I reckon you sent a couple of your employees to deliver your regards."

Dalton's eyes sparked at that. "You can't think I had anything to do with that business with Bob Wills or this thing with Ed Hatcher. I don't need to result to underhanded tricks to beat my competition."

"Well, let me put your mind at ease, Mr. Dalton. Miss Baskin and I intend to run Lost Coyote just the way it's always been run — the way Jim Vickers started it. We ain't interested in stealin' any of the business from the Golden Rail. You're welcome to it. We'll just continue to operate kinda quiet-like. And I might suggest you should come in sometime when you're lookin' for a quiet place for a drink." He waited for Dalton to smirk, then went on. "As for the question you came in here with, I don't give a damn if Sheriff Bragg lets your boys outta jail right now or keeps 'em another day or two. Just so you know, though, you'd best make sure they understand I won't be so easy on 'em next time."

Dalton found it impossible to sneer in the face of Ben's implied threat. "My men will do what I say," he declared. "But I should point out to you that a big man, making big talk, might find himself looking at the business end of a Winchester rifle. And I ain't responsible for what alcohol does to a man's brain."

"I thought you just said your men will do what you tell 'em," Ben replied.

"I'm just sayin' nobody can talk sense to a damn drunk, and I won't be responsible for anybody who drowns in a bottle of whiskey," Dalton said.

"So's I don't misunderstand what you're sayin'," Ben countered. "You can control your men as long as they're sober, but you can't control them if they get drunk. If that's the case, you've got a helluva problem."

Dalton had held onto his temper for as long as he could stand it. His words were getting twisted around when they came back out of Ben's mouth. "You're a cocksure one, aren't you? I shouldn't have wasted my time trying to talk sense with you." He turned, preparing to walk out.

"Least I can do is offer you a drink, since you went to the trouble to come to see me," Ben said. "Might be a chance for you to enjoy a quiet drink for a change." He couldn't resist saying it.

"Thanks just the same," Dalton snapped. "Come on, Spade, let's get out of this dump." He headed for the door.

Ben called after him, "I'm tellin' Sheriff Bragg to go ahead and let those two outta jail. Just tell 'em next time I'll shoot 'em down instead of takin 'em to jail."

Hurrying out the door after Dalton, Bragg asked, "Did you hear what he said? He says he's droppin' the charges against 'em, so I ain't got no more reason to hold 'em. Sounds like he's tryin' to be reasonable about workin' with you."

"Let's just get it done," Dalton replied. "We're wasting time here." He was still fuming after what he could only see as an unsuccessful visit to the Lost Coyote Saloon. His purpose in agreeing to go and talk to Ben Savage was to intimidate him by a show of command over a crew of dangerous men. He was long accustomed to respect for his commanding persona and he saw no evidence that this crude drifter realized who he was dealing with. He was more determined than before to do anything he could to make sure that saloon run by a woman and an ex-Ranger failed. He thought it a miracle that the saloon had survived as long as it had under Jim Vickers's ownership.

"They're back," Marty Jackson sang out

when he heard the rattle of the padlock on the front door of the sheriff's office. "They sure weren't gone very long."

"Don't surprise me," Ed Hatcher said. "I bet ol' Daniel Dalton gave 'em hell for lockin' us up in here. You wait and see. I'll bet we're gettin' outta here now." They both got up and walked to the front of the cell and stood at the bars, in anticipation of the news. In a few minutes, they heard Sheriff Bragg unlocking the cell room door.

Bragg walked into the cell room. "I'm lettin' you boys outta there now. Ben Savage dropped his complaint against you." He unlocked the cell door and held it open while they filed out.

"What'd I tell ya, Marty?" Hatcher brayed. "I knew the boss wasn't gonna let 'em keep us in here." They hustled into the office to retrieve their weapons and found Dalton and Spade waiting for them. "I knew we wouldn't be in here long after you showed up, boss," Hatcher said.

"Shut up and put your gun on," Spade told him. He could sense how angry Dalton was with Hatcher for not doing the job he had sent him into town to do.

Mack Bragg walked outside with them while Hatcher and Jackson were strapping on their gun belts. "You'll have to pay

Henry Barnes for boardin' your horses overnight, but at least you won't have to pay any fines," Bragg said. "You boys try to stay outta trouble when you come into town from now on." He got a grin and a grunt from Hatcher in return.

Dalton saw fit to make one final remark to the sheriff before leaving. "You know, Bragg, when a man gets elected sheriff, he's expected to serve the interest of all the citizens and merchants in the town."

"Yes, sir, Mr. Dalton," Bragg replied, respectfully. "You're right, and I'm very much aware of that." His response was met with nothing more than an accusing glare before Dalton turned and headed back up the street. Spade followed, leading their two horses, followed by Hatcher and Marty.

When the four Double-D men were comfortably out of range for the sheriff to hear him, Dalton paused to address Ed Hatcher. "How in hell can you not call a man out to fight?"

"I called him out, clear and simple, but he wouldn't face me." He turned to Jackson for verification. "Didn't I, Marty?"

"He sure did, boss, called him out to settle it with six-guns, and Savage said he didn't want to. Said he already had a gun drawn on Ed."

They recounted the entire episode in the Lost Coyote once again, but Dalton saw no excuse for Hatcher's failure. They continued up the street toward the stable then. When they passed the Lost Coyote again, Dalton didn't even glance in that direction, but a thought occurred to him. The more he thought about it, the more he was convinced that it was a good idea. "Spade," he said, "I think the men ought to spread their business to the competition a little more. The Lost Coyote deserves a chance to take care of Double-D cowhands a little more than they do now. It'll give the boys a chance to see what entertainment they have to offer."

"Whaddaya want me to do about this Ben Savage jasper?" Hatcher asked.

"I want you to kill him," Dalton answered. "He's going to be trouble from now on."

"It's gonna have to be from a distance," Hatcher said, " 'cause he's afraid to face me in the street. But I ain't too anxious to get my name on a wanted list. I druther call the dirty rat out for a shoot-out."

"Then I guess next time you'll have to get the jump on him, and you be the one with a gun already out. Then you can give him a choice, fight or die. He'll have to try to save his life."

"How do you know how fast he is?" Spade asked.

"I don't," Hatcher answered, "but I know how fast I am. I ain't worried about it," he boasted as they reached the stable.

"He's sitting pretty right now," Dalton remarked, after the bill was paid and they were mounted and started up the street, "king of the town, now that he's faced you down. Not only laughed at you when you dared to think he would duel with you, then dragged you down the middle of town, so everybody could see him throw you in jail." Dalton watched Hatcher's reactions to his taunting words. He knew the man was too prideful about his reputation as a fast gun to ignore much provocation to prove his skill. "I'm wondering why we've never heard his name before, but I suspect we'll hear about it in the future," Dalton continued. Hatcher made no verbal response, but Dalton was satisfied to see his eyes narrow and his teeth clenched. "After this thing with you today, I doubt anyone else will have the guts to face him. I expect one of the boys will have to take him down at long range. Deacon Moss comes to mind. He's pretty accurate with a rifle."

"Hold on, boss," Hatcher blurted. *The seed was planted.* "I'm the one that rattlesnake dragged through town, so I claim first call on settlin' up with him." He reined his horse sharply to a stop.

"What are you gonna do?" Dalton asked when he pulled up beside him.

"I ain't leavin' town till I settle with him for what he done to me," Hatcher declared.

"Well, we can't deny you the right to take your vengeance out on this man," Dalton said. "God knows he's insulted you enough to give you that right. I just wasn't sure you'd want to tangle with him again."

"You boys go on back to the ranch," Hatcher said, knowing now what he had to do. "I'm goin' huntin'. I'll bring you back that tin star he pulled out of his pocket yesterday."

"I respect your decision," Dalton said, "good hunting." He felt satisfied that Hatcher would flush Savage out somehow — face-to-face, or in the back, it didn't matter to him. And it was not his concern if Hatcher was arrested and hanged, as long as he got rid of Ben Savage.

"Well, you managed to get a visit from his majesty, Daniel Dalton, king of the Double-D," Rachel said as she set a cup of coffee down on the table before him. "That's something neither Jim nor I have ever accomplished. Must make you feel kinda special."

"Ought to make you feel like you've got a target on your back," Tiny Davis suggested. "What'd you let those two outta jail for?"

"It didn't make a whole lot of difference," Ben answered. "Bragg was only gonna keep 'em another night, anyway. Might as well let 'em get on out and let's see what they're gonna do."

"Best be sure you don't set down nowhere with your back to the door," Tiny advised.

While they were sitting there talking, Ham Greeley came in. Seeing Ben and Rachel, he walked over to join them. "Don't mind if I do," he said before anyone asked.

"We're drinking coffee," Rachel said with a wide smile.

Ham pretended to shudder. "I'm gonna need somethin' with a little more bite than that." He looked back at the bar. "Tiny, how 'bout a shot of that rye whiskey you've got? I might need somethin' strong if I'm gonna have to talk business." He looked back at Ben and explained. "You said you needed some carpentry work done. Said to come talk to you about it."

"That's a fact," Ben said. "I want you to take a look at the north side of the front porch where that mule tried to jump up on it and tell me how much you want to fix it. There's about six floorboards that need replacin', and I expect you might need a new joist."

"Dang," Ham responded, "you sound like you could fix it yourself. Thank you, Tiny," he said when the bartender set his drink on the table.

Ben smiled. "I reckon I could, if I had to, but you'd most likely do a better job."

"I'll take a look," Ham said and tossed his drink down. "Damn, that's nasty stuff. Wish I had a barrel of it." Then he got around to something he was more interested in. "I was across the street at Howard's and I saw ol' Daniel Dalton and three of his hands walkin' toward the stable. Two of 'em were those fellers Mack Bragg had in jail." He looked directly at Ben. "Did you know that damn Ed Hatcher was loose again?"

"He knew," Rachel answered for him. "Dalton and Spade Gunter were in here before they got out." She shifted her gaze toward Ben, as well. "He told Mack to let 'em out."

Ham was about to ask why, but Annie Grey came from the kitchen before he got his question out. "I'm ready to go home, Rachel. I cleaned up everything after dinner. There's a fresh-baked batch of biscuits

148

and I sliced up a plate of ham, if somebody needs something to eat."

"All right, Annie, thanks," Rachel said. "We'll see you in the morning."

Annie smiled at Ben and joked. "Are you gonna build a fire in my stove in the mornin'?"

"Don't count on it." Ben laughed. "I'm gonna try to get used to sleepin' a little later." Even as he said it, he doubted he'd be able to stay in bed any longer than he had that morning. When she walked out the door, he asked Rachel, "How far does she have to walk to get home?"

"It's not but about a mile and a half to her house," Rachel answered. She knew he asked because he wondered about her safety. "She always leaves about this time, before it starts to get dark, so we don't worry about her. Just in case, Johnny gave her a little derringer to carry in that shopping bag she's toting. Once in a while, if we've got something special going on, and she needs to stay after dark, somebody usually walks her home." She studied his face while she talked, wondering how this seemingly gentle man who looked concerned about Annie getting home could be the same killing machine that reacted to Bob Wills's attack.

"I'd walk her home, if it was real dark," Ham japed. "But I don't like the dark, myself, so Johnny would have to walk me back." He got the chuckles he was going for.

"It won't be long before suppertime," Rachel commented to Ben. "Are you gonna go down to the hotel to eat?"

"I thought I might," Ben answered. "How 'bout you? You care to join me?"

"No thanks. I always find something to eat in the kitchen. I'll eat one of Annie's biscuits. Besides, it's probably a good idea for one of the owners to stay here."

"Well, maybe I oughta stay here and let you go to supper," Ben said. "But big as Tiny is, he can most likely hold the place together." Saying that, brought up another question. "What about you, Tiny? What do you do for supper?"

"Annie fixes me a big dinner. I don't need a big meal at suppertime," Tiny explained.

Rachel smiled at Ben and winked. "You hear Annie say she baked a fresh batch of biscuits? Half of them will be gone in the morning, and we won't sell more than two or three tonight. Something happens to them."

"Rats," Tiny said. "You know we got rats in here."

150

■ ■ ■ ■

"You're a little early," Lacy James greeted Ben at the door to the hotel dining room, "but it won't be but about fifteen minutes before we're ready to start serving. Ordinarily, I'd tell you to come back in fifteen minutes. But since you're one of our distinguished business owners, I'll invite you to come on it and take a seat and I'll get you a cup of coffee to work on 'till we're ready. All right?"

"That's mighty neighborly of you," Ben replied. "I 'preciate it." He couldn't help thinking she could have saved a lot of words and just told him to take a seat. He shed his gun belt and rolled his six-gun and holster up in it, then left it on the table by the door. That done, he paused to let Cindy Moore pass, carrying a large stack of napkins for the tables, before continuing on to a small table against the wall. He had just settled into his chair when Lacy appeared again, carrying a cup of coffee for him. While he had the time, he thought back over what had been a fairly busy day for him. He had been eager to meet Daniel Dalton face-to-face to get an idea what type of man he was, because he had a feeling he

151

was going to be concerned with Dalton more than a little.

CHAPTER 9

His stomach full, he said yes when Cindy asked if he wanted more coffee. He watched while she poured and signaled for her to stop when the cup was about half full. "Don't give me anymore even if I ask you for it," he said then. "I'm afraid I'm gonna float outta here already. But I want you to tell Myrtle that was one fine supper."

"I'm tinkled pink to hear you were satisfied with the food," Lacy commented, overhearing his remark to Cindy. "Maybe we can look to see you coming back to see us."

"I think you can count on that," he replied.

She pulled a chair out and sat down with a cup of coffee to join him. "I declare, Ben Savage, you've had a right busy introduction to this little town of ours."

"A little busier than I had hoped for," he said. "I'm hopin' I'll get a chance to settle in a little better now that I've met the owner of my competitive saloon."

"I'll bet that was an interesting meeting." She chuckled. "Have you met Wilson Bishop yet? Dalton owns the Golden Rail, but Wilson is the one who manages it. He comes in here occasionally."

"No, I've not had the pleasure of meetin' Mr. Bishop," Ben answered. "Maybe I oughta go and introduce myself and we could talk about our different methods of runnin' a saloon."

He laughed and she laughed with him, knowing he had no illusions about his lack of experiences in the business of managing a saloon. She got up then, saying she had to help Cindy. "Don't be a stranger," she said as she pushed her chair back under the table.

He finished his coffee and got to his feet. Leaving the money for his supper on the table, he walked to the door and paused to strap on his gun belt. As he stepped down from the little porch by the outside door, there were only a few rays of the setting sun peeking up from the western horizon. The town took on a peaceful look as the street grew dim in the twilight and all was quiet as he walked up the street toward the Lost Coyote. The quiet gave way to the familiar noise of a saloon in the early evening hours as he approached the Golden Rail. When he became even with the front door, he remembered his conversation with Lacy and their joking about his getting to know Wilson Bishop. Hearing the sound of voices laughing and talking, he thought, just for the hell of it, it might be interesting to meet the manager of his competition.

He stepped up to the doors and looked inside. It was not a large crowd, most of the laughter and noise he had heard on the street came from a card game with six participants and a couple of saloon girls watching the game. Mickey Dupree greeted him when he walked up to the bar. "What are you drinkin'?" Mickey asked, not certain if he had ever seen Ben before.

"How 'bout a shot of corn whiskey?" Ben said. He watched while Mickey poured. "How 'bout Mr. Bishop, is he around?"

"Yeah," Mickey answered. "That's him standin' at the end of the bar, talkin' to Charlene. "Whaddaya need to see him about?"

Ben smiled. "I just wanna meet him. I'm the new co-owner of the Lost Coyote."

"No foolin'!" Mickey blurted without thinking and took a step backward, never expecting the owner of the Lost Coyote to set foot in the Golden Rail. He hesitated for a long moment, not sure what he should do. Finally, he turned his head toward the end of the bar and called out. "Hey, Wilson, there's a fellow here wants to meet you."

Wilson Bishop turned to look at Ben, and like Mickey, he was looking at a stranger. He took a longer look before walking over to meet him. "You lookin' for me?" He asked. "What can I do for ya?"

"My name's Ben Savage. I'm the new owner of the Lost Coyote. I thought it would be a good idea to know the fellow managing my competition." He gave him a friendly smile.

Like Mickey had been, Bishop was speechless for a few moments, since it was the last thing he expected to happen. Having to look up to the imposing stature of Ben Savage, he was befuddled at best, finding himself at a disadvantage. "What for?" was all he could come up with in response to Ben's statement.

Ben shrugged and answered. "Just because we're in the same business, and I figure we're both interested in helpin' the town grow. Right? I mean, there ain't no reason why we both can't do a good business here." He could see right away, by the blank expression on Bishop's face, that he was

156

wasting his time. Rachel would probably have told him that, if he had asked her opinion first, but it hadn't been anything he had planned to do. It had been a spur-of-the-moment decision.

"My business is makin' sure this saloon is runnin' like it's supposed to," Bishop finally responded. "I ain't got the time or the interest to give a damn about the Lost Coyote." He glanced at Mickey for support as he gained confidence. "If you're lookin' for advice, since I heard you ain't got the first notion on how to run a saloon, I can tell you one thing. Startin' out by shootin' one of our customers and causin' another two to get throwed in jail ain't the best way to expect us to be friendly." He glanced at Mickey again, feeling smug in the way he handled Ben's attempt to lower the barrier between the two saloons. "So I reckon you wasted your time payin' us a visit. Anything else I can help you with?"

"No, I reckon not," Ben replied calmly. "I'm glad I stopped in, though, and I appreciate your honesty. I think it can't ever hurt to know your competition, and I know now that what other people told me about the Golden Rail seems to be true. It's run by a real horse's ass. Thank you again." He tossed a coin on the counter to pay for his drink and nodded to Mickey as he walked back to the door, leaving them both speechless for a few moments.

When he went out the door, Mickey and Bishop looked at each other, hardly able to believe the surprise visit just ended. Mickey was the first to find his voice. "As I live and breathe . . ." he started, then paused. "I never in hell expected to see that man in here." They both turned then to look up at the top of the stairs and the man who had stood watching the entire encounter at the bar.

He had been tempted and he almost pulled the trigger, but he knew he would have had to be on the run for murder, and he didn't want that. There were too many witnesses there in the saloon. So he cursed under his breath as he released the hammer, holstered the Colt, and hurried down the stairs. Hatcher didn't look at Mickey and Bishop as he swept past the bar, stopping at the door to peek out before going outside. When he got outside on the rapidly darkening street, he looked toward the Lost Coyote and spotted Ben Savage walking in that direction. By the size and brawn of the figure, it could be no other, so he immediately followed him, hurrying in an effort to catch him before he reached the saloon. There were no longer any thoughts about calling Savage out again. The more he had thought about the way Marty Jackson had described the man's lightning response when Bob Wills tried to kill him, the more he had decided it was not worth the risk.

The street was already dark enough that he could shoot Savage down without being seen. He just needed to get a little closer, so as not to take a chance on just wounding him. *That's close enough,* he thought when he closed the distance a little more. A few seconds after having just thought it, Savage suddenly stepped into Howard's General Merchandise. *Damn!* Hatcher swore to himself, *I should have shot him!* That was twice he had missed the opportunity to shoot Savage in the back. It made no difference now, he would shoot him head-on when he came back out of the store. So he hurried back against the side of the harness shop across the street from the store. Tuck Tucker had already closed the shop and gone to supper. There in the dark shadow of the small building, he waited and watched the door for Ben to come out. Ready to shoot just as soon as Ben stepped out, his Colt .44 cocked and aimed at the door, he could feel his heart pounding in his chest.

He thought about the humiliation he had endured at the hands of Ben Savage and the sweetness of the revenge he was about to take.

What the hell is he doing in there? he thought, when seconds that seemed like minutes began to build up with still no reappearance of Ben Savage. Then another thought occurred, *It will be even better if he walks out with his arms loaded with packages.* He continued to wait with still no sign of his target. Finally, his patience expired and he decided to look in the window of the store to see what was taking so long. Before leaving the shadow of the harness shop, he took a quick look up and down the street. When he was sure no one was coming, he stepped out in the street and started immediately across. He was in the middle of the street when he was stunned to see the man he stalked taking a step away from the front corner of the general store, his pistol in hand. They both fired at almost the same time. Half a second quicker reaction time was the slim difference that sent Hatcher to his knees, his own shot impacting in the store's front wall before he keeled over on his side.

Careful to make sure Hatcher was hurt too bad to get off another shot, Ben moved up to stand beside him. Hatcher grimaced as the pain burned in his chest, and when he was aware of Ben standing over him, he tried to lift his hand to shoot. But Ben stepped on his wrist and reached down to pull the .44 out of his hand. "You wanted to have it out with me, face-to-face," Ben said to the dying man. "Was this face-to-face enough to suit you?"

"You low-down scum," Hatcher whined, "you kilt me."

"Wasn't that what you were tryin' to do to me?" Ben asked.

"You damn right," Hatcher stated boldly. "You were lucky."

"Yeah, I reckon I was," Ben admitted. He noticed the blood coming from Hatcher's mouth when he tried to talk and knew the pain the man was suffering. "I'll get you something to ease the pain," he said.

"I 'preciate it," Hatcher rasped, growing weaker and fully aware of Ben's meaning. Ben walked around behind him and put a final round in his head.

Knowing Sheriff Mack Bragg would likely be coming any minute, Ben looked back at Howard's store. Cecil had not thought it safe enough to come out yet, but Ben could see him peeking through the window. He thought he owed Cecil and his wife an

161

explanation, so he went back in the store. "I'm sorry I didn't have time to explain what I was doin', but I was kinda in a hurry before."

"We thought you'd gone crazy," Cecil said.

"When you came walking in here like that," Sarah Howard said, "didn't say boo or howdy-do, just walked right on through the store, into the back, and out the back door, I thought something was chasing you."

"Matter of fact, something was," Ben said, "somebody, anyway. I wasn't sure 'cause I couldn't clearly see who was comin' up behind me. And I figured, if it was a friend, they'da called for me to wait up." He shrugged. "I'd best get back outside to talk to the sheriff, but, anyway, I wanna say I'm sorry I ran through your place like that." He turned to leave.

"Who got shot?" Cecil asked.

"Oh," Ben said, realizing he hadn't said. "Ed Hatcher," he answered as he went out the door.

When he went back outside, he saw Mack Bragg coming, carrying a lantern. When he got to the body, Bragg held the lantern up as if to make sure it was Ben, although it wasn't that dark yet. A matter of habit, Ben figured, and he couldn't help commenting, "If there were any more shooters out here,

162

that lantern would give 'em a good target."

"Hell, I knew it was you," Bragg said, halfway serious. "You're the only one shootin' anybody in town lately. I brought the lantern so I could see who got shot this time." He held it briefly over the corpse. "I figured this was gonna happen when they left town this afternoon. I knew damn well Hatcher wasn't gonna let it lie, and I'm afraid this ain't the end of it. Tell me how it played out, just so I'll have your version of it."

Cecil came out of the store as Ben talked the sheriff through the incident and anywhere he could, Cecil nodded and said, "That's right, just like he said." When Ben finished, Bragg thanked Cecil for his report on the shooting, even though he had remained inside the store while it all happened. "Glad I could help you, Sheriff," Cecil said, oblivious to Bragg's sarcasm.

When the usual spectators gathered to see what the shooting was about, Cecil took the responsibility to inform them what had taken place. Bragg took that opportunity to pull Ben aside to ask him another question. "I'm satisfied it all went down just like you said it did. But just to be sure, that shot in the back of his head, was that to put him outta his misery?"

163

"Yes, it was, Sheriff. He was dyin' and in a lotta pain. It wouldn't have been more'n fifteen or twenty minutes before he cashed in from that bullet in his chest. But there wasn't any reason to let him suffer that long."

"I figured that was the case," Bragg said. "But I had to hear you say it. It'da been a whole different story, if that shot in the back of his head was the first one. Wouldn't it?"

"I reckon it woulda," Ben said, "but I think it was the shot he was fixin' to hit me with."

"I'd best go get Merle," Bragg said.

"I'm already here, Sheriff," Merle Baker announced. "I heard the shots and figured somebody would most likely be lookin' for me pretty soon. I'll go get my cart." He paused then to ask, "You suppose ol' Daniel Dalton's gonna want the body for burial out at his ranch? He didn't want Bob Wills."

"I don't expect he'll want this one, either," Bragg said. "But he'll be comin' in here complainin' like Hatcher was his favorite son."

"I'll give him till tomorrow afternoon," Merle said, "then I'm gonna dig a hole for him beside the other one up in the bone garden."

164

"Did Hatcher get him?" Wilson Bishop asked Stump Jones when the Golden Rail handyman came back to report on the gunshots.

"Hell, no," Stump replied. "Ol' Hatcher's layin' out yonder in the street in front of Howard's store. Two bullets in him, one in the chest and one in the back of his head." He went on to give them the story of the shooting as Cecil Howard had narrated. "Sounds to me like Hatcher was followin' Ben Savage, but Savage went in Howard's, came out the back door, and surprised Hatcher."

"Damn Hatcher," Mickey said. "He had Ben Savage cold when he came in here to talk to Wilson. He shoulda shot him while he had the chance."

Wilson shook his head. "Mr. Dalton ain't gonna like this." Back to Stump, he said, "I expect you'd best ride out to the Double-D and give him the news."

"Tonight?" Stump asked, not especially excited about taking the one-hour ride to the ranch this late.

Wilson hesitated a moment. "I reckon it won't make any difference. You can wait and

165

go out there in the mornin'."

Up at the Lost Coyote, Tuck Tucker followed Ben in the front door, chattering away about the brief gunfight. "I was just on my way here to have me a drink after I et. When I heard them shots, I thought somebody was shootin' up my shop. By the time I got down there, you'd already took care of business." When they walked inside the saloon and saw the inquisitive faces gathered near the door, he immediately began to verbally recreate the incident for them.

Tiny and Rachel waited until Tuck was finished before Rachel asked Ben, "Is that the way you remember it? You mighta had a closer look than Tuck," she japed.

"Pretty much, I reckon," Ben replied, "except for the part where Tuck said Hatcher called me out and we decided to face off in the middle of the street. There wasn't time to do any deciding about what to do. There wasn't time to do anything but try to shoot him before he shot me as soon as we saw each other, and I reckon I was the lucky one this time."

"Come on," Tuck cajoled, not willing to let Ben downplay the contest between him and the gunman, Hatcher. "You was just quicker'n him on the draw. Ain't that right?"

"I don't know if I was quicker than Hatcher or not," Ben tried to explain. "Both of us already had our guns out and we both fired as soon as we saw each other. I was just lucky."

"If you say so," Tuck said, preferring to believe his own version of the gunfight. He turned to Tiny then. "I'm ready for that drink of likker I started for before I heard the shots." He followed Tiny back to the bar.

"Come on, partner," Rachel said, "I'll bet you could use a drink, too." She led him over to a table next to the kitchen. "Sit down and I'll get it for you." She went to the bar then and picked up a bottle and a couple of glasses. He nodded his thanks and sat down. When she returned, she poured them both a drink and sat down at the table with him.

"Well, thanks a lot for the service," he said and tossed his drink down.

"I expect we need to treat you to some good service while we can," she said as she refilled their glasses. " 'Cause if you keep going the way you have been your first couple of days, you might not be around that long." It was said in jest, but she was not certain but what it might prove to be his fate.

"Maybe I might better get myself a will drawn up, like Jim did," he japed. "I could name you as my heir, but if I did, I'd have to watch my back around you then." They joked about it, but in the brief time Ben had been exposed to Daniel Dalton, he had learned that he was dealing with a man who lived by a set of principles suited to his own desires and ambitions.

An hour's ride from Buzzard's Bluff, Daniel Dalton sat at the dining room table with his wife. There was seldom much conversation between them at the table, and this night was no exception. Estelle suspected his business in Buzzard's Bluff had not gone well for him, for he was especially mute on this evening. When Maria Gomez came into the dining room with fresh coffee, Dalton was prompted to break the silence. "Has Spade Gunter asked to see me since we've been sitting here?"

"No, señor," Maria answered.

Maybe it was too soon to expect Hatcher's return from Buzzard's Bluff, but he decided to ask on the chance that he had. Unless it was extremely important, Maria would not usually interrupt his dinner or supper and

168

she might not realize that this matter was important. "If he does, or Ed Hatcher, either one of them, let me know right away."

"Sí, Señor Dalton," Maria answered. She turned her attention to Estelle Dalton then. "You do not eat enough, señora. Is not good?"

"It's very good, Maria," Estelle responded. "I just don't have much appetite for food lately."

"You need to get out of the house once in a while," Dalton said, a comment she often heard from him. "Do something besides sitting in that damn chair in your room. Get some fresh air and maybe you'd have an appetite."

"Thank you for being concerned about me, dear," Estelle said. "But I'll be all right."

That was the final bit of conversation between them until he had finished eating. Once he had, he wasted no time excusing himself and withdrew from the dining room. She knew that was the last she would see of him until breakfast.

His mood was no better the next morning when he walked into the kitchen while Maria was still in the middle of preparing breakfast. "Spade?" he asked and she shook her head. "I'll be back in a minute," he said and went out the back door. He walked briskly across the yard to the bunkhouse and the little cook shed where Ned Snyder was busy cleaning up after breakfast for the crew.

"Mornin', boss," Ned greeted him. "You need somethin'?"

"Where's Spade?" Dalton asked and when Ned said he thought he was still in the barn, Dalton asked, "Did Hatcher come in last night?"

"No, sir," Ned answered. "Ed ain't come back yet. You want me to tell him you're lookin' for him when he does?"

Dalton didn't answer for a moment, then said, "Yeah, tell him." Then he turned around and started back to the house. Could be good news, could be bad. Knowing the kind of man Ed Hatcher was, he knew there was a very good possibility that he had stayed at the Golden Rail to celebrate his killing of Ben Savage. There were two other possibilities for his late return. One was the chance he had killed Savage, but Mack Bragg had jailed him for it. That possibility didn't concern Dalton. The other was one he didn't want to hear — that Savage had killed Hatcher.

There was nothing he could do but wait to hear of Hatcher's success or failure and shortly after he had eaten his breakfast, he

170

received the answer when Stump Jones arrived at the ranch. When Maria told him that Stump had come to the kitchen door asking to see him, Dalton got up from his desk and followed her back to the kitchen.

"Mornin', Mr. Dalton," the saloon handyman began. "Mr. Bishop sent me out here to tell you that Ed Hatcher's dead — said you'd wanna know."

"The damn fool!" Dalton uttered before he could catch himself. "He should have shot him in the back." As soon as he said it, he realized he had lost control of his emotions in front of the lowly handyman.

"I hear tell that's what he tried to do, but that Ben Savage feller turned it around on him and shot him down," Stump said.

This was not the news Dalton wanted to hear. He was not sure if Savage was a threat to the Golden Rail's business or not. He had just outlasted one ex-Ranger, only to have another one take over the Lost Coyote. This one was younger and said that he was going to continue to run Lost Coyote just as Jim Vickers had. As far as competition between them, Dalton wasn't worried about that, for he would continue to attract the drifters and outlaws. But he had aspirations of making Buzzard's Bluff talked about in the same circles as Dodge City and Tombstone, wide-open towns that attracted cowhands, drifters, gamblers, outlaws, and prostitutes. If that happened, he could expect to pull in a lot more money than he did now. And he saw saloons like the Lost Coyote as a hindrance to that image and encouragement to settlers — farmers who didn't spend their meager incomes on whiskey and painted ladies. The unforeseen arrival of Ben Savage had caused Dalton to take actions he would not have needed to take. He saw immediately that Savage was a danger to his plans and had to be eliminated. His encouragement of Ed Hatcher to take the ex-Ranger out was strictly a business decision in his mind and he felt no guilt attached to it. Without the renewed threat of Savage, he was confident that he could have eventually run the woman, Rachel Baskin, out of business. He was just sorry now that Hatcher was not the gunman he had claimed to be.

He glanced up from his thoughts then and realized that Stump was standing there, waiting for instructions. "All right, Jones, you can tell Wilson I got the message." Stump nodded solemnly but did not turn to leave. Dalton realized the simple handyman was sniffing the aroma of baked biscuits still lingering in the kitchen. "Maria, give Mr. Jones a cup of coffee and a biscuit, if you have any left over."

"Thank you, sir," Stump replied at once. "That'ud be mighty nice of you. I sure would enjoy some coffee and biscuit before I ride back to town."

"You're welcome," Dalton said. He considered himself a compassionate man. His dealings, when it came to the business of making money, had nothing to do with that. He did an about-face and returned to his study. When he had decided what next to do, he would call Spade in and give him his instructions.

CHAPTER 10

The next few days brought a more peaceful atmosphere to the little town of Buzzard's Bluff. There was nothing from Daniel Dalton after the shooting of Ed Hatcher even though Sheriff Bragg was convinced it would only be a matter of time. It was still a time of indecision for Ben Savage, however. He felt relatively useless around the saloon, since it was obvious that Rachel was accustomed to handling the operation of the daily business without help. The only job he was supervising was the repair of the north side of the front porch. And Ham Greeley took only one full day to complete that job. After that Ben was idle again. In fact, he felt that every time he volunteered to do any chore, more often than not he made it more difficult. At the same time, he found he was not suited to sitting around doing nothing. Luckily, Rachel came to his rescue. She approached him one evening.

"There's something I thought I'd talk to you about and see what you think of it. Remember when we first went over the books? I told you we were gonna need a shipment of whiskey. Well, I was thinking you might wanna go with Johnny Grey to pick that up. It's a five-day ride from here in a wagon, but we get it a whole lot cheaper if we go pick it up and haul it back, ourselves."

"Where do you go to get it?" Ben asked.

"Houston," she said. "Tuck went with Johnny last time, and I was worried the whole ten days till they got back. On the trip before, they told them at Houston that some outlaws robbed one of their freighters. They said they took what money they had and as much whiskey as they could carry on their horses. Then they set the wagon on fire and burned up the rest of the whiskey. Like I said, I didn't go to sleep until they got back to Buzzard's Bluff. Johnny said the time I shoulda been worrying was when they drove down to Houston with an empty wagon. If the outlaws were smart, that's when they woulda hit them — when they still had the money to buy the whiskey. I told Johnny I wouldn't ask him to go again. It's not worth the money we'd save to put them in danger. Besides that, he doesn't like to leave his little farm that long." She paused to give him a sweet smile, then said, "I'll bet Johnny might change his mind if he knew you were gonna escort the wagon. I'll bet Tuck would go again, too. Of course, he claims he wasn't worried about outlaws."

He smiled back at her. "Sure, I'll go with either one of 'em to get the whiskey. You say it saves us money to haul it ourselves?"

"About a hundred and twenty-five dollars," she replied. "And that's counting the cost of the supplies for Tuck and Johnny, plus fifty dollars apiece for them to haul it."

"Whenever Johnny's ready," Ben said. "Tomorrow mornin', if he's ready."

"I doubt he'd be ready to go on that short notice. I'll tell Annie to ask him if he wants to go again. He'll be in here to eat breakfast in the morning, so we'll find out then. Tuck Tucker will be in tonight to have a drink, that's for sure."

"You sure this ain't some wild idea to get me out from under your feet for a while?" he joked.

She laughed and replied, "I'll never tell."

As Rachel had speculated the day before, Johnny Grey decided not to make the trip to Houston because he didn't want to leave his farm for the time it would take, just when he had a sow about to have pigs. But she was accurate in her prediction that Tuck Tucker was always ready to go. Tuck furnished the wagon, anyway, and insisted on doing the driving. That suited Ben just fine, because he intended to ride his horse. Cousin needed the work and Ben was a hell of a lot more comfortable in the saddle. They started out, following a wagon road down the Navasota River, Ben on the big dun gelding, Tuck driving a team of mules. Rachel and Tiny waved to them from the porch of the Lost Coyote when they drove past. The little redheaded gnome driving the wagon sat up and gave them a proud salute in return, while Ben touched the brim of his hat with his forefinger. It worked out that the first stop to rest the mules would be Tuttle's Trading Post, which was only a little over ten miles from Buzzard's Bluff. Ben smiled when he thought how surprised Tuttle and Rosa would be to see him show up again.

He was surprised when Daniel Dalton failed to come to Buzzard's Bluff to complain to the sheriff the day after the death of Ed Hatcher. Ben suspected that Hatcher was not acting without Dalton's knowledge or direction in the matter. But Dalton had made no visit to town since it happened, to pick up Hatcher's horse and belongings, or to pay Merle Baker for the burial of the body. Ben had to wonder if he might be wrong in judging Dalton's limits when it came to violence. He could only hope that was the case and the reason Dalton didn't show up in town to protest Hatcher's death. Whatever became of it, he saw no advantage in hanging around in case Dalton made some effort to seek revenge for his two dead cowhands. It would be him that Dalton would be after, anyway. *He'll just have to wait till I get back,* he thought.

As far as this morning was concerned, he was glad to be back in the saddle, on his way to Houston — a trip that would take him five days, to a town he hadn't seen in a long time. Cousin was wearing new shoes and it would be an easy trip for the big dun, since the rate of travel would be half his usual to accommodate Tuck's mules. As he rode along beside the wagon, he was subject to a near-constant stream of observations on a countless number of things — on most of which, Tuck spoke as an expert. On topics he claimed no expertise about, he still commented, however. To rest his ears, Ben found it necessary to occasionally ride on ahead of the wagon, supposedly to scout the trail before them. In spite of the wear on his ears, Ben came to like the fiery little man who resembled a fictional character out of a children's book of fairy tales.

They arrived at Tuttle's store at midmorning, and Ben received his usual warm welcome. After he and Tuck took care of Cousin and the mules, they went up to the store where Rosa had made coffee for them. Ben told Wilfred and Rosa about the great change in his life that had happened in the short time since he had last been there. "I declare," Tuttle marveled, "if that ain't somethin', Ben Savage, owner of a saloon." He looked at Rosa as if to see if she could believe it. She beamed her response, already convinced that Ben could do anything. "I'll be . . ." Tuttle went on. "So I reckon you're a Saloon Ranger now. What did you say the name of it was?"

"The Lost Coyote," Ben answered. Then he told him how Jim Vickers had come to name it that. "At least, that's what Rachel Baskin told me."

"Well, that's a pretty good name," Tuttle commented.

"I never knowed that was the reason Jim Vickers called the saloon that," Tuck confessed. Ben almost laughed, thinking that it must be one of the very few things Tuck claimed no knowledge of.

"Buzzard's Bluff," Tuttle mused. "That place has sprung up like a weed in the last couple of years. It sure cut into my business. I used to deal with a lot of the small ranches and farms between here and there. I even did a fair amount of trade with the Double-D, but that's all dried up. I don't know why I don't look into stockin' my store in Buzzard's Bluff, instead of Navasota. Heck, Navasota's about twice as far from here as Buzzard's Bluff. I've just been doin' my business with Navasota for so long." He looked at Rosa and grinned. "We still do enough to keep us goin', though, don't we?"

His comment cut to the bone of Ben's thoughts. He hadn't thought about the harm the town could do to a small trader like Wilfred Tuttle. And he immediately felt guilty about the supplies he had bought from Cecil Howard for this trip to Houston. If Tuttle's situation had occurred to him, he would have waited to buy some of the supplies from him. It was too late now. The money he was carrying was to pay for the whiskey he was going to pick up. He tried to think of some personal items he might need but could think of nothing. Finally, it occurred to him that he could use some .44 cartridges, so before they left, he bought a couple of boxes. Tuck bought some smoking tobacco and a box of matches, so that helped. And Ben insisted on paying for the coffee Rosa made for them.

When the mules were rested, Ben and Tuck said farewell to Tuttle and Rosa and continued on down the Navasota River toward the town of Navasota, planning to stop for the night about ten miles short of the town. When they reached Navasota, the wagon trail to Houston left the river and angled in a more southeast direction. Tuck was familiar with the trail, since he had taken the journey before. And when they reached Houston, Tuck guided them to the Baldwin & Sons Shipping Company, where they loaded a three-month supply of corn whiskey. They tied their full load down under a canvas sheet and started back that afternoon, planning on stopping at a popular camping site by a wide creek about ten miles north of Houston. They had decided on that spot on the trip down because of the presence of a couple of freight wagons parked there and evidence of many campfires. They figured there might be less danger of outlaws attacking wagons this close to Houston, especially if there were several wagons there.

When they reached the camping spot,

181

there were no other wagons there, so they picked the best spot, close to the creek bank where there was a good patch of grass. Tuck unhitched his mules and took them, along with Ben's horse, down to drink while Ben volunteered to get some wood for a fire. The one drawback about the place they camped was that, because of its popularity, there was no firewood close by the creek. It had all been cleaned out, so Ben had to walk up the creek a good distance to find wood to burn. He found a good source a couple of dozen yards farther on when he saw a tree that lightning had knocked down. It was only halfway burned, so there were plenty of limbs and branches unburned.

Hearing another wagon on the road some thirty yards away, he looked over to get a brief glimpse of it through the trees. He couldn't see enough of it to tell much about it, other than the fact it was a covered farm wagon. Probably a family, he figured, *I'll tell them about this firewood.* He continued to load up wood for his fire.

Riding up the creek, downstream from the campsite, two riders guided their horses up just short of the clearing. Toby Jenkins reined his horse to a stop and waited for his partner, Dan Ward to come up beside him. "There's two of 'em," Toby said, "that one we've been followin' and another'n already here."

"Wonder what he's haulin' on that wagon?" Dan asked. "He's got it all tied down under that canvas like he don't wanna get it wet."

"I don't know," his partner answered. "But he's got a good-lookin' horse down at the creek with them mules."

"I'd like to know what he's haulin'," Dan said. "Might be somethin' real valuable. Maybe worth a lot more than what that couple's got in that wagon we've been followin'."

"Hard to say, ain't it?" Toby responded. "That family's movin' to someplace with everything they own, I expect, and maybe a little money to buy some land, or somethin', too."

"Hell, let's just go ask that little feller what he's haulin', and if it ain't nothin' we want, we'll go pay the family a little visit." That seemed like the reasonable thing to do to Toby, so he agreed, and they rode out of the trees toward Tuck, who was coming up from the creek, leading the mules.

"How's it goin'?" Toby called out a greeting as he and Dan walked their horses up on either side of Tuck.

"Ain't never been better," Tuck answered.

Toby took a good look at the stubby little man with the red hair and bushy red beard. He looked over at Dan and winked. "Me and my friend was curious. Whatcha haulin' under that canvas?"

"Vinegar," Tuck sang out confidently.

"Vinegar?" Toby echoed. "Vinegar, like regular vinegar?"

"That's right," Tuck replied, enthusiastically, "a whole wagonload of vinegar, all packed in bottles."

"Where you takin' it?" Dan asked.

"To the vinegar mill," a smiling Tuck answered, looking back and forth at each of them, hoping to stall long enough for Ben to return. "Wanna see it?"

"Vinegar mill?" Toby looked toward Dan, and both men shook their heads. "No, we don't wanna see it," Toby said. "Come on Dan, we're wastin' time." He wheeled his horse and Dan followed.

Tuck watched them ride across the clearing toward a wagon that had just pulled into the other side of the clearing. "Those fellers are up to no good," he said to his mules. "Where the hell is Ben with that firewood?"

Across the clearing, the two riders pulled up by the wagon with a two-horse team just as Robert Grier started to unhitch them. At once wary of the two riders, Robert looked

184

anxiously at the shotgun now out of his reach by the wagon seat. "Evenin'," Toby said. "Where you folks headed?"

"Buzzard's Bluff," Robert answered.

"Buzzard's Bluff," Toby repeated. "You got a pretty good piece to go yet. That your missus in the back of the wagon? Tell her to come on out, we'd like to meet her."

"I'm sure she'd wanna meet you, too, but she's been sickly of late, so she'd best stay in the wagon where she can rest," Robert said.

With a look of bored impatience, Dan drew his pistol. "Look here, mister, we've been doin' this for a long time. You can make it easy on yourself, or you can take it the hard way. Don't make no difference to us, but I can guarantee ya, you ain't gonna like the hard way. Tell your wife to get her ass outta the back of that wagon where we can see her. Her hands better be empty unless she wants to see how you look with a bullet hole in your head. Now the sooner we get this done, the sooner we'll be gone, so call her out."

With no choice in the matter, Robert called, "You hear him, Sue Ann? I reckon you'd best do what he said and maybe nobody will get hurt."

"Now, you're actin' smart," Toby said. He

185

climbed down off his horse, his pistol pointed at Robert. "That money you got hid in there, where'd you hide it? It'll be a whole lot easier on you and Sue Ann if you just go ahead and tell us. 'Cause we're gonna go through that wagon and turn everythin' upside down till we find it. My partner's got a terrible temper when he's riled, so if we don't find that money, he'll burn that wagon up and everythin' in it."

Terrified, Sue Ann climbed down out of the wagon and hurried to stand by her husband. "That's a good girl," Toby said. "Now, get us our money, all of it, and we'll be biddin' you folks a good evenin'."

"Please," Sue Ann pleaded, "We don't have but a little bit of money, and it's all we've got to try to start a new life."

"You both look young enough to start all over again," Toby told her. "And you ain't that bad a-lookin' woman. I bet if you was to start whorin', you could make that money up in no time a-tall — and maybe enjoy yourself while you're doin' it. Whaddaya think, Dan? Think she could make it?"

"I'd pay her for a ride or two," Dan allowed. "Maybe I'll look you up next time I'm in Buzzard's Bluff," he said to her. "Right now, I've got other places to go, so get that money."

186

"The next place you're goin' is hell." The sinister warning came from behind the wagon, startling the two bandits. It was only for a split second and they both turned to shoot, firing wildly while Ben took dead aim, knocking Toby down with his first shot. Then, as Dan's hurried shot embedded into the side of the wagon, Ben's second shot slammed into his chest. Shocked into a state of paralysis, Robert and Sue Ann Grier were introduced to Ben Savage.

He didn't speak until he checked both men to make sure they were no longer a threat. After collecting both their firearms, he turned to the startled couple who were now holding onto each other in desperate thankfulness to still be alive. "Are you folks all right?"

"We are now," Robert said, "thanks to you." He tried to say more, but words failed him.

"It took me a while to see what was goin' on, but I was ready to back you up," another voice rang out, and they turned to see Tuck Tucker holding a shotgun.

Even more confused by the sudden appearance of angels from every direction, Sue Ann was finally able to speak. "God bless you both. You saved our lives. I know they wouldn't have left us unharmed."

"It's my fault," Robert confessed. "They warned us back in Galveston that there were outlaws attacking the freight wagons coming out of Houston, and in most cases leaving the drivers dead. But I thought the outlaws wouldn't be interested in a farm wagon loaded with nothing but a plow, a little bit of furniture and some plants in pots."

"It's a terrible thing," Tuck allowed, "when a man and his wife can't travel to a new place without havin' to watch out for no-good outlaws."

"Where are you folks headin'?" Ben asked.

"We're goin' to Buzzard's Bluff," Robert said. "My father is the postmaster there."

"Sam Grier," Tuck said. "I heard he had a married son. Well, ain't that somethin'?"

"Buzzard's Bluff," Ben commented. "That's where we're headin'. If you want to, you can join up with us and we'll make the trip together."

"Mister," Robert said, "we sure would like that! And we'll surely be grateful for your company." Sue Ann added her thanks, and Robert introduced themselves. "We're Robert and Sue Ann Grier," he said.

"I'm Tuck Tucker, and this is Ben Savage," he said, "and we're plum tickled to meet you folks."

188

Ben couldn't help being curious about one thing, so he asked Tuck. "When those two rode over to your wagon, what did you tell 'em to make 'em move on?"

Tuck shrugged. "I don't know. They asked me what I was haulin', and I told 'em vinegar."

"And they believed you?"

"I reckon," Tuck answered, " 'cause they asked me where I was haulin' it to."

"Where'd you tell 'em?"

"I told 'em to the vinegar mill," Tuck replied.

Puzzled, Ben hesitated before asking, "What's a vinegar mill? I ain't ever heard of a vinegar mill." He looked at Robert and Sue Ann. They looked equally puzzled.

"I don't know," Tuck said. "I ain't ever heard of one, either." When all three of them looked at him in amazement, he shrugged again. "It just sorta dropped outta my mouth — sounded like there oughta be such a thing."

Ben just continued to look at the comical, elf-like figure of a man for a few seconds before shaking his head and grinning. "Does sound like there oughta be such a thing," he said before suggesting that Robert should leave his team hitched long enough to pull his wagon over to the other side of the clearing. "You'll be handier to the water and we can build one big fire and share it."

"That sounds like a good idea to me," Robert said at once.

"Good," Ben said. "You move on over to join up with us, and I'll get us a fire goin' after I do something with these bodies." He paused to look around them. "Over on the other side of those trees, I reckon."

So, while Robert and Sue Ann moved their wagon over to the other side of the clearing, Ben and Tuck disposed of the bodies after taking inventory of the possessions of the two outlaws. Their reward didn't add up to much, and outside of two fairly good horses, their combined estate was worth little more than a night of drinking at the Lost Coyote for Tuck — if he so desired to invest it that way — or the price of a month's supply of flour for Sue Ann's kitchen, if she was frugal with her use of that staple.

Ben and Tuck used the late road agents' horses to drag their bodies away from the clearing. And using a shovel Tuck carried on his wagon, they dug a shallow grave wide enough to contain both bodies. This was done as a courtesy to other folks who might stop there to camp. When they were finished with that chore, they returned to their camp to find Sue Ann already in preparation for making some pan biscuits to have with their supper. "Well, we've got a couple of horses and their saddles to decide what to do with," Tuck said, since no one had brought it up.

Robert was quick to insist that he and his wife felt no right to claim anything that belonged to the two men who had accosted them. "You took care of those two," he said. "I didn't do anything. So, as far as I'm concerned, everything they have is yours." He looked at Sue Ann for confirmation, and she nodded her agreement.

"Robert's right," she said. "As far as I'm concerned, we still have our lives to live because of what you did. And that's as much as we could hope for."

"Why don't we do this?" Ben suggested. "Tuck owns a harness shop in Buzzard's Bluff. Saddles and harness are his business, so give him the saddles. I understand Henry Barnes buys and sells horses. See what Henry will give for the two horses, then you and Sue Ann take half of that and Tuck take the other half."

"What do you get out of it?" Robert quickly asked.

"I reckon I get the right to say I didn't kill those two men for money," he said. His simple answer was met with an awkward silence that lasted until Tuck ended it with a comment.

After gawking at Ben for a long moment before deciding he was sincere, he said, "Well, makin' a little profit offa you gettin' rid of those two sorry criminals don't bother my conscience one bit. So that deal is fine by me."

"Good, then that's settled," Ben declared. "How long before those biscuits will be done?"

Spirits were high at supper that night, and to welcome the couple to the Buzzard's Bluff community, Ben untied one corner of the canvas and pulled one bottle of corn whiskey out, so they could all drink to the meeting of the two parties. As befitting a lady, Sue Ann took only a few sips from Robert's cup. It having never occurred to either of them to ask what business Ben was in, Sue Ann was tempted to ask, "Won't you have to answer to the owner when he finds out there's a bottle of his whiskey missing?"

Tuck chortled as he answered for Ben. "No, ma'am, it's his whiskey." Not understanding, she gave him a look of confusion, so he pointed to Ben and said again, "It's his whiskey." She was still not certain, for like her husband, she had assumed Ben might be a lawman, riding with Tuck as a guard for his cargo. Still chuckling, Tuck said, "Ben's the owner of the Lost Coyote Saloon. This whiskey is for the saloon."

Ben was quick to clarify. "What Tuck means is I'm half-owner of the Lost Coyote. I'm a partner with a mighty fine lady named Rachel Baskin."

Robert was still shaking his head in amazement. After witnessing Ben take down two outlaws who already had their weapons in hand, he had been convinced that he was a lawman or a gun for hire.

Four days' travel found the two wagons approaching Tuttle's store on the bank of the Navasota River. Wilfred Tuttle walked out into the yard to greet them as Tuck and Robert pulled their wagons to a stop. "I declare, Ben, looks like you doubled your wagon train since you came through here before."

"Howdy, Wilfred," Ben returned. "Say howdy to Robert and Sue Ann Grier. They're on their way to Buzzard's Bluff. Robert is Sam Grier's son, and they're comin' to look for a piece of land to settle. Robert's a farmer."

"Is that a fact?" Tuttle responded. "Well, welcome to Brazos County, folks. What kinda farmin' do you do, Robert?"

Robert paused to help Sue Ann down from the wagon before answering. "Well, sir, I can grow most anything, so I'll be wantin' to grow food for my family to eat. Once I get a food crop established, I'll want to start on a peach orchard. I know how to grow the best peaches you'll ever eat. That'll be my money crop." He smiled at Sue Ann and said, "We're plannin' on another crop that'll cost more money than it produces."

Sue Ann blushed sweetly and patted her stomach. Ben hadn't noticed until then that she was showing a little baby bump. "I'm hopin' for a boy," Robert joked. "I'll put him to work as soon as he can walk."

"Well, congratulations on the start of your family," Tuttle said. "As young as you two look, you must notta been married long."

"Six months," Robert said.

"Newlyweds," Tuck declared, "and you've decided to settle in Buzzard's Bluff. How'd you decide that? 'Cause your daddy's in Buzzard's Bluff?"

"Well, I reckon," Robert answered, "that had a lot to do with it, but that ain't the only reason. My dad said the land and the climate around here would be right for growin' my peaches."

"Is that what that is in them little pots in the back of your wagon?" Tuck asked.

"That's right," Robert answered. "Those little seedlings will be bearing peaches some-day."

Finding the conversation interesting, Tuttle was moved to ask a question. "So you're gonna be lookin' for some land to grow your peaches on, right?" Robert said that was the first thing he had to find. "I know where you can get forty acres right on the river for nothin'," Tuttle said. When he saw Robert's eyes open wide with interest, he said, "Old man Mutt Oakley had a forty-acre patch not two miles from here. He passed away last winter. and there ain't nobody claimed that farm. There's a right stout cabin on it, too. I expect that'ud be a good place for your farm, if you could move in there before somebody else finds it."

Tuck grinned slyly and commented, "And he'd be real close to the store, here, to get most of his supplies. Right?"

"Why, that's right," Tuttle said with a chuckle. "I hadn't thought about that." He received a cynical snort from Tuck for his comment.

"Well, that sure sounds like something I'd like to take a look at," Robert said, im-mediately interested. He looked at Sue Ann and she nodded at once.

"I know where Mutt's place is," Tuck

volunteered. "I sold him some harness. I'll take you out there when you're ready to go look at it."

"I'd sure appreciate that," Robert said and looked again toward Sue Ann. "I told you comin' out here where my dad is was a good idea. And it sure looks like the Lord's sendin' us a lotta good help to get us here."

CHAPTER 11

As soon as the horses and mules were rested enough to continue, the two-wagon train left Tuttle's store and pulled in to Buzzard's Bluff a little over two hours later. They split up then, with Ben and Tuck heading for the Lost Coyote, while Robert and Sue Ann pulled around behind the post office. Robert and Tuck agreed to take a ride out to look at the forty acres Tuttle had told them about. "Better take a day or two to see your pa," Tuck said. "Then just give me a holler, and we'll go see that place."

"I thought you might show up sometime today," Rachel greeted Ben when he walked in the back door, looking for help to unload the whiskey. "You have any trouble?"

"Nothin' to speak of," Ben answered. "We hooked up with some new folks on their way here. Sam Grier's son and his wife, they're lookin' to settle around here."

"I didn't know Sam had a son," Rachel

remarked. "He's never mentioned it that I recall."

"Hell, maybe Sam don't know he's got one, either," Tuck japed. "I bet he was a pistol when he was a younger feller."

Rachel acknowledged his attempt at humor with no more than a look of exasperation and turned her attention back to Ben. "Johnny Grey's here to take Annie home. Maybe he'll give you a hand unloading the wagon." She went into the saloon to get some more help and took over the bar while Tiny and Johnny went out to help Ben and Tuck unload the crates of whiskey. With all that help, it didn't take long before it was stacked in the storeroom. Then they all had a drink to celebrate the acquisition of a two to three months' supply, depending upon how busy they were. When that was done, Rachel wanted to bring Ben up to date on what had happened in town while he was away. "We've got a lot more business from the Double-D," was her first statement. She waited for his reaction before saying more.

"The Double-D?" he asked to be certain he had heard her correctly. "Are you sure they're from the Double-D?" She nodded slowly, a wry smile upon her lips.

"What happened to the Golden Rail? Did they close down or something?"

"Nope," she replied. "I've seen several of these Double-D cowhands from time to time before now, but this past week, there've been four or five of 'em in here almost every night. And you might think it's been good for business, but some of our regular customers have been leaving mighty early in the evenings. So far, the Double-D men have just been loud and a little obnoxious, making comments that could cause trouble. But our regulars have been real careful not to rise to any bait from them." She made a little face and sighed. "It's a good thing Tuck was with you, 'cause if he'd been here on a couple of nights, he'da been into it with those boys."

Picturing the little red-haired gnome, Ben said, "I expect you're right. Sounds to me like Daniel Dalton is hopin' to run our regular business off. Have you seen any sign of him in town?"

"I haven't seen hide nor hair of him ever since you shot Ed Hatcher," she said. "I would ask Cecil Howard if he's seen him at the store, but Cecil hasn't been in for the last three nights. Johnny has been coming here to pick Annie up every day this week, just in case, he says."

"Have you talked to Mack Bragg about it?" Ben asked.

"I told him I was a little worried about the possibility of trouble from the Double-D crew of roughnecks, but he said there's nothing he can do unless they start some real trouble." She paused and shrugged. "Like one of 'em shooting somebody, I suppose."

"I reckon we'll just have to wait and see what happens from now on," Ben said. "And we'll deal with it then. Everything else all right?"

"As far as I know," she answered. "Are you going to the hotel to eat supper?"

"Yeah, I was thinkin' about it. I'd like to sit down to a good hot supper. I've gotta take care of my horse first, then I'll head up to the dinin' room right away." He sensed that, although her question was quite simple, she was hoping he wouldn't be too long at the supper table. Even though he knew she never went to the hotel for supper, he invited her to join him anyhow, and she declined, just as he expected.

"Well, look who's back," Lacy James greeted him when he walked into the hotel dining room. "Where have you been? I thought you mighta drifted right outta town, just like you drifted in one day."

"I had to go to Houston to pick up some

200

whiskey for the saloon," he said, "just in case you come in sometime and want a drink."

She laughed and said, "Don't be surprised if I do one night. Sometimes we get some of that ornery bunch from over the river, and I feel like I might be in the wrong business."

"What else would you do?" he asked.

"Hell, I don't know," she insisted. "I don't know anything else. Maybe I'll come to see you one day, looking for a job. Clarice must be stacking up some years."

He laughed with her even though he knew she had far too much class for that. "Yeah, but she's got a heart of gold," he teased, "she ain't got that mean streak like you have."

She gave him another hearty laugh. "You want your usual table?" He said he did, and she reminded him to park his gun at the table by the door. "I'll get you some coffee. Anybody joining you?"

"Nope," he said, but five minutes after he sat down, he was joined by Cecil Howard.

"I saw you go by the store," Cecil said. "You musta just got back in town. Mind if I sit down for a minute?"

"Yep, I just got back. What's on your mind?"

"As you know, I'm the mayor of Buzzard's

Bluff, so I'm talkin' on behalf of all the members of the city council." He hesitated before going forward, obviously uncomfortable in what he was about to ask. "I don't know how else to ask this, so I'll just put it to you bluntly. Is there some history between you and Daniel Dalton, like some bad blood or something?"

His question struck Ben as kind of strange. "I never heard of Daniel Dalton before I rode into town a couple of weeks ago. Why would you think there was?"

"The fact that you gunned down two of Dalton's men would seem to have something to do with it. And you mysteriously show up here to take over a saloon that is Dalton's competition. The council is worried that there's gonna be a gang war over control of the town. We've had a little trouble with some of Dalton's cowhands, but all of a sudden, since you hit town, they're showing up in larger numbers than before."

He paused and sat back in his chair for a moment when Cindy brought Ben's supper. "Are you gonna have supper, Mr. Howard?" she asked.

"No, no thank you, Cindy, I'll be leavin' in a minute."

Ben took a bite out of a large golden-brown biscuit, then looked Cecil in the eye. "So what are you tryin' to get at, Cecil? You askin' me to get outta town because some of Dalton's men are raisin' a little hell?" He found it hard to believe. This, the same man who gave him a big welcome when he first found out he had become a partner in the Lost Coyote — the same man who gave an inspired accounting of Ben's shoot-out with Ed Hatcher? "I think you're forgettin' something when you say I gunned down two of Dalton's men. What you meant to say was that I was attacked by two men I never saw before I came here, and I was successful in avoiding gettin' killed. If you're seein' more Double-D riders all of a sudden, it ain't because of me. More likely, it's because Dalton thought he was gonna run Rachel outta business as soon as Jim Vickers died. And you and the other members of your city council would have to go to the Golden Rail for a drink of whiskey. Don't that make more sense?"

Cecil didn't reply for a few moments, until he thought about what Ben had said. "Yes, but why does he seem to be going after you and nobody else?"

"Because when I showed up, it was just the same as when Jim was still here running the Lost Coyote," Ben said. "He figured Rachel couldn't keep runnin' it by herself." He cut off a piece of the steak on his plate and started chewing it while Cecil thought for a few more moments. "You're right, Mr. Mayor, you've got problems with Daniel Dalton, but they ain't gonna go away if I leave." He carved off another piece of his steak. "I will say this. I'll do whatever it takes to take care of my saloon, so people like yourself won't hesitate to go there for a drink and some conversation without worryin' about some gunslingin' drunk." He paused briefly to stab a piece of potato with his fork. Pointing it at Cecil to emphasize his next comment, he said, "Rachel tells me you ain't been in the Lost Coyote for the past week. She figures you've taken your business to the Golden Rail."

"Of course, I haven't!" Cecil exclaimed at once. "I just haven't felt the need for a drink in the last few days."

"Good," Ben responded. "Rachel will be glad to hear we ain't lost your business."

"Well, I guess I'd best let you eat your supper in peace," Cecil said, fumbling with his words while thinking he had not handled the matter very well. "It's just that the council . . . me being the mayor, I mean . . . I told them I'd check . . . you can understand there's nothing against you personally . . . certainly not from me."

"I know that, Cecil, and I respect your position in this problem for the town. We'll just keep doin' the best we can to make this a first-class town, right?"

"Right," Cecil responded. "Glad we could talk this over." He pushed his chair back from the table and got to his feet. "Enjoy your supper. I hope I haven't disturbed you."

"Anytime, Mr. Mayor."

"You want some more coffee?" The voice came from over his shoulder. He recognized it as Lacy's. She started pouring it before he had a chance to say he would appreciate it. "I couldn't help overhearing part of what His Honor the mayor was whining about. He needs to go out to the Double-D if he wants to complain to somebody."

"Oh, I wouldn't come down too hard on him," Ben said. "He's just afraid something's gonna start tearin' this town apart and none of us wants that. Right?"

"If you say so," she answered.

His supper finished, he left the hotel and walked back up the street toward the Lost Coyote. When he walked past the sheriff's office, Mack Bragg stepped out the door and hailed him. "See you got back from

Houston," Bragg said. "Any trouble?" Before Ben could answer, Bragg said, "I saw Tuck comin' back from the stable."

Preparing to answer Bragg's question with a simple, "Not much," he instead remarked, "then I reckon Tuck gave you a detailed account of our trip."

Bragg nodded. "I swear, Ben, trouble just wants to come to you. But I'm damn glad to see you back in town. Now there's one saloon I don't have to keep an eye on. I suppose you've heard we seem to have more Double-D men in town than usual and most nights they all come at the same time."

"Is that a fact?" Ben asked. "Almost sounds like they're bein' sent in on purpose, don't it?"

"That was my first thought," Bragg answered. "But I might be expecting more trouble from Dalton than he intends to make. I thought he'd show up at my office the day after you shot Hatcher, raising hell about you, but he never showed up."

"I'm hopin' he's got enough sense to know he can't fight the whole town to win whatever he's after. And the only thing I can think that might be, is him owning both saloons and makin' the town wide open for gamblin', prostitution, drinkin', and all the problems that come with those things."

"I reckon we'll just have to wait and see," Bragg said. "But I don't intend to stand by and let 'em take over this town."

"As a business owner here, I'm glad to hear you say that," Ben said with a smile. "I'll do what I can to help you out, Sheriff."

The sheriff was counting on it. "Thanks, Ben, I 'preciate it."

He noticed three saddled horses and two packhorses tied at the rail in front of the Lost Coyote when he was still walking past the Golden Rail. He couldn't help wondering if they would have usually been tied in front of the Golden Rail. But then it occurred to him, if they were Double-D riders, they would not likely be leading packhorses. So it was just somebody passing through town. When he got back to the saloon, he walked in and paused to look the room over. He spotted the three men right away, seated at a table, playing three-handed poker. He glanced over toward the end of the bar where Rachel was talking to Tiny. She saw him at the same time and smiled. "Did you have a big supper?" she asked when he walked over to join them.

"I did," he answered, "and it was pretty good eatin'." He motioned with his head toward the three cowhands playing cards.

"Double-D?" He asked to be sure, even though he had already assumed they were not.

"No," Rachel answered. "They're from the RBJ ranch, down south of here. It's a ranch owned by Ross Jacobs. Some of those boys have been in here before, but it was quite a while ago. They're on their way back to the RBJ after they escorted the owner's wife to Waco. The older man with them is Ross Jacobs's brother."

While she was telling Ben about the three men, Ham Greeley walked in, and seeing them at the bar, walked over to join them. "Evenin', folks," he greeted them. Looking at Ben, he said, "I heard you and Tuck was back from Houston. I hope you brought some good corn whiskey back with you. I don't wanna run out."

"Ha," Tiny responded. "We ain't seen much of you in the last week. I thought you mighta give up drinkin' for good."

Feeling all their eyes upon him as they waited for his reply, Ham answered sheepishly. "I just didn't come in the last couple days. I think I caught me some stomach problems from somethin' I et."

"There's a lot of that goin' around this last couple of weeks," Tiny taunted. "Them stomach problems, ain't that right, Rachel?"

"That seems to be the case," Rachel confirmed. "It drove our business down, and that's a fact. Quite a few of our regular customers stayed away. We did get some of the Golden Rail's regulars and that helped us businesswise." She looked at Ben and winked. "But I don't expect that's gonna last very long. Do you, Ben?" Before Ben could answer, she looked toward the front door and remarked, "Speak of the devil . . ."

Ben turned to see what had interrupted her train of thought. He at once recognized Marty Jackson as the man who had been with Bob Wills the night he had shot him. He was accompanied by two other men, and they entered the saloon with the kind of swagger that suggested they expected to be catered to. Ben looked back at Rachel. "Double-D," he stated simply and she responded with a distinct nod of her head. "Well, let's just treat 'em as nice as we treat all our customers," Ben said. He waited and watched when one of the men, who looked to be a shade older than his two companions, walked over to the bar and bought a bottle of whiskey. While he was paying Tiny for the whiskey, his friends sat down at a table across the room from the three RBJ hands. Ben was aware of Marty Jackson's eyes locked on him while his partner was busy watching Ruby, who was standing beside one of the RBJ men, encouraging him to bid on a hand of poker.

"Here you go, boys," Deacon Moss announced as he set the bottle down in the middle of the table, "courtesy of Mr. Daniel Dalton." He pulled a chair back and sat down heavily.

"You didn't bring no glasses," Shorty Dove said. "Whaddaya expect us to do, take a swig and pass the bottle?"

"The bartender's bringin' the glasses," Deacon said. Then, seeing Marty's attention distracted from the bottle, asked, "What are you lookin' at, Marty?"

"Spade said he was outta town," Marty replied, clearly worried.

"Who?" Deacon asked.

"That big ape, standing down at the end of the bar, Ben Savage," Marty answered.

"Ben Savage?" Shorty responded, that being sufficient to interrupt his concentration on the young woman watching the card game. He had never seen Ben Savage, so he turned, as did Deacon, to look toward the end of the bar where Ben was still talking to Rachel and Ham. "Is that the gunman who done for Bob and Ed?"

"He's a full-grown boy, all right. I'll say that for him," Deacon commented. "Are

210

you sure that's him? Spade did say he was out of town."

"I'm sure, all right," Marty insisted. "It was right here in this saloon. He got the jump on us, and we was leavin'. But Bob went back to settle it with him." He shook his head slowly, recalling the way Ben had turned and cut Bob down, quicker than Bob could pull the trigger.

"Well, that was Bob's fault," Deacon said. "If it was like you told it that night, this jasper had his back turned to Bob. There ain't no way any man's gonna beat me if I'm lookin' at his back, with my gun in my hand." He paused to shake his head. "Bob did somethin' wrong somewhere, hesitated, or didn't cock his pistol, somethin' to get his ass shot like that."

"Uh-oh," Shorty warned, "he's up to somethin'. He musta recognized you, Marty." While they watched, the subject of their conversation intercepted Tiny on his way to their table and took the three glasses from him. "He's comin' this way." All three dropped a hand to rest on the handles of their pistols.

"Evenin', boys," Ben greeted them cheerfully. "I'm Ben Savage. I'm one of the owners of this saloon. You fellows ride for the Double-D, right?" He didn't wait for an answer. "I just thought I'd welcome you to the Lost Coyote. We're glad to see that a lot of your crew have decided to try us out for your drinkin' and windin' down after a hard day workin' with cattle." He parked an empty glass in front of each man. "We're hopin' you'll find out you like it a little better here where we try to make sure nobody disturbs you and you don't disturb anybody. So enjoy yourselves. We're glad to see you and your friends in our saloon."

He turned around and returned to an amazed partner and bartender. "Well, that was a right pretty little welcome for our troublemaking competition," Rachel declared, a devilish grin on her lips. "What are you up to?"

"Like I said," Ben answered, "treat 'em like our best customers." He grinned and said, "It'll give 'em something to think over."

He was right in thinking that, for it left them puzzling over what his play was, for he could not possibly be welcoming them to his saloon. "This is a setup," Shorty finally blurted and immediately turned to look behind him as if expecting the sudden appearance of a firing squad of vigilantes to wipe them out.

"I don't think so," Deacon said. "We'd

212

already be dead, if that was what he's up to."

"You reckon he's really tryin' to get us to behave ourselves and not start any trouble?" Marty asked. "It is a lot more peaceful in here. Ain't like the Golden Rail, is it?"

"Damn it, man! What's the matter with you?" Deacon demanded. "What the hell do you think the boss sent us in here for? Bought us a bottle of whiskey and told us to go have ourselves a good time at the Lost Coyote. You think he wants us to like this place and quit spendin' our pay at the Golden Rail?"

"I reckon not," Marty replied sheepishly. "I reckon I wasn't thinkin' there for a minute."

"You sure as hell weren't," Deacon said, "so let's drink up and raise a little hell. It ain't gonna be every day we get sent into town with money to buy a bottle." He looked around them at the other customers in the saloon. In addition to Tiny, Rachel, Ham, and Ben at the far end of the bar, there were a couple of men standing at the near end. Other than the three cowhands playing cards across from them, there was no one else in the saloon. "This place is kinda dead," Deacon announced. "Let's liven it up a little." He took another drink,

213

wiped his mouth with the back of his hand, and got to his feet.

He walked over to the table where the RBJ men were playing cards and put his arm around Ruby's shoulders, startling her. "Hey, darlin'," Deacon said, giving her a hard squeeze, "why don't you come on over to my table? It don't look like you're gettin' the attention a pretty little thing like you oughta be gettin'." He flashed a wide grin at the three cowhands when they all looked up at him. "You oughta know by now that Double-D cowhands treat women better'n these small ranches do."

Ruby took a cautious look at the baleful man leering at her and replied, "Thanks for the invitation, honey, but I'm keepin' company with Jimmy, here, right now." She tried to maintain a friendly tone to keep from offending Deacon. "Right now, I'm tryin' to help him win this hand."

"Come on," Deacon said, "I'll take you to the men's table. We'll have a drink and maybe you can make a few bucks." She tried to pull away from him, but he held her tightly, hard up against his body.

"I'm sorry, honey, but I'm visitin' with Jimmy right now," she told him. "Maybe some other time, all right?" He continued to leer at her, squeezing her even tighter until she was afraid she wouldn't be able to breathe if he continued. "All right," she said sternly, no longer trying to sweet-talk him, "you've convinced me that you're strong as an ox. Now you can let me go, so I can breathe. Clarice went to get some supper. She'll be back in a few minutes. She's bigger'n I am. Maybe she'll feel like rasslin' you."

"To hell with Clarice," Deacon insisted, "I've got a cravin' for you."

The discussion between them was intense enough to interfere with the card game. When it was obvious she was not going to be successful in rejecting Deacon politely, the dealing of the cards came to a halt. All three men of the RBJ ranch turned to glare up at the intruder. The young man named Jimmy said, "Mister, she's done told you she's busy, so why don't you just leave it at that?"

"This business is between me and the whore, Sonny, and it ain't none of yours," Deacon told him. "So why don't you keep your nose on your little card game?"

Jimmy put his cards facedown on the table and started to get up, but Frank Jacobs put his hand on the young man's forearm to keep him from rising out of his chair. Ross Jacobs's brother had sat silently, witnessing

215

the baiting game that Deacon seemed intent upon playing until he felt he had to respond. "Did I hear you say you were from the Double-D?"

"That's right, Pop, the Double-D," Deacon answered. "You've most likely heard of us 'cause we're probably double the size of whatever little outfit you ride with. That's why they call it the Double-D."

"Oh, I've heard of you, all right," Frank said. "We work for the RBJ. We border your range on the south side of Wray's Creek. We ain't as big as the Double-D, but we'd be a good bit bigger if we didn't keep losin' cows along that creek."

"What's that supposed to mean?" Deacon demanded.

"I think you know what it means," Frank said. "It's called cattle rustlin'."

Deacon released his hold on Ruby and drew up to his full height. "Old man, you just talked yourself into an ass whuppin' unless you don't start apologizin' right quick." He pulled his coat back away from his holster and struck a pose as if ready to settle the issue with six-guns.

"I ain't apologizin' for callin' you a cattle rustler 'cause that's what you are. You riders from Double-D cut out portions of another man's herd and change the brands. That's what horse thieves do. So I ain't apologizin', and I'm not gonna participate in a gunfight with you, either. 'Cause that don't prove the right or wrong of anything. It just proves who's been practicin' the most to see how fast he can draw." He continued to gaze calmly at the fully frustrated gunman. "If you're wantin' an apology so bad, I suggest you make one to this young woman. I think she's the only one here who deserves one."

Deacon was getting madder by the second. It didn't help that he felt like he was coming off looking foolish in the face of Frank's calm. "You smartass loudmouth cowpuncher!" he roared. "I'll shoot you down right where you sit, if you don't get up from there!"

Of those struck speechless by the disagreement that suddenly exploded into a full altercation, Ben had followed it closely to the point where he intended to intervene. When Deacon was provoked to the point of drawing his pistol, Ben feared he may have waited too late to act. So he moved purposefully at this point to defuse the situation. With no display of urgency, he strolled slowly over behind the table, so as not to pull Deacon's intense gaze away from Frank Jacobs. When it looked like he was about to pass directly behind Deacon, he made a quick move toward him. Suddenly aware of the man behind him, Deacon spun around to meet Ben's right fist flush on his nose and his gun hand yanked straight down by Ben's left. In reflex, Deacon pulled the trigger and sent a shot into the floor that barely missed his right foot. In response, Ben landed another right that dropped Deacon to the floor, stunned.

Struck as motionless as every other witness to the unlikely drama taking place, both Marty Jackson and Shorty Dove reacted too slowly. By the time they jumped to their feet, it was to find themselves looking at the business end of Ben's six-gun, waiting for the first one to make a move. When neither man was willing to risk going for his weapon, Ben said, "Unbuckle your belts and let 'em drop." While they did, he kicked Deacon's pistol across the room toward the bar and Ham picked it up. Still covering the two Double-D men with his six-gun, he directed them to come over and help Deacon up on his feet. "I'm sorry to have to tell you that you three are no longer welcome here at the Lost Coyote. We were hopin' you'd become regular customers, but it's against the rules to shoot people here in the saloon when they're mindin' their own business. And you broke that rule, so you've

218

gotta be on your way. I might recommend the Golden Rail. I understand they encourage the kind of behavior you just demonstrated here. You can pick up your weapons at the sheriff's office tomorrow. We're still lookin' for good customers, so you might wanna tell your friends back at the Double-D we'd be glad to welcome them, if they're content to behave themselves." He followed them to the door and watched until they rode off down the street.

While Ben was seeing the Double-D men off out front, Rachel walked over to make sure the men from the RBJ weren't expecting to be asked to leave as well. The two younger cowhands were still in a mild state of amazement to find themselves still alive. "I have to apologize for the intrusion on your card game," she told them.

As for Frank Jacobs, he could only explain his state as one of utter astonishment. "That's the damnedest thing I think I've ever seen," he said when Ben came back inside. "That blanket-head was determined to kill somebody, pardon my language, ma'am." He nodded to both Rachel and Ruby. "But it's a rare thing to see somebody tryin' to prevent a quick-draw contest in a saloon. Some saloons hope for one, but you handled that like you were dealin' with a couple of schoolboys."

Ben smiled and said, "I think that approach worked this time because I doubt if any one of those three got as far as grade school before their brains stopped growing. On the good side, you fellows get a round of drinks on the house for refusing to participate in a gunfight. That all right with you, partner?" Rachel laughed and said it was all right with her.

"Well, we'll thank you kindly, won't we, boys?" Frank said. "And while I'm at it, I'll thank you for steppin' in when you did. I thought I was gonna get shot there for a minute."

"I did, too," Ben said. "Matter of fact, I thought for a minute you were as determined to get shot as that fellow was to shoot somebody."

"My name's Frank Jacobs," he said. "This is Jimmy Whitley and Ron Corbett. I'd like to shake your hand." He extended his.

"Ben Savage," he said, taking the hand offered. "This nice lady, here, is Rachel Baskin. She and I own this saloon."

"I know I may have sounded suicidal back there, but I swear, we've had so many of our cows disappear along the boundary with Double-D. And we know they're stealin' 'em. I reckon I'm gettin' too old to keep my mouth shut. When I heard that jasper shootin' off his mouth about the Double-D, I just couldn't help myself. I had to say something."

Ben glanced at Rachel while Jacobs spoke his piece, then back at Frank, he said, "We've had our problems with the Double-D, too. Matter of fact we're still havin' 'em. What you saw just now is a sample of the trouble we're havin'. Some of it has already led to a couple of shootings. So we can understand your feelin's about that bunch. They're not above dry-gulchin' you, either, so just to be sure, why don't you bring your horses around to the back of the saloon and tie 'em there at the steps. Then stay and finish your card game, and nobody will know when you leave." He paused a moment to judge what Frank thought of that advice. "Besides, unless I miss my guess, I think Jimmy and Ruby have got some more things to talk about." That brought a tinge of red to the young man's face and a knowing smile to light Ruby's countenance.

"That's not a bad idea," Frank said. "I could use a couple more drinks, so I'm not in any hurry. We're stayin' here tonight, anyway, got us a couple rooms at the hotel."

"In that case, you might wanna take your

horses to the stable," Ben suggested. "Henry Barnes will take good care of 'em for ya. Of course, the hotel's got a little corral out behind it, and they won't charge you anything for keepin' your horses there. We've got a right conscientious sheriff here in Buzzard's Bluff, and I know he takes a good look around the town late at night, but he doesn't patrol the town all night. So that means there really ain't anybody watchin' those horses that might be in the hotel corral all night. And if you're as particular about your horse as I am about mine, you'll wanna take him somewhere where he'll get water and good food and he's locked up in a stable. But that's up to you."

"You know, I never even checked," Frank said. "When that young desk clerk said we could keep our horses there, I automatically thought they had a stable."

"Freeman Brown's the owner of the hotel," Ben said. "They ain't got a stable now, but he said it's in his plans to have one before long."

"Well, I reckon you've made a decision for me," Frank said with a chuckle. "Ron, let's you and I take those horses to the stable. Jimmy's busy right now. We'll re-deal that last hand when we come back here."

"Seems like a real nice fellow," Ben commented to Rachel after Frank and Ron went out the door to stable their horses for the night. "I reckon I'll walk over to the jail-house and give Mack these guns and let him know we had another visit from the Double-D. I'll be right back."

CHAPTER 12

After leading his two companions out the end of the street, Deacon pulled his horse to a stop a few dozen yards past the hotel. When Shorty and Marty pulled up on either side of him, Shorty asked, "Where we goin', Deacon?"

Still in severe pain from a broken nose, but a little clearer in the head now, Deacon answered. "That's a damn good question. We let him buffalo us, just because he got the jump on us. Where the hell *are* we goin'? That big weasel mighta run us outta his saloon, but he sure as hell can't run us outta town."

"That's right," Shorty said. "He ain't the sheriff. Why don't we go to the Golden Rail? I believe I could use another drink right now."

"If he hadn't sneaked around behind my back and slugged me when I wasn't lookin', he'd be layin' back there on the floor,"

Deacon continued, re-creating the scene in his mind. "Caught me by surprise, he did, or he'da never got away with that." He wiped some more blood from his upper lip with his bandanna, grimacing when he touched his nose with it. "Damn him! Nobody pulls a trick like that on me and gets away with it. The boss wants that man dead, and I'll damn sure do the job for him."

"We'd best be extra careful," Marty Jackson warned. "I've seen that man do some things."

Fired up by his own failure to dominate the situation in the saloon and a burning need to make up for it, Deacon chastised him. "And do what, Marty, run for home, like you did when that gunslinger shot Bob Wills?"

"You weren't there that night," Marty countered. "I didn't have a chance to do anything, and there were some others there to help him."

"That ain't the way I heard it," Deacon said. "But that don't make no difference now. I'm aimin' to take care of Mr. Ben Savage for breakin' my nose, and I wanna know if you two are gonna help me. I'm gonna kill him whether you do or not. Maybe you druther ride on back to the Double-D and tell Mr. Dalton you went

225

into the Lost Coyote to raise some hell, but you got throwed out and hightailed it for home. And thank you for the bottle of whiskey." He paused to let that sink in.

"No, hell no," Shorty replied at once. "I ain't goin' back to the ranch. I say let's get that jasper tonight."

"Count me in," Marty said, although he still had doubts about going up against the ex-Ranger. "What are we gonna do?"

"The first thing I've gotta do is go back to the Golden Rail and see if I can get my nose to stop bleedin'," Deacon answered. "Then we'll decide how we're gonna flush him out and kill him."

"What about the sheriff?" Shorty wondered. "What if he gets into it? I don't know if Mr. Dalton would like it if we got the sheriff after us."

"That's the reason we don't just go back to the Lost Coyote, walk right in, and start blazin' away," Deacon answered, not sure how best to accomplish what he was determined to do. It needed to get done without the sheriff knowing who did it. "Let's go get my nose fixed and we'll decide how best to catch Savage without anybody seein' us."

They turned around and rode back to the Golden Rail Saloon. Inside, they walked straight to the bar, surprising Mickey Dupree and Stump Jones. "I swear, Deacon, what happened to you?" Stump asked. "You look like you got kicked by a mule."

"Give us a shot of whiskey," Shorty ordered, but Mickey was more interested in what happened to Deacon's nose.

"I got punched when I wasn't lookin'," Deacon answered, "and I need a little doctorin'. I need to have somebody take a look at it to see if there's anything she can do to fix it, so I can breathe." He looked at Bonnie Cruise, who walked up to the bar when she saw them come in. "Take a look at my nose, Bonnie, and see if you can doctor it up, so I can breathe."

The young prostitute made a face when she stared at the bloody nose. "Not me," she exclaimed. "Lookin' at all that bloody mess makes me wanna be sick. Tell Charlene to do it."

"Who done it to ya?" Mickey asked.

"Ben Savage," Shorty answered for him. "Pour us a drink of likker," he repeated, needing a shot or two of courage to brace himself for whatever was going to happen that night.

"I mighta guessed that," Mickey said and reached under the counter for some shot glasses. "Charlene," he called while pouring three whiskeys. "You boys oughta stay out of that wild saloon," he couldn't resist saying. When Charlene walked over to the bar, Mickey pointed to Deacon and said, "He needs some doctorin' on his nose."

"I can see that," the seasoned prostitute remarked. "What did you run into, honey? Did your horse stop, but you forgot to?"

"You know, right now I ain't in no jokin' mood," Deacon replied curtly. "Can you fix it so I can breathe outta it?"

"Let ol' Dr. Charlene take a look at it." She stepped up close to him and peered up his nose. After a few moments, she said, "It's hard to tell, it's so full of blood. Ain't no doubt, though, it's broke all right."

"Hell, I know that," Deacon barked. "Can you do anything for it? I'm havin' to breathe outta my mouth."

"I'll do what I can," she said. "Come on back of the bar." He went around behind the bar with her and stood there while she pulled a drawer open and took out a couple of old bar towels. "Set down on Mickey's stool, there, and tilt your head back." She got down on her knees and squinted up his nose. "What a mess." She got up again. "Just set right there. I gotta get something from the kitchen." She was gone for only a minute before returning with a pan of water and a wooden spoon. Watching, fascinated

228

by the procedure, Shorty and Marty had another drink while Charlene, down on her knees again, began her assault on Deacon's nose. After cleaning away some of the blood, she turned the wooden spoon around and stuck the round handle in one side of Deacon's nose. Just as he started to grab her arm to stop her, she gave the spoon a sharp thrust. Deacon yelled in pain. She pulled the spoon back out and began mopping up the flow of blood that came with it. That was as much as young Bonnie could take and she headed for the front door to get some fresh air.

When he could talk again, Deacon cursed her. "Damn you, you crazy bitch, you damn-near kilt me! I could hear the bones crackin'." For the second time that night he felt faint.

"You can breathe through that side of your nose now, can't you?" she asked stoically. "Like I told you, your nose was all broke down in there. Ain't nothin' I can do to fix it. I could only rearrange the broke-down part some, but it oughta heal up just like it is. You just ain't gonna win no beauty contests." She watched him trying to regain his senses for a few moments before asking, "You want me to fix the other side now?"

"Hell, no!" he roared and jumped to his

feet, almost stumbling over the stool. "I shoulda knowed you didn't know nothin' about doctorin'." He looked at Mickey, who had a smile of amusement on his face. "Pour me a drink of that likker," he ordered.

"You'll thank me when that nose stops hurtin'," she said and returned to the table she had been occupying with two drifters when Deacon and his friends came in.

Standing up to the bar then, holding a bar towel under his damaged nose, he managed to tilt his glass under the cloth to down the whiskey. When he was calm at last, he asked Mickey if any of the other boys had been in that night. "Not so far," Mickey said while he studied the results of Charlene's work. "You three are the only Double-D boys I've seen." After a moment, he remarked, "That feller packs a helluva punch, don't he?"

"Anybody does when the other feller ain't lookin'," Deacon protested. "It'da been a helluva lot different if I'da seen him comin'."

"Maybe so," Mickey said, "but I believe it'd be a good idea to try to catch that feller when he ain't lookin'."

"I want him facin' me right out in the middle of the street," Deacon claimed. "But he won't stand up to me fair and square, same as when Bob and Ed called him out, he wouldn't face up to 'em. That's why we gotta catch him outta that saloon."

"He's outta the saloon right now," Bonnie informed them, having heard Deacon's comment as she came back in from outside. "He just walked by and he's standin' out in the middle of the street holding some guns and talkin' to Sheriff Bragg." When they all showed immediate interest in what she said, she opened the door again and stood in the doorway. "Him and the sheriff are goin' in the jailhouse. You'd better hurry if you're thinkin' about shootin' him!" All three of the Double-D men ran to the door, as well as Wilson Bishop, who had joined them when he heard what was going on. They got there just in time to still see Ben Savage's broad back as he entered the office door.

"Dammit to hell!" Deacon blurted when he saw the golden opportunity presented to him. Without hesitating, he reached for his pistol, only then realizing his holster was empty and he grimaced in frustration when he remembered that Savage had taken their pistols. And in fact, he was turning them over to the sheriff at that moment. Looking quickly around him for a weapon from some source, he was frantic to act quickly before his target disappeared into the sheriff's office. But no one of them was armed.

"Quick!" he exclaimed. "Our rifles on the horses! We can get them before he comes back outta there."

"Hold on, there, Deacon!" Wilson Bishop interjected, suddenly realizing what was actually about to happen. "You can't shoot that man from this saloon. Daniel Dalton would raise holy hell, if you tie the Double-D and the Golden Rail to the shooting. Damn it, man, you just said, yourself, that it has to be an unknown shooter to keep the sheriff out of it. That damn city council will be trying to close this place down."

"I ain't gonna miss this chance to put that lily-livered lowlife in the ground," Deacon swore. "You're right, I ought not shoot him from the saloon, but I can sure as hell shoot him from down behind the hotel. Come on, boys," he said to Marty and Shorty. "Let's get out of here and get our rifles off the saddles while he's in there talkin' to the sheriff. If we hurry up, we can get outta sight behind the hotel and shoot him down right in the middle of the street." They followed him out the door, desperate to get their rifles before Ben came back out. "Hurry!" Deacon prodded. "We gotta be outta sight when we shoot."

Forgetting his painful nose in his haste to

dry-gulch Ben when he walked unsuspecting out of Mack Bragg's office, Deacon took the two porch steps in one leap. Shorty and Marty, caught up in his determination to kill, were right behind him. All three arrived at their horses at almost the same time, and all three were struck dumb at the moment of discovery — their rifle slings were all empty! Beside himself with rage, Deacon uttered a moan between clenched teeth that erupted into a howl of complete frustration.

Inside Mack Bragg's office, the sheriff paused for a moment to listen. "What was that?" he asked. "Did you hear that?"

"Yeah," Ben answered, unconcerned. "Sounded kinda like a coyote howlin', didn't it?" He grinned and said, "Maybe it's the Lost Coyote tellin' me to get back to work." They stopped their conversation to listen, but there were no other sounds except that of horses galloping away. He had to smile even more when he realized that Deacon and his two friends just found out their rifles were missing. He had recognized the three horses when he walked by the Golden Rail, having watched the three ride away from the Lost Coyote. Thinking it a wise precaution, he took the opportunity to ease the three rifles out of the saddle scabbards and turn them over to Mack with their pistols.

Feeling the need to verify what he suspected, the sheriff walked to the door and looked out. "Yep," he confirmed, "that was the three horses that were tied in front of the Golden Rail." He walked back inside, slowly shaking his head. "Ben, I reckon you know what you're doin', but I've gotta tell you, you're playin' a dangerous game. I know what you're gonna say, and I agree with you. You have every right to throw troublemakers out of your place of business." He cocked his head in a show of indecision. "But confiscatin' their firearms, I ain't sure you're standin' on legal ground there. Maybe forbiddin' 'em from wearin' them in the Lost Coyote woulda been more in line with what most business owners woulda done. 'Course, you bein' a former Texas Ranger, I know you understand the law as well as I do." He looked Ben in the eye. "And that's the reason I go along with everything you've done, so far. And you did tell those three they could have their weapons back tomorrow, so I reckon it ain't complete confiscation." He paused for a long moment before continuing. "I swear, I forgot what I was fixin' to say." He paused again but couldn't recall what he had intended. "Anyway, I just hope you know you're paintin' a great big target on your back, and you've got yourself a passel of enemies in one helluva short time in this town."

"Mack, I appreciate what you're tellin' me, and I don't deny anything you said. But I can't see how any of this can be my fault. The way I see it is that all I'm guilty of is inheriting a saloon and not changin' one thing about the way it operates. It wouldn't be fair to Rachel and Annie and Tiny, or Ruby and Clarice, if I let Daniel Dalton run us out of business."

"I expect you're right about that," Bragg replied. "No argument from me, but it ain't gonna help them any, if you get yourself shot, either. That's all I'm sayin', so watch your back."

"I'll do that," Ben said. "Now, I'd best be gettin' back to the saloon, or they'll think you locked me up for stealin' firearms."

Outside, he paused to inhale the night air. All the dust from the daily travel up and down the street had settled, leaving a fresh, clear evening, set to receive a new moon. Even though he could think to enjoy the evening, he couldn't help thinking what a clear target he was, walking down the middle of the street. Maybe it was a damn good idea he had, to take those rifles when he had the chance. The thought ran across his mind that being a Texas Ranger might not have been as dangerous as owning a saloon.

When he walked back in the Lost Coyote, he saw that Tuck Tucker had come in and was already in a card game with his usual opponent, Ham Greeley. They had engaged Frank Jacobs and Ron Corbett in the game to make it a four-hand. Tuck was busy telling Frank and Ron how he and Ben had saved a young couple on the way back from Houston. He interrupted his story when he saw Ben walk in but only long enough to tell Ben he was fixing to come after him if he hadn't showed up pretty soon.

"You want something to drink?" Tiny asked when Ben walked over to the bar to join him and Rachel. He declined the offer of a drink.

"You want a cup of coffee?" Rachel asked. "There's some left in a pot I made a little while before you went to the sheriff's office."

"No, thanks anyway. I don't really want anything right now. Might have a drink later." It occurred to him at that moment that he had been many years without family. And now, he guessed this was his little family. It felt like it, anyway.

■ ■ ■ ■

Deacon Moss, Marty Jackson, and Shorty Dove rode into the barnyard at the Double-D after a hard hour's ride and pulled their saddles off before releasing the tired mounts to go to water. Buster Pate was at the barn, and he walked out to meet them. "You boys are back pretty early, I figured . . ." He interrupted himself to ask, "What in the hell happened to you, Deacon?" Deacon didn't answer him and continued into the stable to put his saddle away.

"Better not bother him about it," Marty said to Buster. "Things just didn't go to suit Deacon tonight. Didn't go to suit any of us, I reckon. And I'm pretty sure Mr. Dalton ain't gonna like it a bit." He went on to tell Buster all about their mission to raise hell in the Lost Coyote and how the whole thing turned upside down.

When Marty finished, Buster asked, "And now the three of you have gotta go back to the sheriff's office to get your guns?"

"That's a fact," Shorty answered him, "and I'm tellin' you, ol' Deacon is as hot as a boil in the middle of your fanny. He ain't said a word all the way back from town, did he, Marty?"

"Not a word," Marty answered, "and we near 'bout wore our horses out to keep up with him."

Buster remarked, "Mr. Dalton ain't gonna be happy about this. He was dependin' on Deacon to draw that feller out. I wouldn't wanna be in any of your boots when he finds out. You goin' to tell him now?"

"I figure that's Deacon's job, but if it was up to me, I'd wait till mornin' before I owned up to it," Shorty said.

When Deacon came back out of the stable, they quickly went silent until Marty asked, "Are you gonna report to Mr. Dalton tonight?"

Still steaming, Deacon didn't answer at once. He was still making that decision in his mind. "I don't know," he finally spoke. "I don't see as how it'll do Mr. Dalton any good to tell him tonight. It won't make any difference in what happened, if we wait till in the mornin'." He turned and headed for the bunkhouse, leaving them to stare after him.

"There ain't no doubt in my mind," Shorty commented. "He's goin' after that Savage feller. Deacon ain't gonna bother about a fair shoot-out. He just wants to kill him any chance he can get. I just hope the boss don't come down hard on me and

Marty 'cause it was Deacon's show right from the start. He called all the shots."

Marty didn't say anything, but he was as concerned as Shorty when he thought about Daniel Dalton's likely reaction to this latest confrontation with Ben Savage. He secretly wished that Dalton would send Deacon to do his dirty work alone, instead of involving him and Shorty. He had never actually killed a man, and he was not really sure how he would respond if it happened that he found himself face-to-face with Ben Savage. At this stage in his young life, he had to admit that it may have been a mistake to join the Double-D's crew of outlaw cowhands. But the Double-D was all he had, and he was reluctant to let it go. So he saw no alternative other than to continue to imitate the bold-talking swagger of the rest of the men.

CHAPTER 13

"Mornin', Maria," Spade Gunter said when she opened the kitchen door. "I think Mr. Dalton wants to talk to Deacon this mornin'. He said to report to him when he got back, and Deacon didn't wanna bother him last night."

Maria nodded. "Sí, he has asked already this morning if you have come." Staring at the bruised and swollen face of Deacon, she stepped back to let them in the kitchen but made no comment. "Wait here, I go tell him." In a few minutes, she returned to tell them Dalton would see them in the study, then stepped aside to let them pass through to the hallway.

"Well?" That was all they were greeted with from the owner of the Double-D and the Golden Rail, although his heavy frown indicated his immediate displeasure upon seeing Deacon's face. Overnight, the heavy bruising, combined with the flattened effect on the bridge of Deacon's nose, made his injury appear even worse. Without hearing the first word of Deacon's report, Dalton could read the result in the faces of both men. He was still irate over Ed Hatcher's miserable failure to eliminate the roadblock Ben Savage presented in his intention to run Rachel Baskin out of business. And now he expected to hear of another failure.

"Yes, sir," Spade responded respectfully. "Things didn't go like Deacon and the other boys wanted 'em to."

"Let him tell it," Dalton interrupted. His accusing gaze having never left the battered face of Deacon Moss, he said, "Tell me the man who did that to your face is dead." He already assumed the man to be Ben Savage.

The normally bold and cocksure Deacon sputtered painfully as he sought to explain his failure to carry out Dalton's wishes. "I surely wish I could, Mr. Dalton," he started humbly, "but some things didn't work out like they shoulda." When Dalton's eyes narrowed under heavy dark eyebrows, like a thunderstorm building, Deacon hastened to assure him. "It ain't done, though, not by a long shot. He got the jump on me this time, but it wasn't because of anything I done wrong. It was all bad luck, but luck ain't gonna go his way every time. I can take that man down and won't nobody blame me after what he done to my nose. He'll have to fight me, or be branded a low-down coward. I was gonna get him last night, but I didn't have a gun. None of us did, Marty or Shorty neither. That's the only reason he ain't dead."

"What do you mean, you didn't have a gun?" Dalton interrupted. "Why didn't you have your guns with you?"

Deacon's heart sank. He hadn't meant to mention that part of their folly. "The sheriff's got 'em. He took 'em away from the three of us, so we couldn't use 'em last night." That sounded better than the actual fact — that Savage took the guns away from them and gave them to the sheriff. "He said we could have our guns back today, so we have to go get 'em."

The look of disgust on Dalton's face was sign enough to express his feelings on the matter, but he preferred to express them, so there would be no misunderstanding. "Do you know why I pay you higher wages than any of the other ranches in this part of Texas, and hire you year-round? I'll tell you why. It's because I thought I hired men who could do more than nursemaid a herd of cattle. Spade will tell you that." He paused to glance at his foreman. "At least I'm assuming he has."

"Yes, sir, boss," Spade immediately piped up. "I told 'em, all right."

Dalton continued. Looking Deacon square in the eyes, he said. "This thing between you and Ben Savage, it looks to me like this is a personal problem. And I don't hire a man who's got personal problems, so you go take care of yours, or don't come back to the Double-D. Do you understand that?"

"Yes, sir, I do," Deacon replied at once and turned toward the door.

Spade hesitated long enough to ask, "What about Shorty and Marty? You want me to send them in to town to get their guns back?"

The look of disgust returned to Dalton's face. "Yeah, I reckon so. We're already short a couple of men or I'd tell you to fire them." Spade nodded and started to follow Deacon out the door. "And Spade," Dalton stopped him, "I think I'd best ride into Buzzard's Bluff this morning. I'd better check on a few things, myself."

"Yes, sir," Spade said. "I'll have your horse ready. Are you wantin' anybody to go with you?"

"No, I think I'll go in alone." He thought it might be better if he was not accompanied by the men who had been making trouble for the merchants of Buzzard's Bluff of late. His last visit to town, when he accompanied the sheriff to go talk to Ben Savage, had not ended that well. In addition, he thought maybe it was time he was seen by more of the merchants as the owner of the Golden Rail and not only referred to as the owner of the Double-D.

After Spade left, he called for Maria to lay out his riding clothes, then went to his wife's room to tell her that he was going into town. When he looked inside her door, Estelle was asleep in her chair by the window. *Good,* he thought, and closed the door quietly. He went back to his room where Maria was waiting to help him into his boots and leather coat. As he was leaving, she told him she would make the señora a pot of tea. He went out to the stable where Spade had his favorite black Morgan saddled and waiting.

Deacon, Marty, and Shorty had not been gone longer than fifteen minutes when Mack Bragg looked out his office window and saw Daniel Dalton pull up in front of the jail. "Oh, hell," he murmured, "here comes trouble." He walked back to his desk and sat down. In an effort to present himself as a person of authority, he took out some wanted posters and pretended to be looking through them. "Well, good mornin', Mr. Dalton," he greeted him when he came in the door. "What brings you in to town this mornin'? If it's about those weapons, I just turned them over to your men not thirty minutes ago."

"Good morning, Sheriff," Dalton returned. "No, I didn't stop in about the weapons. I think you did the proper thing when you confiscated their weapons, if they were threatening anyone." He walked over and sat down in a chair facing Bragg. "I just thought it my place to stop by to let you know that I have been hearing of too many reports on the ill-behavior of my ranch hands. And I wanted to let you know that I'm telling the men to behave themselves in town. There seem to have been several instances of trouble in the Lost Coyote, so I've told my men to stay out of that saloon. After all, I own the Golden Rail, I need their money spent there. That way, we keep the money going round and round between the ranch and the saloon. Right, Sheriff?" He paused and smiled to let Bragg know he was making a joke. "I wish I could say that would put a stop to all the mischief caused by a rowdy cowhand who's had too much whiskey to let him use good sense. But you understand that might be out of my control."

"I reckon that's safe to say," Bragg replied. "But the town of Buzzard's Bluff will sure appreciate your efforts to keep the peace."

"Good," Dalton said. Unable to think of anything more, he got to his feet. "Well, I just wanted to drop by and let you know I'll try to help keep the peace."

Bragg got to his feet as well. " 'Preciate it, Mr. Dalton. Thanks for stoppin' by." He stood in the doorway and watched him lead his horse across the street to the Golden Rail. "Now, what in the world is that ol' dung beetle up to?" he asked aloud. "Wait till I tell Ben Savage about this visit." He would have gone right away, but he didn't want to risk having Dalton see him going immediately to his competition.

Equally surprised across the street, Stump Jones, staring out the window of the Golden Rail, uttered, "As I live and breathe . . ." He turned and yelled at the three men sitting at a table. "Look who's comin'. You boys didn't say Mr. Dalton was comin' to meet you here."

"That ain't funny, Stump," Marty said as he walked over to the window to see what Stump was joking about. "Well, I'll be . . ."

246

he blurted when he looked out and saw Dalton tying the Morgan to the hitching rail out front. He turned immediately toward Deacon and Shorty still sitting at the table. "We got to get outta here! It's the boss! He's comin' here!"

Like three truant schoolboys caught by the principal, the three outlaw cowhands ran out of the saloon to take refuge in the kitchen, where a startled Charlene was eating a late breakfast at the table. "What the hell?" she blurted. "Who's after you?"

"Just sit there and shut up," Deacon said. "It's Daniel Dalton, and I'd just as soon he didn't find me here." He eased up beside the kitchen door in an effort to try to hear what was being talked about in the barroom. He turned back to Charlene to ask a quick question. "Did Wilson say anything about Mr. Dalton coming by here today?"

"Not to me, he didn't," she answered. "Hell, he don't ever come by here. Wonder if Wilson knew he was comin'." She looked over at Peggy, the cook, "He say anything to you, Peg?" Peggy simply answered with her usual scowl of boredom and shook her head, not particularly concerned one way or the other. Deacon eased up close to the open door again to listen when he heard Dalton speak to Mickey Dupree at the bar.

He heard Mickey's greeting to him and heard Dalton ask where Wilson was. Mickey said he was in the office and asked if Dalton wanted him to fetch him, but Dalton said no, he'd go to the office.

When he was sure Dalton had gone into Wilson's office behind the barroom, Deacon said, "I'm gettin' outta here before he comes in the kitchen." He headed for the back door. Shorty and Marty followed and all three were thinking how smart they were to have tied their horses around behind the saloon.

"Wait a minute," Shorty exclaimed as they were climbing into their saddles, "what are we runnin' for? He knows we came to get our guns this mornin'. Hell, he sent us in here to get 'em."

"Yeah, but he didn't say to set around in the saloon after we got 'em," Deacon answered him. "You do what you want. I've already had one chewin' out this mornin'. I ain't hangin' around for another one." He gave his horse a firm kick with his heels and the big bay gelding lunged into action. He had not shared with Shorty and Marty the fact that he had been given an ultimatum by Dalton, kill Ben Savage or don't return to the Double-D. He was afraid if Dalton caught him sitting in the saloon, he might

248

fire him right there. The boss had a temper, and he was pretty riled at the present.

Deacon led them past the hotel and down along the creek bank before he pulled his horse to a stop. "We need to make us some plans," he said when they pulled up beside him.

"Where the hell are you headin'?" Shorty wanted to know. "This ain't the way back to the Double-D."

"For the three of us, there ain't but one way back to the Double-D," Deacon said. "There's somethin' I ain't told you 'bout that meetin' I had with the boss and Spade this mornin'. And I'm gonna tell it to you now, straight. He got his ass jacked up so high about us gettin' ourselves run outta town and our guns took away from us that he gave us one chance to make up for it." He had their immediate attention. "I'll boil it down for ya, we kill Ben Savage or we don't come back to the Double-D." He wanted their help, so he wasn't going to tell them that it was only he who had been given the ultimatum.

They both reacted as if they had just been slugged. "Damn, that's kinda hard, ain't it?" Shorty asked. "He didn't tell us to do nothin' but raise some hell in the Lost Coyote. He never spelled out that he wanted us to go in there and shoot Ben Savage. Ain't that right, Marty?"

"That's the way I understood it," Marty said and turned toward Deacon. "You was the one wantin' to draw Savage out to face you in a shoot-out, and me and Shorty were just goin' with you to help get a fight started."

"That's right, that's right," Deacon quickly agreed. "I'm the one that wants him dead. I'm the one he attacked and re-arranged my nose. But Dalton don't see it that way. He said all three of us are guilty, and so we're all in this together. So the way I see it is we work together to put this jasper in the ground, and things will be all right with the boss again." While Shorty and Marty tried to grasp the severity of their sentence from the boss, Deacon went on. "We ain't got time for no face-to-face quick-draw shoot-outs. We need to kill him any way we can, as long as we do it so nobody can point their finger at any one of us."

"Damn, I don't know," Marty hedged. "That's gonna be pretty hard to do without somebody seein' us do it." He was not at all anxious to risk an attempt on a man who got the best of Bob Wills and Ed Hatcher.

"You ain't goin' soft on me, are you?" Deacon asked. " 'Cause the boss ain't got no use for a man scared to pull a trigger."

"You know I ain't scared, Deacon," Marty quickly responded. "I'm just sayin' we'd best be careful, so nobody can say we done it."

"We'll plan it so nobody can point a finger at us," Deacon assured him.

While the meeting between the three assassins on the creek bank south of town was just in the planning stages, a meeting of a more genial nature was going on at the Lost Coyote. "Well, good morning, Frank," Rachel sang out cheerfully when the three RBJ ranch hands walked in the saloon.

Hearing her greeting from the kitchen door, Ben walked out to say good morning as well. "I thought you boys would be startin' out for home early this mornin'," he said and nodded to each of them. "I was just goin' in the kitchen to get another cup of coffee. You want a cup? Annie just brewed up a big pot."

"No thanks," Frank replied. "But we appreciate the offer. We're packed up and ready to get started. We just thought we'd like to stop by to thank you folks for your hospitality and for how you handled that trouble last night."

While Frank talked, Rachel noticed that

251

young Jimmy Whitley kept looking back and forth and up the stairs and down. She stepped over close beside him and whispered low, "She doesn't usually come downstairs very early in the mornings. But if you just wanna speak to her real quick, she's most likely awake." He answered her with a rapid nodding of his head and a youthful smile. Overhearing the whispered conversation, Ron Corbett looked at Jimmy and just shook his head in playful disgust. "Come on," Rachel whispered and took Jimmy by the hand. Before Frank and Ben noticed, Rachel and Jimmy were halfway up the stairs.

Rachel led him to one of the doors that Jimmy had come to know well. She tapped on the door and called out softly, "Ruby, are you up yet?"

From inside the room they heard her sleepy reply. "Rachel, is that you?"

"Yes, it's me," Rachel answered. "Are you decent? I've got somebody here who wants to say good morning."

"Let me put my robe on," Ruby came back. "Who is it?"

"One of your admirers, I think. Open up, he's in a hurry." She looked at Jimmy and winked. He was almost trembling in his anticipation of seeing her before he left.

They heard the key in the lock and a second later the door opened to reveal Ruby, looking young and sleepy. When she saw who had come to call at this hour, her youthful face blossomed with a big smile. "Jimmy," she said softly. Rachel left them and hurried back downstairs.

When she got back to the men talking, the subject was on the best trail to follow to avoid contact with Double-D cowhands. "I hope we haven't brought you any trouble because of you taking our part in that little confrontation," Frank said.

"Nothing we can't handle," Ben told him. "I hope we get to see you again if you're ever up this way. Wish the RBJ was a little bit closer to Buzzard's Bluff."

"Me, too," Frank said and extended his hand. "Well, we'd best get goin' if we're ever gonna get home. We might have to leave Jimmy here." He laughed, then called out, "Come on, Jimmy, we're leavin'." He came bounding down the steps, happy and sad at the same time. "Mercy," Frank said, "was I ever that young?" They all enjoyed a good laugh and the men from the RBJ went out the door, leaving one young prostitute weeping silently in her room, thinking how things might have been had she made different choices in her life.

When they had left, Ben went back to the kitchen to get that cup of coffee he had been going for when Frank came in. The discussion now returned to the problems that may have hatched after the altercation with Deacon Moss. There was sure to be some trouble. Deacon didn't impress Ben and Rachel as the kind of man who forgives and forgets. They were more than a little surprised to find that the Double-D man they would first encounter was not Deacon but the Double-D, himself, Daniel Dalton.

Tiny was the first to spot the solemn potentate of the troublesome ranch and he gave the warning to Ben and Rachel, who were sitting at one of the tables close to the kitchen door. "Trouble's comin' early this mornin'," Tiny announced, and when Dalton walked to the bar, Tiny pointed to the two people seated at the table before Dalton asked. Without a word to Tiny, Dalton headed to the table. Ben stood up to receive him.

"Mr. Dalton," Ben acknowledged. "What can we do for you?"

"Savage," Dalton responded, then nodded in Rachel's direction. "Miss Baskin." Back to Ben, he said, "I'm in town this morning on some other business, and I thought it would be a good idea to stop by and talk to you."

Not sure what to expect from this surprise visit, Ben raised an eyebrow in Rachel's direction before responding. "We were just havin' some coffee. Sit down and have a cup with us, unless you want something a little stronger."

"Thank you, I will," he replied and pulled a chair back. "I never drink alcohol in the mornings. Coffee will be fine."

Having been listening at the kitchen door as soon as she heard who their visitor was, Annie quickly ran to the stove, poured a cup of coffee, and met Rachel with it before Rachel reached the door. She had to stifle a laugh when she almost collided with Annie. "Thank you, Annie," she said and took the coffee to the table quickly, not wanting to miss any of the conversation.

Dalton nodded a polite thanks in Rachel's direction before beginning. "I'm aware that there has been some trouble caused by my men in your establishment here. I don't know what the reason for that is. I know that I have had some rough men on my payroll, and as we all know, these men are hard to control when they're let out of the cage. But I wanted to let you know I have given orders that they are not to cause any trouble in this saloon. Their behavior has already resulted in two deaths, and I wanted to let you know that's not the way I do business with my competition."

"Well, that's mighty good to know," Ben remarked when Dalton paused to take a few sips of his coffee. "I can guarantee you we won't be sendin' anybody down to the Golden Rail to do damage or cause trouble. And we'll keep doin' what we have to do to defend ourselves and our customers, just like we always have. Looks to me like the town is gettin' bigger every day. I expect it won't be much longer before we'll have another saloon come in to compete for the likker business. So it's a smart idea for you and us to get along now, before that happens."

"Well spoken," Dalton replied, "exactly the way I see it." A long pause followed then, the only noise between them the sipping of their coffee. When it was obvious to them both that there was really nothing more to discuss, he said, "I suppose I'll get along with my other business now. Thank you for the coffee. I'm glad to know where we stand. None of us is trying to run the other one out of business." He got up to leave.

Ben and Rachel stood up as well. "Glad

you stopped by," Ben said as Dalton walked out. They remained standing until he disappeared, then turned to exchange grins and a shake of the head.

"Now, what do you suppose that was all about?" Rachel asked, and both Tiny and Annie came over to join them, also curious about his visit. "I thought he was gonna invite us out to his ranch to have tea with him and that mysterious wife he's supposed to have before he was finished. What's her name, Estelle?" She looked at Tiny, then Annie — neither of them knew. She looked back at Ben and questioned, "You think he meant what he said about not causing any more trouble?"

"Don't get your hopes up," Ben told her at once. "I think the purpose of that little visit was just so he could declare that all the trouble we might have from now on ain't gonna be his doin'. And the biggest lie he told was the last one he said — that he wasn't tryin' to run us outta business. 'Cause that's exactly what he's aimin' to do."

A few minutes later, Tuck Tucker burst through the batwing doors like he was rushing to put out a fire. "What's goin' on?" he exclaimed. "I just saw Daniel Dalton come walkin' outta here!"

"Just Christian businessmen havin' a friendly visit," Tiny answered him, but it was Ben who had to tell the fiery little gnome what was said.

"You didn't believe a word of what that lying dirty bird said, did you? 'Cause, if you did, you'd best lock the henhouse before that fox gets in," Tuck warned. "I swear, I need a drink after hearin' that kinda talk from that devil."

"It's still a little early for you to start drinkin', ain't it?" Tiny teased.

"Why?" Tuck responded as if surprised he would ask. "The sun's up, ain't it? I thought it was before I came in here."

Tiny chuckled as he poured him a drink. Tuck tossed it back, wiped his red whiskers around his mouth, and asked, "Whaddaya gonna do, Ben?"

"What am I gonna do?" he repeated. "Nothin'. What can I do? Just wait and try to take care of whatever happens, unless Mack Bragg tells me it's all right to shoot Dalton's men on sight."

As if he heard his name called, the sheriff walked in the saloon right after that. "Did I see Daniel Dalton comin' outta here a few minutes ago?"

"That you did, Sheriff," Rachel answered. "I don't think anybody in town missed it."

"I was fixin' to come tell you that Dalton was just in my office," Bragg said. "He said he stopped in to tell me he was sorry about the trouble his men had caused, and he was gonna try to put a stop to it."

"Ha," Tuck grunted. "If turds could talk, they might try to tell you what a pretty journey they took to get here."

Bragg ignored Tuck's wisdom and asked Ben, "Whaddaya think? You think that man's turned over a new leaf?"

"I think Tuck's right," Ben answered. "I think Dalton's paintin' a pretty picture of his innocence in whatever trouble is on the way to Buzzard's Bluff — at least to the Lost Coyote. But if the Coyote goes down, it'll be just the first step in Buzzard's Bluff goin' down the path of other wild Texas towns." He gave Bragg a stern look and added, "And that's gonna make your job a helluva lot harder." He saw the immediate understanding, and with it, the concern in the sheriff's expression. "So I reckon we've all gotta keep a sharp eye about us and hope we're ready for whatever happens."

"I reckon," Bragg replied. He didn't express it, but he suspected that, if what Ben said was true, one of Dalton's first objectives would be to take Ben Savage out of the picture. That didn't take a genius to figure out. They had already attempted to do it more than once.

A couple of the saloon's regular early drinkers came in then, sending Tiny back to the bar and Annie back to the kitchen. "You might as well sit long enough to have a cup of coffee, Mack," Rachel said and got up to follow Annie into the kitchen to fetch it for him.

CHAPTER 14

"How do you know he'll go to the hotel for supper?" Shorty asked.

" 'Cause he always does," Deacon said. "That cook at the Lost Coyote don't stay there to cook supper. And if he don't go to the dinin' room at the hotel, the only other place to get supper is at the Golden Rail, and I don't think he's gonna go there. Do you?"

"I reckon you're right," Shorty replied, ignoring his sarcastic tone. "I didn't think about that. What time do you reckon he'll go to supper?"

"How the hell am I supposed to know that?" Deacon answered him. "We're just gonna have to wait him out."

"The dinin' room is open for supper from five o'clock till seven o'clock," Marty said. "That's a long time to wait."

"You got somethin' better to do?" Deacon asked, again sarcastically. "We've gotta nail his ass tonight or we'll be on the road outta here tomorrow." He could tell by the attitude of both of them that they were not very enthusiastic about the job they had to do. He decided he'd better talk up their courage a little. "Hell, there ain't gonna be nothin' to this job tonight. The way we got it planned, don't matter which way he comes outta that dinin' room, one of us will get a shot at him. And when we shoot that jasper, we're gonna be Mr. Dalton's three favorite pets. I guarantee ya." He grinned to try to prime their courage. "We can't miss, if we do it like I say. Let's go over it again, so everybody knows what to do. Where you gonna be, Shorty?"

"I know where I'm supposed to be," Shorty answered, impatient with Deacon's insistence on repetition. When Deacon prodded him to answer, Shorty said, "At the Golden Rail, by the front corner, and it's my job to get the horses ready to go as soon as one of us shoots him." Deacon had decided to leave the horses behind the saloon where nobody would bother them. And when the job was done, they could ride down the creek bank behind the hotel and out of town in minutes.

"All right, Marty, where you gonna be?"

"Beside Howard's store, so I've got a good

angle for a shot if you or Shorty miss him." Deacon said that was right, but Marty had one concern. "I'm gonna be across the street from the Golden Rail, and I'll have to run across the street to get to the horses. What if there's somebody out in the street, and they see me runnin'?"

"They'll all be lookin' at him. Ain't nobody gonna pay attention to you. If he's already in the dinin' room before we get set up, then I'll be the one gets the first shot. And anybody in the street will be looking up toward the hotel where the shots come from. Hell, I'm gonna have to run across the street, too. I ain't worried about it. If things go like they're supposed to, I'll nail him as soon as he walks outta the dinin' room. And likely you and Shorty can stroll over behind the Golden Rail and be in the saddle when I get there."

That seemed to satisfy his two unenthusiastic partners in the planned assassination, so they continued to pass the time away there by the creek. After what seemed a long time, Deacon was about to ask what time it was when Shorty looked at his watch and announced that it was almost five o'clock. Marty jumped to his feet at once and hurried to his horse. "Don't get your long johns twisted in a knot, Marty," Deacon told him.

"The dinin' room opens at five. Even if he gets there right when they open up, he'll have to have time to eat it before he comes out again."

"Right," Marty said, "I didn't think about that. I reckon it's a good thing you're callin' the shots and I ain't."

"We don't need to be hurryin' around, attractin' attention," Deacon said. "We've got plenty of time to ride around back of the saloon, tie the horses, and walk to our spots." *The only thing that would be better would be if it was dark,* he thought, but he didn't say it to his partners. In the saddle then, he led his assassination party up from the creek and loped along behind the buildings until he reached the Golden Rail.

As luck would have it, when they got there, Stump Jones was coming from the outhouse. "Heyo, Deacon," Stump greeted them. "What you boys doin'? I thought you took off for the ranch."

"We changed our minds, and we got a little card game goin' on with some fellers we met back beside the jailhouse. We thought it'd be better if we left our horses here in case Mr. Dalton comes back. So, don't say nothin' to anybody about seein' us, all right?"

"Sure thing, boys, I won't tell a soul,"

Stump assured them.

" 'Preciate it, Stump," Deacon said. "We'll be back to get 'em in a little while." When Stump went inside, Deacon told his partners, "I know Stump, he won't say nothin'. Don't get nervous on me. This ain't gonna make no difference. Let's get to our spots." Before they parted, he had to remind Marty to take his rifle with him. *Damn good thing I set myself in the best spot to shoot. Whether he's comin' out or goin' in,* he thought, *I'll get the first shot at him.* He hadn't counted on running into Stump, so he asked Shorty what time it was as they started out to their ambush. Shorty told him it was already twenty minutes after five. So Deacon picked up his step.

The spot he had picked out for himself was on the opposite side of the street from the hotel, which was the first business structure you came to if you were approaching the town from the south. The only other building was the residence and office of Dr. John Tatum, and it was set back from the road a good fifty yards. There was a small clump of oak trees just short of the hotel, which afforded him ample cover to watch the dining room without being seen. The angle was perfect. If Savage had not yet come to eat, Deacon would see him when he did, provided Savage made it by Shorty and Marty. He could watch him the entire way as he came down the street, and he could wait to let him get close enough, so he couldn't miss. The anticipation of that moment caused Deacon to reach up to gingerly touch the ruins of his nose. He could barely touch it before a needle-like shot of pain made him take his hand away at once. It served to increase his anticipation of the satisfaction he was about to enjoy.

After he had remained there, kneeling beside the trunk of a tree for what seemed like a long time, he began to think of things that he might have done differently. The first thing he thought was that he could have brought his horse with him because the cover there in the trees was enough. No one could have seen his horse and he would almost be out of town as soon as he took the shot. "Damn," he cursed himself for not thinking of that. He cursed himself for being so intent upon making the assassination the work of all three of them. Otherwise, he might not have decided to keep all the horses together. "Damn it, damn it," he repeated again. "I wish I had a watch." It seemed so long, he decided that Savage must have gone in as soon as the dining room was open. He cursed Stump Jones then for delaying them. It meant he wouldn't have the chance to take the easy shot at Savage walking down the street. But that didn't matter, he told himself, the shot would be just as easy when Savage was walking back to the Lost Coyote.

He stood up to change his position for a few minutes before kneeling again, and just as he did, two men came out of the dining room. Neither man was Ben Savage, but it caused him more concern because now diners were starting to come out. He dropped back down on his knee again. When no one else came out right away, he brought his rifle to his shoulder and set the front sight on the back of one of the men walking away from the dining room. It would be an easy shot and would bring him so much pleasure. *Where is that bigshot saloon ranger?*

Up the street, his partners in the planned assassination were experiencing no better success in playing the patience game than Deacon was. After a while, Marty was finding it difficult to remain inconspicuous. He started out simply leaning against the side of Cecil Howard's store, but after what seemed like a long time, he thought passersby were beginning to notice him. So he tried to stroll casually up the street a couple dozen yards, then strolling slowly back, repeating that for a while.

Down the street from Marty, Shorty at least knew the time was a quarter to six, but he was as antsy as his two fellow assassins, checking his pocket watch every few minutes. After a while with no report from a rifle down near the hotel, he decided he looked too suspicious just standing there at the front corner of the Golden Rail. So he thought he might attract less attention if he was just sitting in one of the straight-back chairs on the narrow porch. He stepped up on the porch and quickly dragged the closest chair over away from the window, hoping no one inside would notice. He sat down and tipped the chair back against the wall on its two back legs, his rifle lying on the floor beside him. In a few minutes, Stump Jones came out the front door.

"Hey, Shorty, what you doin' back here again? I thought you and the other boys was goin' to a card game."

"I decided I didn't wanna play no more cards," Shorty answered with the only thing he could think of at the moment. "I just thought I'd set here on the porch for a spell."

"It is kinda nice out here this time of evenin'," Stump remarked. "I'd join you, but Wilson's got me cleanin' out the stockroom. Maybe I'll set with you when I get through."

"Yeah," Shorty said, "but I might not stay here much longer." Stump went back to work, leaving Shorty to peer anxiously down the street toward the hotel. "Come on, Deacon, make it quick and let's get the hell outta town," Shorty muttered under his breath.

Inside the Lost Coyote, Rachel walked in the office to find Ben still poring over the ledger she had given him, so he could trace the activity of the saloon's whiskey business after Jim Vickers's death. "I thought you were goin' to the hotel to eat supper," she said.

"I am," he responded. "Tuck wanted to go with me, so I told him to come by here after he closed his shop."

"He's in the saloon now," Rachel said. "Been there for fifteen minutes. If you're going to eat at the hotel, you'd better shake a leg. They'll be closin' in about forty minutes."

"I swear, I let the time get away from me," Ben reacted immediately. He gave her a big grin and joked, "Your ledger is such interestin' readin' that I forgot about Tuck and supper, too. I'd best get outta here before he comes in after me."

"I'm sorry, Tuck," Ben said when he came out. "I got into some of Rachel's accountin' books back there, and the time slipped up on me. Let's go. I don't want you to get too weak to walk to the hotel."

"We ain't gonna walk," Tuck said. "We're gonna ride. I've got my wagon still hitched up, and after we eat, I'm gonna take a couple of rolls of wire out to my cabin down the creek."

"All right," Ben said and started for the door. "Want me to bring you anything from the dining room?" he asked Rachel as he walked past her.

"No thanks," Rachel replied, "but I'll bet Tiny would be tickled if you happened to bring him back a slice of cake, if Myrtle made one today."

"I wouldn't refuse it," Tiny said.

Outside, Ben climbed up on the wagon seat beside Tuck, and they pulled away from the saloon. They took no notice of the man carrying a rifle walking casually back toward Howard's store. Likewise, Marty Jackson paid little attention to the men in the wagon until they had passed him and he suddenly recognized the man sitting beside the driver. Turning to look at the rolls of wire in the back of the wagon, Ben asked, "Whaddaya gonna use all that wire for?" He didn't get an answer, for Tuck was struck in the back with a .44 slug before he could reply. With no idea where the shot had come from, Ben grabbed Tuck and pulled him off the wagon seat and they both landed in the bed of the wagon. Rapidly scanning the street from side to side, his Colt six-gun already drawn, Ben's eyes came to focus on the man with the rifle, who was raising it to his shoulder again. Ben recognized Marty Jackson at that moment and quickly fired two shots at him, missing both but close enough to rip splinters from the boardwalk by his feet. In panic, Marty ducked back behind the corner of the store. Ben took advantage of that moment to reach for the reins and pop the mules' rumps with them.

The mules responded and pulled the wagon bouncing over the rough street, causing the few people on the street to scatter while Ben held Tuck flat in the bed of the wagon. As startled as everyone else, Shorty Dove dropped his chair back on all four legs and grabbed his rifle as the driverless wagon rattled past the Golden Rail just in time to see Ben reach up to take the reins again. With no time to think, Shorty raised his rifle and shot at him. Wild, the first shot ricocheted off one of the rolls of wire, and the second embedded in the side of the wagon. He didn't try for a third one, since he realized several people taking cover in the doorway of the barbershop next door had seen him take the shots. He turned to threaten them, then thought better of it and ran back around the saloon where the horses were tied. He jumped on his and lit out for the cover of the trees lining the creek.

Hearing the gunshots on the street, Deacon jumped to his feet again, not sure what to do. In a successful ambush, he would have hoped to hear a single shot, but he had heard several and he was not certain what that might mean. Then suddenly he saw a runaway team of mules pulling an empty wagon heading his way. It continued right on past the hotel, out the end of town, and onto the south road. When it was past him, he discovered it was not empty, for he saw the head and shoulders of a man in the wagon. Too late, he realized the man was Ben Savage when he reached up from behind the seat to drive the mules. His initial reaction was a frustrated rage as he ran out of his cover in the trees to watch helplessly as the wagon continued down the road. "Damn!" he cried out in anger for missing his chance to shoot. Then, when he saw the wagon suddenly swerve off the road and onto the path leading to the doctor's office, it struck him that Marty or Shorty had wounded Savage. "They got him!" he bellowed. "He's wounded and he's tryin' to get to the doctor!"

He came out of the trees and looked back up the street. Although there were people in the street, coming out of the stores to gape, there was no sign of anyone giving chase to the wagon. He knew he had a chance to put the fatal round into Ben Savage, if he hurried to get to the doctor's office before anyone else thought to follow the wagon. So he started down the road at a trot.

Nancy Tatum got up from her chair at the table when she heard the wagon come into the yard. "Always at suppertime," she complained as she went to the window to see who it was.

"Doesn't matter that much," Dr. John Tatum said. "I'm about finished, anyway." He took a few quick sips from his coffee cup and got to his feet. "Probably has to do with those shots we just heard."

"It's that new owner of the Lost Coyote," Nancy reported, "that Ben Savage fellow who's been shooting everybody. He's lifting somebody out of the wagon." She paused to see who it was. "It looks like Tuck Tucker. I better go open the office door." She hurried to the two-room addition on the side of the house that served as the doctor's office.

When she opened the door, she found Ben standing there holding Tuck in his arms. "Ma'am," Ben said, "he's got a gunshot wound in his back. I don't know how bad it is."

She stepped back and held the door open for them. "Bring him right on inside and lay him on the table in there," she instructed, pointing to the door of Tatum's surgery. "Dr. Tatum will be right in." With experience from many gunshot victims before, she went straight to the kitchen to put some water on to boil. When she returned, she laid out some instruments she knew her husband would need to examine the patient. She took a look at the short little man lying on the table and started to get him out of his jacket. His eyes, closed tightly until that moment, opened wide when she turned him to try to get his arm out of the sleeve. "I'm sorry," she said, thinking he had been unconscious, "I didn't mean to hurt you."

"You ain't hurtin' me, ma'am," Tuck answered. "I'll set up, so you can pull it off. Gimme a hand, Ben." Ben stepped forward and pulled him up to a sitting position so Nancy could get him out of his jacket and shirt. When the doctor came in, the patient was lying facedown on the table, most of the blood cleaned away from his wound, and several towels spread across Tuck's back.

It didn't take Tatum long to determine the extent of the damage to the little red-haired gnome. "I'd say you were pretty lucky," he said after his initial examination.

"Lucky?" Tuck responded. "If I was lucky, he'da missed me."

"You're lucky the wound isn't serious," Tatum said, patiently. "A few inches to the left and he'd have hit your lung. Now hold still, and I'll dig that slug outta there. I'll give you a little painkiller to make it easier."

"I don't need no painkiller," Tuck insisted. "The ride over here in that wagon was rougher'n diggin' a bullet out."

With concern for his big-talking little friend now relieved, Ben had other things to think about. He knew the man who shot Tuck was Marty Jackson, and he had an idea that Marty ran after he threw a couple of shots at him. But there were another two shots after Marty's. He could guess who that shooter was, so somewhere back around the Golden Rail, Deacon Moss may or may not be hiding. He now needed to find Deacon before Deacon found him. He decided it would be a good idea to move Tuck's wagon out of sight until the doctor was finished with him. "I'm goin' outside to take care of those mules," he told Nancy and went out the office door.

Outside, he took hold of the bridle of one of the mules and led the team around behind the house where he tied them up to a clothesline pole. He took a moment to replace the two cartridges he had spent in his six-gun, unaware of the man who ran in the office door at that moment.

Still winded from running after the wagon, Deacon burst into the office, his rifle aimed at Nancy Tatum. "Where is he?" he demanded. She didn't have to answer, because he then saw the doctor through the open door to his surgery. Hustling the terrified woman before him, he pushed her into the surgery before shoving her aside and raising his rifle to point at the man lying on the table. "What the hell?" he blurted upon seeing the short, red-bearded Tuck on the doctor's table.

"You lookin' for me?" Deacon spun around to face Ben Savage in the doorway, his Colt six-gun leveled at his belly. He started to raise the rifle, but Ben warned

276

him, "Do it and you're dead." A long moment passed while Deacon made his desperate decision. "Drop it and come peacefully and I'll take you to jail," Ben offered.

Deacon froze, undecided. "All right," he finally relented. "I'll drop it." He held the rifle out to his side at arm's length. Then he dropped it, but before it hit the floor, he drew his pistol, grabbing Nancy at the same time and jamming the .44 into her side. "Now, I'll tell you to drop it, or I'm gonna make the doctor a widower. Take me to jail, was you?" he gloated, "You shoulda shot me while you had the chance."

"Let her go," Ben ordered firmly.

"Let her go?" Deacon mocked as he pulled Nancy even more directly between himself and Ben, enjoying his moment with the upper hand. "It's time to put you in the ground." He pulled the pistol out of Nancy's side, pointed it straight at Ben, and said, "Say good-bye." He never heard the sound of the shot that smashed into his forehead.

"Good-bye," Ben said as Deacon's knees sagged and he collapsed to the floor, releasing a still-terrified woman, who might have collapsed, as well, had Ben not moved at once to steady her.

The doctor moved quickly then to help his shaken wife, taking her into his arms.

"You're all right," he tried to assure her. When he was sure she was going to be all right, he glared at Ben. "You might have killed her. That was a helluva reckless shot you took."

"Not really," Ben said. "He was standing head and shoulders above her, and at that close range, his head was a big target to shoot at. I just had to wait till he took the gun outta your wife's side, in case he pulled the trigger on reflex."

In the excitement of the moment, Tuck was completely forgotten until he finally spoke. His question was the only one that seemed logical to him. "Why the hell didn't you just shoot him when you walked in, instead of all that business about takin' him to jail?"

"That's a good question," Ben answered. "I don't rightly know, just too many years as a Ranger, I guess." He looked at Dr. Tatum then. "How long before you're done with him?" There was one more man he had not accounted for, and that was the man who took the last two shots at the wagon as it passed the Golden Rail. He knew now that it had not been Deacon, because Deacon could not have gotten to the doctor's office that quickly, if he had been near the Golden Rail.

"Yeah, Doc," Tuck asked, "how long? I'm gettin' tired of layin' here."

"I don't know," Tatum replied, not fully recovered from the traumatic incident in his surgery, himself. "Not long, I was about to remove the bullet when all this started." Back to Ben, he said, "I'd like to have that man removed from my surgery. Will you need help doing it?"

"No, I'll take care of it," Ben said. "He ain't gonna be as easy as Tuck was, though. If you'll hold the door open, I'll drag him outta here." So, while Dr. Tatum held the door, Ben took hold of Deacon's boots and dragged him outside.

As he dragged him past a somewhat recovered Nancy Tatum, she asked, "What happened to his face?"

"That's another story," Ben said, "but the hole in his forehead kinda completes it, don't you think?"

"You need a hand with that?" Ben heard the question and turned to see Sheriff Mack Bragg riding up the path from the road. "I've been followin' a trail of gunshots. Shoulda known they would lead to you."

"Is that a fact?" Ben replied. "I wish you'da followed it before it ended up here. Before you ask, Dr. and Mrs. Tatum and Tuck, too, will tell you that I tried to get

Deacon to surrender, but he took the other option. And he is a heavy son of a gun. Grab his shoulders and we'll throw him in the wagon."

"Tiny said Tuck was in the wagon with you. Is he all right?"

"He took a bullet in his back," Ben said. "But Dr. Tatum said it was more in his shoulder, and he'll be just as ornery as ever. I got a look at the one who shot him. It was Marty Jackson. I tried to shoot back at him, but he got away. We caught two more shots from the Golden Rail, so I figure that had to be Shorty Dove, but I didn't see him. I don't know where this one was hidin', somewhere near the hotel I would guess 'cause I don't see any sign of a horse around, so he musta walked."

"Well, there ain't much doubt they were set up to ambush you," Bragg said. "There was one horse tied behind the Golden Rail. I expect it belonged to Deacon. Funny ain't it? This happened right after Daniel Dalton came to town on a peace mission."

CHAPTER 15

When Doc Tatum was finished with Tuck,
Ben helped him up in the wagon and drove
it for him, since Tuck's right arm was in a
sling. He was not as spry as he claimed to
be, so Ben talked him into staying in his living quarters in the back of his harness shop
instead of going to the cabin he maintained
on the creek. "You ain't gonna be able to
string any wire till that shoulder heals,
anyway. You might as well stay in town."
Tuck could hardly disagree. "You got anything to eat in that place you stay in town?"
Ben asked. They had been on their way to
supper when the attempted murder took
place, and now it was too late to eat at the
hotel dining room."

"Sure, I got stuff to cook, I just don't feel
much like cookin' right now," Tuck said.

"Hell, I'll do the cookin', if you've got
something to cook," Ben volunteered. "We
could always go get some supper at the

281

Golden Rail, but you'd take a chance on the cook spittin' in your bowl. If you've got the fixin's, I can mix up some pan biscuits. You got any sowbelly?" When Tuck said he did, and had some dried apples, too, Ben said, "All right, then, we can have us a feast." So they dropped Deacon Moss's body off at Merle Baker's place of business, then Ben took Tuck to his harness shop and left him there while he drove the mules to the stable. "I'll stop in the Lost Coyote just long enough to let Rachel know where I am, then I'll come cook us some supper."

There was still the concern for the two would-be assassins who had taken flight. So Ben kept a wary eye about him when he left the stable and walked down to the Lost Coyote. He found it highly unlikely that Marty and Shorty would risk another attempt tonight, but it never paid to be careless. When he walked into the Lost Coyote, he was received as if he had been away for a long time. Rachel and Tiny rushed to meet him before he got as far as the bar. "Ben," Rachel exclaimed, "the sheriff told us you had a close call."

"That's a fact," Ben couldn't help japing. "I was too late for supper." The remark was good for a laugh from Tiny and a look of impatience from Rachel.

"Mack said Tuck got shot," Rachel said. "Is he all right?"

"Yeah, Doc Tatum fixed him up. I took him to his place, and I'm goin' back there now to cook us both some supper. I just thought I'd stop by here to let you know where we were." He went on to tell them about the raid on the wagon and the confrontation with Deacon at the doctor's office, answering all their questions. When Clarice heard that he was going to Tuck's to cook them some supper, she volunteered to go with him and help with the cooking. "He's already got shot," she said. "Ain't no use in him takin' a risk eatin' your cookin'."

"Are you gonna stay with him all night?" Rachel asked.

"No, just gonna get him fed. He ain't really too bad off. He was lucky he got shot where he did. He doesn't need any help, so I'll be right back after we eat. He's in luck tonight. I'm gonna make him some of my pan biscuits."

"Oh, hell," Clarice said, "I know I'd better go with you now. There ain't no tellin' what that poor man will have to end up eatin'."

"You best be careful walkin' around town tonight," Tiny warned. "Those two that were in on this thing with Deacon ain't got

283

a lick of sense. They might still be lookin' for a chance to bushwhack you."

"I ain't worried as long as I've got Clarice with me," Ben joked. He was convinced that the danger of that was not likely tonight. If he wasn't, he would have advised Clarice not to accompany him.

"I thought I'd find you here," Marty Jackson said when he reined his horse to a stop in front of an old line shack on a branch of Wolf Creek.

"It's lucky it's you and nobody else," Shorty Dove replied. "I had my rifle on you the whole time you left the creek and rode up the branch."

"I messed up," Marty confessed. "I didn't expect to see him sittin' on a wagon seat, and he got by me before I knew it was him. I took a shot, but I hit the feller drivin' the wagon. Savage started throwin' shots back at me, and I had to take cover." He was ashamed to say he had run around to hide behind the store, so he didn't mention that. "Did you get him? I heard you shootin'."

Shorty shook his head. "Hell, no. I was surprised just like you was. I heard your shots, but when that wagon came by me, I thought at first it was empty. It had already got past me when I realized that both of 'em was down in the bed of it. I shot at 'em, but I don't think I hit either one of 'em. Then I had to get outta there. There was too many people that saw me takin' those shots."

"You reckon Deacon got him?" Marty asked. "When I got back to get my horse, you were gone, but Deacon's horse was still there."

"I swear, I ain't got no idea," Shorty answered. "Like I said, I had to get gone, or there woulda been people shootin' at me."

"Whaddaya reckon we oughta do?" Marty wondered. "Deacon said if we didn't get Savage, we couldn't go back to the ranch, but if he got him, we can go back. If I can't go back to the Double-D, I don't know where I'll go."

"Me, either," Shorty said.

They talked it over for a long time, speculating on whether or not Deacon got the job done. Finally, they decided there was only one way to find out and that was to ride back to the ranch to see if Deacon was there. "Even if he didn't kill Savage and we're fired," Marty said, "we still have to get all our possibles, bedrolls, and such. Surely Mr. Dalton ain't gonna keep us from gettin' our own property, and he might change his mind about lettin' us stay." That seemed the best thing to do, but it was already getting late by then, so they decided it best to wait until morning. There was the possibility that Deacon wouldn't be back that night, and they preferred to have him there when they went back.

After a long night, with no bedrolls and nothing to eat, trying to sleep in a leaky old shack, they got on their horses and headed for the Double-D. When they got to the ranch, they rode straight to the bunkhouse, looking for Deacon. The first person they saw was Spade Gunter. He was coming from the stables, and when he saw them, he headed toward the bunkhouse to meet them.

"Where's Deacon?" Spade asked. Well aware of what Deacon had set out to do and knowing the two of them had gone into town with him to get their guns, he was anxious to hear if they knew.

Spade's question was bad news for Shorty and Marty, and it was Shorty who answered, "We was kinda hopin' he was here."

"Whaddaya mean, you was hopin' he was here?" Spade demanded. "You tellin' me you don't know where he is?" He looked from one of them back to the other as both simply shook their heads. "What the hell happened? 'Cause I'm gonna have to go in and tell the boss." They tried to tell him all that had taken place as far as their part in the ambush was concerned. But after the point when the wagon rumbled on past the Golden Rail, they could only guess, hoping that Deacon was able to finish the job. Now Spade was slowly shaking his head, dreading the report he was forced to give Dalton. "After what you've just told me, Deacon should be back by now. So he's either dead, or he took off after he missed his chance to kill Savage."

"I reckon so," Marty said. "So I reckon we can pick up our possibles and move on."

His remark was ignored by Spade, for the foreman was shaking his head, thinking about the three-shot ambush they had planned. "There's somethin' else you ain't told me. How the hell did Deacon talk you two into helpin' him set Savage up?" His question brought a blank look of puzzlement to both faces.

"Deacon told us what the boss told him," Shorty answered. "He said the three of us was in this together, since we messed around and got our guns took away from us. Deacon said the boss told him he had to make a plan and all three of us had to get Ben Savage or we couldn't come back here to the Double-D."

Spade just stared at the two young men for a long moment before saying, "Mr. Dalton never told Deacon that. He only ordered Deacon to call Ben Savage out, and if he didn't get the job done, not to come back here. The only thing he said you two had to do was go into town and get your guns back from the sheriff. Deacon lied to you." He saw the immediate despair in both faces and could not help feeling sorry for them, neither one of them having reached their twentieth birthday. "How bad is it?" he asked, thinking back on their telling of the ambush.

"I shot the feller drivin' the wagon," Marty volunteered at once, "and Ben Savage saw me."

"And two or three folks on the street saw me shoot at the wagon," Shorty said.

"In other words," Spade said, "there ain't no doubt both of you were in on it. Too many witnesses and one of 'em is Ben Savage. I'll go in and talk to Mr. Dalton about it, but I don't know how he's gonna take it. He ain't been in a good mood ever since Ben Savage came to town." He looked at the two downcast men for a few moments longer. "Have you had anything to eat?"

"Not since yesterday mornin'," Shorty answered.

"Well, go on in the bunkhouse," Spade said. "Ned ain't finished feedin' breakfast yet. Just stay there till I get a chance to talk to Mr. Dalton." They started to do as he said, but he stopped them. "Hold up a minute. Let's see who this is." He had spotted a rider in the distance, approaching the ranch. They all turned to watch the rider. In a minute, they recognized Stump Jones. "I expect we're about to find out what happened to Deacon," Spade speculated.

Stump started his report while he was still getting down from the saddle. "Wilson sent me out here to tell you Deacon Moss is dead." He paused to look at Shorty and Marty, "I was wonderin' what happened to you two," he said, then went back to his report again. "Anyway, you fellers shot Tuck Tucker when him and Ben Savage rode down the street. And Deacon tried to surprise Savage at the doctor's office, but Savage shot him in the head."

"Is Tuck Tucker dead?" Marty asked, once again feeling remorse for shooting the wrong man. Stump told him he was only wounded, and it wasn't a bad wound.

Spade nodded, then looked at Marty and Shorty. "You boys go on in the bunkhouse and get you some breakfast. I'll go tell the boss all the news."

"I'll go with 'em," Stump said. "I ain't had no breakfast, either." The three of them headed to the bunkhouse, leading their horses, while Spade went to the house to seek an audience with Mr. Dalton.

"Mornin', Maria. Is Mr. Dalton in a decent mood this mornin'?"

"Sí, Señor Gunter, I think he in pretty good mood today."

"Well, he's liable not to be after I give him the report on Deacon, so I'm just givin' you the warnin' in advance."

She smiled at him and nodded. "Gracias, Señor Gunter, I watch my step." She went to tell Dalton that Spade was there to see him.

"Well, Spade, have you got word of Deacon yet?" Dalton asked as soon as his foreman walked in the door. "Did he finally show up?"

"No, sir," Spade answered. "That was Stump Jones that just rode in. Deacon ain't comin' back. He's dead."

Dalton didn't say anything for a long moment. This was the report he had halfway expected, but he had harbored hope that he would be wrong. When he finally responded, it was with just one word. "Savage?"

"Yes, sir, it was Ben Savage. Shot him in the head when Deacon tried to surprise him in the doctor's office."

Dalton did not go into the rage that often accompanied news that went opposed to his wishes, but Spade could read the anger in his eyes. It was as if he was smoldering inside and was just moments before erupting. However, he remained calm and asked, "Anything else?"

"Yes, sir, there is," Spade answered, "Shorty Dove and Marty Jackson." He proceeded then to inform Dalton about the botched assassination attempt and the fact that Deacon had hoodwinked the two young men to help him. "Neither one of them boys is a real gunman. Deacon didn't have no business drawin' them into that ambush."

Still patient, Dalton listened, then calmly told Spade that it was out of the question to consider letting the two of them stay on at the Double-D. "I'm afraid it would be no time at all before the Texas Rangers sent someone after them — and after me, too, for harboring two felons. And I would no doubt be accused of ordering the attempted assassination of a former Texas Ranger."

"Yes, sir, I can see how that would look," Spade said. "It's too bad, though. They're both good boys, just got snookered by ol' Deacon. They'll be gone this mornin'. I'll tell 'em." He turned to leave.

When he walked back through the kitchen, he shook his head at Maria and gave her a shrug of his shoulders. She smiled at him, understanding his frustration. As the door was closing behind him, Spade heard Dalton call out for Maria.

When she went to his study, he told her to come inside and close the door, a signal that always gave her a feeling of dread. "Maria," he said. "I'm having a rough day." She knew only too well what would follow.

Outside, Spade walked over to the bunk-house to find Shorty and Marty sitting at the table with Stump and Buster Pate. As expected, they were discussing the incident in Buzzard's Bluff, and the conversation came to a halt as they all waited for what Spade had to say. Ned Snyder, having been listening to the conversation at the table while he started cleaning out his empty pots and pans, stopped to listen as well. "I'm sorry, boys," Spade started. "You're gonna have to go." Then he explained why Dalton couldn't keep them on without getting the law down on him. They expected as much. When Shorty said they would hurry up and get their belongings together, Slade told them to take their time about it, they could wait till after supper if they so chose. Before either of them thought to ask, Spade said, "Mr. Dalton didn't say anything about it, but you can each take one horse, too.

"Good luck, boys," Spade said and left them to ponder their future while he started thinking about finding men to replace them. He was already short two men because of Ben Savage. Now he was short three more for the same reason. There was also another concern, although he wasn't sure it was anything to worry about. He wondered about the calm reaction Dalton displayed when told of Deacon's failure to take care of Savage. Maybe it was just the calm before the storm that surely must follow.

He had worked for Dalton for a long time now, and he felt a reluctant sense of loyalty to the man who was determined to own the town of Buzzard's Bluff. In the beginning, the idea was to become the biggest cattle ranch in the state, and consequently, become the major source of business for the merchants of Buzzard's Bluff. It was a year or so later that the idea of owning a saloon in town occurred to Dalton as a way to attract more business to "his town." It didn't matter that it was the gamblers, drifters, and outlaws the saloon would attract. At some point, that aspect of the business appealed to him and he began to have visions of creating another Deadwood or Dodge City.

Spade paused as he murmured, "And then along came Ben Savage." That was the point at which Dalton began ordering assassinations. Spade wasn't sure how much longer he could be a part of it. He had never given direct orders to any of the men to seek Savage out and kill him, but he had as much as condoned it by his awareness of the order from Dalton. So he was a part of it. He couldn't deny it. What he wondered now was how far it would go before Dalton ordered him to kill Ben Savage. And he knew that was the day when he would have to leave the Double-D.

CHAPTER 16

Daniel Dalton's lack of response to the killing of Deacon Moss was surprising to the folks in Buzzard's Bluff, even though Dalton had made it a point beforehand to state that he did not condone any of his men's unlawful behavior. Once again, there was peace in the town, and Ben decided he could get used to that. He had made up his mind that Buzzard's Bluff was where he was going to stay. But if he was perfectly honest with himself, he wasn't sure he wouldn't be downright bored. It occurred to him then that he had never officially resigned his appointment as a Ranger. Captain Mitchell had told him to take as long as he needed to take care of the will settlement, but Ben had not had any intention to take as long as it had. If there was a telegraph in Buzzard's Bluff, he would have wired Mitchell a couple of weeks ago. He definitely owed the captain the courtesy of a formal resignation, and now that there was time to think about something other than trying to keep from being killed, he felt remiss for letting it go for so long. Thinking maybe the current peace in Buzzard's Bluff would last for a while, he made a decision.

"Partner," he announced to Rachel while they were having breakfast, "I'm gonna be takin' a little trip tomorrow. Be gone about four, maybe five days."

"You are?" Rachel replied, surprised. "Where you goin'?"

"I've gotta go to Austin, do something I shoulda done weeks ago," he answered. "My captain in F-Company doesn't know where the hell I am — whether I'm dead or alive. He knew I was gonna take a little time off, but I don't think he expected me to be gone this long with no word from me. After so many years workin' for the man, I surely owe him the respect of a formal resignation, instead of just not showin' up for work."

"When did you decide to do it?" Rachel asked.

"Just now," he said, "but it's gonna depend on one thing."

"What's that?"

"Well, things have been nice and peaceful around here for a few days, so it just might be that ol' Dalton has really decided to call off the war. So I'm givin' him one more night, and if we don't have any more visits from the Double-D tonight, I'm leavin' in the mornin'. I'll ride down there and turn in my badge, turn right around, and come home."

"I guess we'll make it all right till you get back," she said, while thinking that she wasn't sure she wanted him to go. It didn't escape her, however, that he said he would come *home,* instead of to Buzzard's Bluff. Still, she couldn't help recalling how suddenly he appeared in their lives. And the thought that he might just as suddenly drop out of their lives came to mind. She and Tiny, and Annie, and Clarice and Ruby, they had all come to depend upon him to protect them. She found it hard to believe how confident she had been on her own, before Ben Savage. She shrugged and suggested, "You could just write him a letter, if you didn't wanna go to the trouble to ride all the way to Austin just to say, 'I quit.' "

"I could, I reckon," he said, "but I need to shake the man's hand. Besides, I ain't much good at writin' letters."

"Then I guess you'd best ride to Austin and do the right thing," she said. "Like I said, we'll be all right till you get back."

He grinned to think she even thought to

reassure him. "Just like you were before I showed up on the doorstep, right?"

"Right," she said.

The day passed without incident and in the evening, the usual regulars showed up for a couple of drinks or a game of cards. A couple of cowhands from one of the smaller ranches came to spend some time with Ruby and Clarice. Everything was running smoothly, just like the old days, when Tuck came in. His arm already out of the sling Dr. Tatum had put on him, he walked over to the bar where Ben and Tiny were talking. "I'm takin' Sam Grier's son out to take a look at Mutt Oakley's old place in the mornin'," Tuck announced.

His announcement didn't ring a bell with Ben at first until he remembered a moment later. "That's right," Ben said. "I forgot about that. Forty acres, right? And he's gonna grow the sweetest peaches you've ever tasted."

"That's a fact," Tuck said. "You wanna ride out there with us? Get a look at a right pretty little piece of land."

Before Ben could answer, Tiny answered for him. "Ben's headin' to Austin tomorrow."

"Austin?" Tuck responded. "Whatever for?"

"I've got some business to take care of," Ben told him. "Shoulda done it before this."

"If I'da known that . . ." Tuck started, seeming flustered. "This thing with Robert Grier, that don't have to be tomorrow. I can take him to see that land anytime. That land ain't goin' nowhere. So if you need me to go with you . . ."

"Now, why would he need you to go with him?" Tiny asked. With an impish grin on his face, he was obviously intent upon getting the little runt wound up. Tiny and Rachel had joked about Tuck's tendency to shadow Ben.

"It's just a good idea to have another gun hand with you on a trip that far," Tuck declared. "Like that trouble we had with them two fellers that tried to rob Robert Grier and his wife when we was comin' back from Houston. I was there to back him up."

"He sure was," Ben said, trying to keep Tiny from getting Tuck too wound up. "He was right there with his shotgun." Talking directly to Tuck then, he said, "I won't be needin' any backup on this little trip, and I think it's important to take Robert Grier out to see that land so he can get started on growin' those peaches."

"Well, if you're sure," Tuck said. "I'll keep an eye on the Lost Coyote while you're gone, in case the Double-D starts raisin' hell again."

"I'm sure Tiny and Rachel will appreciate that," Ben said. Looking over Tuck's head, he frowned and shook his head at Tiny, who looked about to comment.

Ham Greeley walked in then, so he and Tuck sat down to play their usual two-handed poker. The evening went well with a good crowd, and at closing time, Ben sat in the office with Rachel while she counted the proceeds for the night. "Not a bad night," she commented. "Best one we've had in a while." He nodded in response. "So I guess you'll be leaving in the morning," she said.

"Looks that way," he replied.

She walked over and put the cash drawer in the safe and locked it. Then she smiled at him and asked, "You remember the combination?"

He chuckled, embarrassed. "No, not offhand. I know you told me, but I can't call it to mind right now."

She laughed with him. "I declare, you're unbelievable," she said. "I guess I don't have to worry about you running off with all our money, do I?"

"Reckon not," he said and shrugged indifferently. The next morning, he waited until

Annie got there before setting out for Austin. He decided he might as well eat a good breakfast before starting. While he waited for her, he went to the stable to get Cousin and his packhorse and loaded it with the supplies he had bought the prior afternoon to take him to Austin and back.

It was still not quite suppertime when he pulled Cousin to a halt in front of Fred Pritcher's stable in Austin after a two-day ride from Buzzard's Bluff. There was no sign of Fred, so he dismounted and walked back in the stable and found him cleaning out one of the back stalls. "You gettin' that cleaned up for me?"

Startled, Fred turned around to squint at him. "Ben Savage!" he exclaimed then. "I thought you musta took off forever."

"Well, tell you the truth, I reckon I have. I'm just back in town for tonight. I'll be leavin' again in the mornin'." When Fred seemed puzzled by that, Ben went on to give him the news about his inheritance.

"A saloon, huh?" Fred was obviously surprised. He couldn't imagine the man he knew for so long as a Texas Ranger in the business of operating a saloon. "I betcha found out that was a helluva lot different from bein' a lawman."

"You can say that again," Ben responded. "You don't know the half of it, but I've got a partner who knows the business." He didn't bother to tell him about all the trouble he had seen already during the short time since he took over. "She's been runnin' the business for quite a while and doin' a good job of it."

"She?" Fred asked. "Your partner's a woman?"

"Yep. And she's as sharp as a shoe tack when it comes to managin' a saloon," Ben boasted. Fred asked no further questions about his lady partner, so Ben said, "I need to leave my horses here tonight, all right?"

"Sure thing," Fred said. "You can use this stall right here."

"Good. I expect I'll sleep at the boardin' house tonight, if they ain't figured I'm dead and rented my room out to somebody else." He figured he'd settle up with the man who owned it and pick up anything he might have left in the room. When he went to Buzzard's Bluff, he hadn't expected to stay there.

"Come on," Fred said. "I'll help you unload your packhorse. You gonna leave the dun now, or you gonna need him some more today?" When Ben commented that every place he was going to was in walking distance, Fred led him out of the stable to fetch his horses. "A woman operatin' a saloon," he mumbled to himself as if amazed.

He walked about half a mile to the state capitol building and the annex behind it that held Randolph Mitchell's office, his rifle in one hand and his saddlebags on his shoulder. He was hoping the captain hadn't left the office early for supper and when he got there, he was pleased to see the door open. As surprised as Fred Pritcher had been to see him, Randolph Mitchell was even more so. "My God!" Mitchell blurted upon seeing the familiar image of Ben Savage in his doorway. "I thought I'd never see you again. What the hell happened to you?"

"Sorry 'bout that, Captain," Ben started out with an apology, "but I reckon I kinda had my hands full, and there ain't no telegraph in Buzzard's Bluff." He went on to explain what had caused him to be so busy, from the first day he hit town, until only recently.

Mitchell listened to Ben's accounting of the trouble he had run into and the steps he was forced to take to keep his saloon from being run out of business. When he had finished, Mitchell nodded his head slowly and said, "So I gather that you've decided to keep your saloon after all that. Is that right?"

"Yes, sir, that's right," Ben said and paused to form a grimace before continuing. "So I reckon I came in to hand you my badge and to tell you I appreciated workin' with you. You've always been a fair man with me. I hope there ain't no hard feelin's because of the way I handled this." He laid his badge on Mitchell's desk.

"No, no hard feelings," Mitchell replied. He paused for a long moment, obviously thinking hard on what he was about to say. "I don't blame you for grabbing on to something that would fix you and your future for good. I have to tell you, you're maybe the best man in this whole company when it comes to getting the job done."

"I appreciate that," Ben responded humbly and almost wished he hadn't said he quit.

Mitchell nodded his head, still thinking, then he said, "Tell you what, I'm getting ready to go to Bowen's Restaurant for supper. Why don't you go with me?" When Ben shrugged as if trying to make up his mind, Mitchell said, "You haven't made any plans to eat anywhere else, have you?" Ben shook his head. "Well, you're probably gonna eat somewhere, so come on and go with me."

"That sounds good to me," Ben said. "I appreciate the invitation."

"Good. Let me lock up my desk here and we'll go." He took Ben's badge off the desk, picked up his hat, and they went out the door. Ben waited while Mitchell locked up. "If you like pork chops, Bowen's got a new cook who knows how to cook 'em," he said as they walked out to the street. "He's got everything else you could want, too, but I like the chops."

After all the years Ben had worked for Mitchell, this was the first time he had ever been invited to share a meal with him. *It took me quitting to get an invitation,* he thought as he parked his rifle and saddlebags just inside the door. He hoped they wouldn't be too conspicuous. The restaurant was not crowded, since it was early for the supper rush, and the pork chops were as good as Mitchell had advertised. They finished it up with more coffee while the waiter cleared the table of their dirty dishes. Mitchell had more questions about the Lost Coyote and the town of Buzzard's Bluff.

"You're a good deal younger than Jim Vickers was when he quit the Rangers. I expect he was about ready to retire into

305

something with a little less stress. But you're still young enough to get a little antsy if you have to sit around too long, so I've been thinking about something that might interest you." He reached in his pocket and pulled out the badge Ben had laid on his desk. "Why don't you keep this, and I won't accept your resignation just yet. Maybe if I need your help on something in your area, you could lend a hand. From what you've been telling me about this Dalton fellow, that sheriff might need some help and you'd be the closest Ranger to send. Whaddaya say? Of course, I can't keep you on full wages. I'd only pay you for days you worked for me."

Ben couldn't help smiling. It sounded like the perfect solution to the quandary he had been laboring under. He needed no time to consider the offer. "I accept," he said and they shook on it.

"There's something else I need to tell you," Mitchell continued. "Billy Turner was let go a week ago. Turns out he had another prisoner try to jump him and he had to shoot him. The fellow he shot stole some cows, and Billy had to transport him back to Fort Worth for trial. There had been so many times that happened, and it was usually mostly with a few Rangers in

B-Company. My boss asked me about that business with you and Billy and those two prisoners you picked up over at Navasota. I told him the story, just the same as you told me it happened. And I think that carried a lot of influence on the colonel's decision." He looked Ben straight in the eye. "I'm telling you this so you'll know Billy might have it in for you. I don't know as how you'd have any chance of running into him, but I wanted you to know about it."

"Thanks for the warnin'. I don't see any chance of runnin' into him. I'm not goin' anywhere near Fort Worth, and I doubt he'll pass through Buzzard's Bluff."

They parted outside the front door, Mitchell back to his office, Ben to the boardinghouse that had been his home for the last few years. He had picked the rooming house owned by John Coleman and his wife, Bertha, because it was closer to the stable than any of the other places he looked. It had suited him just fine. He was not in town for most of the time, and the boardinghouse was just a bed and a meal when he had been in town. Consequently, he had never gotten to know any of the other full-time residents very well. For that reason, he got a couple of curious looks from two men sitting on the front porch when he turned in at the walk. "Evenin'," he offered as he walked past them and went in the door. Since there were two more still sitting at the dining room table, he looked there first, reasonably sure he would find John Coleman there, as well. Coleman usually sat at the table long after supper, drinking coffee while his wife helped their cook clean up the kitchen.

"Well, Mr. Savage," John Coleman announced when he saw Ben. "You've been away for a long spell this time. You lookin' for supper? You're a little bit late, but Bertha can maybe fix you up with somethin' to eat, if they ain't throwed it all out."

"Thank you just the same," Ben replied, "I've already had supper, ate at Bowen's Restaurant with my boss. But I need to settle up with you. I'll be here tonight and most likely eat breakfast here in the mornin'. I'll move out then." He thought he detected a genuine look of disappointment on Coleman's face. "I believe I'm paid up to the first of the month and that ain't but four days from now."

"Found you a place you like better?" Coleman asked at once. " 'Cause, if you've got some complaints . . ."

"No, ain't nothin' like that. I'm leavin' Austin permanently. I've got no complaints. I'm just startin' out in something new, and it's in a little town called Buzzard's Bluff about ninety miles from here."

"Oh," Coleman responded. Like most people, he'd never heard of the town. "Buzzard's Bluff," he repeated. "Well, we'll be real sorry to see you go. You say you're paid up to the first? I reckon you're wantin' some kinda refund on some of your money." Ben could tell by the anguished look Coleman now wore, that he didn't like the thought of refunding money.

Feeling generous, since he was now the half-owner of a saloon and a part-time Texas Ranger, as well, Ben said, "How 'bout this? You give me my breakfast free in the mornin' and we'll call it all square on the room rent, okay?" All the other guests paid a rate that included their meals. He had made a deal for a special rate, paying for his room only, with no meals included. He was away for so much of the time, and he had to pay for the room, but he would just pay for the meals when he ate there.

"Yes, sir," Coleman answered with a wide smile.

"That'll work just fine. I'll tell Bertha you're all paid up through breakfast." He got up from the table to shake Ben's hand. "It's been a pleasure to have you as our guest."

With that settled, he went upstairs to his room and was happy to see it had not been disturbed since he was last in town. Breakfast the next morning was typical for him when he was in town. The few other guests who were down for breakfast as early as he was, stared at him when he walked in. It seemed they were not sure they should say good morning or not and would generally return his good morning, but not cheerfully enough to start a conversation with him. He thought about his new "family" in the Lost Coyote. In comparison, this breakfast was like going to a funeral service. That is, until he finished eating and left the room. He could hear the conversation liven up behind him. Bertha had made it a point to tell him she was sorry to see him go and to come back to visit them again when he was back in town.

Not much time was spent talking to Fred Pritcher at the stable. He saddled Cousin and loaded his remaining possibles onto his packhorse and he was soon on his way out of Austin. Since he had been lucky to catch Mitchell in his office the night before, and get that business taken care of, he should make the round trip in four days.

As he had figured, he raised the buildings

of Buzzard's Bluff above the horizon in the early afternoon of the fourth day. A short time later, he was walking Cousin up the street toward the stable. Jim Bowden called out to him as he went past the blacksmith shop. "Howdy, Ben, glad to see you back." Ben returned the greeting and kept on going. Hearing Jim Bowden's greeting, Tuck Tucker ran out of his harness shop and hustled up to the stable after Ben.

Henry Barnes walked out to give Ben a hand with his horses. "See you got back in one piece," he said. Then he glanced down the street to see Tuck. "Here comes your deputy," Henry said with a grunt. Ben looked behind him to see the little redhead hurrying along on his short little bowed legs. "Tuck's been guardin' the town ever since you left," Henry remarked.

Ben snorted a chuckle. "I reckon Mack Bragg oughta appreciate that," he managed to comment before Tuck arrived.

"I was thinkin' it was about time you showed up," Tuck said. "Everything turn out all right?"

"Yep," Ben answered and pulled his saddle off the big dun gelding.

"Well, that's good," Tuck declared. "Everything's under control here."

"Is that so?" Ben responded. "Well, I

reckon you musta done a good job then."

"You goin' to the Lost Coyote?" Tuck asked.

"That's where I'm headin'," Ben answered, "soon as I take care of my horses."

"Me, too," Tuck said. "I'll go on ahead while you're doin' that and tell 'em at the saloon that you're back and you're on your way there."

He hurried away then to deliver his message. Ben and Henry exchanged glances, then just shook their heads. "I swear, Ben," Henry commented, "he's gone completely loco since you've been gone, running up and down the street half the night. I hope he'll settle down now that you're back." He paused to scratch his head. "What I can't figure out is why he thinks it's your responsibility to take care of the town. I thought that was Mack Bragg's job."

"I think the same as you," Ben said, "and I'm damn sure Mack thinks so, too." He picked up his rifle and saddlebags and walked back to the Lost Coyote.

When he walked into the saloon, he found most of his little "family" gathered at the end of the bar, having been alerted by Tuck. "Glad to see you back." Rachel was the first to greet him. "I don't need to ask you how your meeting with your captain went, since you *did* come back."

"I told you I would," Ben replied.

"We thought you mighta gone back there and got yourself talked into stayin' with the Rangers," Tiny spoke up. "We even had a bet on it, me and Rachel."

"Is that so?" Ben asked, interested now. "Who won?"

Tiny hesitated, suddenly wishing he'd kept his mouth shut about it. "Rachel," he finally confessed, then quickly sought to explain his reason. "I was just thinkin' that you looked like you didn't have enough to do around here half the time, and I thought you mighta missed the action you had when you was a Ranger. The way you took care of them Double-D boys, there ain't no doubt that's the kinda life you're suited for."

Ben glanced at Rachel, then back at Tiny, and was interrupted when he started to comment. "Hell, I told 'em you'd be back," Tuck declared. "There's still unfinished business here. Ain't that right, Ben?"

"I reckon so, Tuck," Ben answered. "But that's Mack Bragg's business. We'll just take care of our own." He said it to remind him that Bragg was the sheriff and the whole town was Bragg's responsibility and not his. Even as he thought it, he was pretty sure any trouble from the Double-D would focus on the Lost Coyote. "Right now, the only thing I feel real responsible for is to put away some of Myrtle Johnson's cookin' down at the hotel. I ain't had a whole lot to eat today."

"That sounds like a doggone good idea," Tuck said. "I'll go with you."

"Well, it's a little early yet. I need to carry my saddlebags back to the room and wash up some, so Lacy will let me in the dinin' room."

Tuck hesitated a moment, trying to decide what to do. "All right, then, I'll meet you down there when they open."

Just as he said he would, Tuck was sitting on a small bench outside the dining room door when Ben walked down the street to the hotel. Lacy James gave Ben her usual cordial greeting when he and Tuck walked into the dining room. "You've been away for a while," she said. "I was afraid you weren't getting the nourishment a growing boy like you needs. I see you brought your bodyguard with you."

"Good evenin' to you, too, Lacy," Ben returned. "It don't pay to hang around a place as rough as this one without some kind of protection." He grinned at Tuck, who grinned back at him innocently, unaware that Lacy was japing him. "You still serve food in here? We didn't come in here to talk. Did we Tuck?"

"You got that right," Tuck answered.

"You heard 'em, Cindy, better get Myrtle back in the saddle," Lacy told her young waitress. "I'll get 'em some coffee."

When Lacy left to get their coffee, Ben said, "You ain't said anything about Robert Grier and his wife. Did you take him out there to see that property?"

"I sure did," Tuck replied, "took him out there and he thought it was just what he was lookin' for. He didn't waste no time at all decidin' on it, came back here and got his wagon. The next day, he was already moved in and workin' on Mutt's old cabin. I told him he was doin' the right thing. Jump on it quick 'cause somebody else is liable to." He paused to chuckle then before continuing. "His daddy was complainin' in the Coyote last night. Said he hadn't seen his son in two years and hadn't never even met his daughter-in-law. They popped in and popped right back out again." He shook his head and chortled, "That boy sure is anxious to get started."

"That sounds like a good thing to me," Ben commented. "We need more and more hardworkin' young families to keep this town growin'." Their conversation was interrupted then when Cindy brought out two plates piled high. "Now, this is what I've been thinkin' about for the last two nights," Ben commented. Cindy stood back to watch them attack Myrtle's Cowboy Stew. Back standing just inside the kitchen door, Myrtle watched, as well, pleased by their reaction to her cooking. Had he been able to see their faces, he might have been more convinced than ever that he had found a place to call home after so many years adrift.

CHAPTER 17

Back in Austin, a man riding a Palouse gelding and leading a sorrel packhorse pulled up to the walk at a large two-story house and stepped down from the saddle. He paused to take a look toward the front porch of the house and the one person sitting in a rocking chair as he looped his reins over the gatepost. "Afternoon," the stranger said when he stepped up on the porch.

"Afternoon," Louis Watts returned, eyeing the stranger in curiosity.

"I'm lookin' for the Coleman boardin' house. Am I in the right place?"

"Yes, sir," Louis answered. "You're in the right place, and if you're lookin' for Mr. Coleman, he's right inside in the parlor. Least he was when I came out on the porch just a few minutes ago."

"Maybe I'll go in and talk to him. I'm lookin' for a friend of mine who's supposed to have a room here, Ben Savage. Have you seen him, today?" When Louis seemed to be trying to associate someone with the name, the stranger added, "He's a Texas Ranger." Then he saw the light come on in Louis's eyes.

"Oh, the Ranger, right," Louis remembered. "I declare, I never did catch that fellow's name. He was gone most of the time. Yeah, he used to live here, but he moved out a few days ago."

"Moved out? Do you know where he went?" the stranger asked. "To another boardin' house maybe or outta town?"

"I'm sorry, friend, I ain't got no idea," Louis said, shaking his head. "John Coleman might know, he's the owner. Like I said, he's right inside the door in the parlor. You could ask him."

"Much obliged," Billy Turner said. "I'll do that." He opened the front door and walked inside where he found Coleman sitting in an easy chair, reading his newspaper. "Mr. Coleman, feller on the porch said you might be able to help me out. My name's William Smith, and I'm tryin' to catch up with a friend of mine, who I ain't seen in years. Ben Savage, last I heard from him, he was rentin' a room here at your house."

"You just missed him," Coleman replied. "You're right, Mr. Savage used to rent one

318

of my rooms. But he moved out four days ago, outta town somewhere. Town with a funny name, I can't rightly recall the name of it now."

"Buzzard's Bluff, John," Bertha Coleman said as she walked in the room. "That's the name of it. He told me that the other morning when he left here — Buzzard's Bluff. I don't have any idea where that is." Then she remembered. "He did say that it was about ninety miles from here."

"Thank you, ma'am," Billy said politely. "I know where it is. Looks like I've missed him this time, but it wasn't nothin' important. Just thought I'd visit with him, if he was here." He took his leave then, cursing his luck, but still determined to settle with Ben Savage.

It had been quite some time since he had been to Buzzard's Bluff. And at that time, there were only three or four buildings there, but there were several cattle ranches close by. One of them was a sizable outfit, as he recalled. He wondered what Ben Savage had been sent up there for and how long he might be there. He wished he had found out Ben was there when he started out from Fort Worth. He could have saved himself a lot of time and trouble, if he had ridden straight to Buzzard's Bluff, instead of riding all the way down here to Austin. "Just take a little longer, Ben," he said aloud. "But that's all right 'cause thanks to you, I've got nothin' better to do." There had been investigations regarding several killings he and a couple of his fellow Rangers had been involved in. But it was the damning testimony of Captain Randolph Mitchell that slammed the door on his career as a Ranger. And that testimony came straight from what Ben Savage had reported to Mitchell. Thinking back on his trial, he supposed he could say he was lucky to have escaped time in prison. One of the lawyers wanted him executed, but the prosecutor was not bent toward pampering prisoners, so he held out for kicking him out of the Texas Rangers. "So, Mr. Ben Savage, you signed your own death warrant for shootin' off your mouth about another Ranger."

He started out for Buzzard's Bluff right away, riding right through the center of Austin, since with Ben out of town, there was no reason to keep from being seen. It crossed his mind that it might bring him extra satisfaction to settle up with Captain Mitchell while he was here in Austin. His better judgment told him that might be too big a risk. Even if he managed to get close enough to Mitchell to kill him, the act would set every Ranger in the state on his trail. No, he decided, it was better to take his vengeance out on Ben Savage. One Ranger turning up dead in the remote cattle country around Buzzard's Bluff would hardly cause a ripple.

He didn't spare the Palouse as he pushed the gelding with the odd markings along a trail that led in the general direction he desired. He knew he would strike the Navasota River somewhere near Buzzard's Bluff, if he continued on that path. He had not taken time to eat breakfast, electing instead to keep pushing his horses until he was forced to rest them. In the early afternoon of the second day, he struck the river and made the decision to stop. Thinking he couldn't be far from Buzzard's Bluff at this point, he would have preferred to keep going. But he knew he could not afford to push his horses any farther. So he walked them along the river, looking for a spot that suited him when he suddenly stopped.

Up ahead, he spotted a thin column of smoke beyond a crowded grove of trees hugging the riverbank. *A camp?* He wondered. Cautious now, he pushed the weary Palouse forward, entering the trees ahead and continuing until he could see where the smoke was coming from. "Would you look at that?" he muttered when he saw the cabin. There was a wagon parked alongside and a couple of horses grazing nearby. The fire that produced the smoke he had seen was outside, in front of the cabin. "Well, now, this looks convenient," he said to himself and rode on out of the trees. Just as he did, a young woman came from the cabin carrying a bucket. She proceeded down to the edge of the river to fill it, taking no notice of the man riding out of the trees. "Hello the house!" Billy yelled, causing her to start. A few moments later, a young man came out of the cabin to see who had called. "Howdy, folks!" Billy called out again. "Mind if I come on in?"

"Come on in," Robert Grier called back to him and stood to watch him approach. Sue Ann hurried on up from the water's edge to stand by her husband.

Billy rode up to them and stepped down from the saddle. "I declare," he said, "I didn't have no idea there was a cabin here till I rode outta the trees back there. My horses are plum near wore out, and I was fixin' to rest 'em and cook myself somethin' to eat. But I don't wanna intrude on you folks' home here. I'll just push 'em on a little farther up the river."

"Why, you'd be welcome to rest your

horses here," Robert said. "We'd offer you something to eat, but we don't have anything fixed right now. We don't wanna be inhospitable, but we haven't got our cabin fixed up yet to cook inside. We can offer you some coffee and if you've got something you were gonna cook, we've got a good fire already goin'."

"So you're just movin' in this old place?" Billy asked.

"That's right," Robert replied. "We've taken over the house and the forty acres it's settin' on." He looked at Sue Ann and smiled. "And so far, it's been a good bit of work just tryin' to clean the house up."

"Well, I can sure appreciate that," Billy said, taking another critical look at the cabin. "If you're sure you don't mind, I'll take you up on the offer to use your fire. I'll try to stay outta your way. I've got some sowbelly I'll cook up. That'll hold me till I get to Buzzard's Bluff."

Feeling as if she was terribly lacking in common hospitality, Sue Ann was moved to offer something. "I'm downright ashamed we don't have anything cooked up to offer, but I've got flour and baking powder, I could mix up some pan biscuits for you."

"I wouldn't trouble you for that, ma'am," Billy replied in his most humble manner.

"I'm used to goin' without. I'll just take care of my horses and let you folks get on with what you were doin' before I interrupted."

"Won't be any trouble at all," Sue Ann insisted, and went to fetch her flour at once.

"Hate to put you folks out," Billy said to Robert as he pulled his saddle off the Palouse, then pulled the packs off his pack-horse.

"Like my wife said, we're sorry we ain't really set up here yet." He watched Billy getting the sowbelly from one of his packs. "You say you're headin' to Buzzard's Bluff?"

"That's a fact," Billy answered. "How far is it from here?"

"About ten miles," Robert answered.

"That's about what I figured and I'da kept on goin', but I'm afraid I'd break my horses down if I pushed 'em another mile." He was thinking there was little chance these people knew Ben Savage, but he decided to make sure. "I'm on my way to see an old friend of mine and I heard he was up this way. You folks bein' new here, yourselves, you ain't likely run into a feller named Ben Savage, have you?" He was surprised by the immediate smile on Robert's face.

"Sue Ann," Robert said, "our guest wants to know if we know Ben Savage."

She reacted as he had upon hearing the

name. "Well, I expect you told him we surely do."

Seeing the look of complete surprise the stranger displayed, Robert said, "Excuse our manners. I'm Robert Grier and this is my wife, Sue Ann, Mr. . . ." He waited for Billy to respond.

"William Smith," Billy said. "Pleased to meet you."

"Same here," Robert said, then went on to tell Billy how Ben Savage literally saved their lives when they were attacked by a pair of outlaws on their way here from Houston.

After Robert finished telling of their fateful meeting with Ben Savage, Billy commented. "That sounds like ol' Ben, all right. 'Course, bein' a Texas Ranger, that's what he was trained to do."

"Well, it sure came in handy to my wife and I," Robert said. "Ben's not a Ranger anymore, though, if you didn't know. He's in the saloon business." Robert paused, obviously enjoying Billy's total surprise. "He's half-owner of the Lost Coyote Saloon in Buzzard's Bluff."

"Well, I'll be . . ." Billy started. It was difficult to believe, but it couldn't be better for his purposes. He now knew exactly where to find Ben, and he could be sure he would be there. This chance meeting with these two tenderfoot settlers was the best piece of luck he'd ever had.

Judging by the expression on Billy's face, Robert was prompted to remark. "I expect Ben will be real surprised to see you. Do you two go way back?"

"Yes, sir, we sure do — way back. We used to be Rangers together. And you're right, Ben's gonna be plum tickled to see me again." *And if you think so much of him, you can come to his funeral,* he thought. "Yes, sir, Ben's gonna be plum tickled," he repeated.

It turned out to be a pleasant time for Billy Turner, visiting with the Griers while his horses were watered and rested. Even though he was anxious to get about the business he had traveled far to accomplish, just knowing his reward was sitting and waiting for his appointment with Mr. Colt and his six friends was enough to make his spirits soar. He knew in his heart that he would kill Ben Savage. Everything pointed to that end. Maybe it was pure luck, but if it was, it was the luck of the devil. He could have taken any number of directions out of Austin to reach Buzzard's Bluff. There was no road from Austin to Buzzard's Bluff, no wagon track, no old Indian trail. He just pointed the Palouse's nose in the general direction of the Navasota River, and the trail he picked took him right to this cabin and two people who could tell him exactly where to find Ben Savage. By the time his horses were ready to go again, Robert and Sue Ann were convinced that they had met one of Ben's old friends, and they were glad they had helped them get together again.

Billy wished the couple luck with their plans to grow their peaches and promised that he would be sure to come back when he was in this part of the territory again. They watched him as he rode away. "What a nice man," Sue Ann remarked. "He said he couldn't wait to surprise Ben."

"Damn, I'm impressed," Billy said to himself when he reined his horse to a halt by the hotel and paused there to look up the main street of Buzzard's Bluff. It had grown considerably in the years since he had been there. On his ride from Robert Grier's cabin, he had tried to decide how best to execute his plan to kill Ben Savage. His initial plan was to simply take him by surprise, walk up to him and shoot him down, jump on his horse, and make tracks. But that was with the picture of the town in his mind as he had last seen it. Looking at Buzzard's Bluff now, he had to consider the possibility that instant escape might not be as easy as he thought. There was even a jail here now. There was the option of calling Ben out to face him in a fair fight, but Billy didn't believe in fair fights. Those who did were fools as far as he was concerned. He needed an advantage, and surprise was the best advantage he could count on.

He considered the option of waiting in ambush and taking Ben down with his rifle, but as he walked his horse slowly up the street, he couldn't see a spot where he could sit unnoticed while he waited for Ben to walk by. He discarded that plan. When he went past the sheriff's office, Mack Bragg stepped out on the porch and stood there to look him over. Billy nodded. "Sheriff," he acknowledged. Bragg returned the nod. Billy rode on by the Golden Rail, then a little farther up the street, he saw the sign he was looking for. "The Lost Coyote Saloon," he murmured under his breath, "a dumb name for a saloon." He felt the muscles in his forearms tense up, and all thoughts of clever plans to assassinate this man he hated were overwhelmed by the primeval desire to walk in and shoot him down. With that thought only, he rode up to the hitching rail and dismounted. He paused to look right and left to make sure he didn't spot Ben or that sheriff who had just given him a looking over. Satisfied that no one was giving him a second look, he looped the Palouse's reins over the rail and walked up on the porch. Before walking inside, he stopped at the batwing doors to peer into the saloon. Seeing no sign of the man he hunted, he pushed through the doors and stopped to scan the lightly crowded room again. He looked from one side to the other, up at the top of the stairs and back down. Ben wasn't there. He headed toward Rachel, who was talking to Cecil Howard at her usual spot at the end of the bar.

Moving down the bar to meet him, Tiny greeted him. "Evenin', stranger, what's your pleasure?"

"I'll take a shot of rye whiskey, if you've got rye," Billy said.

"We sure do," Tiny assured him and produced a bottle from under the bar. "Don't believe I've seen you in before."

"I've been here before," Billy said, "but this place wasn't here the last time I passed through Buzzard's Bluff." He took another look around the room to be sure, then tossed his whiskey down.

"Is that a fact?" Tiny asked. "What brings you back this time? You just passin' through this time, or you plannin' to stay a while?"

Billy gave him a slow smile, thinking he asked a lot of questions. "I came to look up an old friend of mine. I heard this was where he hung out."

"Oh?" Tiny responded. "Who's that?"

"Ben Savage."

At the sound of Ben's name, the conversation between Rachel and Cecil stopped, and they both turned to see who might be inquiring after him. "Good evening," Rachel greeted him. "Ben isn't here right now. You say you're a friend of his?"

"Yes, ma'am," Billy answered politely. "Me and Ben rode together when we was both Rangers. I couldn't ride through this way unless I stopped to see ol' Ben."

"He just stepped out for a little while," Rachel said. "He should be back pretty soon. Why don't you sit down and have another drink? I'm sure Ben will be glad to see an old friend from the Rangers."

He sure will, Billy thought. To her, he said, "That's a good idea. That's what I'll do." He waited for Tiny to pour him another shot of rye, then walked over to an empty table on the side of the room, thinking Ben would more likely glance toward the bar when he walked in. He pulled a chair back and sat down facing the door. When he was sure Rachel and the two men at the bar were no longer looking at him, he eased his Colt .44 out of his holster and put it in his lap. Ready to welcome Ben, he sat waiting. He took another glance toward the bar to make sure Rachel was still there, just in case she was somehow suspicious. Evidently, she wasn't, so he returned his full attention to the front door.

After about fifteen minutes, with no sign of Ben, Rachel walked over to the table. "I thought Ben would be back by now," she said to Billy. "He just went to eat supper. I'm sure he'll be back any minute now. Can I get you another drink?"

"No, ma'am," Billy replied. "I'm gonna hold off for a while, 'cause I expect I'll do plenty of drinkin' when Ben gets here. Don't you worry 'bout me. I've got plenty of time." She smiled at him and returned to the bar.

"Are you gonna need another cup of coffee?" Cindy Moore asked when she came up to the table carrying the coffeepot.

Ben gave Henry Barnes a questioning look, but Henry shook his head. "I reckon I've had enough, too, Cindy. That's gonna do it for me. You be sure and tell Myrtle that she's outdone herself again."

"Tell her I agree with him," Henry said, then turned back to Ben. "You goin' back to the Coyote now?" Ben said he was, so Henry said, "I'll walk with you. I'm goin' back to the stable."

Lacy James came over to the door to dispense her customary sassy nonsense to Ben while he paused to strap on his six-gun. "All our customers appreciate the fact that you didn't shoot anybody while you had your supper."

"If I had, it wouldn'ta been any of your customers," Ben returned, "maybe some of the hired help."

"I'm gonna tell Cindy and Myrtle you said that," she joked. "There might be a little something extra in that soup next time." He laughed with her, and he and Henry walked out to the street.

"Seein' as how I'm supposed to be a businessman now, it doesn't seem right to be wearin' a gun belt and a six-gun around town, does it?" He looked over at Henry. "You don't ever wear one."

"No, I reckon not," Henry remarked as they took a casual walk past the sheriff's office and the Golden Rail. "I ain't seen many occasions when I thought I needed one. I couldn't hit nothin' with one, if I did wear it. It's a different situation with you,

332

though." He was thinking of the confrontations Ben had survived in the short time since he had arrived in Buzzard's Bluff. "If I was you, I wouldn't take it off."

Ben started to respond, but his thoughts were interrupted by something that caught his eye, causing him to become immediately alert. Tied at the rail in front of the Coyote, he saw a Palouse horse and a packhorse. Although an unusual breed of horse, you might occasionally come across one, but he knew for sure one man who rode one, and Captain Mitchell's warning about Billy Turner came to mind. There was no reason to believe Billy could know he was here in Buzzard's Bluff. His appearance here might be strictly coincidence, or the horse might not be the one that Billy rides. Whatever, he decided, it wouldn't hurt to take precautions. So, as they approached the Lost Coyote, he said, "I'll say good evenin', Henry. I'm gonna go in the back door. I think I might need to visit the outhouse."

"You think that soup mighta already had somethin' in it," Henry said with a chuckle. "I'll see you later." He continued on and Ben headed toward the back of the saloon.

CHAPTER 18

He truly hoped he was wrong as he unlocked the back door of the saloon, but with a man like Billy Turner, it was better to be cautious. If it was Billy, Ben decided he was in Buzzard's Bluff for only one purpose, so he wanted to make damn sure before he walked in that barroom. Inside the back hallway, he walked as quietly as possible past the rooms located there. When he got to the kitchen door, he paused to take a quick look inside to make sure Johnny Grey had already picked Annie up. When he confirmed that, he continued on to the door to the saloon. He opened the door slowly, a little bit at a time, until he could view the entire room. There were a few customers, but not the usual crowd, since it was still early. He glanced at the bar and saw Tiny and Rachel talking to Cecil Howard. Then he scanned back across the broad room and stopped on the back of a lone customer.

There was little doubt. It was Billy Turner, seated facing the front door, waiting for him to come walking in.

Trying not to make a sound, Ben walked in the door, his eyes on Rachel and Tiny. As soon as he took two steps into the room, Rachel caught sight of him and started to call out. But she hesitated when she saw his finger pressed to his lips, signaling her not to speak. She thought she understood at once, he wanted to surprise his friend, so she told Tiny and Cecil not to give it away. All three turned to watch Ben's surprise move with wide smiles of anticipation upon their faces.

So intent upon watching the front door, Billy was totally unaware of the big man moving silently up behind him. When he was close enough to see the pistol Billy was holding in his lap, Ben was sure then that there was no chance Billy was there for any reason other than murder. He drew his six-gun then and said, "You lookin' for me, Billy?"

Startled, Billy's reaction was akin to an explosion. His natural instinct was to turn and fire without time to see what he was shooting at. Ready for such a move, Ben caught him beside his head with the barrel of his pistol, as hard as he could swing it, knocking Billy flat and sending a shot into the ceiling before he hit the floor. Stunned from the force of the blow, Billy could offer no resistance when Ben snatched the Colt out of his hand and rolled him over on his belly. "Tiny!" Ben yelled. "Go out front and get a rope off that Palouse tied at the rail."

Tiny stood frozen, his eyes and mouth wide open, until Rachel punched him on the shoulder and yelled, "Go!" She looked back at Ben, kneeling on Billy, his knee in the middle of Billy's back. She had seen Ben in action before, against Bob Wills and Ed Hatcher, but this was different. This time he was angry. It was apparent in his face and in the force with which he struck Billy down.

At that moment, Tuck Tucker walked in the front door, stepping aside to keep from being bowled over by Tiny on his way to get the rope. "Hey," he blurted, "what was that shot I heard?"

"Go get Mack Bragg!" Ben ordered. Tuck sputtered, confused for a few seconds, before going back out the door. By the time he was back with the sheriff, Billy's hands were tied behind his back and his ankles tied together. It was unlikely he could have struggled, even had he not been tied, for he was still not recovered from the blow to his head.

Mack Bragg was no longer surprised by the confrontations Ben Savage seemed to have with those on the wrong side of the law. So he was very calm when he looked at the trussed-up body of a stranger he had seen riding through town less than an hour before. After taking a close look at Billy, he looked up at Ben. "Trouble?"

"Yeah. This one's gonna be a lotta trouble, but it's gonna be mostly me that has to deal with it. Let me tell you right off that this is a legitimate arrest, so let's take him to jail till some arrangements can be made. I'll explain it all after we put him in jail."

"All right," Bragg said. "You usually know what you're doin'. That's his spotted-lookin' horse out front, ain't it?" Ben nodded. "I'll take it to the stable after we put this one in a cell. You wanna throw him across the saddle?"

"That's as good a way as any," Ben allowed. He reached down and grabbed Billy by the shoulders and stood him up on his feet. He bent over and let Billy fall across his shoulder, then stood up and walked out the door. Tuck ran out the door in front of him in a hurry to get the horse turned around, but the spirited Palouse was suspicious of the little redheaded gnome and continued to pull away, at times lifting Tuck's feet off the ground. Impatient and not entirely over his anger at having Billy come after him, Ben said, "To hell with it, the jail ain't that far." And he walked down the street to the jail with his bundle on his shoulder. Mack Bragg walked along beside him asking questions.

"Who is he?" Bragg asked.

"His name's Billy Turner. He was a Texas Ranger, workin' outta Fort Worth. He was just thrown out of the Ranger service for executing prisoners while he was transportin' 'em back for trial. I had the misfortune of workin' with him to arrest two outlaws down at Navasota. The low-down varmint tricked 'em into makin' a play for a gun he knew was empty. Then he shot 'em down when they went for it. I didn't like it, and I told him so. He blames me for gettin' his ass kicked out of the service." Bragg hurried on ahead as they approached the jail to unlock the door. "I wish to hell there was a telegraph line near this town," Ben commented as he carried his package inside.

Once they had Billy laid out on a cot in one of the cells, Bragg started to question Ben. "What am I supposed to do with him?"

he asked. "I understand what you told me he did, but as sheriff of this town, I don't know what to do with him but hold him in jail for a while. From what you told me, he needs to be picked up by the Rangers. And like you just said, there ain't no telegraph near here to wire the Rangers to come get him. You know the town ain't gonna pay to feed him but for so long, and I'll have to let him out. So he's liable to be after you again."

"Like I told you back at the saloon, it's gonna be my problem and not yours. I'd appreciate it if you'd keep this just between the two of us." Bragg nodded, anxious to hear what Ben was going to tell him. Ben continued to explain the predicament. "The thing is, I'm still a Texas Ranger. I went to Austin to resign, but my boss talked me into keepin' my badge and givin' him a hand when there's something in this area that needs my help. So what it boils down to is I made an official arrest of Billy Turner, and it'll be my responsibility to transport him back to Austin for trial."

"Damn," Bragg swore. "That's a helluva note. Why didn't you just shoot him instead of knockin' him in the head?"

"Now you sound like him," Ben cracked, nodding toward the cell room. "That's what got me in all this trouble in the first place."

"I swear," Bragg said, shaking his head. "What gets me is, how did you manage to stay alive up to now? Operatin' a saloon and still a Texas Ranger, but you're gonna still be stayin' right here, right?"

"That's right, but don't let it concern you. I won't be interferin' with the town's business at all. You're the sheriff, and it ain't none of my business."

"I understand," Bragg said. "There won't be no problem." To himself, he thought, *The hell you ain't. I'm gonna be calling on you anytime I need help.* "Are you gonna transport him to Austin right away? I need to know what to tell Lacy about feedin' him."

"Keep him a day or two, or at least till he acts like he knows which side is up. I don't know how hard I hit him and I wanna be sure he ain't outta his head, if I'm gonna be ridin' with him all the way to Austin."

"Well, I hope he's just got a headache," Bragg declared. "I ain't set up to run no mental hospital."

"Don't worry, I'll take him off your hands." Ben assured him and started for the door. "I'll take his horses up to the stable and tell Henry what's goin' on." With a shake of his head, he added, "I'll see if Tuck is still swingin' on the reins of that Palouse."

When he got back to the saloon, he found it unnecessary to tell Henry. Henry was at the Coyote when Ben got there. So were quite a few other people who were curious about the one gunshot. Rachel, Tiny, and Cecil were the ones most anxious to hear the story, for they were the three who watched what they thought was a practical joke on an old friend. "Honestly, Ben," Rachel marveled, "we thought you just suddenly went loco." She was especially chagrined that she had been so cordial to the man, oblivious to the fact that he had come to kill Ben. He told them the story behind the whole bizarre occurrence. Later on, when it was just the two of them, he could tell her about the trip he was going to have to take to Austin. *It's a damn good thing she's the one who really runs this place,* he thought. There was still the worry about what was going on at the Double-D, and that was the main reason he hated to leave for the time it would take to get Billy to Austin. All had been peaceful, but he couldn't bring himself to believe Daniel Dalton had come to the peace table.

Their customers stayed around a little later than usual on the night just passed, so Ben decided not to tell Rachel about his trip to

Austin. He decided to wait until morning and not even then until he had a chance to see what kind of shape Billy was in. The prior night's activity was played over again by Rachel and Tiny for Annie's benefit. After breakfast, Ben went to the jail to see how his prisoner was doing. When he got there, Billy was in the process of eating his breakfast, delivered by Mack Bragg. He didn't have to wait long to discover that Billy had recovered his mental faculties.

"Well, well, well," Billy drew out, "if it ain't my old friend, Mr. Goody-goody Savage."

"Glad to see you're feelin' your old self," Ben told him.

"Yeah, I'm just fine and dandy, if you don't count this damn cut on the side of my head. But everything on the inside is workin' just fine, especially my memory. I'm rememberin' real good how you snuck up behind me and slammed me upside my head when I wasn't lookin'. That's the kinda thing a feller don't forget."

"It's kinda like when a fellow set himself up watching the door with a gun in his lap, waitin' to shoot you when you walk in, ain't it?"

"I was just gonna challenge you to a fair fight out in the street," Billy claimed, caus-

342

ing Ben to chuckle in response.

"Is that a fact? If I was like somebody I know, I reckon I woulda just shot you in the back, wouldn't I, Billy?"

"You *shoulda* shot me," Billy replied. "The sheriff told me you were gonna transport me back to Austin. And I'm tellin' you right now, I ain't goin' back to Austin. I'll kill you first chance I get, first chance you get careless. You think about that."

"Fair enough," Ben replied. "I 'preciate the warnin', so I'll give you one. I'll give you the chance to have a fair trial, the same as any prisoner the Rangers capture is entitled to. The same as 'Big Foot' Kelley and Jack Queen down in Navasota were entitled to but didn't get." He looked Billy straight in the eye to deliver the rest of the message. "Make no mistake, Billy, I will shoot you down if you make the first wrong move."

"Then I reckon we both know the rules," Billy remarked. "When are we gonna get started?"

"When I tell you," Ben answered and walked out of the cell room. Mack Bragg followed him outside. He went down the two steps to the street before he stopped to talk to the sheriff. "Mack, I probably don't have to tell you this, but I will anyway. You be damn careful around that man. You heard him say he would kill me first chance he got. Well, the same goes for you. He's as dangerous as any prisoner you've ever locked up, so don't get careless around him."

"I don't intend to," Bragg said. "I'm just thinkin' about that two-day ride you're fixin' to take with that scoundrel. You'd better not go to sleep till you turn him over to the authorities in Austin."

"I might not," Ben said. "Looks to me like he's ready to go. Maybe I didn't hit him as hard as I thought, so I reckon I'll take him tomorrow mornin'. It's a little too late to get started today, so I'll ask you to keep him just one more night." He started to leave but paused again. "You know, I've been thinkin', I arrested him for what he was fixin' to do. If he was to behave himself and make it to trial, a good defense lawyer might say he couldn't be sentenced on what would amount to bein' nothing but my word."

"Maybe," Bragg replied, "but he was sittin' there watchin' the front door with his pistol in his hand. That pretty much shows what he had in mind to do. And he did fire off one round."

"A lawyer could say he was just actin' in self-defense when I sneaked up behind him." He shook his head and grimaced. "I'd just hate like hell to tote his ass all the way to Austin and have him find a way to get acquitted."

"I heard him say he was gonna kill you, first chance he got," Bragg insisted. "I could testify for you." He shrugged and thought to add, "I don't know if I could be away from Buzzard's Bluff to go to Austin. I ain't even got a deputy to watch the town while I was gone."

"There's no use sweatin' about it," Ben finally decided. "Takin' him in and lettin' the court decide what to do with him is the only thing to do now unless we let him go. And I ain't ready to do that right now — or ever."

"Amen to that," Bragg stated.

"So I'll take charge of him first thing tomorrow mornin'. You can tell Lacy you won't need breakfast for him in the mornin'. We're gonna get away from here before breakfast. I'm goin' to the stable now to see if he's got any supplies in his packs. No sense in spendin' my money on supplies for him, if he's already got some."

"Howdy, Ben," Henry Barnes called out from the hay loft of his barn when Ben walked past on his way to the stable door.

345

"You fixin' to get your horse?"

"Nope," Ben answered, "but I'll be takin' him out first thing in the mornin' — that Palouse, too. Right now, I'm gonna look through Billy Turner's packs to see if he's got enough food to take both of us to Austin."

"He might have," Henry remarked, "I ain't looked to see what he had in them packs," he lied. "I don't reckon a man like that feller does much cookin'." When he went through the sack the night before, he had found nothing in the line of food but bacon, hardtack, and coffee. "I'll be right down to help ya." He hurried back to the ladder and was in the stable alleyway by the time Ben walked in.

After a few minutes, Ben announced what Henry already knew. "Nothin' but bacon, hardtack, and coffee, but there's enough to take us to Austin. So I'll let Billy pay for our chuck on the trip. If he complains about the food, I'll just tell him he shoulda put more thought behind his shopping. I'll take his packhorse, too. It looks better than mine, and it's used to followin' along behind that Palouse. I expect I'll be here about the time you get here in the mornin'. I wanna get an early start — before breakfast. So give 'em some grain tonight." Henry said he would, and he would make sure they were watered well.

With that settled, he said so long to Henry and went back to the Coyote where he found Rachel waiting with questions of her own. Her first one was "What will Mack do with that man? Cecil was already complaining last night about the cost of keeping him in the jail for any length of time."

"Nothing for the mayor or the rest of the town council to worry about," Ben assured her. "Billy will be gone tomorrow."

"Where's he goin'?" Tiny asked, overhearing Ben's answer.

"He and I are gonna take a little trip to Austin, where we'll let the Rangers decide what to do with him."

"You just got back from Austin," Rachel complained. "You leaving me here to run this place by myself again?" He smiled at her in reply and she realized how silly that sounded, since she was really the one who took care of the business whether he was there or not.

"Oh, I think you'll know what to do," he japed. "If you run into something you aren't sure of, ask Tiny what to do."

"Kiss my foot," she responded.

"If there's any real trouble, don't worry, I'll ask Tuck to keep an eye on the place."

Although he was just joking with her, he still had concerns about the business with the Double-D. It was way too soon to accept the recent peace as a lasting one. *Damn you, Billy,* he thought. *You would have to show up here right now.* Getting serious then, he told them there was really no choice in the matter of transporting Billy to Austin. He was the only one who could do it.

The early rays of daybreak found Ben leading Cousin, the Palouse, and Billy's packhorse down the street to the jail. When he tied the horses at the rail, he was surprised to see Mack Bragg already up and standing in the open doorway. He had halfway expected to have to bang on the door to wake both sheriff and prisoner. "Have any trouble?" Ben asked Mack, who was standing there holding a double-barrel shotgun.

"No, no trouble," Bragg answered, "but I'll be honest with you. If I got any sleep at all last night, it was with one eye open. I don't believe he closed his eyes all night. Every time I checked on him, he was awake and most of the time talkin' to himself." He led Ben into his office and proceeded to unlock the door to the cell room.

"It's about time you showed up!" Billy

greeted him when he followed Bragg into the cell room. "I'm ready to get started — coulda started last night, in fact," he went on. "I'm ridin' my horse, ain't I? I didn't hear no jail wagon pull up out front. Let me use this honey mug one more time before we get in the saddle. How 'bout some coffee? You bring my breakfast with ya?"

Bragg turned to look at Ben. "See what I mean? He runs his mouth all the time, even when there ain't nobody with him. You're liable to be plum loco by the time you get to Austin."

"I expect he's tryin' to do that very thing, anything to keep you distracted," Ben replied. "I rode with him for a couple of days before this, and he didn't run off at the mouth then. I reckon he's tryin' to wear you out, so you don't watch him too close."

"It's sure as hell workin' on me," Bragg declared.

"Well, let's get him outta your hair," Ben said. "I brought a pair of handcuffs with me. I'll put them on him before we let him outta his cell."

"Hey," Billy blurted. "Ain't you gonna feed me no breakfast?" He stared defiantly at Ben. "You remember what I told you, I ain't goin' to Austin." He looked at Bragg then. "Hey, Sheriff, I musta got hold of some rancid bacon last night. I had to sit on that slop bucket again." He cast an evil grin in Bragg's direction. "I didn't wanna mess your bucket up, so I dumped it out on the floor. You might wanna clean it up before you put another prisoner in here."

"You son of a . . ." Bragg started, then raised the shotgun and aimed it at Billy.

"Uh-oh, un-oh," Billy mocked him. "Look at that, Ben, he's fixin' to shoot me! You're supposed to protect your prisoner. Ain't that the code of the Texas Rangers?"

"It's like this, Billy," Ben finally answered him. "You're goin' to Austin one way or another. If you quit brayin' like a donkey and behave yourself, you can go sittin' up in the saddle. If you keep actin' like a horse's ass, you'll go gagged, bound hand and foot, and thrown over the saddle. Might as well make up your mind which way it's gonna be 'cause I don't intend to put up with any trouble outta you. You'll get breakfast when I get breakfast. So, what's it gonna be?"

"I'll set in the saddle," Billy said. "I'll be good. It's my saddle, ain't it — on my horse?"

"That's right," Ben answered, "your saddle, your horse. I want you to have a real comfortable ride to Austin. So put your

350

hands behind you and back up to the bars."

"Ah, come on, Ben, is that necessary? I told you I'd be good."

"Put 'em behind you and back up, or you're gonna ride lyin' on your belly across the saddle," Ben threatened.

"All right, all right." He backed up to the bars and put his hands behind him. Ben quickly locked the handcuffs on his wrists. "You'll take these off while I'm in the saddle, right? It's inhumane to make a prisoner ride all day with his hands behind him."

"Maybe," Ben allowed. "It's a lot more humane to shoot the prisoner, so he won't mind the trip at all. If I remember correctly, that's your way, ain't it? You won't need your hands, anyway 'cause I'll be holdin' the reins of that fancy Palouse. All you'll have to do is relax and enjoy the ride."

"All right," Billy said, "I'll admit, I was havin' a little fun with you, but I can't even scratch my nose with my hands cuffed behind me. As one Ranger to another, I give you my word, I won't try nothin'. I'd just be a helluva lot more comfortable with my hands free. And like you said, you'll be holdin' my reins. I can't do nothin'."

"I appreciate your attitude, Billy. Oh, and by the way, when I saddled your horse this mornin', damnedest thing! There was one of those little two-shot pocket pistols stuck back up in the gullet under your saddle horn. Well, don't you know I pulled that outta there. You mighta accidentally shot yourself."

"You dirty swine," Billy growled.

"Open the door," Ben said to Mack as he drew his six-gun and the sheriff unlocked the cell and stood back to let Billy out. Billy took a couple of steps back as if about to refuse to come out. Then he suddenly lunged toward Mack, pretending to attack. Startled, the sheriff jumped backward, almost stumbling, causing Billy to throw his head back and laugh. That was enough to make Ben lose his patience with Billy's efforts to intimidate the sheriff. He placed a boot in the center of Billy's behind with sufficient force to knock him off balance and send him stumbling out the cell room door. With his hands behind his back, he couldn't catch himself, and crashed to the floor belly-first. "How much more do you wanna play?" Ben growled as he lifted him up on his feet. "Now, walk out that door, or do you need another boot in the ass to help you?"

With an assist from Ben, Billy was settled in the saddle, sullen and silent until Ben grabbed one of his boots and slipped a loop of rope over it. "Hey!" Billy protested. "What the hell are you doin'?"

"Just wanna make sure you don't fall off and hurt yourself," Ben said and tossed the other end of the rope under the horse's belly, then went to the other side to tie it to Billy's other foot. Satisfied that Billy couldn't jump off the horse, even if he tried, he climbed up on his horse after securing Billy's reins to Cousin's saddle. To Mack, standing there watching the preparation to ride, Ben said, "If I don't have any trouble with my prisoner, I oughta be back in four days, maybe five, depending what I have to do when I get to Austin." He cocked his head to give Billy a look. "If I do have trouble with him, I'll most likely be back sooner." He started to turn Cousin away from the rail but paused. "I forgot about this." He reached in his pocket and pulled the two-shot derringer out, then tossed it to Bragg. "It ain't loaded. I took the bullets out." Scowling, Billy made no comment.

"Keep your eye on that black-hearted devil," Bragg cautioned him. "He'll kill you if you give him half a chance."

Ben nodded, saying nothing, but Billy leaned toward the sheriff as they pulled away from the jail. "You can count on it,

Sheriff."

The initial signs of an awakening little town began to appear as lights in several store windows suddenly flickered into life. But there was no one on the street other than the two men riding down the middle of it, a long ride ahead of them.

CHAPTER 19

On a trail now familiar to him, Ben led his prisoner across a wide-open stretch of prairie toward a camping site he had used on his last trip to Austin. It was on a creek bank a little over twenty miles from Buzzard's Bluff, and there was grass for the horses as well as plenty of wood for a fire. No longer japing and noisy, Billy Turner rode in stoic silence, a state brought about when he learned of Ben's discovery of his hidden pocket pistol. Before that, his mood had been downright carefree, knowing that once he was back on his horse, he would have a weapon handy and the broad back of Ben Savage for a target. He was faced with a much more difficult task now to secure his freedom. There was nothing for him but to be ready when the slightest opportunity presented itself. And he knew from his brief period riding with Ben Savage that the opportunities would be rare. He had never harbored many fears in his life, and he had always enjoyed the powerful feeling he experienced when taking another man's life. When he had joined the Texas Rangers, it gave him the opportunity to enjoy that feeling without fear of reprisal. There was only one fear that haunted him, and that was the fear of dying of strangulation by hanging. He had often been placed in circumstances that might have caused him to be shot. He had never experienced any fear of that possibility. But to be hanged by the neck, like a helpless pig at a hog killing, was abhorrent to his inner soul. For that reason, he was sincere when he said he would not permit Ben Savage to hand him over to the hangman.

They rode on in silence until reaching the first camp site. Ben picked out one of the occasional trees on the bank of the creek and pulled the horses under the shade of its branches before dismounting. He said nothing to Billy as he went about the business of unlocking his hands but leaving the cuffs on one wrist. He let him stretch his arms for a couple of minutes, his gun in hand, before he ordered him to put his hands together in front of him. Billy hesitated, the cocky smile returning to his face. "What if I don't?" he threatened. "You gonna shoot me?"

"That's exactly what I'm gonna do," Ben replied. "But I'm not gonna kill you. I'm just gonna give you a round in the shoulder, maybe another in the leg, to make sure you ain't gonna give me any more trouble. If you ain't willin' to cooperate with me, I don't plan to give you anything to eat till I turn you over to Captain Mitchell in Austin. So make up your mind now on whether or not you're gonna put those hands in front of you, so you can eat." To show he meant what he said, he cocked the hammer back on the Colt six-gun.

Billy gazed stoically at him for a few moments before putting his wrists together. "You would, too, wouldn't you?" He sneered as Ben quickly snapped the cuff closed around his other wrist.

Ben untied the rope around one of Billy's boots, so he could get his feet out of the stirrups, then stood back from the horse, covering him with his pistol. "All right, get down off the horse." When Billy did so, Ben said, "Walk over to that tree and sit down with your feet on both sides of it."

"Ah, hell," Billy protested. "There ain't no need for all this fuss. You're holdin' the gun, I can't do nothin'."

"All right, then," Ben replied casually, "which leg do you want it in?" He cocked the Colt again and prepared to shoot.

"Wait a minute, damn it!" Billy blurted. "I'm goin' to the damn tree." He did as Ben instructed, walking over to the tree, dragging the rope behind him, then sat down facing the trunk. "The trunk's too big. I ain't gonna have no room to eat."

"It ain't as big around as that horse's belly. Set!" When Billy stuck his legs out, Ben took the loose end of the rope and tied it to his other boot. "Now you just sit there and rest while I do all the work." He left him then to take care of the horses. When they were taken care of and left at the edge of the creek to drink water, he gathered wood for his fire. Once the fire was going to his satisfaction, he went to the creek, upstream from the horses, to fill his coffeepot.

Billy could only sit there with his legs around the tree trunk and watch Ben prepare some breakfast for them. When it appeared to him that Ben was preoccupied with slicing off some of the bacon from the packs, he thought to make an attempt to free himself. He was sure he might be able to just reach the knot on one of his boots, even though his wrists were cuffed together. He watched and waited until Ben was halfway turned away from him as he situated his frying pan on a couple of burning limbs. When it appeared Ben's attention was focused on getting the pan just right, Billy reached around the trunk, stretching as far as he could in an effort to get his fingers on the knot. He was almost there when he was suddenly startled by the sound of the .44 and a piece of bark ripped off the trunk just above his hands. "You're actin' like somebody who don't wanna get fed," Ben commented.

"I was just tryin' to ease my foot a little bit!" Billy insisted. "Wasn't no need for you to go off half-cocked."

"Well, I'm fixin' to bring you a cup of coffee in a minute or two, and that'll ease you all over. I'm fryin' you some bacon and hardtack. I know that's what you like to eat, 'cause it came outta your packs. Next time we stop to rest the horses, you'll know the drill, and maybe it'll run even smoother."

"I reckon you're gonna go arrest all the Rangers who've ever shot a prisoner after you're done with me," Billy remarked sarcastically.

"No," Ben said and paused, "just the ones who set up an ambush and wait to shoot me."

"You were damn lucky you came in the back door of that saloon, or you'd be dead right now."

"I was more lucky that you were ridin' that Palouse geldin' and tied him right out front, so I'd know you were waiting for me inside."

Billy just snorted in response, but he realized that it had been a clear case of his not thinking of that because he had been so anxious to shoot him. *We've still got a day and a half of riding to do,* he thought. *He's got to slip up somewhere between here and Austin.*

Once the horses were watered, fed, and rested, they got underway again, following the same trail Ben had followed when he had ridden to Austin to resign from the Rangers. They reached the stop for the night without incident and he had to wonder if Billy had really given up any ideas of escape. *Too much to hope for,* he thought as he prepared to get his camp ready. He was more particular about the placement of the camp for an overnight stay. For one thing, he wanted more trees in the event he needed protection, but also for the sleeping arrangement. He planned to tie Billy hand and foot when it was time to sleep and he needed two trees fairly close together. This was because he planned to tie his hands to a rope from one tree, and his feet to a rope from the other tree. That way, he could give his prisoner enough slack between the two ropes to permit him to lie comfortably, but not enough to let him reach his feet with his hands.

While they were eating their supper, Billy, his legs tied around the tree, decided to try a different approach and appeal to Ben's sense of honor. "I'll admit I've done some bad things in my life, but one thing I'm proud of is I ain't ever turned my hand against another Ranger." When Ben jerked his head back in surprise at that statement, Billy was quick to explain. "Oh, I know what you're thinkin', but in the Ranger company I was trained in, it was a common practice to execute prisoners, if their crime had to do with killin' or somethin' that was gonna get 'em the rope for the crime. But one Ranger never turned on another Ranger. I know now that I done wrong when I came after you, but it was because I thought you was out to smear the name of the Texas Rangers. I ain't got nothin' against you no more. And as one Ranger to another, why don't we just say we're even? You go your way and I'll go mine, and we won't ever cross paths again. And the good name of the Texas Rangers won't get drug in the dirt. Whaddaya say?"

Hardly able to believe what he had just heard come out of Billy's mouth, Ben didn't answer him right away as he simply stared at him in amazement. It was such a surprising attempt by one so brazen and cocky, that he had to think a moment before answering. "Billy," he finally asked, "do I really look that stupid to you?"

The two of them stared at each other for a long moment before Billy shrugged and said, "What the hell? You never know, it woulda made things a helluva lot simpler. We'd split, I'd go one way, and you go the other and that woulda been the end of it."

"Except for the part where you sat waitin' to ambush me when I walked in the Coyote," Ben said. He shook his head in disbelief. "I gotta hand it to you, Billy, you've got one hell of an imagination. You'd best hang on to that in case they throw you in prison, instead of hangin' you."

"To hell with you, Savage," Billy responded, sliding back into his own skin. "You ain't got me to Austin yet, so you'd best watch your step. I told you back yonder in that two-bit sheriff's jail that I don't plan to go to Austin and you can bet on that."

Still finding it hard to believe the man could threaten him in his situation, Ben couldn't help pressing him. "If I untie you and hand over your gun, will you let me go free?"

"Yes," Billy answered him. "I'd let you go, and no hard feelin's."

Ben looked at him as if seeing him for the first time. "You're just as crazy as a coyote eatin' locoweed. Finish that bacon, it's time to put you to bed. Maybe your head will be straight again in the mornin'."

"I don't want that bacon. I don't need no food, and I ain't gonna need no sleep, either. I'll just stay awake and hug this tree while I watch you sleep."

Ben was beginning to think there was something mentally wrong with the man, so he tried to appeal to him logically. "The way I'm gonna tie you tonight, you'll be comfortable enough to go to sleep and that'll make the ride tomorrow a lot better for you."

"I'll set right here. I don't need no sleep, but I'll be watchin' you while you sleep."

"I reckon not," Ben stated emphatically. "I think you've got your mind turned upside down. I'm the one callin' the shots here, not you. So I'm gonna untie your feet so you can get up. Then I'll tie you between this tree and that closest one there." He nodded toward a tree about twenty feet away. "You understand?" Billy did not respond. He continued to stare at Ben as he bent down and untied the rope on one of his feet. "All right, get up."

Billy slowly got to his feet, his eyes cast down at his handcuffed wrists. When he was fully erect, he lifted his gaze to lock onto Ben's, causing him to become immediately alert. Something was going on in the brain behind those eyes and it looked as if it was about to happen if he didn't do something to prevent it. "We'll get an early start in the mornin', get into Austin early enough to get you settled for the night. They'll fix you up with a nice bunk." His attempt at civility had no apparent effect upon Billy, who continued to stare.

Finally, he spoke. It was with a flat lifeless tone, void of emotion. "I ain't goin'." To the tree, or to Austin, Ben wasn't certain, but before he had a chance to find out, Billy lunged at him, his handcuffed hands reaching for Ben's throat.

Ben easily stepped aside, stuck his foot out, and tripped the charging maniac. Looking down at Billy sprawled on the ground, Ben said, "That was a dumb damn thing to try. I coulda shot you just as easy." Billy made no reply. Instead, he got up on his feet again, still with slow, deliberate movements to face Ben. "Now, you've had your

364

little try, don't make that mistake again." Billy's response was to hunker down like a charging bull and launch another attack upon him. Finding it hard to believe the man had suddenly gone crazy, Ben again stepped aside at the last second. But this time, instead of tripping him, he quickly shifted his six-gun to his left hand and met Billy's charge with a hard-right fist flush on nose. The force of the blow laid Billy flat on his back, stunned once again by the bigger man. Ben watched him for a few seconds as he struggled to roll over in an effort to get up. It struck Ben at that moment! Billy was determined to overpower him or get shot in the process. It amounted to an attempt to gain his freedom, or to commit suicide by gunshot, a much quicker death than hanging. This was why he kept repeating that he was not going to go to Austin.

Ben was torn between two different thoughts at that moment. Would it be the more humane between the two, to simply shoot him and put him out of his fear of hanging? He didn't debate the issue very long before deciding. Like he had told Billy before, it wasn't his job to punish. His job was to capture. Looking down at the stunned man, trying to gather his senses, Ben suddenly became angry. "You're goin' to trial, you sick puppy, but you ain't gonna enjoy the trip." Working quickly then, before Billy had time to regain his faculties, he tied Billy's ankles back together again. Then he took the rest of the coil of rope and tied his arms against his body. Once he had him sufficiently hog-tied, he stood him up against one of the trees and tied him tightly against the trunk. "Now, damn it, we'll turn in for the night."

The next morning, he found his prisoner sagging slightly, but still firmly bound to the tree trunk. He had to admit that he wasn't in a much better mood than his captive. It had been impossible to get more than brief snatches of sleep, even though he knew Billy was secured to that tree. He left him there while he got the horses ready to travel. When they were saddled and ready, he went back to the tree to get Billy. He stood there a few moments, taking a look at his prisoner. He had been so put out with him during the night that he planned not to take any more chances with him. He was going to leave him bundled up and throw him over the saddle to ride the rest of the way to Austin on his belly, a distance he figured to be about forty miles. Looking at him now, sagging with fatigue, and dried blood all over his lips and chin, he had a change of heart. *Just a weakness, I reckon,* he thought. So he untied him and walked him to the creek where he let him drink and wash his face. There was not a word from Billy as he obeyed each order Ben gave him, getting down on his knees and washing his face with both hands still shackled. "I'll feed you when we stop to rest the horses," he said when he settled him in the saddle the same as he had the day before. "If you get any more ideas like you did last night, I will shoot you. But like I told you yesterday, I'll cripple you, but I'll be damned if I'm gonna help you commit suicide. They might not hang you. You might just have to spend some time in prison."

"You're just the perfect goody-goody Ranger, ain't you?" Billy responded.

"I reckon so," Ben replied, "and if you keep your mouth shut, I might let you take a leak before you climb on that horse."

In spite of Billy's tendency to make smart remarks, he was surprisingly quiet after his unsuccessful attempt to jump Ben the night before. With the one rest stop for the horses, when Ben made coffee and cooked more bacon and hardtack, they reached Austin fairly early in the afternoon. Ben rode straight to the jail to turn his prisoner over to the sheriff to be held for trial. Deputy

Sheriff Joe Farmer was on duty at the jail, and he knew Ben well. "I swear, Ben Savage," Joe greeted him. "Whatchu doin' back here in Austin? I heard you was in the saloon business in some little town up on the Navasota."

"I am," Ben replied, "but it still looks like I've gotta do the Rangers' business for 'em. I wanna drop this fellow off for you to keep till Captain Mitchell decides what to do with him. I'm gonna go see Mitchell now to tell him you've got him here in jail."

"Sure thing, Ben," Joe said. "What did you arrest him for?" Ben told him the story behind Billy's release from the Rangers and his attempt to kill him and warned him that Billy was dangerous. "I swear," Joe remarked, "a Ranger, was he? That sure is bad."

" 'Preciate you takin' care of him," Ben said in parting.

As he walked past the cell Billy had been put in, Billy was standing up close to the bars and he gave Ben a parting remark. "I ain't goin' to no gallows," he said softly.

"Maybe not, Billy," Ben returned and walked out the door with a wave of his hand to Joe Farmer.

His next stop was Captain Randolph Mitchell's office to deliver a report that would take the captain very much by surprise. "You brought in Billy Turner?" Mitchell asked in disbelief. "On what charge?"

"Attempted murder," Ben answered. When Mitchell asked who the intended victim was, Ben said, "Me, and I've got witnesses to back up the charge." He went on to give him all the details that led up to Billy's arrest. Mitchell decided the best thing to do would be to turn the case over to the U.S. Marshal Service and let them try it. "Makes no difference to me," Ben said, "just as long as he's not Buzzard's Bluff's problem anymore. We've got other problems to deal with." That prompted Mitchell to ask how he was getting along in his new life as a saloon owner. "My partner is a very patient woman," Ben replied with a chuckle, "and it's a damn good thing 'cause I had no idea there was so much to runnin' a successful business. And so far, it is successful."

"Good to hear it," Mitchell said, even though he would have rather heard Ben say he was ready to come back to work for him full time. "You gonna stay in town for a while?"

"No, sir. I've got some things I'm concerned about back in Buzzard's Bluff, so I'm fixin' to start right back before dark.

I've got to leave Billy's Palouse geldin' and all his stuff at the stable, but if it's all right with you, I'll take the packhorse back with me. It belongs to Billy, but I didn't wanna take two packhorses for that short a trip."

"I'll write you a letter when I find out what they'll do with Billy," Mitchell said. "I know they let him off with a permanent suspension from the Ranger Service and a warning of prosecution if he was involved in any unlawful activity after his release. And it looks like this sure qualifies."

Ben left Mitchell's office and took the horses to the stable where he told Fred Pritcher about the Palouse. "It sure is," Ben replied when Fred commented that it was an unusual looking horse. "And Billy is kinda unusual, himself. I wanna leave Cousin and this packhorse with you for an hour or so. Figured I'd walk down to Coleman's boardin' house and see if they'll let me eat with 'em one more time. I'd appreciate it if you would give all three of the horses a portion of oats, and I'll pick up Cousin and the packhorse after they've had a chance to get a little rest."

John and Bertha Coleman gave him a cordial welcome when he showed up at the boardinghouse and asked if he could buy a meal. Bertha was quite pleased when he said he had come there to eat because she served the best cooking in Austin. There were, of course, many questions about his venture into the saloon business, which he answered as briefly as possible. Most of the other people at the table were still in the dark about who he was. It amused him that it wasn't much different when he had been living there, since he was gone for a majority of the time. When he figured the horses should be rested enough, he took his leave, promising to visit again the next time he was in Austin.

By the time he had Cousin saddled and ready to go, he figured he had only two hours of daylight left, but he figured he'd rather get started back right away, instead of waiting until morning. He had a spot in mind about ten miles out of town where he intended to camp that night.

CHAPTER 20

Ranger Captain Randolph Mitchell heard the shots fired. His office was not that far from the city jail. *Somebody's having a little trouble,* he thought. It was unusual to hear gunshots in the city of Austin. A short time later, one of the guards from the jail appeared at his office door. "Mr. Mitchell," the guard reported, "Sheriff Cowan sent me to fetch you to the jailhouse. There's been some trouble with one of the prisoners, and Sheriff Cowan says he's a Ranger prisoner. He thinks you might wanna come to hear what happened."

"Damn," Mitchell swore softly, knowing immediately it had to involve Billy Turner. *That's what I get for working late in the office,* he thought. "Any of the sheriff's men hurt?"

"Well, no, sir, depends on what you call hurt — more like, are they in trouble," the guard answered. "You'll see what I mean if you'll come down to the jail."

"All right, let me lock up here," Mitchell said as he hurried to close his office for the day, then followed the guard out the door.

When they got to the jail, Mitchell found Sheriff Pete Cowan and Deputy Joe Farmer in the office. As soon as he saw Mitchell, Sheriff Cowan immediately apologized for having to contact him. "I swear, Randolph, I'm sorry to have to call you down here for this, but we've had a little trouble with the prisoner Ben Savage dropped off here this afternoon."

"What kinda trouble?" Mitchell asked.

"Well, he's dead," Cowan said and turned to look at Deputy Farmer, who stared back at the sheriff as if shaken. "Joe, here, was fixin' to take him in some supper and he had to open the cell door 'cause he was carryin' his coffee and everything on one tray. This fellow, Turner, acted like he'd gone crazy." He turned to Farmer again and asked, "Ain't that what you said, Joe?" When the deputy just nodded, Cowan said, "Tell Captain Mitchell what you told me."

"Yes, sir," Farmer began. "When Ben Savage dropped him off, he told me this feller could be dangerous, so I'd best keep a close eye on him. But he didn't make no fuss a-tall till I brought him some supper. He looked at me kinda crazy-like and said he didn't want no supper and said, 'Why don't you stick that tray up your ass?" He paused to let that register with Mitchell. "Well, I sorta told him that I didn't hardly think I was gonna do that and that maybe he needed to learn some decent manners. I reckon that riled him some more 'cause he took a step toward me and took his foot and kicked the tray outta my hands. That's when I drew my .44 and warned him. I told him to back off, but he just stood there, still lookin' crazy. I warned him again to back off, but he started comin' at me till I backed outta the cell. He said he weren't goin' to no hangin'. And that's when he charged at me like a bull. I shot him, I had to. I hit him in the shoulder and spun him around, thought that'd about do it for him. But damned if he didn't yell at me, 'You can do better than that,' and came at me again." He looked from Mitchell to Cowan, then back at Mitchell. "Well, I reckon I said I sure as hell could, so I let him have one right in the center of his chest. He's still a-layin' there in the door to the cell, if you wanna take a look at him. Sheriff said to leave him there till after you got a chance to take a look. The prisoners in the other cells watched the whole thing. They oughta tell you the same thing I just told you. I shouldn'ta carried the tray in. Shoulda just slid it in the door."

"After hearing Ben Savage's report when he brought Turner in, I don't doubt a word you said," Mitchell told him. "I don't think there was any question about it, the man was crazy. It wasn't your fault. He was trying to get you to shoot him. He was that afraid of the gallows. So don't feel guilty about this shooting. You did what you had to do." He thought it unnecessary to tell them that he had had his doubts about any possible actions a court would have imposed on Billy Turner, the principals in the trial being highly unlikely to have been gathered together in one court room. Most likely, Billy would have been released after all was said and done. *At least he got what he wanted,* Mitchell thought, *he got shot instead of hanging. I guess I'll send a message to Ben tomorrow in the mail.* To Pete Cowan, he said, "Nothing more we can do about this. I haven't even had time to notify the U.S. Marshal, so go ahead and get rid of the body." He left them with it while he went to have a late supper at Bowen's Restaurant.

At roughly the same time Captain Mitchell left the jail after seeing Billy Turner's body,

Billy's nemesis was coaxing his campfire into life by a narrow stream about twelve miles northeast of Austin. Since he had treated himself to a fine supper at Bertha Coleman's table, his fire was really unnecessary. He was building it just to give himself something to do with his hands while he was considering where things stood between the Lost Coyote and the Double-D. He found it difficult to believe Daniel Dalton would discontinue the war between them. Dalton had declared that he would order his men away from the Coyote, after claiming that the attempts on Ben's life had not been ordered by him. "Just a big ol' misunderstandin'," Ben said to Cousin, wondering if the big dun could detect the sarcasm in his tone. He took a critical look at his fire and decided it was pretty pitiful. The place he had stopped for the night was lacking in wood for a fire, since there were no trees of any size. But there was water, although little more than a healthy trickle, and there was grass. He had planned to stop at a better campsite about two miles short of where he was now. But when he reached it, there was still a bit of daylight left, so he pushed the horses a little farther. He should have noticed the packhorse starting to lag a bit, but when he did notice, they were two miles past the better campsite. He should have remembered they had already traveled forty miles that day when he reached Austin. Cousin was up to it, but Billy's packhorse wasn't. "We've had worse campsites," he declared to Cousin as he unrolled his bedroll and prepared to get some sleep — maybe make up some of what he lost the night before when he still had Billy.

Off to an early start when the sun came up again to send rays of light probing the gullies and ravines in the line of hills on the distant horizon, he would ride about twenty miles before breakfast. He figured to arrive in Buzzard's Bluff in the middle of the afternoon on the following day.

At approximately the same time Ben was arriving at his overnight campsite on his way back to Buzzard's Bluff, a young cowhand tied his reins over the rail at the Lost Coyote Saloon. Inside, he was greeted warmly by Rachel Baskin. "Jimmy, right?"

"Yes, ma'am," he replied, all smiles. "Jimmy Whitley." His eyes searched the entire saloon as he spoke.

Rachel smiled as she recalled his first visit to the Coyote. "She's upstairs. She should be back in a minute or two." When his wide grin immediately drooped upon hearing that, Rachel quickly assured him. "She's not up there with anybody. She just went up to comb her hair. She'll be right back." The grin reappeared as rapidly as it had faded before. "So what brings you back to Buzzard's Bluff?" As soon as she said it, she realized she could guess the answer to that question, so she asked, "Is there anyone with you?"

"No, ma'am, just me," Jimmy answered, his eyes still focused on the top of the stairs. "Frank said we could take half a day off, since we ain't had any time off for so long, only we couldn't all pick the same day."

"Frank," she repeated, as Tiny stood there grinning as widely as Jimmy was. "That would be Frank Ross, right?"

"No, ma'am, that's Frank Jacobs. He's Ross Jacobs's brother, and he's the foreman of the RBJ ranch."

"You took a pretty long ride over here from the RBJ," Tiny said.

"No, sir, it weren't all that long. Only took me two hours. I cut across part of the Double-D range near the river."

"You'd best be careful cuttin' across the Double-D," Tiny said. "They ain't the friendliest spread around here."

"I reckon," Jimmy said, beginning to become impatient. "All their crew ain't that bad, though. Frank just hired on two hands that used to work for the Double-D. That's the reason he was able to let some of us take a little time off to kick up our heels."

That spiked Rachel's interest right away. "Your boss hired two men from the Double-D? I never would have expected that to happen. I thought the RBJ was having trouble with the Double-D rustling your cattle."

"Well, yes, ma'am, that's a fact," Jimmy replied. "But these two fellows quit the Double-D because they didn't like stealin' other ranches' cattle. They were lookin' for honest work. And RBJ is an honest outfit. They ain't been with us very long, but so far they look like real good workers."

Finding the conversation extremely interesting now, Rachel asked, "What are their names, the two new hands?"

"Marty and Shorty," Jimmy answered.

"Marty Jackson and Shorty Dove?" Tiny recited and glanced at Rachel to see her reaction. It was the same as his. He started to ask more questions, but at that moment, Ruby appeared at the top of the stairs.

She paused to look the room over before taking the first step, wearing the same bored expression she had worn when she went up to comb her hair. She looked toward the bar then and the light went on in her eyes when she saw who Rachel and Tiny were talking to. The frown was immediately replaced by a joyous smile as she hurried down the steps to join them. "Jimmy!" she literally squealed. "You came to see me!"

He blushed unashamed as she placed both her hands in his. "I told you I would," he blurted. "This was the first chance I got."

"Took him two hours to get here," Tiny announced, his grin matching Jimmy's.

"I saved up every penny I could lay my hands on ever since I left here that mornin'," he volunteered.

She leaned forward and gave him a kiss on the cheek. "Come on," she said, "let's go upstairs to my room where we can talk." She dropped one of his hands and led him with the other toward the stairs.

"Better not talk so much you'll be too sore to ride," Tiny was inspired to say, accompanied by a big horselaugh.

"Tiny!" Rachel scolded. "Hush your mouth. Don't tease those young folks. This is the only chance Ruby has to be a girl again."

Tiny shrugged, contritely. "Well, he said he's got a two-hour ride back home." That was all he could think to say in his defense. "Oughta open the door for Clarice tonight, though. She won't have no competition."

They watched the young couple hurry up the stairs before discussing the news Jimmy brought with him about Marty and Shorty. "That's gonna be mighty interestin' to Ben when he gets back. Both of 'em took a shot at him and Tuck," Tiny said.

As if cued by the mention of his name, Tuck Tucker walked into the saloon at that moment. "Hey, Tiny," he bellowed, "pour me a drink of whiskey while you ain't doin' nothin'."

"You sure you're old enough to drink hard likker?" Tiny japed in return and nodded at Rachel. "The boss, here, told me I ain't supposed to serve nobody who don't stand at least a head above the bar."

Tuck looked at Rachel and asked, "When are you and Ben gonna put a piano in here, so Tiny won't be the biggest noisemaker in the saloon?" They all shared a chuckle while Tiny poured Tuck's drink. Tuck took a look around the room to see if there was anyone there he wanted to talk to. Seeing none of his regular drinking pals, he asked, "Who belongs to the wrung-out roan at the hitchin' rail?"

"I expect you probably saw Jimmy's horse," Rachel told him.

"Jimmy who?" Tuck asked.

"Jimmy Whitley," she answered. "You remember him, don't you, the young cowhand from the RBJ who's sweet on Ruby?" Tuck drew his head back, remembering then. "He's upstairs with Ruby now," Rachel said, "and probably will be for a long time." She winked and teased, "You can get Tiny to explain it to you."

While she and Tiny laughed, he nodded his head slowly and said, "It might be hard for you two to understand, but I was young once. Nowadays, I'm more concerned about that tired horse standin' at the rail that could use some water and some grass."

Tiny couldn't wait any longer. "You ain't heard what that young feller said about some new hands the RBJ just hired. He said they used to work for the Double-D, two of 'em, name of Shorty Dove and Marty Jackson." He paused to wait for Tuck's reaction. "Whaddaya think of that?"

"I think Ben's gonna wanna hear about that!" Tuck exclaimed. "Is that true?" he asked Rachel, and she said that it was. "When's Ben comin' back? I hope to hell he ain't had no trouble with that savage he rode off to Austin with. Maybe I oughta be doin' somethin' about those two."

Already regretting telling Tuck about Shorty and Marty, Tiny said, "Just wait till

Ben gets back. He'll know what to do. It ain't up to you to do anything."

"Why ain't it?" Tuck demanded, drawing himself up to his full five feet. "Hell, I'm the one they shot!"

"Whaddaya think you're gonna do?" Tiny asked. "You gonna ride down to the RBJ and call 'em out?"

"Maybe I am," Tuck blustered. "Ain't no use to go tell Mack Bragg about it. He ain't gonna ride down there to arrest anybody. So maybe I'd best take care of it, myself."

"No, you don't," Rachel said. "Tiny's right, nobody should do anything until Ben gets back. He'll know what's best to do. You just settle down and wait for Ben. Tiny, pour him another drink. This one's on the house," she told Tuck.

Not really prepared to ride down to the RBJ, he took the drink and let himself be calmed down by Rachel and Tiny. "Maybe you're right. I told Ben I'd keep an eye on things while he was gone, anyway."

"That's right," Tiny said and winked at Rachel. "He's probably countin' on you." The issue was left unsettled then because Ham Greeley came in and immediately challenged Tuck to a game of two-handed poker. "I reckon he's forgot about ridin' down to the RBJ to call out those two fellers," Tiny commented to Rachel.

"I surely hope so," she replied. "I don't want him putting any ideas in Ben's head about going down there to settle that business with Shorty and Marty. Ben's not the law around here, and I'd be really surprised if those two ever show up here again."

It was sometime after eight o'clock when Ruby and Jimmy came back downstairs in search of nourishment. "I'm gonna see if I can find something to eat in the kitchen," Ruby said to Rachel as she led Jimmy by the table where Rachel was sitting with Merle Baker. "Jimmy ain't had nothing to eat since this morning. I'm gonna make some coffee, if you want some." Before Rachel had a chance to remind her, she said, "Don't worry, I'll clean up my mess so Annie won't have to in the morning." Rachel nodded and gave Jimmy a smile. He responded with a sheepish grin.

"I was wonderin' where Ruby was tonight," Merle commented. "Who's the young fellow? He must be carryin' a lotta money on him."

Rachel had to chuckle. "I'd be surprised if he had enough to pay for more than one quick ride. What you're witnessing is young love." She paused, then added, "After a fashion. Tomorrow morning they'll wake up and find out it was all just a dream."

"I swear, Rachel, you're talkin' like an old woman," Merle said.

"Looking at those two, I feel like an old woman," Rachel replied. Ready to change the subject then, she commented, "I guess your business has slowed down since we're not seeing many Double-D men in town lately."

He smiled and said, "I reckon we can thank your business partner for that, but I have to say he brought me some business when he first came to town. What I need is some customers who wanna pay for a top-line coffin and a formal burial. 'Course, I don't wanna wish any bad luck on any of my friends or neighbors." He looked at her and made a face. "How are you feelin' lately?"

"I'm not that old," she said at once, then paused when Ruby and Jimmy came out of the kitchen. "Find anything to eat?" she asked.

"Yeah," Ruby answered. "Good ol' Annie. She left some biscuits in the oven and we spread some of that apple butter on 'em — went pretty good with that coffee. Didn't it, Jimmy?"

"It sure did," Jimmy responded, then look-ing sheepish again, he said, "I reckon I owe

385

you somethin' for the food, but if you'll trust me for it, I guarantee you I'll bring the money next time I'm here."

"Forget about it," Rachel said. "We don't charge anything for cold biscuits. You better save your money for other things." She smiled at Ruby, who blushed in return.

"Well, I'd best be goin'," Jimmy said after thanking her for the coffee and biscuits. "I've gotta be back at the ranch for work in the mornin'." Ruby walked him out the front door of the saloon. In a few seconds, they returned. "My horse is gone!" Jimmy blurted. "Somebody stole my horse!"

"Oh, I forgot," Rachel said, "Tuck took your horse out back of the saloon and tied it down by the creek so it could get some water and graze while you were busy upstairs."

"I reckon I shoulda thought about that, myself," Jimmy confessed. "I sure do appreciate it."

CHAPTER 21

"Señor Dalton wants to see you," Maria Gomez said. "He send me to tell you."

Spade Gunter hung the bridle he was holding on a corral post. "All right," he said, "I'm on my way." He turned and walked with the petite Mexican woman back to the house. They went in the kitchen door. Spade was surprised to see Estelle Dalton sitting at the kitchen table. She usually ate in the dining room with her husband. "Good mornin', ma'am," Spade greeted her respectfully.

"Good morning, Mr. Gunter," Estelle returned politely. "How are you, this morning?"

Surprised again, for he couldn't remember when she had spoken to him before, he replied, "Very well, thank you, ma'am. And yourself?" She answered with a smile, and he followed Maria into the hallway where she motioned for him to wait while she informed Dalton that he was there. When she came back, she held the door for Spade and closed it after him while she returned to the kitchen.

"Come on in, Gunter," Daniel Dalton invited. "I think it's time we built our crew back up. We need to replace those five men we've lost, since that barbarian came to town. I thought we had a tough crew, but I guess I was wrong. This time, you'd best ride up to Fort Worth and see if you can find some men who know how to handle a gun."

Spade hesitated, reluctant to say his peace. "Beggin' your pardon, sir," he started. "But don't you expect we'd best try to pick up some men who can work cattle?" He was thinking about the small amount of honest work he had gotten out of three of the men they had lost. "We've got the fall roundup comin' up, and we need more men who know how to round up cattle and brand 'em. I'm afraid, if we don't . . ."

That was as far as he got before Dalton interrupted him. "That's the trouble with you and every man around here lately. You're all so damned afraid of one man. One man!" he repeated angrily. "And with him out of the way, that woman running the saloon wouldn't last another six months." He was thoroughly convinced of this, even though there had been no signs that it would happen before the arrival of Ben Savage. "With Savage out of the way, I could buy that bitch out for pennies." To control the town, which was his intent, he felt he had to have control of all the saloon business. And from where he stood, all he could see to prevent that was one man. His eyes seemed to flash with anger when he pointed his finger at Spade as if it was his foreman's fault. "One man!" Dalton roared. "Hell, I could go into town and shoot one man."

"I don't know what to tell you, Mr. Dalton," Spade replied in his defense. "I thought Ed Hatcher would get the job done. He was the fastest man with a gun that I'd ever seen. And Deacon was cut outta the same stock. That Savage fellow just figures out a way to turn the tables on 'em. Bob Wills tried to shoot him in the back, but Savage wheeled and got him first. At least, that's what Marty Jackson said. He's got more lives than a damn cat."

"You sound like you're building that man up as more than human!" Dalton exploded. "Damn it, man! Anybody could walk up to him and put a bullet in him before he knew what they were about. I could do that!" He snorted in contempt. "Maybe that's what it's gonna boil down to."

Spade became afraid that Dalton was working himself up into doing something crazy. "I sure hope you ain't thinkin' about doin' something like that, sir. They've got a pretty good sheriff that tries to keep the peace. He might throw you in the jail."

Thoroughly steamed up by then, Dalton just stared at his befuddled foreman for a long moment before calmly stating, "In the event that actually happened, I would expect you and the men would break me out at once. Am I wrong about that?"

Spade was not sure how to answer the question, unsure if Dalton could actually consider doing something that drastic. He could imagine the chaos an incident like that would create in the town, more than likely with the Rangers and the U.S. Marshals coming in to restore order. He decided it best for him, however, to give Dalton the answer he expected. "No, sir, you ain't wrong about that. Every man we've got would be ready to come after you."

Dalton got up from his desk and stood gazing at his foreman as if making up his mind about something. Finally, he spoke. "Saddle my horse. I'm going into town."

"Yes, sir," Spade said, and turned at once

to leave the room. When he walked back through the kitchen, Estelle Dalton was no longer there, so he spoke to Maria. "He told me he's gonna ride into town. He say anything to you about it?"

"No, he don't say nothing to me," she replied.

He was just naturally curious because Dalton went into town so seldom, and if he said anything to anybody, it would more often than not be to Maria. He couldn't help being concerned after Dalton's foolish talk about shooting Ben Savage. "Well, I expect he'll be tellin' you pretty soon. Do me a favor, will ya? Let me know if he says anything about shootin' Ben Savage."

His request was more than enough to arouse her curiosity. "Sí, I tell you," she said and walked with him to the door. About to ask why he wanted to know what Dalton might say, she was interrupted by the whistling of the teakettle on the stove. She went at once to fix the tea to take into Estelle's room. Before the tea was ready, she heard Dalton yelling for her to come help him with his boots. She ran to his bedroom door, "I be right there," she said, "I fix the señora's tea now."

"Well, hurry up," he told her, "she's got all day to sit there and drink tea."

Spade had the black Morgan gelding saddled when Dalton finally walked out of the house and started walking toward the barn. Spade immediately took the horse's reins and went to meet him. "You need anybody to ride in with you?" he asked.

"No," Dalton answered. "I just think it's time I had a meeting with Wilson Bishop to see how my saloon is getting along. I need to go over the books to see for myself." He climbed up into the saddle. "Maybe I'll visit my competitor while I'm in town and see if they've enjoyed the recent peaceful time they've had."

"You figure on being back before supper?" Spade asked. He wanted to know when he should be concerned. Dalton said that he planned to return in plenty of time for supper. Spade was still watching him ride out of the yard when Buster Pate walked up to him.

"He's goin' into town?" It was a question because a couple of times that week Dalton had ordered his horse to be saddled and he never went anywhere.

"That's what he said," Spade answered. "Said he's gonna go talk to Wilson Bishop."

"You notice the boss actin' kinda funny lately?" Buster asked.

"Funny, how?" Spade responded.

"Like day before yesterday when you went with Elwood to drive that bunch of strays back up to the herd. I was forkin' some new hay down in those two back stalls and he came walkin' in, lookin' for you, I reckon. Anyway, when he saw me, he acted like he didn't know who I was. Then, when I asked him who he was lookin' for, he couldn't remember your name." When Spade looked askance at that, Buster said, "I swear."

"I don't know," Spade responded. "I reckon he's got a helluva lot on his mind right now and sometimes he can't keep everything straight." He shrugged and added, "He ain't a young man no more, ya know."

Spade was dead-on with his comments about Daniel Dalton. He did have a lot on his mind, and he wasn't as young as he used to be. His loss of what he had felt was the upper hand in his competition with the Lost Coyote was a major setback in his mind. He sometimes suspected that Wilson Bishop might not be doing the job he expected of him, even to the extent that possibly Wilson might be skimming cash off the Golden Rail's profits. That could explain the drop in income during the last several weeks. These were the thoughts swimming around inside Dalton's head when he saw the buildings of Buzzard's Bluff rise up from the horizon.

Riding up past the hotel, he noticed very little activity on the street. There was no sign of anybody at the sheriff's office, which sat diagonally across the street from the Golden Rail. He noted that between the two saloons in town, there were more horses tied up in front of the Golden Rail than there were at the Lost Coyote. That gave him some satisfaction, if only for the moment as he tied the Morgan at the rail. Upon seeing him come in the door, Mickey Dupree called out from behind the bar, loud enough for Wilson Bishop to hear, "Mr. Dalton, how you doin'? What can I get you, sir?" In a few seconds' time, Charlene hurried out of the office, followed immediately by Wilson Bishop, who hurried to meet Dalton, while Charlene scurried over to a card game in progress.

"Mr. Dalton," Wilson welcomed him. "What brings you to town today? If I'd known you were gonna be here, I'da had Bonnie or Charlene get in the kitchen to cook you up some dinner."

"I'm not hungry," Dalton informed him. "I just thought I'd come in to see how our peaceful little town is makin' out. Anything new going on that I should know about?"

"No, sir, we're gettin' along about like usual. Set yourself down, and I'll have Mickey bring out a bottle of that rye you favor." Without waiting for Dalton's response, he yelled, "Mickey, bring Mr. Dalton that special bottle you keep for him." He pulled a chair back for Dalton at a side table, then sat down, himself. "Would you rather go in the office?"

"No, this is fine," Dalton said.

"I thought you might wanna look at the books or somethin'," Wilson said.

"No, this is fine," he repeated. "I'm sure the books aren't gonna tell me if you're skimming anything off the top, anyway."

"Ah, no, sir," Wilson was quick to respond. "Ain't nothin' like that goin' on here. You've been more than generous to me. I wouldn't never cheat ya."

"That's not on my mind right now," Dalton said. "I want to know what that troublemaker has been doing. Is he still in tight with the sheriff?"

"I swear, boss, I can't say for sure. I ain't seen hide nor hair of the man all week. Stump said he's been outta town the whole week."

"Out of town?" Dalton reacted as a wild thought struck him. "You don't suppose he's gone for good from Buzzard's Bluff, maybe? Maybe this whole business with Ben Savage was a lie in the first place. And that woman hired a gunman to come in and pull a few of my teeth. Now that he's done his work, he's gone to the next job for hire."

Wilson could see that Dalton was working himself up to the possibility that Savage was actually gone. He hated to contradict him, but he had to set him straight. "Well, sir, I reckon that coulda looked that way, but Stump said he talked to Ham Greeley, and Ham told him Savage was just outta town for a few days, and he'd be back." He could see the instant disappointment wash across Dalton's face and wished he could do something to encourage him. *Of course,* he thought as an idea struck him that he should have thought of before. Suddenly all smiles, he said, "Boss, I'm gonna tell you somethin' you might be interested in."

Dalton showed no excitement over what that might be, but Wilson continued. "See that card game over there on the other side of the room?" Dalton took a casual glance. "Pay a little closer attention to the feller facin' us, wearing the black derby hat. "That's Pitt Ramsey. You ever hear that name?"

"No, can't say as I have," Dalton said.

"Should I have?"

"I expect if you ever lived up in Missouri or Kansas, you most likely would have," Wilson replied. "I was in that dance hall in Kansas City, tendin' bar the night he shot Billy Bob Tannehill and Billy Bob's two brothers — three shots so quick they sounded like one. One of the brothers got off a shot that hit one of the gals that worked in the dance hall. I'll never forget that night, and I ain't never seen anybody that fast since, and I've seen Ed Hatcher. That was six months before you hired me to manage this place."

"How'd he happen to show up here in Buzzard's Bluff?" Dalton asked. "Is he working for one of the small ranches?"

"No, sir, Pitt don't work for nobody, never has. He's in business for himself. He showed up here in Buzzard's Bluff 'cause things were gettin' a little hot for him in Kansas. Seems he shot a feller down in a saloon in Dodge City, but he didn't wait for him to turn around to face him. It was kinda like the time Bob Wills tried to shoot Savage in the back in the Lost Coyote, only this feller wasn't lucky enough to turn around before Pitt got him."

"We're a long way from Dodge City," Dalton remarked. "How did he stumble on

Buzzard's Bluff?"

"He didn't stumble on us," Wilson crowed. "He came here on purpose, on account he heard about the Golden Rail and he heard I was runnin' it. He remembered me from that dance hall, and he figured he could hide out here. He's rentin' one of the rooms upstairs. I told him his identity was safe with me, and you're the first person I've told."

"You say he's in business for himself?" Dalton asked. "Are you telling me his gun's for hire?"

"That's what I'm tellin' you," Wilson said, feeling highly pleased with himself and the opportunity he was offering. "And it looks to me like he's the man to solve one very big problem we've got."

Dalton was at once excited, thinking it an act of providence that made him decide to come into town this morning. "How long has he been here?" he asked.

"Day before yesterday," Wilson answered.

"Why the hell didn't you send word to me?" Dalton demanded.

"Uh . . ." Wilson stumbled. "I was fixin' to today. I was gonna send Stump out to tell you, but I thought you'd want me to make sure Pitt was still in business before I did."

"I want to talk to him. Go over and tell him I want to talk some business with him, and I don't have time to sit around and wait for his poker game to break up."

"Uh, yes sir," Wilson responded. He was not sure Pitt would jump at Dalton's command. "I'll go over and tell him what you said." He got up from the table, walked across the room, and stood by Pitt Ramsey's shoulder.

Ramsey turned at once, a scowl on his face. "Damn, Wilson, I thought you were one of those cows you've got workin' here."

"I don't wanna bother you while you're playin' cards, but my boss told me to give you a message."

"Your boss?" Ramsey responded. "I thought you owned this place."

"No, a lotta people think that, I reckon, but I'm just runnin' the business for him. Daniel Dalton owns the saloon. That's him settin' at the table against the wall over there. This saloon ain't all he owns. He owns the Double-D cattle ranch, and it's the biggest ranch in this part of Texas."

Aware then that the game was waiting for him to call or raise, Ramsey threw his cards in. "I fold," he said and turned back to Wilson. "All right," he asked, "what's the message?" Prepared to hear a complaint because of his reputation and possibly a request to find another saloon to hide in, he scowled up at Wilson, expectantly.

"Mr. Dalton would like to discuss a business proposition with you," Wilson said, almost in a whisper.

Ramsey reacted with immediate interest. "Is he ready to talk right now?" Wilson said that he was. "Good 'cause I'm damn tired of throwin' my money away in this game. I'm done, boys." He raked what money he had left off the table and pushed his chair back. Then he followed Wilson across the room to Dalton's table. "Wilson said you wanted to talk to me about something."

"That's right," Dalton replied. "Have a seat." He paused while Wilson made a quick introduction, then said, "Wilson, why don't you go get Mr. Ramsey a glass?" By the time Ramsey was settled in his chair, Wilson was back with his glass. When he set it on the table, and was about to sit down with them, Dalton looked up at him and remarked. "I expect it's best if Mr. Ramsey and I be left alone to discuss this."

"Right," Wilson said at once, already in a half-crouch, preparing to sit. "I was goin' to suggest that." He turned immediately and withdrew to the bar, where Mickey was already alert to an important meeting in progress. "I told 'em it was best they talk about it without me puttin' my two cents' worth in," he told the bartender.

"Wilson tells me you're a man who specializes in jobs that require a lot of skill with a firearm," Dalton opened the discussion bluntly.

Ramsey took an appraising look at Dalton before answering. "Let's just say I've found myself in life-or-death situations more than most men, and I've always come out on my feet." He paused then, knowing Dalton was eyeing him intensely as well, hesitant to come right out and say what he wanted done. "Sometimes it's best to eliminate a problem that happens to be in the way of your plans when you find out you can't go around it. That's what I specialize in, Mr. Dalton. I eliminate problems that get in the way of folks like you."

This was what Dalton wanted to hear, a professional by all standards, a man who was cold and businesslike without the brash boasts and claims like Ed Hatcher or Deacon Moss. "I'll get right to the point, I've got a problem that's standing in the way of what I plan for this town, and so far, nobody has been able to get the job done." He poured them both another drink. "I could use a man like you, Mr. Ramsey. How'd you

401

like to come work for me?"

"Sorry, Mr. Dalton, I don't work for nobody. I'm an independent contractor. You want a problem removed, I'm interested in talkin' about it, but I don't work no cows or mend no fences." He sat back in his chair and smiled. "And I don't work cheap." He reached for the drink Dalton had just poured and tossed it back. "Thanks for the drink. That's better stuff than what Wilson is pourin' at the bar." He made motions as if to get up but paused when Dalton spoke two words.

"How much?" Dalton asked. "I wasn't talking about hiring you as a ranch hand."

Ramsey settled back down in his chair. "That depends," he said. "Who's the target? Is it just one man, or will his death trigger a reaction from one or more others? Will he answer a challenge to face me in a fair fight? Or am I gonna have to ambush him?"

"His name's Ben Savage," Dalton replied. "He's the owner of the other saloon up the street, and he's standing in my way."

Ramsey gave a small nod and smiled. He had heard some of the men in the saloon talking about the big jasper at the Lost Coyote. "I heard talk of him," he said. "I heard he shot three men down who came after him one at a time. And I heard all three of those men worked for you."

"You heard right, Mr. Ramsey. All three were my men, and he caused two more of my men to have to run to escape arrest. That's why it's important now that Savage's death is the result of a duel and not a shot in the back. I've talked to the sheriff and to Savage and his partner about the attacks. I told them I ordered my men to stay away from the Lost Coyote. And they know damn well my men don't dare go against my orders. That's why I want to know just how good you think you are with that gun you're wearing. Hell, I could hide behind a building, shoot him myself, and save my money."

"Then, why don't you?" Ramsey asked.

"Because everybody in town would know that I did it — or I had one of my men do it," Dalton answered. "If you shot him, a stranger just passing through, with no connection to the Double-D, got the best of him in a fast-draw contest, they couldn't lay it on my doorstep."

Ramsey snorted the start of a chuckle. "If I could get him to face me, then I wouldn't have to get the hell outta town, either." He snorted again, amused by the thought of hanging around Buzzard's Bluff to enjoy the notoriety that always accompanied a duel in the street. Back to Dalton then, who was fidgeting nervously with his empty shot glass, he said, "It's gonna cost you. It would be a helluva lot cheaper just to shoot somebody in the back for you. But if I've got to put on a show for the town while I gun this jasper down, it'll cost you."

"How much?" Dalton asked again.

"Four hundred dollars," Ramsey replied, "and free rent for that room upstairs for as long as I'm in town."

"Done," Dalton accepted at once and extended his hand. He would have gone eight. "When will you do it?"

"As soon as I can find him and take a little time to see how he handles himself," Ramsey said. "I reckon I'll start hangin' around the Lost Coyote for a spell, so I can work him up to wantin' to meet me out in the street. That way, it won't look like I came to town just to kill him."

"That's good, that's smart," Dalton said. He was already congratulating himself for contracting the assassin.

"I'm gonna need half of the money to start," Ramsey informed him, "the rest when the job's finished."

"I never carry more than one hundred dollars with me when I come to town," Dalton said. "I didn't know I was going to strike a deal with you, obviously, or I would

404

have brought more. A hundred should show you that I'm acting in good faith and I'll have the rest for you right here in the Golden Rail when the job is done."

Ramsey saw no need to haggle over an advance payment, so he didn't hesitate to accept Dalton's terms. "Well, Mr. Dalton," he said with a little smile, "looks like you're fixin' to lose some business here. I'll be doin' most of my drinkin' up at the Lost Coyote."

CHAPTER 22

With absolutely no thoughts that he might now have a price on his head, Ben guided Cousin onto the south end of the main street of Buzzard's Bluff. He had made good on his estimate that he would reach the town in the middle of the afternoon. He was tempted to see if the hotel dining room was still open, but he knew Annie would have fixed something for the noon meal back at the Coyote. So he would grab something there to hold him until suppertime when he had already promised himself a big supper that night.

As Cousin plodded slowly up the street, Ben couldn't help experiencing a peaceful feeling about the little town he now called home. Approaching the sheriff's office, he felt thankful that he was not responsible for keeping law and order in Buzzard's Bluff. He was satisfied that the town had an honest and reliable sheriff in Mack Bragg. With recent signs that Daniel Dalton had backed off his aggressive approach toward ruling the town, it appeared Buzzard's Bluff still had the potential to grow into a thriving city. Thinking of the sheriff and his warning to him about how dangerous Billy Turner was, Ben decided he should stop in and tell Mack that the package had been delivered and locked up in the Austin jail.

An interested party in the Golden Rail Saloon, located diagonally across the street from the sheriff's office, stopped to stare out the window when he caught sight of the rider. "I'll be damned," Wilson Bishop uttered, "there's that devil now. He's back in town." His immediate thought was to bring Pitt Ramsey to the window so he could get a look at the man he was being paid to kill. He turned around at once and looked back and forth across the room. Not seeing Ramsey, he yelled at Mickey. "Where the hell's Pitt?"

"You mean Mr. Pete Wood?" Mickey came back, using the name Pitt had given them to call him by. "I'm afraid he's busy at the moment, upstairs with Bonnie, sowin' some oats." He chuckled in appreciation of his humor.

"Damn it," Wilson swore. "Ben Savage is back in town, and Pitt could get a look at

him if he would come down here right now."
He turned to take a look at the stairs, trying
to decide.

Guessing what Wilson was thinking,
Mickey informed him, "I ain't goin' up
there to get him. You can, if you want to,
but I ain't about to disturb him right now."
Wilson understood Mickey's thinking, and
he was aware of a definite risk in disturbing
Pitt at this particular time. Still, he thought
Pitt would like to take a look at Savage.
After giving it a little more thought, he
decided it not worth the risk and just stood
there watching as Ben guided his horse up
to the jail.

Seeing the big man on the dun gelding
through the window of his office, Mack
Bragg walked out to meet him. "Well, I see
you got back all right," the sheriff greeted
him. "You made good time. You didn't have
to shoot him before you got there, did you?"

"Nope," Will replied. "We made it all the
way to Austin and I turned him over to the
sheriff. So I reckon that's the last we'll hear
outta Ranger Billy Turner. How is everything goin' back here in Buzzard's Bluff?"

"It's been so quiet, it's beginnin' to worry
me," Bragg said and laughed. "Even the
Golden Rail ain't made much noise." He
turned serious for a moment and asked,

"You reckon ol' Daniel Dalton has finally given up on the idea of takin' over the town? I saw him this mornin'. He was over there at his saloon — wasn't there long before he rode on out of town."

"I don't know, Mack," Ben answered. "It doesn't seem likely. He's just that breed of cat, I reckon, but stranger things have happened."

"It could be that he's just waitin' till he hires more men," Bragg speculated. "Before you came to town, there was really only three or four of his men that caused most of the trouble in town. It was always Hatcher, Wills, or Deacon that got into it with somebody here in town, or some of the ranch hands from one of the smaller spreads. But those three are gone." He paused to give Ben a little grin. "You might know something about that. I expect he's havin' trouble findin' any men right now, gunslingers or just honest ranch hands. It bein' roundup time of year, most of those ridin' the grub line all summer have probably signed on with somebody."

"You could be right," Ben allowed. "Reckon we'll just have to wait and see. Hell, you never know, ol' Dalton might turn around and wanna join the city council — maybe run for mayor."

"That'll be the day," Bragg commented.

Ben touched his finger to the brim of his hat and turned Cousin back toward the stable. He looked at the Lost Coyote as he rode slowly by, but there was no one occupying the two chairs out front. *Hope there's somebody inside buying whiskey,* he thought, in fitting with his role as an owner.

"Howdy, Ben," Henry Barnes called out from the corner of the corral where he was pumping water into the watering trough. "Glad to see you got back all right. Have any trouble?"

"Nothin' to speak of," Ben replied. "Everything all right with you?"

"Ain't had nothin' to complain about all week," Henry confessed. "Somethin' terrible must be gettin' ready to happen."

Ben pulled Cousin's saddle and bridle off and released the dun gelding into the corral while Henry relieved the packhorse of its burden. "They haven't had anything but grass for a couple of days," Ben said, "so they'd most likely appreciate some oats."

"I'll take care of 'em," Henry said. He helped Ben carry the remaining supplies from the Austin trip into the barn. Since the packs and the horse, too, had been the property of Billy Turner, Ben told Henry to look through the packs, and he was welcome

410

to anything he wanted. Telling him he'd see him later, Ben took his rifle and saddlebags and walked to the Lost Coyote.

"Well, welcome home, partner," Rachel greeted him when he walked in the door of the saloon. "There's a fresh pot of coffee on the stove, and Annie's got some ham biscuits and beans still warm in the oven. She made a second batch of biscuits because she said you'd be here, but you'd most likely be a little after everybody else ate. So you'd better not tell her you ate before you came here, if you did."

"No, I didn't eat." He laughed. "I thought Annie might have something left, so I came straight here after I took care of the horses. How'd she know I'd show up today?"

"Beats me," Rachael said. "Annie just knows things like that. I've quit trying to figure her out. She walked in here a little while ago and said she just put a fresh pot of coffee on because you'd probably show up pretty quick. It wasn't five minutes later when Clarice looked out the window and saw you taking your horse to the stable." When Ben reacted with a look of disbelief, Rachel asked, "Am I lying, Tiny?"

"She's tellin' the truth," Tiny said. "That ain't no lie." The oversized bartender grinned and nodded. Ben looked from Tiny to Clarice, who nodded, as well.

Ben decided to let the subject lay. Annie was kind of spooky, anyway. "Well, I'm ready to help her get rid of some of that food and coffee," he said, "just as soon as I dump this stuff in my room." He went out the back door to the hallway and would have bumped into Annie if she had not backed away from the door. She was carrying a tray with his food on it. "Oh, sorry, Annie, I almost lost my dinner, didn't I?"

"That's all right," she replied, "I knew you were comin' in the hall."

Astonished by her reply, after just hearing Rachel say Annie just knew when things were going to happen, he had to ask, "How did you know I was coming into the hall?"

Matching his look of astonishment with one of her own, she said, "When I saw the door opening."

"Right," he said, feeling a little foolish, "that would give it away, all right. I'll be right back to eat that," he said then, holding the door for her.

Before he had finished his dinner, Tuck Tucker and Ham Greeley came into the saloon. As expected, Tuck was quick to sit down at the table with Ben, seeking a full report on the transport of Billy Turner. "Did he give you any trouble?" Tuck wanted to know. "I shoulda gone with you," he said. "You're lucky that sidewinder didn't get the jump on you."

"Yeah, I reckon I was," Ben replied, satisfied to let it go at that.

"Well, here's a piece of news, you'll be interested to hear," Tuck announced. "I know where we can find Marty Jackson and Shorty Dove." That seemed to spark Ben's interest, so Tuck told him about the visit Ruby had just had with Jimmy Whitley. When he had finished, he asked, "Whaddaya thinkin' we oughta be doin' about it?"

"I don't plan on doin' anything about it," Ben answered. "They've both run from here. If they show up here again, then I'll do something about it. I'm satisfied they're gone."

Completely surprised by Ben's reaction, Tuck stammered, "But one of 'em shot me!"

"I know, Tuck, but look at it this way, he was tryin' to shoot me. He didn't mean you no harm. I'm willin' to let him get by with takin' a shot at me. I expect you're man enough to forget about it, too."

They were interrupted then when Annie came back in to announce she was going home. "The kitchen's pretty much cleaned

413

up. There's coffee still in the pot, if you want some and I put what's left of the biscuits in the oven. Anything else you want me to do before I go?"

"No, Annie," Rachel answered. "You've already done more than we would expect, just so Ben would have something to eat when he got here."

"That's right, Annie," Ben quickly spoke up. "I surely did enjoy those biscuits. I appreciate it." He looked past her then to see if Johnny Grey was there, but when he didn't see him, he asked, "Is Johnny comin' to pick you up?"

"No, sir," Annie answered. "Everything's been so peaceful for a while now, that I told Johnny not to bother quittin' work just to take me home. It ain't but a mile and a half, and I enjoy the walk."

"I'm not doin' anything right now," Ben volunteered. "I'd be glad to walk you home. A little walk might do me some good." It wasn't even close to dark yet, but he still felt like she should have some kind of escort.

"Oh, no, sir, I wouldn't make you do that. It ain't that far, and it's broad daylight right now."

Then he had an idea. "Can you ride a horse?"

Annie laughed. "Yes, sir, I can ride a

414

horse, but I ain't got one. That is, we've got two horses, but Johnny uses both of 'em on the farm."

Ben thought about Billy Turner's packhorse. "I'll tell you what, I find myself with an extra horse on my hands, and I've been wonderin' what I was gonna do with him. He's a gentle little sorrel geldin' that I used for a packhorse when I went to Austin last week. That little horse would be just right for you." He looked over at Tuck then. "I'll bet Tuck's got a saddle in his shop that'd be the right size for a lady like you. Is that right, Tuck?" He gave his dwarflike friend a stern eye.

Understanding his message, Tuck said, "Why, I sure do. I know just the one and a bridle to go with it."

Dumbfounded, for it was coming at her too fast, Annie didn't know what to say. She looked at Rachel for help, then back at Ben before she managed to speak. "I ain't got no money to pay for a bridle and saddle."

"Who said anything about money?" Tuck asked, fully in accord with the gesture now. He glanced at Ben, who was grinning back at him. "It'll take me a little while to dig it outta my storeroom. What about if I have 'em ready for you tomorrow by the time you're ready to head for home?"

Completely astonished by then, Annie found it impossible to respond, so Ben spoke for her. "That oughta work out all right, don'tcha think, Annie?" She still could find no words. "Then you'll be ready this time tomorrow to ride home, and today I'll walk you home," Ben continued. They were all caught up in the generous contribution to Annie's transportation needs, and Ben was telling Annie how she could keep her horse out back of the saloon where it could graze as they walked out the door. "There's a lot of grass out back, and we can tie him on a long-enough rope so he can reach the creek."

By the time Ben returned, the usual regular customers were beginning to wander into the saloon. Among them was a tall slender stranger wearing a black derby hat tilted slightly forward on his forehead. He stood at the bar and watched the other patrons while he tossed a drink of whiskey back. He tapped the empty glass on the bar a couple of times to get Tiny's attention. "You ready for another'n?" Tiny asked. Ramsey nodded. "First time in here," Tiny said as he poured his drink. "First time in Buzzard's Bluff?"

416

"That's right," Ramsey replied, "first time."

One look at the vest and morning coat the stranger wore told Tiny that the man was not a settler or a cowhand. The Colt six-gun resting in the quick-draw holster told him even more, and he wondered if the man had intended to visit the Golden Rail and not the Lost Coyote. "Well, welcome to Buzzard's Bluff," Tiny said. "You gonna be with us a while, or are you just passin' through?"

"Ain't decided yet," Ramsey answered. "Depends on what I find here and whether or not I can strike a good card game."

Tiny noticed the stranger was eyeing a table in the back where Tuck, Ham, and Jim Bowden were playing cards. And it occurred to him that the man was most likely a professional gambler. "Those three fellers back there playin' cards," he felt the need to say, "ain't big-money gamblers. They just have a little friendly game to pass the time."

Ramsey smiled at him. "Ain't nothin' wrong with that," he said. "I might join 'em." He stuck out his hand. "My name's Pete Wood."

"Tiny Davis," he returned. "If you're really thinkin' about playin' with those fellers, I'll introduce you, if you want me to."

"That would be a right friendly thing to do. I'll take you up on that. Might as well get off to a good start." He picked up the drink Tiny had just poured and followed him back to the table.

"Got a feller here who's new in town," Tiny said in introduction. "He'd like to join in the game, if you don't mind."

"Sure," Tuck said at once without waiting for Ham or Jim to comment, "long as you know we set a bet limit. Ain't none of us millionaires."

"Don't matter to me if it's penny-ante," Ramsey said. "Poker's poker, whatever the stakes are. I'd be pleased to take some of you fellers' pocket money."

"Uh-oh!" Ham said, "we better watch out. Have a seat, stranger." Ramsey sat down and introduced himself as Pete Wood. Tuck identified each of them and the game was on.

It was not long after that when Ben returned from his walk with Annie. Seeing the usual card game at the back table, he figured he had some explaining to do to Tuck, so he went back to the game. He couldn't help being curious about the fellow in the black derby hat, but he thought he'd ask Tiny about him later. "I don't want to interrupt the game, but I need to tell you

418

something, Tuck. Just wanted to let you know, I don't expect you to give away a saddle and bridle for nothin'. I'll pay you for her tack."

"I figured you'd tell me that," Tuck said. "We'll talk about it after 'while. I'm busy takin' these fellers' money right now."

After Ben walked away, Ramsey asked, "Who's the big feller?"

"That's Ben Savage," Jim answered him. "He's one of the co-owners of the saloon."

Ramsey turned in his chair and took a good look at him as he walked back to the bar. His initial thought was what a big target he was. He liked what he saw, because a big man was ordinarily slower in his reflexes. And he was wearing a six-gun, which would indicate he wouldn't hesitate to use it. *Perfect,* he thought. He turned his attention back to the card game and thoughts about how he was going to stage the shooting, so it wouldn't appear to be planned. "You boys play here every day?"

"Usually five days a week," Ham replied. "I expect we'll play tomorrow, won't we, Tuck?" Tuck said he planned on it.

Good, Ramsey thought. He stayed there until close to suppertime, playing the cards that were dealt, and when they decided it time to be thinking about supper, they quit with all four committing to resume the game the next day at the same time. Ramsey thanked them for inviting him back, saying he was going to recover the small loss he had suffered.

"I was just takin' it easy on you today," Tuck boasted. "Tomorrow, I'm gonna clean you all out."

"I reckon we'll just have to see about that," Ramsey came back in kind. *You're gonna be my trigger,* he thought as he grinned at the little red-haired gnome. He took a closer look at Ben when he walked by the bar on his way to the door and gave Tiny a nod of his head.

"Who's the stranger?" Ben asked Tiny after Ramsey had left.

"Fellow by the name of Pete Wood," Tiny replied. "Looks like a big-time gambler or somethin', don't he? But he just got in that little poker game with Tuck and the boys. No trouble, seemed to have a good time."

He had that look, all right, Ben was thinking. But he also had the look of a gunslinger. "Is he just passin' through town?" Tiny said that he was. "Where's he stayin'?" He wondered if it might be at the Golden Rail.

"I don't know," Tiny answered. "Maybe at the hotel?"

"Maybe," Ben replied. After twelve years

as a lawman, he thought he saw signs of a dangerous breed of outlaw. He wondered if Mack Bragg might have paper on somebody by that name, even considering odds that Pete Wood was an alias.

"I was wonderin' if you were gonna give all your business to the Lost Coyote," Wilson Bishop said when Pitt Ramsey walked in the Golden Rail. He looked around him to make sure no one could overhear him before continuing. "I didn't hear any gunshots while you were up the street."

"Just like I told your boss," Ramsey said, "this job has to be set up, so that it don't look like a planned assassination. It's got to look like a face-off between the two of us, so nobody can lay it at Dalton's feet, or say that I came to town just to kill him. You can tell your boss that I'll finish the job at about this time tomorrow, and that's when I'll expect to get the rest of my money."

Wilson didn't hesitate. Knowing how crucial this was to Dalton, he went to the back room to find Stump Jones. Hearing Wilson calling, Stump came out of the closet, where he was building some new shelves. "You wantin' me?"

"Yes," Wilson replied. "Saddle your horse and ride out to the Double-D. I want you to give Mr. Dalton a message. Tell him that job will be done by this time tomorrow. On second thought, tell him by five o'clock tomorrow, since it's gonna take you an hour to get out there."

"Will he know what job you're talkin' about?"

"He'll know," Wilson assured him. He was sure Dalton didn't want him to discuss it with Stump. "Just tell him what I said."

CHAPTER 23

Just for the hell of it, Ben decided to stop by the sheriff's office on his way to supper. He found Bragg in the office about to go to the hotel dining room, himself. "Trouble already?" Bragg joked. "You ain't been back but half a day."

"No," Ben responded, "I just thought I'd ask you if you've gotten any wanted papers on a man named Pete Wood."

"Don't recall seein' that name," Bragg replied. "We can take a look through 'em, if you want to." He went to his desk and pulled out a cardboard box. "This is everything I've gotten so far this year." While he divided the papers into two stacks, so they could both search, it occurred to him. "Is this about that stranger in the derby hat I saw come outta the Golden Rail this mornin'?"

"As a matter of fact," Ben replied. He started going through the wanted papers.

"Did you say he came outta the Golden Rail this mornin'?" Mack said he did. "And he ended up in the Coyote this afternoon, playin' cards with Tuck and Ham and Jim."

"Cause you any trouble?" Bragg asked. When Ben said no, Bragg shrugged and said, "Sounds like the Golden Rail mighta been a little too rough for his taste." They continued searching the WANTED notices with no luck. Then toward the end of them, Bragg said, "Look at this drawing on one I got two months ago. Don't this remind you of that fellow you're talkin' about?" He handed the notice to Ben. "Derby hat and all," he added.

"Wanted for the murder of a man in a saloon in Dodge City, Kansas," Ben read aloud. "Name's Pitt Ramsey. Sketch sure kinda favors this fellow I just saw in the Coyote." He handed it back to Bragg to take another look.

"Hard to tell for sure," Bragg said. "This drawin' looks a little heavier than the man I was lookin' at this mornin'. Maybe I oughta go see if I can find him and have a little talk with him. Accordin' to this, he ain't wanted for robbery or rustlin' or anything but that one shootin' in a saloon."

"He was in the Coyote for a couple of hours playin' cards," Ben said. "And he was just as quiet as could be — got along fine with Tuck and the others."

"Sounds like his name might be Pete Wood," Bragg decided, "and he ain't caused no trouble, so let's go eat supper. I'll keep an eye on him. I can't arrest him till he breaks a law."

"Well, well," Lacy James announced when they walked in the door. "Look what the sheriff caught. You bringing your prisoners to the dining room now, instead of feeding them down at the jail?"

"Good evenin' to you, too, Lacy," Ben replied.

"Oh, that's Ben Savage with you," Lacy continued to jape. "He's been gone so long I forgot what he looked like." She favored him with a big smile. "Myrtle cooked pork chops tonight. She musta known you'd be back."

Maybe she's got the same kind of powers Annie's got, he thought. In response to Lacy, he said, "It'll be my pleasure to get rid of some of 'em for her." He unbuckled his gun belt and left it on the table by the door, then followed Mack to the sheriff's favorite table in the back corner of the room.

The cooking was every bit as good as he had built it up to be during his ride back

425

from Austin, while living on bacon and hardtack. When the meal was finished, they remained to have another cup of coffee. It was then that the stranger walked in the door, and it was obvious that he had not eaten there before. "I believe that's our Mr. Pete Wood," Bragg commented quietly.

"That's him," Ben said. "Lacy's gonna have to lay down the law to him." He and Mack watched Ramsey's reaction when Lacy stopped him from going directly to a table. They were close enough now for Ben and Mack to hear the conversation.

"This is your first visit to our dining room," Lacy said. "So, if you don't mind, we'd like to ask you to leave your firearm on the table placed there for that purpose."

Ramsey looked around then and saw the table. "What if I do mind?"

"Then I hope you find another restaurant with food as good as ours, and they'll let you eat with your gun on," she said.

He laughed. "All right, I'll take it off." He had started to unbuckle his belt when he noticed Ben and Mack sitting at the table in the corner. "Wait a minute," he said, "feller back there is wearin' a gun. How come?"

"He's the sheriff," Lacy said with a sassy smile. "He can keep his on. Show me your badge and I'll let you wear your gun."

426

Ramsey returned her smile. "Oh, that does make a difference, don't it? Gives you a good feelin', too, to know the sheriff is protectin' us while we eat. Matter of fact, I'd like to go say a word to him."

"I'm sure he'd be glad to meet you," she said. "He always likes to meet newcomers. And after you say hello to him you just sit yourself down at any table and Cindy will be there to take care of you in a minute or two."

Ramsey selected a table toward the middle of the room, removed his derby and hung it on the back of the chair, then walked back to their table. "Don't wanna interrupt your supper, Sheriff, but I'd like to introduce myself. My name's Pete Wood. I'm a gambler by trade, an honest one, and I always like to let the law know what I'm doin' in their town."

"All right, Mr. Wood," Bragg responded. "We don't have any problem with professional gamblers in this town. So, if you're playin' an honest game, good luck to ya."

Ben was aware that Ramsey's eyes seemed to be studying him while he talked to the sheriff. After Bragg wished him good luck, Ramsey said, " 'Preciate it, Sheriff." Then he addressed Ben. "You're the owner of the Lost Coyote, right?"

427

"One of 'em," Ben answered.

"Right," Ramsey said, "I saw you in there today. I promised those boys I'd be back tomorrow to play cards. Will you be there?" Ben nodded. "Good, I'll see you tomorrow. Nice talkin' to you, Sheriff." He returned to his table.

"Now, tell me why I feel like I oughta check my pocket to see if my wallet is still there," Bragg commented as they watched him walk away. Ben responded with a chuckle, but he knew what Mack was referring to. The name, Pete Wood, just didn't seem to fit the man they were looking at.

"Maria!" Daniel Dalton yelled from his study, and when she didn't arrive immediately, he yelled again. He was suffering another one of the severe headaches that had recently begun to attack him for no reason at all. When the weary little woman appeared in his doorway, he scolded, "Where the hell were you? I've got another damn headache."

"I am sorry," she explained, "I was in the señora's bedroom, fixing her tea. I will make you some strong coffee." There was nothing else she knew to help his headaches. She wondered if they had anything to do with his recent bouts of dizziness. There was a doctor in town, but Dalton would not go to see him. His stubbornness would kill him, she sometimes thought. He would probably call her to come into his bedroom when he was ready to go to bed, and she always hated that. He should call his wife to do that. She knew that Estelle was suspicious of what she thought the two of them were doing in there with the door closed. Maria didn't know if she should tell the señora what she was doing in there. She was not convinced that massaging the old man's feet gave him the relief he claimed, anyway. His wife should have to be the one to rub his crooked old feet. Her thoughts were distracted then when she heard someone knocking at the kitchen door.

She opened the door to find Spade Gunter standing there. "I need to give the boss a message from Wilson Bishop," he said. "Has he gone to bed yet?"

"No, he is in his study," she answered, "but his head hurt, he say."

"Well, Stump Jones just rode in from town and he said Wilson told him to make sure the boss got this message tonight."

She shrugged. "I tell him." She turned and went back to the study. In a couple of minutes, she returned and said, "He said for you to come in."

"What is it, Spade?" Dalton asked when his foreman stuck his head in the door.

"Sorry to bother you, sir, but Stump said you'd wanna know. It ain't much of a message. He just said to tell you that the job will get done at about five o'clock tomorrow. Said you'd know what that meant."

"Okay, Spade," Dalton said, "I know what he means." Spade started to pull the door closed again, but Dalton stopped him. "And, Spade, I'll be going into town again tomorrow."

"Yes, sir, I'll have your horse saddled. Just tell me when you're ready."

Annie came in the next morning to find that Ben had already started the fire in her stove, even though she was a little earlier than usual. "Give it another minute or two," he told her, "and that coffee oughta be about ready."

"I reckon I'm gonna have to get here about midnight to beat you to the coffeepot," she said. She was feeling a little jumpy this morning for some reason and she attributed it to all the talk yesterday about a gift horse. Now, she purposefully made no mention of it to Ben, thinking that he may have had more to drink than she knew about. And maybe this morning he would realize he had promised to give a horse away. If that was the case, she could not in good conscience, hold him to his word. Best not to mention it, she decided.

"Why don't you sit down and have a cup of coffee before you get started?" Ben suggested. She hesitated. "You afraid to drink my coffee?" he teased. She said she wasn't and promptly poured herself a cup along with one for him. "Did you tell Johnny you were gonna ride home this afternoon on your new horse?"

She flushed with excitement at that, realizing that it had not been whiskey talking the day before. He was really giving her a horse! "Yes," she said. "I told him, but I don't believe he thinks it will happen. I wasn't sure," she confessed. "He asked how much you had been drinking. I told him that he could ask you that when he comes in to breakfast."

He laughed. "I talked to Tuck last night. He'll have your tack ready, and he said he'd saddle your horse and bring it here after dinner."

"I declare, I don't know if I'm gonna be able to do anything proper today or not. How can I ever thank you enough? And Tuck?" she remembered.

"That's easy," he grinned. "Just keep fixin'

breakfast and dinner like you've been doin'."

"Well, after I treat myself to this cup of coffee you made, I'll do just that. I'll fix you a big breakfast. You're gonna need it."

"Good." He paused, then asked, "Why'd you say I'm gonna need it?"

"I don't know," she answered, wondering herself. "It just popped out." Even in her excitement, she still felt troubled about something. Maybe it was because she didn't think she deserved a present she hadn't worked for. Later, when Johnny came in to breakfast, Ben told him all about the sorrel gelding and the fact that the horse seemed to be in sound condition. He guessed the age to be about four years old. "She said she was gettin' a saddle, too," Johnny joked. "I told her I wished you'da gave her a plow instead."

"Just for that crack, I'm not gonna let you ride him," Annie told him.

Rachel showed up before they had finished eating, but Tiny, Ruby, and Clarice trailed in a little later, as usual. Johnny Grey left as soon as he finished eating, and Ben sat there until he had all the coffee he could hold for the time being. Then with nothing better to do, he walked up to the stable to check Cousin's and the sorrel's shoes. The shoes weren't bad on either horse, but he decided to take Annie's horse to Jim Bowden to be shod. *Might as well start her out ready to go,* he thought.

He waited and talked with Jim while he shod the horse and when he was finished, he climbed on the sorrel and rode it bareback up the north road out of town for about a mile before returning it to the stable. He wanted to make sure the horse had no objection to being ridden. Reassured as to the gentleness of the sorrel, he felt it would make Annie a good horse. Almost before he knew it, he had used up the morning, so he walked back to the saloon, leaving the horse with Henry until Tuck came with the new saddle.

He got back in time to join Rachel and Ruby for dinner, Tiny and Clarice having already eaten. When Annie brought the coffeepot for refills, she commented to Ben, "This might not be as good as yours was first thing this morning."

He only chuckled in response. When she went back into the kitchen, Rachel joked, "We might be buying some new dishes before long. I think I heard two hit the floor in there this morning."

"She is nervous about something today," Ruby said.

"She's just excited about that horse," Rachel declared. "If Tuck gets here too soon, we might have to clean up the kitchen for her."

Tuck's timing was good, however, because Annie had just finished her work for the day when he walked in the door. "Hey," he blurted, "anybody know who owns this little sorrel out front?" He was answered by a little squeal of excitement as Annie ran by him. She was followed at once by Rachel and Ben.

They found her outside at the hitching rail. She was holding the horse's bridle with one hand and stroking its neck with the other. "Oh, he's beautiful," she cooed.

"Step up in the saddle and we'll adjust the stirrups," Tuck said. Ben offered a hand and she jumped right up on the horse. "We'd best shorten 'em a little," Tuck suggested and adjusted them. "There you go, just right," he decided. Rachel couldn't help thinking if they were shortened a little more, they'd probably be just right for Tuck. She had better sense than to say it, however. "I ain't got no sidesaddle," Tuck declared. "I didn't think you'd wanna ride that way, even if I had one."

"I don't," Annie said, "and I wore my long knickers this morning, anyway."

"Take him for a little ride," Ben said, "and see how he feels."

She turned the sorrel away from the rail and started down the street toward the hotel at a trot. Halfway down the street, she urged the horse to lope, causing Ben to comment that she knew how to ride. Past the hotel, she turned around and came back up the street at a gallop. Almost even with the front door of the saloon, she reined the horse to a sliding stop and cried, "I love him!" She hopped down, put her arms around the sorrel's neck, and hugged him.

"I swear, if I didn't know how old that woman is, I'd think we were watching a kid on Christmas morning," Rachel commented aside to Ben.

"That was some fancy ridin' for a little lady like you." They all turned to see who made the remark. Pitt Ramsey stood on the boardwalk, smiling at them. "Yes, ma'am, that was some fancy ridin'." He turned and walked into the Lost Coyote.

The look of joy on Annie's face turned immediately to a troubled frown and she placed her hand on Ben's forearm. "You be careful," she said.

Puzzled by her remark, he was about to question her when he was interrupted by Ruby, who came out of the saloon carrying

Annie's cotton sack she brought back and forth from home every day for her personal items. "You don't wanna forget these," she said.

Annie took the bag and tied it on the saddle horn. "Thank you, everybody, especially you and Tuck," she said to Ben. "I'm gonna ride home to show Johnny. I'll see you in the morning."

She rode away at a lope, passing Ham Greeley and Jim Bowden on their way to the saloon. Ben and Rachel stood there watching her until she rode out of sight. "I don't care what they say about you, you did a really nice thing there, partner."

"Every once in a while," he came back and they filed back into the Coyote behind Ham and Jim.

"You couldn't find no big card game, I reckon," they heard Tuck razzing the stranger called Pete Wood. "You shoulda tried the Golden Rail. Mighta found a bigger game."

"I wouldn't have missed a chance to set down with you boys again," Ramsey said. "I left a little on the table here yesterday, and I plan on gettin' it back today."

"All right, then, let's get her goin'," Tuck said. "Everybody chip in for the bottle." Tiny brought a bottle and four glasses over to the table and collected the money for it, and the game was underway.

Chapter 24

Everything went as it had the day before, with a lot of boastful talk and complaints of bad luck until Pete Wood said, almost casually, "That last card came off the bottom of the deck."

Since Tuck was dealing, he naturally jerked his head back in surprise. "What are you talkin' about?"

"I'm just sayin' you dealt that last card off the bottom of the deck," Ramsey said, his voice absent any emotion. "I want one off the top." Jim and Ham both looked at Ramsey, astonished by his charge.

"I didn't deal no card off the bottom," Tuck said. "You're seein' things."

"All right, if you say so," Ramsey said. "Maybe I am seein' things." The game continued, although now the atmosphere was somewhat more chilled. With nothing more said about it, the deal went around to Tuck again. By that time the chill had warmed a little until Ramsey commented, "There you go again." He flipped the last card over that Tuck dealt to him. "Three of diamonds," he said. "That card was on the bottom of the deck."

"Mister, you've got eye problems," Tuck said. "I don't deal off the bottom. I ain't slick enough to deal off the bottom."

"He's right," Ham said. "He ain't slick enough to deal off the bottom."

"Well, he damn sure did that time," Ramsey charged, "and it's the second time he's done it. I wasn't gonna say any more about it as long as he didn't try to get away with it again. But I don't like gettin' skinned by a cheat, especially one that ain't no better at it than he is."

Flabbergasted by the first charge, Tuck was at a full boil by this time. "I don't know what in the hell you've been chewin' on, but it musta been locoweed. I ain't never cheated nobody in a card game. Anybody around here can tell you that."

"I make my livin' playin' cards," Ramsey said. "And I can spot a cheat a mile away, especially one as bad at it as you are."

"I don't know what kinda game you're playin'," Tuck charged, "but you're a damn liar."

"You best watch your mouth, old man, or

439

I'm gonna fix it for you." He pushed his chair back a little to give himself more room. Both Ham and Jim tried to calm Ramsey down to no avail. The argument became loud enough until finally Ben realized what was going on. He at once hurried over to the table when it looked like Tuck was about to square off with the stranger, Pete Wood. "Hey, settle down, settle down. What's the trouble over here?"

"This banshee is callin' me a cheat," Tuck blurted. "Said I was dealin' off the bottom."

"That's because he was," Ramsey said. "I saw him both times."

Ben looked directly at the stranger and said, "No, he wasn't cheatin'."

"How the hell do you know that?" Ramsey demanded.

"Tuck doesn't cheat," Ben said. "That's how I know." There was a silent standoff for a long second while each man measured the other. "You didn't see him cheat."

"So, now you're callin' me a liar?" Ramsey demanded.

Aware at last as to what was actually going on, a wry smile broke out on Ben's face when he answered. "That's right, Pitt, I'm callin' you a liar."

It was so subtle that Ramsey didn't catch it until a moment later. A smile matching

Ben's appeared on his face then. "Well, Ben Savage, what are we gonna do about it? I don't stand for no man callin' me a liar."

"I'll tell you what we can do about it, Mr. Ramsey," Ben said. "We can escort your ass out of here and you can go back to the Golden Rail and tell Daniel Dalton your little plan didn't work. On second thought, I've got a better idea. I think we'll just march you down to the jailhouse. I believe Sheriff Bragg has got paper on you for a murder in Dodge City, Kansas."

Ramsey was startled for a moment when he realized Ben knew who he was, but he recovered quickly. "You talk like a crazy man. My name's Pete Wood, and I ain't ever been in Dodge City. I won't stand for a man talkin' to me like that, so I'm callin' you out. You're wearin' a gun. I wanna see if you know how to use it." He started to get up out of his chair and was halfway up when Ben's right hand against his chin snapped his head around and he fell back into the chair. While he was still stunned, Ben quickly relieved him of the Colt he was wearing. He grabbed a handful of his shirt then and pulled him out of the chair and walked his would-be assassin toward the front door. Ramsey stumbled and staggered as Ben forced him to walk, holding him up in the process. Tuck ran after him with Ramsey's derby and plopped it on the confused man's head.

"He ain't gonna make it," Tuck predicted when Ramsey's legs began to buckle. "We gonna have to tote him. You hit him too hard."

"Take his feet," Ben said and Tuck got between Ramsey's feet and picked his boots off the floor. They carried him out the door then. "Right on down to the jail," Ben directed, and they hauled him down the middle of the street.

"Ben, what the hell?" Mack Bragg exclaimed when he opened the door to discover Tuck and Ben carrying an apparently woozy prisoner.

"Evenin', Mack," Ben announced. "We're bringin' you one Mr. Pitt Ramsey. I believe you've got paper on him."

"I do," Bragg said. "Drop him in that chair there, and I'll relieve him of that gun belt. Then we'll put him in a cell."

They dropped his limp body in a chair in front of Bragg's desk, unaware that he was not as helpless as he would have them believe. The sheriff unbuckled his gun belt and pulled it off him, then took the pistol Ben handed him and put it back in the holster. When Bragg rolled the belt and put it on his desk, Ramsey saw his chance. Suddenly coming to life, he jerked his pistol out of the holster and aimed it at Ben, who was opening the door to the cell room.

"Ben!" Tuck yelled. In the same instant, Ben drew and fired as he spun around. Ramsey dropped his pistol and stared down at the ugly black hole in his white shirt. He glanced up briefly at Ben in disbelief before he dropped to the floor.

Standing frozen in shock, Bragg could only stare at the body now lying on the floor while Tuck helplessly mumbled, "I swear," over and over. In a sudden fit of anger, Ben reached down and grabbed the corpse by the shoulders, pulled it to its feet, and dropped it across his shoulder, then walked out the door with it. It was enough to break Tuck and Bragg out of their trance. "Ben!" Tuck yelled. "Where you goin'?" He ran out the door after him.

Ben marched straight to the Golden Rail, diagonally across the street. With Tuck and Bragg following, he stormed into the busy saloon and stood there looking for Wilson Bishop. When he spotted him, he was gratified to see Daniel Dalton sitting at a table with him. He walked through a gang of customers who parted to make him a path. When he got to Dalton's table, he heaved his grisly burden off to land in the middle of it, sending dishes and glasses crashing on the floor. "I believe this belongs to you," he said to Dalton, turned and walked back out.

As he neared the door, one of the men standing there reached for his .44. "I wouldn't if I was you," Mack Bragg warned him, his weapon already in hand. He backed out the door after Ben and Tuck.

Outside, they could still hear the sounds of the chaos created by Ben's delivery of Dalton's gunman. Not quite cooled down as yet, Ben asked Bragg, "You need anything from me?"

"No," Bragg answered, "not officially, I reckon. I was a witness to the shooting. It was sure as hell self-defense." With no thoughts of going back in to take charge of the incident, he said, "I think I'll go back to the Coyote with you. I need a drink."

"That makes all three of us," Tuck said.

Inside the Golden Rail, there was another development, one that no one in that saloon saw coming. With Wilson yelling for Mickey and Stump to remove the body lying across the table, no one noticed the sudden confusion that overwhelmed Daniel Dalton. It was not until Ramsey's corpse was pulled off the table that Wilson realized that Dalton was acting strange. When he asked Dalton if he was all right, Dalton seemed to have trouble talking, and one side of his face looked as if it was sagging. Alarmed then, Wilson asked him if he was feeling all right. Dalton tried to answer but could not get the words out. "Stump!" Wilson yelled. "Help me. Something's wrong with Mr. Dalton!"

With Mickey's help, Stump and Wilson carried the stricken man into Wilson's bedroom and laid him on the bed. "Go get Doc Tatum. Tell him to hurry!"

"First time I've ever been called to come here when it wasn't a gunshot," Doc saw fit to comment when he walked in. "Where is he?"

Wilson led him back to his bedroom, and Doc started to examine a seemingly peaceful patient at that time. But when he tried to question Dalton, he seemed confused and unable to answer the simplest of Doc's questions. Doc asked Wilson how Dalton was behaving before he appeared to lose it all. When he got all the information Wilson could give him describing Dalton's behavior before the incident with the body on the table, Doc came to his conclusion. "Based on everything I see here and what you've told me, I'd say Mr. Dalton had a stroke."

■ ■ ■ ■

Spade Gunter was in the bunkhouse when Stump rode into the Double-D barnyard to deliver the news about his boss. It was his sad duty to carry the news to Estelle Dalton. She was in her room when he, with Maria escorting him, told her that her husband had suffered a stroke. "He ain't dead, ma'am," Spade hurried to assure her. "He's just bad off, is what Stump says. The doctor said he would do what he could for him tonight and for us to send a wagon in to carry him home in the mornin'."

Estelle was surprisingly calm when hearing the news. Spade had expected her to come to pieces when she heard and that was why he wanted Maria to go in with him. "A stroke," she asked, "isn't that in the brain?"

"I don't know, ma'am," Spade answered and looked at Maria for help.

"Sí, señora, it affects the brain," Maria told her.

Estelle turned back to Spade. "I'm sure Daniel will expect you to take over the operation of the ranch, so I'll expect the same."

"Yes, ma'am, I'll see to it that everything's took care of."

"I know you will, Mr. Gunter," she said. "Maybe we can concentrate on raising cattle and forget about Ben Savage and the town of Buzzard's Bluff."

Spade stood speechless for a few moments, surprised to hear what sounded like treasonous talk behind Daniel Dalton's back. He was surprised to think she had even the faintest notion of her husband's ambitions. When she stood, patiently waiting for his response, he wondered if he was meeting the real Mrs. Daniel Dalton. "Yes, ma'am," he finally replied. "It's time we got back to the business of raisin' cattle. I'll go into town in the mornin' and bring Mr. Dalton home."

In the days that followed the death of Pitt Ramsey, Buzzard's Bluff enjoyed a period of quiet that the town had not seen in some time. Ham Greeley brought reports from the Double-D that Stump Jones told him. According to Stump, things were mighty different around that ranch now with Daniel Dalton confined to an easy chair all day long and his long-silent wife consulting daily with foreman, Spade Gunter. "Don't ol' Daniel Dalton complain about that?" Tuck asked.

"Shoot," Ham replied. "He couldn't if he

wanted to. The stroke left him paralyzed and he can't even talk."

Tuck was about to make a comment about how quiet it was at the Golden Rail when he suddenly hesitated, when he saw who came in the door. Seeing the look on Tuck's face, Ham and Tiny turned to see what had captured his attention. "Evenin'," Spade Gunter said. "I'm lookin' for Ben Savage."

"You're in the wrong saloon, ain'tcha, Gunter?" Tuck challenged.

Spade fixed on him with a patient eye. "Not if Ben Savage is here," he answered.

"I reckon we've got kinda cautious when somebody from the Double-D comes in 'specially to see Ben," Tiny said. "The last one was Pitt Ramsey and that didn't turn out too good for ol' Pitt."

"Is he here?" Spade pressed.

"I'm here," Ben said from the back door. He motioned for Rachel, who was coming in with him, to stay back away from the door. "What can I do for you? Spade, ain't it?"

"That's right," Spade replied. "I understand you and the lady standin' by the door are partners in this business."

"That's a fact," Ben answered, wondering where Spade was going with it.

"Well, I came in to let you know there's a

new partnership out at the Double-D. A man and a lady, just like you've got here, and we're callin' off the war between the Golden Rail and the Lost Coyote. Mrs. Dalton is hopin' you'll accept our offer of peace."

Knowing a true sign when she saw one, Rachel stepped forward and extended her hand before Ben could respond. "You go back and tell that lady that we certainly will accept your offer." As Spade took her hand, Rachel turned to Ben. "Isn't that right, partner?"

"I reckon I know better than to get in the way when two ladies make a deal," Ben said.

"Well, I'll be go to hell," Tuck muttered, astonished.

An hour's ride from Buzzard's Bluff, at the Double-D, the shell of the man for whom the ranch was named sat in a chair by the window, staring out. What he stared at, no one knew, for the stroke he had suffered left him unable to move or speak. Not noticing when his wife walked into the room, he was startled when she began cleaning the drool off his face with a wet cloth. "Well, Daniel," she spoke softly, "we've come full circle, haven't we? Now it's you, sitting by the window all day, instead of me." She wasn't sure he understood what she was talking about, but she continued. "The Double-D is solely in the cattle business. I'm sending Spade back into town today to let Wilson Bishop know that I've decided to sell the Golden Rail." She hesitated then, her face breaking into a broad smile when she saw a glint of understanding in his eyes. "I'm going to let the owners of the Lost Coyote know I'm taking offers. I'm sure you'd agree that Ben Savage should have first chance at it."

When she walked out of the room, her smile still in place, Maria was prompted to ask, "A good day, señora?"

Estelle paused, considering the question. "Yes, it is, Maria." She laughed. "A very, very good day."

ABOUT THE AUTHORS

William W. Johnstone has written nearly three hundred novels of western adventure, military action, chilling suspense, and survival. His bestselling books include *The Family Jensen; The Mountain Man; Flintlock; MacCallister; Savage Texas; Luke Jensen, Bounty Hunter;* and the thrillers *Black Friday, The Doomsday Bunker,* and *Trigger Warning.*

J. A. Johnstone learned to write from the master himself, Uncle William W. Johnstone, with whom J. A. has co-written numerous bestselling series including The Mountain Man; Those Jensen Boys; and Preacher, The First Mountain Man.

The employees of Thorndike Press hope you have enjoyed this Large Print book. All our Thorndike, Wheeler, and Kennebec Large Print titles are designed for easy reading, and all our books are made to last. Other Thorndike Press Large Print books are available at your library, through selected bookstores, or directly from us.

For information about titles, please call:
(800) 223-1244

or visit our website at:
gale.com/thorndike

To share your comments, please write:
Publisher
Thorndike Press
10 Water St., Suite 310
Waterville, ME 04901